Mystery Kes
Keskinen, Karen
Blood orange

Blood Orange

Blood Orange

KAREN KESKINEN

MINOTAUR BOOKS
A THOMAS DUNNE BOOK
NEW YORK

A THOMAS DUNNE BOOK FOR MINOTAUR BOOKS.
An imprint of St. Martin's Publishing Group.

BLOOD ORANGE. Copyright © 2013 by Karen Keskinen. All rights reserved. Printed in the United States of America. For information, address St. Martin's Press, 175 Fifth Avenue, New York, NY 10010.

"Separation" by W. S. Merwin, currently collected in MIGRATION by W. S. Merwin. Copyright © 1962, 1963, 2005 by W. S. Merwin, used by permission of The Wylie Agency LLC.

Excerpt from MYTHOLOGY by Edith Hamilton. Copyright © 1942, 1969, by Edith Hamilton, used by permission of Little, Brown and Company.

www.thomasdunnebooks.com
www.minotaurbooks.com

Library of Congress Cataloging-in-Publication Data

Keskinen, Karen.
  Blood orange / Karen Keskinen.—1st ed.
      p. cm.
  "A Thomas Dunne book."
  ISBN 978-1-250-01233-3 (hardcover)
  ISBN 978-1-250-02833-4 (e-book)
  1. Women private investigators—Fiction.   2. Teenage girls—Crimes against—Fiction.   3. California—Fiction.   4. Secrets—Fiction.   I. Title.
  PS3611.E834B58 2013
  813'.6—dc23

                                                        2013006983

Minotaur books may be purchased for educational, business, or promotional use. For information on bulk purchases, please contact Macmillan Corporate and Premium Sales Department at 1-800-221-7945 extension 5442 or write special-markets@macmillan.com.

First Edition: June 2013

10   9   8   7   6   5   4   3   2   1

This book is for Thor

1973–2011

brave heart,
sweet soul

Your absence has gone through me
Like thread through a needle.
Everything I do is stitched with its color.

—W. S. Merwin

Chapter One

Lili Molina was alone in the dressing room, the last to finish, taking her time. She slipped on the elbow-length gloves with their fingers of leaves and bent twigs. Daphne's fingers, a sign of the Greek nymph's transformation from girl into tree. A living death, horrible really. Yet only Lili seemed to see it that way.

A drum out in the central workroom rapped a call to attention. She stepped from behind the screen and paused before the tall mirror, captivated by the beauty of the young woman gazing back at her. For the first time in many hours, Lili smiled.

Streams of bright copper twined through her dark hair. Her brown skin shimmered with gold dust, and layers of silver diaphanous netting floated over her apparently naked body. Underneath the netting Lili wore an opaque body stocking, but you could hardly tell. Her figure—ordinary in real life, she thought—looked stunning in the costume, all its imperfections somehow transformed.

More drums joined the summons. Lili's spirits warmed, then flared like red roses. She flounced the netting, flicked her hair over her shoulders, and skipped out to the hall.

Everyone gathered in the cavernous workroom—the dancers, tailors, makeup artists and float builders—burst into applause as she entered. She stepped up to join Jared, now dressed as Apollo, on the float platform. The mambo beat surged faster and louder. Lili kissed two fingertips and held them to her medallion, the image of La Virgen de Guadalupe, resting as always in the hollow of her throat.

Then the big double doors burst open, and the magnificent Apollo Guild float trundled out under a fierce solstice sun. It was high noon.

The sun had scorched a path westward by the time Lili recrossed the pavement on foot, inserted her key in the lock, and tugged open one of the heavy doors. Now the Guild workshop was still and semi-dark, lit only by light sifting down from the high clerestory windows. Behind her, the door thudded shut.

So many happy hours spent here. Six months working on the float and costumes, singing and dancing and ordering in pizza. And three weeks ago, right here in this room, the announcement was made: Lili was selected to be Daphne, exactly the way she'd dreamed. Smiling at the memory, she began to thread her way through the tables and sawhorses scattered about the dim open space, heading for the dressing room in the east wing. Then she heard something.

A tapping sound was coming from one of the cell-like rooms in the back. Lili halted and held her breath, listening. Who would be working during Solstice, with the party in full swing up at Alameda Park?

But then she understood. It was Danny, of course. It could only be Danny Armenta. Relieved, she turned and entered the narrow hall on her right.

"Danny?" she called. "It's me, Lili. Danny, are you here?" She reminded herself not to startle him—he was so easily frightened these days.

When she arrived at Danny's tiny work space, he was looking expectantly at the open doorway. But confusion clouded his expression when he saw her. It was her makeup, Lili realized, the gold skin paint, sequins, and glitter.

"It's me, Danny—Lili. Just me in my costume, OK?" She wagged a leafy hand at him playfully. "I came back to change."

Danny's expression cleared. "Hi Lili."

"Guess you didn't see me when I got on the float. Otherwise you'd've of known it was me."

"No, I . . ." He lifted one shoulder in a shrug. "I stayed in here."

Danny was still cute. Still had that reddish-brown hair and those light hazel eyes. He was heavier now—probably from the meds he had to take—but it didn't totally wreck his looks.

"What are you doing?" She nodded at the hammer in his hand.

Danny looked at a pastel chalk drawing tacked to the wall. "Hanging that up."

"Wow—is that . . . me?"

He studied the portrait. "Yeah," he said softly. "It's you."

"It's way too beautiful."

He squinted at her, obviously puzzled. "But that's—that's what you look like."

"I wish." Lili laughed. "But thanks. Thanks for drawing me and making me look so pretty."

"I worked on it when nobody was around. For about two weeks." Danny tugged at his old baseball cap. *Santa Barbara High School Dons.* Once maroon, it was nearly gray now. The brim was caked in grease where he'd lifted it, maybe a thousand times.

Lili had never seen him without his cap. He'd played first base, and some guy told her once that Danny Armenta was the best hitter the Dons ever had. But that was two years ago.

Danny had abruptly dropped out of school in his senior year. He'd seemed really confused for nearly six months, and then—at eighteen—he'd totally lost it. *Mental,* all the kids whispered.

Mental. A scary word. A word that didn't fit him, as far as Lili was concerned. And never would.

"I gotta go change out of my costume. But then, do you want to go back up to the park with me? There's music and food and tons of people. . . ." But she saw Danny's face tighten. Noise and tons of people—not what he liked, she realized, not at all.

"Um . . . I just want to stay here." He picked up a stick of pumpkin-colored chalk and rubbed it fretfully on the back of his hand. "OK?"

"Sure it's OK. Listen, I'm going to the dressing room. When I'm finished I'll come and say bye." Then Lili did something she'd never done before: she planted a sisterly kiss on Danny's cheek.

He took a step back and averted his gaze. But she didn't take it personally. She understood it bothered him a little to be touched, even just a hand on his arm.

The dressing room door cried its usual suffering sound when Lili opened it. The high-ceilinged space seemed ghostly this afternoon, the open alcoves bulging with costumes from past solstice celebrations. The lone window, frosted glass over wire netting, was shoved open, and a whisper of a breeze flowed into the room, stirring the air. A good idea, she thought: the dressing room always smelled so funky.

Lili closed the door behind her, then stood before the mirror one last time. *Daphne* . . . She admired once more her silky gold skin, flashing eyes. For nearly a year she'd secretly longed to be Daphne. And then, the unbelievable miracle: she was chosen. From that moment on, everything was perfect . . . except for last night.

She turned away from the mirror. *Hurry up and change, then go back to the park and have fun,* she ordered herself. *This is your time, don't let anything spoil it.*

Lili lifted her street clothes from her locker, carried them behind the folding screen, and set them on an old wooden chair. For the last time, she slipped out of the leafy gloves and draped them over the chair back. Then, carefully, Lili raised the layers of silver netting over her head. She folded the netting, placed it under the gloves, and began to peel the body stocking from her arms, first the left, then the right.

The spandex was tight and she worked slowly, taking care not to snag the knit fabric on her sparkly gold fingernails. Lili rolled the stocking down to her waist, over her hips to her knees.

She reached out a hand to the chair to steady herself—and halted at the sound of a sharp *click.*

"Hello? Who's there?" Her voice quavered.

No one answered, and Lili felt foolish. The old building was heating up in the sun, that was all. She bent down again and reached to her calf.

"Bitch!"

Lili was seized from behind by strong arms. She screamed, and something rough was forced in her mouth. She bit down hard, closed on coarse filthy leather.

"You dirty slut."

Lili grew limp with fright and in that instant she was smashed face-first to the concrete floor. Her nose crumpled, erupting in a gush of blood. She gasped to breathe, sucked in blood and choked on it. Then she gathered her strength and forced the leather from her mouth, screaming once more. But as she struggled to rise to her knees, the full weight of his body dropped down on her back.

Now Lili fought with every ounce of her strength. But both her legs were trapped in the stocking and the smothering weight pressing down on her was much greater than her own. Something slithered around her neck and slowly tightened— No—no—she did not want to—did not want to— Please help me, dear God!

"Feel that? Do what I say or I'll kill you," he hissed in her ear. *"Now keep your filthy mouth shut."* His breath was hot on her cheek.

So, it was him. It was him after all. Petrified, stunned, Lili grew still. She knew he would rape her. But she would live, she would live. She heard him breathe thickly as he fumbled with his pants—

Dear God, did she hear someone knocking at the window?

She tried to scream, but the cord bit into her neck. Only a gurgle came from her throat.

Again she heard the soft knock. She listened hard and prayed . . . tried to call out . . . and the knocking grew faint.

"Didn't I tell you, shut up? Didn't I say, do what I tell you or die?" He whispered in her ear, whispered like a lover from hell as the ligature tightened.

Chapter Two

I wove my bike in and out of the flotsam deposited the night before: smashed cascarones, confetti, splashes of candy-colored vomit. It was the morning after Solstice, and I'd managed to avoid the frivolities. At thirty-seven, I was apparently too old to hear the siren call.

Rounding a corner, I cruised to a stop in front of 101 West Mission, lugged the faded blue Schwinn over the curb and up the cracked steps of the 1930s bungalow court. Two years before, when I'd opened for business, I'd screwed a shiny brass plaque to the board facing the street: JAYMIE ZARLIN, SANTA BARBARA INVESTIGATIONS—SUITE D. Thanks to the salt-infused air, the plaque was already tarnished.

I wheeled my bike down the crushed shell path, heading for the back. Reborn in the sixties as a collection of tiny offices, 101 West Mission was moldy, its stucco walls crumbling. Shimmery clouds of termites filled the courtyard after every warm rain. But the rent was low, extra low if you signed the disclaimer.

Not low enough, though. And today I'd promised myself I'd do the accounts—what there were of them—and face the music.

"Ever heard of the early bird?"

I halted in my tracks. Perched on the top step to suite D

was a short plump Mexican woman wearing a nylon track-suit, hot pink trimmed in silver and black. "Jaymie Zarlin?" she said. "Santa Barbaria Investigations?"

Barbaria? Was this some kind of joke? "Santa Barbara Investigations," I corrected.

"You sure?" The woman, somewhere around fifty, put a hand to her lower back and grimaced as she got to her feet. She reached into her pants pocket, managed to extract a bent card with two fingers, and held it out to me. "Your eyes. They're two different colors."

"Last time I looked, that was the case." I rested the heavy old cruiser against my thigh and read my own business card, the card I'd been handing out for nearly two years now. *Jaymie Zarlin, Santa* Barbaria *Investigations.* "Where did you get this?" I spoke sternly, as if I were the victim of a misspelling conspiracy.

"From a cop. Big guy, sexy? Dawson, I think. Pretty sure he likes you. I can see why—except for those eyes and maybe the way you are dressed, you're a chica guapa."

A beautiful girl? She was flattering me: I knew damn well what I looked liked. Yep, my eyes were different, all right: one was an innocent blue and the other a sly and cynical green. My olive complexion was scattered with obstinate freckles left over from childhood, and I preferred to tether my horsey brown hair into a no-nonsense ponytail. Too serious to be pretty, I'd have said. Just good-looking enough to get by.

But what the hell was wrong with my black jeans, tennies, and best vintage T-shirt? I coolly decided to not take the bait. "Mike Dawson? Sure, I know the guy."

"Uh-huh, I bet you do." The woman held open the screen door and waited as I bolted my bike to the wrought-iron banister. "By the way, I'm Gabi Gutierrez. Let's go inside, OK? And could I please have a glass of water? I've been here one hour

and it's so hot, the sweat's rolling down the crack in my butt."
Relentless, she followed hard on my heels.

Suite D's signature perfume of damp plaster and dry-rot
welcomed us as we stepped inside. I tossed my bag on the desk
and began to ease up one of the brittle old window blinds.
Then I jumped: a tiny wizened face peered at me through the
glass.

"Deadbeat! Crawk! Deadbeat!" The screech was loud enough
to drown out a siren. The repo woman next door had parked
her yellow and green parrot outside, tethering it by one scaly
leg to a perch. As usual, the bird flapped itself into a frenzy at
the sight of me.

"Kinda musty in here. Want me to open the windows?" Ms.
Gutierrez didn't wait for an answer but proceeded to snap up
the rest of the blinds and raise the sashes. "Whoa, look at that
dust! And that bird—*pft*! Ugly as sin."

She leaned out the window and shook a warning finger at
the parrot. I stared past her in disbelief: Deadbeat was studiously, silently polishing his beak on his perch.

I headed for the kitchen, sneaking a backward glance as I
went. The woman was running a speculative finger over my desk
and smiling.

"You should get a new bicycle, aluminum," she called after
me. "Something lighter than that old thing. How many rooms
you got here?"

"Rooms?" I returned with a glass of water and handed it
to her. Then I dropped into my office chair, assuming what I
trusted was an authoritative position behind the desk. "Three
including the bathroom, I guess. By the way, what you called
'that old thing' is the bike I got in fifth grade. I earned it with
my babysitting money."

"OK, I get it. It's special to you." Her eyes roved the walls,
taking in the sum of my decor: a creased map of Santa Barbara,

last year's tide calendar, and a shadow box holding mounted butterflies. "This place needs the creative touch. Some nice velvet curtains maybe, I know a lady on San Andres who sews them really—"

"Ms. Gutierrez?" I'd wrangled the papers scattered across the desktop into a stack. Now I anchored the stack with a chunk of sandstone. "How may I help you?"

"Please, call me Gabi." She sat down in the client's chair and folded her hands in her lap. "Well, yesterday . . . my sister's boy Danny . . . Danny, he . . . *Dios mío.*"

Ms. Gutierrez dabbed at her eyes with the sleeve of her hot-pink top. I located a box of tissues and placed it in front of her on the desk. "Just take your time."

"Sorry." She yanked out a tissue and trumpeted. "I guess I had to let everything go."

"When you're ready."

"OK, I'm ready. I'm here for Alma, my little sister. And for her kid Danny, but mostly for Alma." She drew in a deep breath, let it out. "See, I raised all my brothers and sisters. I got six, one is dead. Alma, she was the little one, the sweet one. And then she fell in love with a mean guy and I couldn't stop her. She had some really bad years. . . ."

The narrative was wandering. "Is this about him, Ms. Gutierrez? The mean guy?"

"Call me Gabi. No, that one is long gone, gracias a Dios," she glowered. "Alma had three kids with him before she got free. Chuy, Aricela, and Danny. Danny's the oldest, he's eighteen. My sister says he's sick. To me he's just crazy. *Loco!*" The word ricocheted around the small room like a bouncy ball.

I cleared my throat. Crazy, loco—I detested those words. "So this is about your nephew, who is *mentally disabled?*"

Gabi Gutierrez was quiet, staring off into space. When she met my eyes, I saw that her anger was gone and only sadness remained. "Don't get me wrong. Danny was a great kid, my favorite nephew growing up. But I just don't—don't know if maybe he *did it*."

I pushed back my chair, got up, and walked over to the window. Devil bird caught sight of me and stuck out his pointy black tongue.

"Look, Ms. . . . Gabi." I turned back to the room. "I guess Deputy Dawson didn't explain what I do. I'm an investigator, not a detective. I find missing people, that's pretty much it. So unless your nephew's missing, I'm afraid you've come to the wrong person."

"No!" Gabi jumped up, sending her handbag toppling. A jumble of objects fell to the floor: purple-handled scissors, a pink cell phone, a fat bundle of coupons in a money clip.

"You *are* the right one, I already know it. Listen to me: Danny—they say he killed a girl! Two kids found him yesterday, sitting by her body, covered in blood. She was Lili Molina, a good girl, Danny's friend. Maybe even his only friend. I don't think Danny would hurt a bug, but what do I know? He's—he's *mentally disabled* now. And this is killing my sister, she can't move. I mean it. Alma cannot get out of her bed."

"I wish I could help." I felt squishy with sweat. "But Dawson shouldn't have given you my card. I've never investigated a homicide—it's outside my area of expertise." This wasn't entirely true. I'd investigated two homicides, on behalf of the families of mentally disabled victims. But this was different, wasn't it?

"I'm sorry, Gabi. Look, I can give you the names of several attorneys who might be able to help you. If they can't, they'll give you referrals."

"Hey, come on. Do you think Alma has money for a lawyer?" Gabi stood up and stretched to her full five-foot-flat height. "She cleans houses, like me."

"Well, there's the public defender—"

"You don't get it. Everybody except Alma thinks Danny did

it. Especially the cops! No public anything is gonna help him. Even me, I'm not sure." She held out her hands to me, palms up. "I want the facts, that's all I'm asking."

"I'm sorry, I really am." I dropped back into the desk chair. "But I'd be misleading you if I took this on. I'd be out of my depth, and I might even damage your nephew's case."

"The reason he gave me your card—the sheriff? He said you would help. *Pft!* What did he know." Gabi Gutierrez stomped over to the door, yanked it open, and shut it smartly behind her. Five seconds later, she jerked it open again.

"Mentally disabled. Yes, that's a nicer word. So you use nice words, so what?" Again the door slammed.

I looked out the side window. Deadbeat was hunched like a mini vulture, muttering into his chest.

God knows I wanted to help. But a voice in my ear warned me to stay away. Danny Armenta and his troubles hit too close to home.

Besides, I had to be practical, didn't I? What I needed was a paying client, as in cash on the barrel. I suspected Gabi Gutierrez planned to reimburse me with her energetic services. That was all I needed: someone stirring up dust, bouncing off the walls to a funky salsa beat. My head throbbed just thinking of it.

Deputy Dawson, just wait till I . . . till I what? Apparently even a mental image of the guy could heat me up. And now, thanks to Ms. Gutierrez, I suspected I was about to make contact with more than an image.

I sat down at the kitchen table while I waited for my coffee to drip, and stirred a loose pile of paper with one listless finger. Honestly, I didn't need to look at a bunch of numbers to know the score. Santa Barbara Investigations had never operated in the black. I'd shored up my venture from its inspired beginning, two years ago now, with my savings. And those savings, which also helped pay the mortgage on my house, had nearly run out.

I poured the coffee into my mug and walked over to the east-facing window at the back of the kitchen. If I couldn't be outside on this achingly lovely June morning, at least I could hang halfway out. I shoved the protesting sash up with one hand, parked my rear on the sill, and rested my eyes on the bougainvillea draping the block wall.

But my thoughts wandered back to the nagging subject of money. Specifically, the lack of it.

I'd squirreled away gleanings throughout the mind-numbing decade I'd worked for the San Joaquin Grape Growers Association. Nearly ten years spent sending out bulletins warning of bunch rot and glassy-winged sharpshooters. I tipped back my head and groaned: the fruits of all that tedium, down the disposal in just over two years.

A hummingbird sporting a purple gorget zoomed in out of nowhere, the beating of his wings as loud as a lion's purr. He studied me for a moment, then dashed over to stab zealously at the glowing pink bougainvillea flowers.

Down the disposal? Come on, I chided myself, that just wasn't true. In the past two years I'd located twenty-seven missing people, eighteen of them mentally disabled. I'd helped save several lives. Did none of that matter?

I tossed the last of the coffee out the window, then hopped off the sill to rinse the mug at the sink. The cup, with its worn image of Santa Barbara's harbor, was precious to me. I smiled as I dried it gently with a dish towel. My brother found it in a thrift shop and gave it to me on my thirty-fourth birthday. Brodie had apologized because the gift was secondhand, but even back then, the mug was worth its weight in gold. Now it was priceless.

I returned the cup to its place on the shelf and walked over to the paper-strewn table. The fact was, I needed more work. Finding missing people was a labor of love, all I really wanted to do. But if I also wanted to survive, I'd need to broaden my horizons.

Just now, what I needed was fresh air. I turned my back on the table and headed for the door.

As I pedaled down Anacapa Street, I told myself I was out for a spin, heading nowhere in particular. Anacapa, like a grande dame sweeping her skirts through the city, descends slowly but surely to the ocean, and I was enjoying the ride. But as I glided past the Lobero Building and approached the main post office, a line of newspaper dispensers caught my eye.

I popped my bike over the curb and scanned the offerings. The headline on the local paper had me digging for change. *Murder at Solstice: Apollo Guild's Daphne Found Dead.*

A light breeze clanked the lanyard on the post office flagpole as I studied the grainy photograph. A lovely young woman with a shy smile gazed up at me: Lili Molina, Danny Armenta's friend.

I decided to pedal on down to the Apollo Guild warehouse. Couldn't hurt. Didn't mean I was getting involved.

Chapter Three

Santa Barbara's uptown streets are lined with beds of exotic flowering plants, brick sidewalks, and swanky shops. But the warehouse was located down in the sin-and-light-industrial zone, on Indio Muerto Street. This was the city's funky back side, packed with auto-detailing shops, massage parlors, junk stores, and many one-of-a-kind enterprises such as the skateboarders' Church of Skatan.

Speeding along on my steed, it took me no more than ten minutes to get to the warehouse from the PO—thanks to the car-clogged streets, no longer than a vehicle would have taken. And hey, I'd enjoyed the health benefit of sucking up a liter of exhaust.

Deputy Dawson must have received my frazzled brain waves. Because it was none other than tall-dark-and-handsome himself who pushed open one of the big warehouse doors as I labored up the sidewalk, cruiser in tow. Mike's gold-flecked brown eyes narrowed, and his curvy lips fought down a smile. It was early summer, but his skin was already darkly tanned, thanks to his Native American grandma.

"Hey, Jaymie." He tilted his chin in a hello. "It's been a while. I see you're still dragging that clunker around."

"Mike. How are you?" I tried to sound professional, but my voice came out kind of prissy.

He gave in and grinned. "Not bad." At six foot four, big-boned and broad-shouldered, Mike was no kid. But somehow his smile said otherwise.

"So what's a deputy sheriff doing in town?"

"Hell, I don't know. Except this block is county land. The city never incorporated it—too many improvements to make, I suppose. The city cops are conducting the investigation, but my boss asked me to keep tabs on the case." His smile snuck back. "You know, I was just thinking about you. This must be fate."

"Uh-huh, fate. By the way, I don't know whether to thank you or kick you in the rear for giving my card to Gabi Gutierrez. Loads of money in that job."

"Since when do you care about that?" Mike's goofy look vanished. "That family needs help—I thought you could give it to them. Nobody's twisting your arm."

"No, course not." I kept my tone flippant, but I was chastened. "Look, do you have a minute? I'll admit, I'm curious about the case. You could brief me, maybe."

"OK . . . sure, why not." Mike held open the door, and I wheeled my bike into the entry hall.

"Listen, Jaymie." Mike hooked a thumb in his belt. "I should warn you. Deirdre Krause is in the main workroom, conducting interviews."

"Dear Deirdre." I pushed the bike against the wall, shoving it harder than I meant to. "She still hot for you?"

"What?" He frowned. "I don't know that she ever was. What makes you think that?"

"Give me a break, Mike. She never could keep her dimpled little hands off you. Or hadn't you noticed?"

"Nope, hadn't noticed a thing. Come on, we'll slip past her and talk in the hall."

I followed him into a two-story-high open workroom, where

a massive parade float stood in a far corner. Card tables were set up in various parts of the room, separate from one another. Plainclothes cops, plus a few uniforms, were interviewing teenagers. Half a dozen more kids were draped over folding chairs, awaiting their turns.

I caught sight of the back of Deirdre's curly blond head, and suppressed an urge to step over and bait the Kewpie doll.

"They're talking to every single kid who worked on the float this year," Mike said as we crossed the space. "Fast, before they start swapping stories."

We came to a dark windowless hall leading to the left. It was cordoned off with yellow tape.

Mike stopped and put his big hand on my wrist. "You know I shouldn't be talking to you about this."

"I know. So I'm figuring you've got a reason. Same reason you sent Gabi Gutierrez to see me. Same reason you're even here today, I'd guess."

"Yeah, well." He frowned. "I've got a few buddies in the police department. What I'm hearing from them . . . I don't like it, that's all. Let's put it this way: the higher-ups have already made up their minds."

"Ah. The wheels of justice are spinning a little too swiftly. So . . . you'd like to throw a cog in those wheels." I smiled sweetly. "Cog—meaning me."

Mike grinned. "Your head's hard enough."

I could have responded, but my thoughts were racing on.

I knew Mike pretty damn well, and I knew he wasn't one to rock the boat unless he had a good reason. It was none of my business . . . but now I really *was* curious about the case.

"Mike? I'd like to visit the murder scene."

"You know that's going too far." He gave me a long hard stare. "But I suppose it's for a good cause. And I'd like to know what you think."

"Great," I said brightly.

Mike shrugged. "The rope's already around my neck. Suppose I might as well go and hang myself." He detached the yellow tape and we passed on through.

I followed him down the narrow hall. "The body's gone?" I said to his back.

"It's gone, all right. The cops removed it straightaway. Not by the book, and Deirdre's pissed. But when you look at the photos, you'll see why they did it."

Chaos and violence were evident the moment we entered the dressing room. I stopped just inside the door and took inventory.

A big three-part folding screen lay flat on the floor, and an old bentwood chair was upended. A circular storage bin was tipped over in one corner, and the contents—old hats, purses, theatrical props—were strewn about. Clothing lay scattered over the pitted gray concrete: a seashell-pink bra and matching underpants, nice jeans and a lime-green top, brown costume gloves with leafy green fingers, and layers of silver netting. Every single article of clothing was either slashed or torn.

The lone window was shut tight, and the space was claustrophobic. A bad smell hung in the room—sweetish, sick. Splashes of blood, already rusty and dried in the summer heat, spread like an angel's halo around the chalk outline of a head.

I turned to a double line of photographs stuck with blue masking tape to the wall. "Dear God—" I pressed a hand to my mouth.

"Ugly, isn't it. That's why the first responders didn't wait to move her. One of the cops knows the victim's mother, and he didn't want her seeing her daughter like that. How can you blame them? Truth is, I think the guys couldn't stand it themselves. . . . I'm surprised they didn't wring the perp's neck on the spot."

I forced myself to look closer at the photos. Lili Molina's

slim naked body was spread-eagled, stripped, badly beaten. Her light-brown skin was carved into bizarre patterns, swirls and crosshatches. A hank of what looked like her own hair, clotted with blood, was stuffed in her mouth. And her sliced face . . . cartilage and bone were exposed.

I glanced up at two photos placed higher on the wall: Lili's graduation portrait, the one I'd seen in the paper, and a picture of her costumed as the goddess Daphne. "She was a lovely girl, wasn't she, Mike? Not exactly beautiful—better than beautiful, really. Her good nature showed through her looks."

"Yeah. I know what you mean."

I told myself it was time to cordon off my emotions. "So. Who discovered the body?"

"Couple of girls, members of the Guild. They snuck back here yesterday afternoon, to do what fifteen-year-olds do. Freaked them out—they're getting counseling. They won't be playing house again anytime soon."

"What exactly did they see?"

"Danny Armenta was mumbling to himself, crouched near the body. A knife lay beside him on the floor. The forensics report isn't back yet, but it's fairly certain it was the same knife that inflicted the wounds."

"Not the murder weapon, though." I pointed at one of the photos. "Those marks on her neck? Lili was strangled to death, with some kind of cord."

"Right. The stab wounds were most likely postmortem— thank God for that." He looked at me appraisingly. "We'll make a detective out of you yet. You've got a good eye."

I ignored the backhanded compliment and glanced over the room. "Everything but the body has been left just as it was?"

"All still in place. You won't find anything new, Jaymie. The detectives have their own opinions, but when it comes to the evidence, they do their job." He crossed his arms over his chest.

"I have to tell you, I think the guy probably did it. I mean, look how crazy the killer was—all those weird cuts, like it was a ritual or something."

"Pretty convincing, all right." But I wasn't convinced. I walked over to the corner, knelt down, and sorted through the items that had been tipped from the prop bin. I came across two belts and a sash, but nothing that matched the marks on Lili's neck in the photo. I glanced up at Mike. "Did the police find the murder weapon?"

He shook his head. "Nope."

As I rose to my feet, a movement caught my eye: a big june bug bumbled in the top corner of the window frame, wanting out. Its carapace sounded a rhythmic *knock-knock* on the pane.

I walked over to the window. Industrial style: wire netting embedded in hazy glass, set in an old redwood frame. "That's odd. The sill's wiped clean." For a moment, I watched the efforts of the june bug.

"Tell me something, Mike. Why was Lili down here, if the party was on? And how did she get here from Alameda Park?"

"The cops are still working on that. They don't know why she came back. But it's not all that far—maybe seven blocks. She probably just walked."

"Kids don't walk these days. Not without cattle prods at their backs." I turned back to examine the frame and sill, then peered through the grimy glass into an asphalted alley. "When we're done here, I'll take a look outside."

"Sure." Mike shrugged. "But remember, the window was shut tight when the girls came in, and the door was wide open."

"The window was shut. . . ." I circled the room, then stopped before one of the open alcoves holding a fifteen-foot-long garment rack. The rack, nothing more than a thick dowel stretched end to end and braced at three points, was packed tight with costumes spilling and frothing from their hangers. "Looks like the Guild's running out of storage space."

"They ran out a while back," Mike said. "For the past few years the new parade outfits have been stored in a locker out in the manager's office. These costumes aren't used anymore, they're the old ones. And I mean old. The Apollo Guild was in existence a long time before the citywide Solstice Celebration started up. Since the nineteen thirties, as a matter of fact."

"Seriously?" I stepped close to the alcove, breathing in a fusty unwashed odor. "So what was the Apollo Guild originally, some kind of private club?"

"Was, and still is. Private and restricted, only for the very wealthy. And men only, even today. After World War Two the Guild became a charity too, a way for the rich to help disadvantaged local kids. Made the members look better, I suppose, community-minded. When the city started up their own solstice celebration, the Guild was the first to sponsor a parade float."

"Hm. Got a flashlight?"

Mike reached into his Windbreaker and pulled out a silver penlight. "Thought you weren't getting involved."

"Just being nosy." I ducked under the clothes at one end of the rack and squeezed sideways, step-by-step, shining the intense light on the dowel. My nostrils filled with dust and the funk of old sweat and perfume. Two-thirds of the way along, I halted. "Right here, Mike. No dust."

"What?" He stepped over to the alcove. "Far as I know, nobody's said anything about that."

"Maybe nobody looked. But this is the spot: I'm standing where Lili's killer waited for her."

"Waited for her? But Danny Armenta—"

"Let's not jump to conclusions, OK? If I part the costumes a little, I can see into the room. And not just into the room. Mike, go over to where the dressing screen stood. You'll see rust stains from the old iron feet on the floor."

"But like I said—"

"OK, stop. I can see you now. From here I could watch you undress."

"Michael, what are you doing back here?" A female voice screeled like a gull from the doorway.

Michael? Ugh! The ultra-high voice made my teeth ache.

"Hey, Deirdre," Mike muttered. "We were just, uh—"

"'We'? I only see one of you, Michael."

I couldn't stand it. I ducked under the costumes and popped back into the room. "Ta-da!"

Deirdre Krause's sulky baby face scowled. "Zarlin? What the hell are you doing at my crime scene?"

Her crime scene? "Just looking around."

"Well, you can just get the hell out. I could have you arrested for this." She raised a viciously plucked brow and looked over at Mike. "I'm surprised at you, Michael."

My skin prickled. "Listen, Krause—"

"Jaymie's here at my invite, Deirdre. She's—" He glanced at me, then made up his mind. "She's investigating the case on behalf of Danny Armenta's family."

"She would be." Deirdre Krause trilled out a laugh. "Jaymie Zarlin, Patron Saint of the Insane."

"That's uncalled for," Mike said quietly.

I clamped my mouth shut and ordered myself not to think of my brother. Instead, I stared the woman down. She was cute enough, theoretically speaking, with a face like a three-year-old cherub. But damn, she looked like a devil now.

"This one doesn't need defending, Michael. I wouldn't bother." Deirdre's voice dripped with saccharin, the way a rattler's fangs dribble with venom before it strikes. "Come find me in five, and we'll get a coffee. I know the sherriff's department isn't involved in this case, but still, you and I have things to talk about."

◆   ◆   ◆

"Deirdre's not as bad as she sounds." Mike followed after me as I banged the cruiser out the door. "She's always at her worst around you."

"I wonder why, *Michael*."

"Hey." He stepped ahead and caught my bike by the handlebars. "Does it matter?"

I looked down at Mike's broad hands and remembered just how good they'd made me feel. . . . "Um, I—"

"Jaymie . . ." He brushed my cheek with his fingertips, then snatched his hand back as if he'd touched fire.

I smiled crookedly, then waved an awkward good-bye and rode around the corner into the alley. I shoved thoughts of Mike Dawson where they belonged, into a closet at the back of my mind.

Only three windows were set in the entire rear wall of the warehouse. The dressing room window had to be the one at the far end. I pedaled down the asphalted alley, leaned my bike against the wall, and balanced upright on the pedals.

Sure enough, someone had swiped away the dirt and grime on the outer sill, just as they had on the inner. Only a few flecks of dust rested there. And you could see where a flat tool, most likely a screwdriver, had recently been jammed under the edge of the frame to pry open the window. The tool had nicked the paint, and the bare redwood was bright.

So Mr. June Bug had entered the dressing room while the window was open. Dumb as a chunk of wood, he'd fixated on the inside of the pane and hadn't been able to find his way back out. And the killer? I wanted to think he'd come in through the window, too. Because if the killer had climbed in through the window, that pretty much took Danny right out of the picture. Cogitating hard, I shifted my weight on the pedals.

It was true: I wanted Danny Armenta to be innocent. For his sake, for his family's sake, and maybe for reasons of my own, I wanted it. And yet—and yet. Something was wrong with my theory. I glared at the bright nick in the redwood. Problem was, it was all a touch too obvious.

I rolled out of the alley, rounded a few corners, and pedaled up Garden Street under what was now a ravishing blue sky and a hot yellow sun. A superior day for the beach: I was tempted to take the day off.

I thought about Brodie and how much he'd loved the ocean. The die-hard surf guys had told me no one ever put in more time on the waves than my brother did. Day in and day out, he was the first one into the water and the last one to leave. When the world turned its back on Brodie, he turned to the sea.

Mike had been right to recommend me to Gabi. How could I not get involved in this case? My throat tightened. I knew what Mike wasn't saying aloud: the police, and then the citizens of this fair city, were going to railroad Danny Armenta straight to death row, due process be damned.

Yet it also was true that this crime was outside my area of expertise. My business was to locate lost souls and reunite them with their families, for better or worse. What did I know about solving a brutally executed murder and rape?

Danny Armenta needed an experienced investigator, some-one who knew what to look out for, what pitfalls to avoid. An amateur could make matters worse for him, screw up what few chances he had.

Palm fronds glistening in the breeze and the clanging of the Presidio bell failed to raise my spirits. By the time I rolled to a stop at 101 West Mission, I'd persuaded myself Danny Armenta was better off without me.

For the second morning in a row, the front steps of suite D were occupied. This time Gabi Gutierrez wore a black-and-white maid's uniform. Like the tracksuit, the uniform was on the snug side.

"Hola!" Gabi jumped to her feet and thrust a pink and purple spiral notebook aloft. "Remember the early bird? It got the worm!"

Pink and purple must be her favorite colors, I thought sourly. "I'm a little surprised to see you again, Ms. Gutierrez. I thought I explained that your nephew's case is outside what I do."

"It's Gabi, remember? And never mind about that." She swept my protest away with another triumphant wave of the notebook. "Investigator, you have a case!"

I gazed at the roof. As I counted to ten, I noticed that the clay tiles were slipping. "And as I explained—"

"No, no. A *different* case." Gabi folded her arms across her chest. "And this one is your kinda job, you can't say it's not." She opened the notebook, removed a check, and held it out to me. "You weren't here, so I asked for a deposit."

I couldn't help myself. I took the check and glanced at it. Then I peered more closely, to make sure I'd read the right number of zeros.

The check, signed by a Mrs. Darlene Richter, was written for no less than ten thousand dollars.

"That—well, that *is* good-sized," I squeaked. It was by far the largest retainer I'd ever received. "And you say it's my sort of job?"

"Yup. You only gotta find Minuet. Easy! With all the people I know who work in Montecito, I could maybe find her myself."

"'Minuet'? Hold on. Don't tell me someone paid a ten-thousand-dollar retainer for a pet."

"Are you rich? Can you be choosy? This is Santa Barbara—some people are rich and some people are poor. Lucky for you, this one is rich." Gabi opened the notebook a second time and withdrew from its pages a color photo. Heaven help me, I opened my hand and accepted it.

A winsome King Charles spaniel, sporting a lavender collar

and lace ribbons over each perky ear, gazed up at me with soulful eyes.

"I'm not sure what to say," I muttered.

"Say yes! Don't you like animals? How can you say no to that face? Besides, ten thousand dollars—I'm pretty sure you could use it." She herded me into the office.

"I need coffee," I bleated.

"Go ahead, take your time. There's things I can do."

Gabi had opened the blinds, tidied the desk, and rearranged the chairs by the time I returned from the kitchen. I dropped into the desk chair, only to find myself looking at a page of neat handwriting, no doubt torn from the purple-pink notebook, resting on the blotter. *What this office needs to run better: new lightbulb, fix broken string on blind, get rid of dirty old couch* . . . I took a few swallows of coffee before I let myself speak.

"Ms. Gutierrez? We need to talk before we go any further. This morning I visited the murder scene."

"You'll help us," Gabi said breathlessly. "I knew you would!"

Dear God, what was I getting myself into? "I've said no such thing."

"Good, good," she replied, plainly not listening. "And please call me Gabi. Now, I need to talk to you about how I'm gonna pay."

"Stop right there." I held up a hand. "If I decide to take the case, and I'm not saying I will, you'll need to understand something. I'm not an invalid, I do my own cleaning. There's nothing much to clean here anyway. So please, don't ask if you can clean instead of paying cash."

"Who said anything about cleaning?" Gabi arched an eyebrow. "You want to live in dirt, that's your business. But don't forget I got you that check."

"Mm. And I wonder what strings you'll attach."

"Well, I been thinking. And when I start thinking look out." A cagey gleam shined in her eyes. "You need a PA. In case you don't know, that stands for 'personal assistant.' Somebody to answer the phone, keep the books, welcome new clients, organize the desk. Most PAs won't dust and vacuum and make coffee, but I'll do all that too!" The gleam grew stronger. "If you let me be your PA, you won't have to work out here. You can use that table in the kitchen with all the coffee rings on it. See? I already figured out you like that better."

I couldn't help it, I burst out laughing.

"OK! I'll tell my sister Alma you *almost* decided to do it. She'll feel better, I know."

"You're a good aunt and a good sister, Gabi. That I admire."

"Not good. Just . . . just average. You want the truth? Below average, even."

Gabi hurried down the street to her car. She was late for her next job. And Mrs. Talcott did not like late.

What Miss Jaymie said, calling her a good sister and aunt, it made her feel prickly with shame. Being praised for the wrong reason made her feel bad.

Gabi had a secret: she was afraid of crazy people. If she saw somebody acting weird even a block away, she crossed to the other side of the street.

A year and a half ago, when Danny got sick . . . well. She asked Alma and the kids to move out. Danny was OK, he never threatened anybody or anything like that. But he was so strange, talking to himself and seeing things in the mirrors. She was scared to be around him anymore.

So she told Alma the manager complained there were too many people in the apartment. But that was a big fat lie.

Shame. Shame on nobody but her.

Hiring Miss Jaymie to help—even if it meant working eighty hours a week—was the least she could do.

The sun was angling low in the west, preparing to paint the sky in 1970s yellows and oranges, when I pedaled up to the

ancient Vee-Dub bus parked in the beachfront lot. The vehicle
was covered in what might have looked like graffiti to a casual
eye. But to those in the know, a great American novel began at
the driver's door and continued down the side and around the
back, concluding at the passenger's door.

I approached an open back window. The interior was con-
cealed by a frayed Indian bedspread functioning as a drape.
The ancient fabric stirred in the late-afternoon onshore breeze.

"Charlie?" I tapped on the Vee-Dub shell. "It's me, Jaymie."

"Course it's you," answered a voice burred by scarred vo-
cal cords. "We're glad to see you, Jaymie girl. Been a long time,
hasn't it?"

"Come on, not that long. Ten days, maybe. I have to think
for myself sometimes, you know."

"Oh, Annie and me know you do plenty of that." The voice
broke into a fit of strangled hacking. "Lift the folding chair
off the hook there, Jaymie. . . . Stay awhile."

"OK. And here you go." I opened my backpack, took out a
small bag of candy, and held it up to the window. A hand bound
with burn tissue reached around the drape and retrieved the
bag. There was a sound of the packet being ripped open, then a
cessation of the coughing and a phlegmy sigh.

"Horehound drops, bless you. Annie and me, we like the
old remedies."

Annie had died seven years ago, mercifully, in the same fire
that had disfigured Charlie so badly. Mike had told me the hor-
rific story: a faulty camp stove had ignited their tent while they
slept.

"Thanks for the blessing, Charlie. God knows I need it."

"Cup a tar? Got plenty of sugar to cut it."

"No thanks."

"Your boyfriend the cowboy dropped by the other day.
Good man, for a fuzz."

"I don't have a boyfriend. You'll be the first to know when I do."

"Oh, you got a boyfriend, all right. Like it or not, you got one."

I crossed my arms over my chest and tried to keep my expression neutral. I didn't know if Charlie could see me through the threadbare curtain. I couldn't see him. Never had, actually, although I'd met him nearly three years ago, when I'd first come to town to look for Brodie. Charlie stayed inside the van all day and drove out of the lot every night after sundown, to park in some driveway or vacant lot.

"I'm not going to argue with you on the boyfriend thing, Charlie. I came to talk to you about something else."

"Figured you did. Listen, why don't you set yourself in the passenger seat? That's Annie's seat, you know."

"I'd be honored." I opened the rusted old door and climbed in. The front seat was separated from the back by another circa 1965 bedspread. I faced front and studied the dash, which was plastered with shells, dried starfish, and sea glass. There was even a touch of whimsy, a sun-bleached plastic fork with some sort of dried seaweed stuck to the prongs. The novel on the exterior was Charlie's creation, but I knew the dashboard was Annie's.

"Let 'er rip," Charlie coughed from the back.

"OK. Did you hear about the girl who was murdered after the Solstice parade?"

"I heard. They arrested a boy for it, a boy who's a little different in his head."

I nodded. "The way Brodie was different."

"Your brother was a fine young beach bum and a first-rate surfer. What happened to him was a crime."

"Yes. And what's happening to this boy is criminal, too. The cops have already decided he's guilty. But I'm not so sure."

"They already tarred and feathered him?"

"You got it. The thing is, his family wants me to help. I've tried to explain I'm out of my depth. Because if I step in, then mess things up—you understand, don't you? I can't have that on my conscience."

"But on the other hand, I'm guessing, who else'll take it on?"

"Yeah, I can't argue with that." I rubbed a finger over the rough skin of a starfish. "Know what? I need a vacation. Hawaii, the Big Island . . ."

"Plenty of time for that later. Plenty of time for you and the cowboy to ride off into the sunset. Right now, I think you know what you gotta do."

There was silence, and the crinkle of another horehound drop unwrapping. I watched the play of the spangly waves, tinged gold by the light of the lingering sun.

"Charlie," I said after a time, "can I bring a hot-glue gun and reattach a few of these treasures? Think Annie would mind?"

"Annie'd appreciate it mightily. And she'd say you already know the answer to your question. She'd most likely say you know the answer to the boyfriend business, too."

Chapter Four

I thought over Charlie's advice as I pedaled home along Shoreline. Locals and tourists mingled at Ledbetter Beach, clustering under bright umbrellas or leaping for Frisbees and Wiffle balls in the sheltering curve of the sandstone cliff. Just offshore, a dozen or more paddleboarders stood erect, looking as if they were walking on water.

I turned up Loma Alta, crossed Cliff Drive, and entered Vista del Mar, dismounting when the road steepened. The sun had beaten down on the banks all day long, and now the sweet resinous odor of rockroses and sage saturated the air. As I turned to the left and wheeled my bike up El Balcón, the hill blocked the sun and the road was plunged into deep shadow.

A clatter of feet approached from behind. I turned, but not before a tricolor blur nipped me on the Achilles.

"God damn it, dog! You're lucky I'm wearing socks." I grinned in spite of myself: the heeler stood his ground, all four feet spread, ready to cattle-drive me on home.

"OK, let's go, Dex." The mutt barked cheerfully. He could be trusted to keep his fangs off my heels as long as I kept moving forward.

El Balcón was a narrow track cut into a hillside so steep, it made a joke of the angle of repose. Three houses, built back

when planning restrictions were lax, clung to three nearly per-
pendicular lots. My house was the third and last, an after-
thought that hadn't involved too much thinking. Somehow the
builder had managed to carve out a terrace and construct a tiny
house and a separate one-car garage, possibly large enough for
a Mini Cooper. Then a previous owner converted the garage
into a studio and wedged an even smaller garage, ramshackle
now, against the bank.

I'd never planned to own a house in Santa Barbara. The
prices were astronomical. But one morning, biking along Cliff,
I'd spotted a Realtor's sign planted halfway up the oak-covered
hill.

"As is," were the first words out of Tiffany Tang's mouth.
"And you'd need to sign some disclaimers. I won't lie to you,
that hill in the back could be unstable: I'm not saying it is, but
just so you know. . . ."

I didn't really take in her words, because Tiff had wisely
chosen to utter them while we were standing on the five-foot-
wide strip of patio at the back of the house, looking out over
the harbor, the Channel Islands, and damn near to China. It
was a spot you could happily die in, I'd thought at the time. Of
course, if there was a big earthquake and the hill came down,
you might die in it sooner than expected.

I turned up my drive and slowed as the climb steepened.
Another nip found my heel, this one more gentle, encourag-
ing. I left the cruiser in the breezeway, walked around the corner, and unlocked the studio door.

Dexter streaked by me and shot onto the futon bed. The
stubborn mutt had belonged to my brother. I'd found Dex
weeks after Brodie's death, living by his wits and charm around
the marina—much as my brother had done, I'd later discovered. The mutt had kept his bad side hidden until he was certain he'd carved out a place in my heart.

I flopped into the papasan chair and tucked up my legs. "Hey, Brod . . . how's it going?" I tried softly. But as usual there was no reply of any kind, no reason to believe he was present.

I knew what some people thought: *It's been three years now. Why doesn't Jaymie move on?*

I called up an image of Brodie as a kid, freckle-faced, alarmingly hyper, and infuriatingly mischievous. Once, when he was eight, he'd found a Jerusalem cricket in the yard and tucked it between my sheets. I could still recall the look on his freckled face when I screamed: a warring mix of remorse and delight. If I moved on, who would remember my brother? And if no one remembered him, he would be lost.

I sat there for ten or fifteen minutes, allowing a braided river of memories to flow through my mind. At last, I got to my feet. "Dex, want to come? I'm going to the house."

The dog, curled into a tight knot, lifted one tan circular eyebrow and let it fall.

"OK, have it your way." I left the door open behind me. Dex would follow in his own good time.

Inside the house, I filled a glass with white wine from the fridge, then went out to sit in the old redwood chair facing the channel. I took a long sip and shut my eyes, letting the icy-cold liquid trickle down my throat.

Just as I was beginning to relax, my cell jangled in my jeans pocket. I fumbled as I pulled it out.

"Jaymie, it's Mike."

As I hopped to my feet, my free hand shot out and connected with the wineglass I'd balanced on the arm of the chair. The glass shattered on the old concrete pavers.

Annoyed by my distracted reaction, annoyed that I'd broken the glass, I spoke curtly. "What's up?"

"Hey. Take it easy."

"Sorry."

"This business with Danny Armenta. Makes me think about Brodie."

I stepped over to the hip-high stuccoed wall and stared out into the gathering fog. "Yeah. Me too. "

"That's not why I called, but . . . I just wanted to say that." Mike paused before he continued. "As a matter of fact, I'm calling with news about Danny."

"OK. But why call me?" I felt my chest tighten. "I haven't decided to take on the case."

The silence expanded between us. The night's first moans from the foghorn sounded out in the harbor.

"Have to say I'm surprised." Mike's voice was cool.

"Why?" I said stubbornly. "Just because my brother was mentally disabled and this guy is too, it doesn't follow that Armenta's my concern."

"Whatever you say."

"But . . . I'd still like to hear the news."

"Sorry. The news is only for someone who gives a shit."

"Hey!" I squeaked. "That's not fair."

"Maybe not. Anyway, here it is. This afternoon, Danny Armenta was beaten up by a couple of inmates, thugs. I talked to a guy I know at the jail and got the kid moved to a single cell. But I'll tell you what, nobody's in the mood to do him any favors."

"He needs to be out of there, Mike. Have they set bail?"

"Half a mil."

"Might as well be a billion. He'll never raise it." I took a deep breath and exhaled slowly. "It's possible Danny didn't do it. In fact, I don't think he did."

"If that's what you think, then you better get to work and prove it."

"But . . . maybe that's not what I think, just what I hope. How can I tell if I'm fooling myself?"

"Does it matter? Either way, you'll go after the truth. But I wouldn't waste time if I were you. The DA's frothing at the mouth."

"Like I said, I haven't actually decided to—"

"Jaymie? You sound like a broken record. Besides, I think you've decided." Mike's voice slowed and warmed. "You have, haven't you."

"Um, can we talk later? I just broke a glass and I need to sweep up. Before, you know, Dex steps in it or something."

"No problem. I'll call you tomorrow."

What the hell was going on? It had been two years since Mike and I were together, two years since I'd backed out of what had begun to feel like too damn serious a relationship. We'd parted friends, at least on the surface—but I knew he'd been thoroughly pissed with me. Now the ice was thawing, it seemed. And I wasn't sure how I felt about that.

Oh, I liked the guy. I liked him a lot, in more ways than one. A memory of what Mike's body looked like under that chambray shirt, and inside those cowboy jeans, came to mind.

But it was complicated.

Mike Dawson was the marrying kind, the house-full-of-kids kind. And for reasons I didn't need to dredge up, I was not.

I scowled and went for the dustpan and broom. I couldn't trust the man. Nor could I trust myself.

The next morning, I found myself standing across the street from the century-old county jail. The three-story pseudo-Spanishy structure was topped by cyclone fencing gaily interwoven with concertina wire. The giant tiara glittered in the sun.

I crossed the street, weaving my way through the women and kids milling about on the wide broken sidewalk. I circled two little girls kneeling on the concrete. Oblivious to their surroundings, they were busy tossing jacks.

At the jailhouse entrance, I pushed open the heavy door and let it fall shut behind me. A mix of smells invaded my nostrils: sweat, bleach, boiled cabbage, and other substances I didn't need to identify. The narrow room, little more than a hallway, was crowded with visitors. I paused as my eyes adjusted to the dim light.

I'd always thought there was an ugly symmetry to this space. A trough worn into the ancient linoleum led from the door to the desk. Double barriers of glass block, enclosing visiting stalls, faced off on opposite sides. The room reminded me of an abattoir: lambs to the slaughter.

Though I'd visited the jail a number of times since Brodie's death on behalf of clients, I'd never quite gotten used to it. Never was able to walk in the door without gloom falling on me like a shroud. But what I felt about the place was irrelevant. I was here on business.

The desk was unmanned, and a battered sheet of tin had been inserted behind the brass mouthpiece. The line of waiting visitors twisted back on itself like a snake. I walked to the end of the line, which was near the head.

After five minutes, the crowd grew restive. At ten past three, voices were raised.

At twenty past, a smiley-faced jailer appeared. "Take it easy, ladies," he crooned through the mic. "Your men ain't going nowhere." He yanked up the tin sheet and tossed it on the counter, and a ritual of sorts began.

Each supplicant stated the name of the man she'd come to visit. The jailer checked the name on a monitor, then slid a narrow black book into a well beneath the plate glass. The visitor signed the book, returned it to the well, and stepped aside.

Guards began to usher prisoners to the stalls. The inmates wore plastic zip-tie cuffs and held their folded hands at their waists.

At last I reached the head of the line. The grilled opening was set in the glass at the level of the jailer's mouth, and I had to twist my neck and bend down to speak into it. "I'm here to see Daniel Armenta."

The smiling oily-faced man stared back at me through the inches-thick plank of smudged glass, his moist lips slightly ajar. His eyes watched my mouth.

"How are you spelling that?" He tipped his bobblehead to read his screen.

"A-r-m-e-n-t-a."

He peered at the screen. "Armenta. The one that killed the girl?"

"That's for a court of law to decide." My temperature was rising, but I held my tongue. I knew all too well that a so-called bad attitude on my part could make things tough for Danny.

The goon stared again at my mouth. Then he slowly raised his eyes to meet mine. "What's your name and what's your connection to the prisoner?"

I bit down on the inside of my cheek to keep cool. "Jaymie Zarlin. Daniel Armenta's family has hired me to investigate his case."

"That's great." The jailer spread his lips, revealing oddly small teeth in a wide, heavy jaw. "Hey, I remember you." He wobbled his head from side to side. "Joan of Arc, huh? Whatever turns you on."

What would turn me on right now would be to wring your damn neck.

Fifteen minutes later, when two large guards led a bent and broken young man into a chute, my mind cleared. This wasn't about me.

I watched through the plate glass as one man shoved a chair against Danny's knees, and the other dropped a hand on his shoulder and rammed him down.

"Zarlin. Cubicle seven," the loudspeaker squawked. I glanced at the guy behind the desk: he was leering at me.

I walked around the glass wall and approached Danny's booth. He was hunched forward, his chin nearly touching his chest, staring at the tabletop. I sat down in a stained resin chair and leaned forward. "Danny . . ." But of course he couldn't hear me through the thick glass. I picked up the black phone hanging on the wall, and waited.

A full minute passed. I tapped the glass with the receiver.

Danny lifted his head. For a single moment, his eyes met mine.

A large dark bruise filled the socket of one bloodshot eye. Terror filled his gaze. Danny, I realized, was nearly catatonic with fear.

Swiftly, before he could turn away, I motioned for him to pick up the phone. I smiled brightly, with what I hoped looked like encouragement.

He hesitated. Then, miracle of miracles, Danny copied my motion. He picked up the receiver on his side of the wall and held it to his ear.

"Danny," I said as gently as I could, "I'm Jaymie. I know your tía. I'm Gabi's friend." A flicker of understanding lit his stunned face. I knew I had a brief moment to connect, nothing more.

"I'm going to help you, Danny. I'll leave my phone number at the desk. Anytime you want to talk, ask for a phone." I studied his face, no doubt handsome before his illness. Was any part of my message getting through?

"Danny, would you say something? My name, Jaymie—please say it back to me."

He opened his mouth, but nothing came forth. When he did speak at last, his voice sounded rusty, long out of use. "I—I—"

But then his eyes blanked. The phone fell from his hand, dangling on its short cord, and his head lolled forward on his chest.

"I'm going to help you," I heard myself say. "Danny? I promise I will."

I watched as the two bulky guards fetched Danny from the booth. They lifted him like a limp rag doll. I couldn't bear to watch, and looked away. But a moment later, a movement caught my eye. Danny lay sprawled on the floor, and the two men stood over him, smirking.

My breath snagged in my throat. I knew better than to champion Danny now—that would only bring him more grief.

The sun needled my eyes as I stepped out on the street. Blindly, I switched on my phone, then managed to punch in a number. "Gabi? It's Jaymie. I'm ready to start."

"Well, well. Jaymie Zee." The deep, masculine voice, rough and tender as the purr of a big cat, vibrated through my phone. "I was just thinking bout you the other day, baby."

"Drop the sweet talk, consigliere. I know all your tricks, re-member?"

"I remember everything, sweetheart. But you musta forgot a few things. 'Cause you'd have called long before this if you re-membered better."

I laughed out loud at the down-home act. Zavier Carbonel, born and raised in the Bay Area, had enjoyed a moon-shot ride from prep school straight through UC Berkeley and Stanford Law. "Zave? I'm going to say this straight out: I need a favor."

"Sure. But you're not getting it over the phone. You want something from Daddy, you pay him a visit. Catch my drift?"

"I'm not coming up to your office, Zave."

"Why not? I'd have thought a competitive young lady like yourself would enjoy walking in and closing the door on these skinny girls I got working for me. They all want a piece of the Zave—you know they do."

"And they all get it. That's the point."

"OK, Jaymie, OK. Come by the house around eight. I'll have dinner ready. Course, you'll bring the dessert."

I had to laugh. "Sooo smooth. And . . . Zave?"

"Yeah, babe?"

"This is something . . . that matters."

"Hear you." His voice sobered. "Don't fret, Jaymie. We'll sort it out."

Zave's posh office was located on the top floor of the tallest building in Santa Barbara, the Granada, with its three-sixty views. But his home was something else.

I piloted Brodie's old El Camino through the lower Westside. It was a mellow evening, approaching dusk. Already, several young men were conducting business on the corners. They noticed my ride and looked at me alertly, then slid their eyes sideways when they understood I wasn't a customer.

Zave's neighborhood was arguably the worst in town. Trash from overflowing garbage cans, plus a dead skunk and other less identifiable roadkill, littered the streets. But this was also one of the oldest neighborhoods in Santa Barbara. The giant palms were stately, the bougainvilleas heaped in huge haystacks glowing maroon and pink in the dying light.

Zave . . . Zave was fine, but maybe our relationship wasn't. Not for the first time, I wondered whether I should be so involved with the guy.

After all, some people would have a name for what we did. Zave, my connection to the well-heeled strata of town, provided me with info and assistance from time to time. And you could say I paid him back with—hey, what the hell—sex.

But was it as simple as that? The payment, incomparable sex, paid both ways. And in helping me, the shyster had a chance to do some good. So how was it wrong?

Out of the blue, without meaning to, I thought of a certain deputy sheriff. Now I didn't feel so perky.

I drove past a housing project. Tattered curtains hung listlessly from open windows, and in a courtyard, a rail-thin ice cream vendor rang a forlorn bell.

Within a few blocks, the road began to meander up Carrillo Hill, and the streetlights and sidewalks disappeared. I turned into a narrow alleyway, rutted and overgrown.

The track circled several tumbledown properties. The structures were sagging, buried in ivy and abandoned. Then the road made a sharp bend, and I pulled up before a state-of-the-art spiked steel gate. I reached out through the window and pushed a button on an illuminated pad.

"Hey, baby."

"Begging admittance, if it pleases you, sir."

The gate slid open with a rather sinister hiss. Up ahead was La Casa de la Boca del Canon, a strikingly beautiful Spanish colonial constructed by William Randolph Hearst in the 1920s. The mogul had it built for his movie star guests, those who required an overnight respite on their journey from Hollywood to Hearst's castle in San Simeon.

As I pulled up in front, I was zapped by sensor lights. I blindly fumbled my way out of the El Camino to the stone steps.

"Ascend to seventh heaven," Zave's deep voice intoned from above.

"For God's sake, Zave. Switch off the klieg lights."

His laughter boomed out above me. I climbed the steps and was swept into his arms.

"Come into my parlor, you delicate butterfly." He held me lightly but firmly and tickled my neck with his tongue.

"Said the spider to the fly," I corrected. "You're the spider, I'm the fly."

"Then give me a buzz, baby," he murmured in my ear.

Zave was not handsome, objectively speaking. His nose was slightly flattened and bent to one side. His eyes were recessed in his skull—a plus for a boxer, but a tough look on an attorney. You hardly noticed, though. Zave's expression was so pleasing, so alive with intelligence, that the fact that his features weren't classic just didn't register.

"Good to see you, Jaymie. Why has it been so long?"

"You're too much for me, Zave. I require months to recover from your attentions."

"Bullshit you do." He took me by the elbow and steered me through several exquisitely tiled archways to his cozy dining room. "I'm going to suggest compartmentalization, Jaymie. Dinner first, followed by business. Then, whatever your naughty little mind dreams up."

A pair of tapers set in crystal candlesticks burned away on the cloth-covered table, where eggshell-thin china and old silver were laid out for two. Zave was a tease, but I knew that in one matter he was deadly serious: the preparation and eating of food.

He drew out a chair upholstered in mango-colored shot silk. "Madam?"

I perched gingerly on the edge, suddenly conscious of my grubby jeans.

The meal was sumptuous: elegant Cajun style. The flaky caught-that-day snapper was baked in a delectable toasted pecan butter sauce, the shrimp sautéed in cognac. "To die for," I moaned.

When we'd finished, I gave my lips one last pat with the linen napkin, then got to my feet and began to clear the table.

"Leave it," Zave commanded. "Eduardo will get it in the morning."

"Honestly," I objected. "I'd feel better if I rinsed my own plate."

"You're so damn bourgeois, Jaymie. I'm not sure if it's a turn-off or a turn-on."

Zave served me a dry apricot sherry in the living room. I leaned back on the couch and studied the huge oil painting over the fireplace. It depicted a fiesta in colonial Spanish California.

"I think I know that painting. It looks a lot like the famous one missing from the county courthouse."

"Does it?" He sat down beside me. "The guy who gave it to me bought it from some other guy. The courthouse painting went missing eighty years ago, you know."

"Doesn't mean they don't want it back." I gazed at him over the rim of my glass. "So someone *gave* it to you?"

"Uh-huh. For services rendered."

"You might have gotten the short end of the stick. I don't know much about art, but it's not a very good painting, is it? All out of proportion."

"It's crap. But a lot of people would like to own it, therefore I like having it. I know I don't have to explain how I am to you, Jaymie."

"No, you don't. And this is no way for me to talk, considering I'm about to ask for your help."

"You're wrong there. You're being straight, and that's best. Now, what is it you want from me? Besides the obvious, of course."

I ignored the lawyerly foreplay. "I need to locate a large amount of money. Half a million dollars, to bail someone out of jail. Somebody who might meet with an accident in there if I don't get him out."

Zave crossed his long legs. "Let me take a wild-ass guess. Would that somebody be the kid accused of the Solstice murder?"

"Yes. Danny Armenta." I carefully set the finely cut sherry glass down on the coffee table. "But I don't see how you figured that out."

"Your brother, sweetheart," Zave said gently. "This Armenta kid is mentally ill too. Now my question is, did he do it?"

"I don't know for sure. But I don't think he did."

"Forgive me for pushing." Zave's dark eyes drilled into my own, and it occurred to me that I wouldn't want to be interrogated by him in a courtroom. "Why do you think he might be innocent?"

"I went to see him yesterday, down at the jail. He's just not capable of it. Danny Armenta is a gentle soul, and the victim was his friend. Plus, there's evidence." There's no way I'd have passed a polygraph: as I said the word "evidence," my hands grew sticky with sweat.

"Evidence, is there? Sure that's not your wishfulness talking?"

"I can go over it with you if you want." I mentally crossed my fingers: sure, I could tell Zave about the window, but the truth was, I didn't know what it meant.

"Not necessary." The uptown lawyer lifted a skeptical eyebrow. "Sounds like your conclusion is based on intuition, Jaymie. But I'll take your word for it." He smoothed the edge of his pants cuff, then rose to his feet.

"In fact, I don't want to know the details. You're brushing up against the Apollo Guild, did you know that? Historically speaking, the Guild is a network of some of the most powerful men in SoCal."

"Really rich guys? Oh, I'm *so* impressed."

"You should be, Miss Smarty. You're out of your depth. Hell, I'm out of mine."

"Now you *are* scaring me. Does this mean you can't help?"

"Have I ever failed you?" Zave bent over me and unwrapped the band from my ponytail. "As it happens, I know just the person who might be inclined to post bail for your boy. But I'll need to make a couple of calls. Celeste Delaney's not the sort to deal directly with someone of my dusky complexion."

"Celeste Delaney? Good grief. *The* Celeste Delaney, of Delaney Oil?"

"None other. But before you get too excited, there's something you need to be aware of."

"And that would be?"

"Timing. They'll move fast on this, Jaymie. The DA is one of the most unpopular people in town at the moment, because of the way she screwed up the Overton case. She spent a shit-load of the public's money and let a killer go free."

"So I suppose she'll see this as a way to redeem herself."

"Precisely. The deranged killer of an innocent young girl is speedily convicted. Huzzah. Election time isn't all that far away, and the woman needs the votes."

His hands slipped inside the neckline of my top. "You're too beautiful to talk business with. Are we done with all that?"

I tensed, and his hand stilled. "Sweetheart. What's wrong?"

"I don't—don't really know."

"We'll figure it out later. Right now I'm gonna scratch your back, and you're gonna scratch mine."

Later, as we lay pressed together in Zave's moonlight-streaked bedroom, something in me tightened again. I drew a ragged breath.

"Jaymie, what?" Zave murmured. "Is it this murder business?"

"No, it's not that. Something's not right. I don't know what."

"Yes you do, girl." His eyes were inches from my own, and his warm breath brushed my cheek. "I've been watching you tonight. A con man knows when somebody's fibbing, even if she doesn't admit it to herself. Know what I think?"

Mutely, not really wanting to hear, I nodded.

"I've seen that look on you before. Couple years back. To you, what we're doing is cheating."

"No." I groaned and buried my face in the slippery graphite-gray satin sheets.

"Yeah. I'd say the sheriff's back in the picture." He placed his lips to my ear. "And while we're truth tellin, I know you got no damn evidence, girl. You got only one thing, and that's *heart*."

Chapter Five

Zave was possibly the most adept con man on planet Santa Barbara, but he was true to his word once he gave it. Accordingly, Andrew Galton, director of the Las Positas Bank & Trust, contacted Miss Delaney and reported back. Zave informed me in turn that her highness had agreed to grant Miss Zarlin a brief interview.

I'd seen aerial photos of the Delaney estate. Miramar, a robber baron's mansion set in ten or twelve acres of rolling hillside overlooking the Pacific Ocean, was a cross between a Greek temple and a mausoleum. I knew very little about Celeste Delaney herself, the inconceivably rich old woman who resided there. Only the obvious: she grasped a fabulous nineteenth-century fortune in her ancient claws.

I considered all this as I pedaled along Cabrillo Boulevard on my way to Miramar. The afternoon was warm, but a brisk onshore breeze cooled my skin. Several dozen sailboats bobbed at their anchors off East Beach. All the beach volleyball courts were occupied, and lithe, nearly naked bodies repeatedly shot like arrows into the air and fell back to the sand.

It was playtime for everyone but me, it seemed. But I wasn't even tempted to join in the fun. Danny needed Celeste

Delaney's help, he needed it soon, and it was up to me to obtain it.

According to Zave, two factors made Miss Delaney a potential source of Danny's bail. First, she had a connection to the Apollo Guild: her nephew, Sutton Frayne III, happened to be one of the three sitting members on the board, which was called the Guild Triune. But there was a second, more compelling factor at play.

Once upon a time, for a short period, Miss Delaney had been Mrs. Samuel Calden. She and Samuel had one child, Jonathan, and Jonathan eventually had only one child himself. Some fifteen years ago Celeste Delaney's only grandchild, Timothy Calden, had developed schizophrenia. Unable to protect himself, he'd been severely abused and eventually murdered down in LA.

Zave thought Miss Delaney might be sympathetic to Danny's situation, sympathetic enough to put up his bail. Maybe so, but I worried my visit might resurrect painful memories for the elderly woman, memories that could cause her to close the door in my face. I'd need to tread lightly.

I left Cabrillo and pedaled up a wide drive lined with ancient Monterey cypresses. Up ahead was a massive iron gate, and a gatehouse constructed of sandstone boulders.

Was I the only visitor who'd ever arrived at Miramar on a bicycle? The incredulous expression on the guard's haughty face suggested I was. I noticed a security camera peering down at me from a stone column. The guy in the gatehouse might not be the only one watching.

"Good morning. May I help you?" The polite greeting was delivered with an unspoken threat. Steel under suede.

"I'm here to see Celeste Delaney."

The guard's light-gray eyes froze to chips of sea ice. "Are you expected?"

"I have an appointment. My name's Jaymie Zarlin."

The man looked disappointed. He probably wanted nothing so much as to throw me off the property. Instead he muttered into a phone, then clicked it off and turned his back to me.

A few minutes passed. Birds screeched in the surgically trimmed shrubbery growing beneath the funereal cypresses. Then the phone buzzed.

Mr. Gatekeeper picked it up and listened. "Right." He glared down at me. "Proceed up to the house and wait at the bottom of the steps. Someone will meet you and escort you to Miss Delaney."

The tall iron gate fell back. In spite of the corrosive sea air, it made not a sound. As I rode on through and up the drive, I thought about oil, Southern California oil, and the pack of ruthless Delaneys who'd sucked the black gold out of the ground and converted it into vast wealth, cheating and ruining so many hardscrabble farmers along the way.

In the end, all the grasping had come down to this: one very old woman inhabiting a heap of stone, supporting an army of hangers-on.

Off to one side, a bird cawed raucously. I glanced over and saw an elderly lady seated in a garden chair on a grassy hill. Several black crows pecked at the ground near her feet.

I dismounted and propped up my bike on the kickstand, then waded across the plush emerald lawn. The crows, nervous at my approach, flapped off a little.

"Miss Delaney?"

The old woman twisted her upper body to look at me. Though the day was quite warm, she was bundled in layers of clothing. "Who are you"—her wide-brimmed straw hat teetered on her palsied head—"and how did you manage to get in?"

"I'm Jaymie Zarlin." I was wearing my pedal pushers, and the long, luxurious grass itched my bare ankles. "I used the open sesame word on your gatekeeper."

"'Open sesame word'?" The woman's mouth was closed tight, like a small puckered scar. But her piercing blue eyes were alert as could be.

"Yes. *Appointment*."

"Ah. Then you must be the private investigator." She nodded at the crows. "You see? Even the birds want my crumbs."

I recognized the sharp intelligence that resided in this old woman, and realized I must speak to it. "I do want something from you, Miss Delaney. That's why I'm here."

Out of the corner of my eye, I caught sight of a tall, powerfully built man striding rapidly down the hill in our direction. We were going to be interrupted, so I continued quickly. "There's only one difference between me and the crows, I guess. What I want isn't for myself."

"Oh?" Miss Delaney reached up a trembling hand and tugged her cashmere shawl close about her shoulders. "That is original, at least. What might—"

"You there! Miss Delaney, this person didn't follow instructions."

I was surprised to observe the bulge of a gun under the man's Windbreaker.

"Who is that—Ken? Ken, no more out of you. Can't you see I'm conversing?"

Top-heavy Ken halted so quickly he nearly tipped over. When he'd regained his balance, he shot me a menacing look.

"I fear the breeze and the chirping of the birds is disorienting to our Ken. He is more of an indoors person like myself," Celeste Delaney said. "I spend much of my time inside, you see, watching old films. I do not often take the air, so my staff is nervous when I do." She smiled slyly. "But before we allow Ken to scurry back inside, would you care for refreshments, Miss Zarlin? Iced coffee and cookies, perhaps?"

"I'd like that very much." I met Ken's glare. "No sugar or arsenic in mine, please."

Miss Delaney cackled. "Certainly," Ken answered through clenched teeth. He spun on his heel and began the long march back up to the mansion.

"Why, Miss Zarlin, I do believe you and I shall hit it off, as they say. May I call you—what is it? Janie?"

"Jaymie. Shall I explain why I'm here?"

"Oh, I already know the answer to that. For money, of course, even if, as you say, it's not for yourself. What else have I to offer, now that I am so very old?"

"It is money, yes. I'm not sure what the banker told you, but a young man named Danny Armenta has been arrested for the murder of a young woman. The authorities want him to be guilty in the worst way, but I believe he may be innocent."

"You *believe* he *may* be innocent? That is hardly a ringing endorsement."

"Nothing is certain at this point," I said more carefully.

"No. Well, as it happens, I do know something of the matter. This murder occurred at the Apollo Guild workshop, did it not?"

"Yes. The girl had been chosen as this year's Daphne."

"Ah, the forever lovely and innocent Daphne. *I* was never Daphne; Father said I was not pretty enough, and that was that." Celeste Delaney rubbed her cheek with a curled hand. "I know the members of the Guild Triune, of course. My nephew, Sutton, currently sits on the Triune, and Brucie Wiederkehr, I believe—and oh, what is it, Vincent Stella?"

I'd done my homework. "Vincent Stellato."

"Yes, Stellato. Sicilian, I suppose. There was a time, you know, when the Apollo Guild was untainted."

"'Untainted'?"

"By new money, or by names that ended in vowels." She shifted her twisted body uncomfortably. "My late grandson . . . I assume you know Timothy's story?"

"I know a little of it."

"But you do know he was mad, otherwise I suspect you wouldn't be here. This young man also is mad, am I correct?"

"He has schizophrenia, yes."

"And your part in all this?"

The sea breeze was sharpening, and I shivered a little. "Danny Armenta's family has engaged me to look into the matter."

"I see. So, how much do you want from me, and to what purpose?"

"I'd like you to post his bail, Miss Delaney. It's five hundred thousand dollars, far beyond what the family could raise, and I have to get Danny out of jail. He's been beaten up once already, and the police are not going to protect him—the opposite, I'm afraid. The amount is large, but you won't have to forfeit. He won't go anywhere, I can promise you."

"I see. You are offering me the opportunity to do some good. To help a fellow human being, as it were?"

"Yes, I suppose I am." The silence was abruptly profound. I thought I could hear the waves of East Beach thud down on the shore.

"Well then. I want you to hear my grandson's story. That is my price. Do you agree to it?"

"Of course."

She nodded and gazed past me with milky eyes. "Timothy was a favorite of mine, what they called a good boy. One October long ago, when Timothy was ten, his father and grandfather both died in a private plane crash out in the Channel. I'd long since divorced Samuel, who was insufferably spoiled and effete, and reclaimed my family name. I can say I was sorry to lose my son, Jonathan, however."

Celeste paused and peered at me, as if to gage my reaction.

"That must have been terribly hard on Timothy."

"In hindsight, I suppose it was. At the time, however, I saw no evidence of it. Timothy was a bit more withdrawn, perhaps,

but mild as always, never any trouble. Unusual in a Delaney."
She raised a trembling hand to the brim of her hat.

"You know, Timothy was my heir. When he later descended
into insanity, I felt somehow betrayed. I cut him off, the one
family member I daresay I should not have abandoned. Well,
these things happen." She withdrew a tissue from her sleeve
and patted the corner of her mouth.

"Eventually, Timothy became very ill indeed, and disappeared for a time. When they found him at last—"

"Miss Delaney," a female voice called.

I glanced up: Ken and a large-hipped woman wearing a maid's
outfit were advancing upon us. The woman balanced a tray in full
swinging stride, and Ken carried a folding table.

"When they found him, his hands and feet were chained
and he was crawling along the floor for scraps of food. He had
been regularly beaten. My grandson was—"

"Miss Celeste, your coffee—"

"Silence! Put the things down and be gone, the pair of you.
And try to keep your hands off one another. Will you have
the decency to do that?"

Impassively, Ken set up the small table, and his helper set
down the tray. Then the two of them turned and marched off.

"Let me tell you something." Celeste Delaney breathed rapidly now. "My grandson, my own flesh and blood, he drank
from a bowl of water set out for a dog. They used him for—"
She stopped and put a hand to her mouth.

"Miss Delaney? I'm so sorry I had to come and ask you for
this." I reached forward and touched her skin-and-bones arm.
"I'm sorry I've caused you to revisit your pain."

"How very amusing." She glared at me. "You think you know
what goes on in my mind!"

Suddenly, I realized she was right. I didn't understand this
woman, not at all.

"Well. There will be no coffee today. I must go in, and so it is time for you to go. But first, let me be clear. Are you convinced the Mexican boy did not kill the girl?"

"As convinced as I can be," I said quietly. "I can tell you this, I'm setting out to prove Danny's innocence."

"I see. And you do not strike me as one who gives up easily." A corner of her lip curled up in what looked like a snarl, though it may have just been a trick of the light. "Then I must help you, mustn't I? There's nothing else for it, my dear. Believe me, I shall."

Bright and early, Gabi squeezed her Chrysler wagon into a tight parallel park on the street. She'd have to move the car every seventy-five minutes, until she found a driveway she could rent cheap.

The little courtyard was quiet. Santa Barbara was not a town that started early in the morning. It was also not a town that went to bed late. So the residents got plenty of sleep.

Gabi stopped to admire a hummingbird nuzzling an apricot-colored Angel's Trumpet. But then a mangy stray cat slipped through the shrubbery, giving her the evil eye. She hoped the cat wasn't an omen.

She continued along the path to suite D. There she bent down awkwardly, stiff this early in the morning, and lifted a loose Saltillo tile beside the office steps. Gabi retrieved the key, turned it in the lock, and pocketed it. This leaving out of the key would stop right now. Just think of the files, the private information! She would have an extra one cut for Miss Jaymie, and inform her that a new and better system was in place.

Once inside, she dropped her tote bag on the desk, then opened the blinds and raised all the windows. Fresh air and organization, that's what she would bring to this business.

Gabi withdrew a pink paper sack and a half pound of freshly ground coffee from the tote and carried them into the back room. She shook her head and frowned: the cramped area was a sorry mix of kitchen and office. A stack of disheveled file folders, anointed with what looked like chocolate powder and a smattering of sugar crystals, teetered on the drain board.

She filled the stained coffee carafe with cold water, making a mental note to pick up some coffeepot cleaner down at Smart & Final, and rummaged around in the cupboard for a filter. As she waited for the coffee to trickle through, she made more mental notes.

The enameled sink was chipped and stained, and the tap dripped. A smell of mold lingered in the room, most likely due to a slow leak in the cabinet under the sink. A scarred maple table took up a third of the floor space, and a mountainous jumble of files, brochures, bills, and miscellaneous papers encircled a fuzzy blotter. It was obvious Miss Jaymie preferred to work back here, though how she ever managed to find anything was a mystery.

Her boss needed help, Gabi thought with satisfaction.

She reached into the bakery bag and withdrew a chocolate-filled pastry, admired it, and set it on a paper towel so as not to dirty a dish. Mrs. Cavanaugh, her Wednesday lady, had dozens of packets of cute cocktail napkins, left over from a garden party, tucked away and forgotten in a kitchen drawer. Gabi would borrow some next week.

She carried her coffee and pastry back to her desk in the larger room. Yes, *her* desk, she'd already decided. She sat down in the big chair and swiveled all the way around. Just like she expected, it felt like her rightful place in the world.

The phone rang. "Santa Barbara Investigations," Gabi proclaimed.

I locked my cruiser to the wrought-iron banister, then paused to listen. Strains of mariachi music pulsed through the gap at the base of my office door.

"¡Buenos días!" Gabi Gutierrez leaned out sideways from behind the computer screen. The woman was so short she couldn't see over the top of it.

"You start early," I groused. The two-person party at Zave's had continued well into the early hours, and I was short-tempered and short on sleep.

"Yes, and it's good I was here. I already talked to your number one client! She wants to see you this morning at ten."

What the blankety-blank was she talking about? "My number one client?"

"Mrs. Richter. I say numero uno, because except for me and my family, I don't think you got any clients except her. I know this cause I already organized the files."

"'Organized'?"

"Yes and guess what? I invented a system just for this office. I don't like to see the client's name right on the top of the file. Not private, you know? So everything is filed by street."

"Street?" This couldn't be real.

"Sure, where the crime happened. For example, Lili Molina, God rest her soul, was murdered on Indio Muerto."

"Nothing wrong with the old system," I whined. But in spite of myself, my spirit was lifting, for I could smell the heavenly odor of coffee brewing—serious coffee, dark and intense. I followed my nose to the kitchen. There, arranged on a tray I hadn't seen for a year, were two cups, a sugar bowl and a creamer, and two pastries oozing chocolate.

"I thought we could go over some stuff while we have our coffee," Gabi called from the other room.

"OK." I could sense my control slip-sliding away. "But turn down that party music, please. My head's starting to hurt."

"Sure. It's funny, isn't it? Loud music helps me concentrate. Now Miss Jaymie, come and sit down in here. This room is more organized. Just wait, I'll get to that table tomorrow."

Pretending I hadn't heard that, I walked into the front room and sat in the visitor's chair. "So where do I find this Darlene Richter?" A tiny splurt of chocolate escaped my lips. "Hope Ranch or Montecito, I suppose."

"That's right, Montecito, on Hot Springs Road. All the dog stealing happens in Montecito. I know 'cause they put up the reward posters in my neighborhood, the lower Westside." Gabi daintily licked a finger. "I already printed a map to her house for you. You'll find it on your desk."

"My desk?" I was waking up now, thanks to the coffee. "But you're sitting at it."

"No no, the big one in the kitchen. The table," Gabi smiled engagingly. "I know you like it the best." She sent me a sideways look. "I like everything organized. Don't you?"

"I like my mind to be organized," I said as I polished off the pastry. "All the rest of the crap doesn't matter so much."

Gabi grimaced, but quickly recovered. "See? We make a good pair."

I had to smile. There was, after all, a smidgen of truth in what she'd just said. "Speaking of order, I've got someone to meet before I go see Mrs. Richter. If I'm going to fit Minuet's mommy in sometime before lunch, I'll have to hustle."

"How will you get there? Montecito's too far for a bike. You have a car?"

"Mostly my ride stays home, for its own protection. Around town I pedal my bike." No need to explain that my cherished El Camino had belonged to Brodie. After my brother's death, I'd paid the astronomical impound fees, then taken it home.

"Use mine," Gabi urged. "You'll get more done. But as your PA, let me advise you about something. Your appointment with Darlene Richter is not 'sometime before lunch.' 'Sometime before lunch' would be Mexican time. This is American time: ten A.M. *sharp*."

◆   ◆   ◆

I stood at the curb and peered into the big old station wagon. Yep, the woman was organized, all right. A large collection of mops, dusters, brooms, and brushes was arranged with military precision. In fact, a sort of homemade rack system had been constructed from lumber and cleverly installed.

A waft of ammonia braced me as I opened the car door. I dropped into the lamb's-wool-padded driver's seat and pushed the buttons to drop the windows. When I turned the key in the ignition, the engine surprised me, roaring nimbly to life. Gabi obviously knew a moon-lighting mechanic, and a good one at that.

I pulled the station wagon away from the curb and steered down the street. It was a little like piloting a barge down a narrow canal.

I snuck a call on my cell. "Mike? I'm running early—I've got four wheels. Where are you?"

"Near the mission. I'll meet you in the parking lot. But Jaymie? Don't drive while you're on the phone."

"Whatever you say, dep. See you in ten."

Hadn't I promised myself I'd keep my distance from Deputy Dawson? But this didn't count, did it? This was business, after all.

It was too early for tourists, and the mission parking lot was empty. I pulled in beside Mike's pickup. His gun rack was bare, and the cab was meticulously tidy. The man himself was nowhere to be seen.

I walked out of the lot and climbed the sandstone steps of the elegant old mission church. The warm morning sun reflected off the cream and pink stuccoed façade and twin bell towers. The early Franciscans had commandeered the best spot in town, and the view over the city and out to the channel beyond sparkled in the crystalline air.

I scanned the grounds below the church, where the rose garden shimmered in delicate shades of pink and orange, ribboned in deep velvet green. Still no Mike.

Then I noticed a half-opened gate, wrought iron and covered in lichen and rust, set in a high stone wall at one side of the mission. As I stepped through into deep shade, I spotted him. Mike had dropped to one knee to read an inscription chiseled into a gravestone. He looked up when he heard the crunch of my footsteps on the gravel path.

When our eyes met I felt myself drawn, as if to magnetic North.

"Hi, Jaymie." Mike stood and held out a hand, and in spite of myself, I practically danced into his reach. He surprised me by grasping my arm and pulling me close.

"Hey! Ask permission," I squeaked.

"You gave me permission." He grinned. "I saw it in your eyes."

"Baloney." I tried not to match his grin with one of my own. "What are you doing back here?"

"Looking in on the relatives." He swept a hand in a semicircle. "Over four thousand bodies buried in this area—pretty tight quarters."

"I didn't know you were Chumash."

"Not Chumash, no. My abuela was half Spanish, half Salinan Indian. Yolanda was the matriarch of the family, totally in charge. Even Dad had to bow to her will. She'd inherited a Spanish rancho, and our land was part of it."

"Sounds like your grandfather married well."

"He knew an opportunity when he saw it. But Mom always said they were in love."

"You've told me so many good stories about your mother. I wish I'd known her," I said impulsively. Once the words were out of my mouth, I wanted to call them back: they invited intimacy.

"She'd have liked you. More than liked you."

My throat tightened. I turned and stepped away.

"Jaymie? You OK?"

"Sure." I quickly donned what I hoped was a nonchalant smile. "Listen, what did you want to talk about? I've got an appointment at ten."

"OK. Business it is." Mike reached into his shirt pocket and withdrew a sheet of yellow paper, folded in quarters. "I heard you visited the kid in jail. Good for you."

"My, news travels fast. Your fellow peace officers approve too, no doubt?"

"Who gives a damn what they think?" He shrugged. "Any ideas yet on raising Armenta's bail?"

"One or two. I'm working on it." I knew better than to mention Zave Carbonel. When it came to the subject of Zave, Mike wasn't his rational self.

"Well, the forensic report isn't back yet. It'll take three or four more days. But I wanted to tell you, the word is the victim most likely was unconscious when she was raped. Unconscious but not dead. The bad news is, no traces of semen. And the knife—no prints at all."

"Hm. Any other DNA evidence?"

"Yes and no. They're checking for DNA on everything, and finding it. Problem is, half the population of Santa Barbara passed through that dressing room in the last week or so."

"So the killer's scrupulous . . . scrupulous and brutal. A lethal combination."

"You said it." His lips tightened. "By the way, the cops know all about the clean windowsills, Jaymie. They don't miss much."

My eyes followed a brown creeper as it explored the shaggy bark of a pepper tree. "No, I don't suppose they do."

Mike handed me the folded page. "Here. It's against my better judgment, but I've decided to give you this. I figure you'll dig it up in the end anyway, so all I'm doing is saving you time."

"Time matters." I unfolded the paper and glanced at it. It was a list of several dozen names, written out in longhand. "What's this?"

"The names of everyone associated with the case up to now. Most of them are the kids who were active in the Guild this year, members of what they call subguilds: design, construction, painting, costumes, that kind of thing. Just about everyone on the list has been interviewed, and as far as I know, they've all been cleared. For one thing, they all have an alibi: they were up at Alameda Park when the murder took place."

"Thanks, Mike. I can use this." I folded the paper and tucked it into my back pocket. "Did you interview anybody yourself?"

"No, not my job. But I did go over and talk to the suspect's mother and his younger sister and brother, to make sure the sheriff's department wasn't involved. And I spoke to the victim's mother. I don't know what was worse, talking to Mrs. Armenta or Mrs. Molina. They're both nice ladies, both cut up bad."

"Lili Molina—did she have any sibs?"

"Yeah, a younger sister, Claudia. Tough kid, tries to be butch. She wants revenge."

"Understandable, I'd say. Fathers in the picture?"

"No. Lili Molina's father died in some kind of ag accident, two years ago. And Armenta's father isn't around."

"Oh boy, this is going to be tough on those families."

"You can say that again." Mike folded his arms across his chest. "Anyway, that's all I've got for you. I thought it was better to talk face-to-face than to send an e-mail or leave a message on your cell. You know, in case somebody decides to check our computers or phones."

"You sound kind of paranoid."

"Paranoid? Christ, Jaymie, I'm risking my job by talking to you about this."

"OK, so why are you doing it? Don't get me wrong, I appreciate it, and I promise you're safe with me. But . . ." I gave him a hard look. "What's in it for you?"

"Not what you apparently think."

"Which would be what?"

"Don't be cute," he snapped. "You figure I'm trying to score points with you. Right?"

I stared at my shoes. "Maybe something like that."

"And that's crap. Because with you, there's no goddamn advantage in scoring points. Doesn't help." Mike glared at me. "Maybe I'm interested in seeing justice done. That ever occur to you?"

"Sorry. Fair enough." I felt myself blush.

"Odds are, the kid's guilty." His voice still carried an edge. "Thing is, the entire PD, from Chief Wheeler on down, have made up their minds. And it's none of my business, but as far as I'm concerned, it's just too goddamn early to shut the door."

"Mike. Are you saying Danny's being framed?"

"Framed? I don't know about that." He turned away and looked over the walls to the mountains. "What I think is this: SBPD is just going through the motions now—the case is already closed."

"Framed, prematurely closed—it amounts to the same thing in the end. And I don't see it the way you do, by the way. I'd say there's a good chance Danny Armenta is innocent."

"Aw, come on, Jaymie." Mike raised a skeptical eyebrow. "You got any proof?"

"Maybe not actual proof, not yet. But—" At that moment, a Franciscan brother, garbed in a brown cowl and robe, crossed the side yard to the main church. A massive twelve-foot-high wooden door closed on his sandaled heels with a thud.

"Mike, listen. Part of it's a gut feeling, I admit. But I swear, there's more to it than that. The other day, when I went around to the alley and checked on the sill? I noticed the dressing room window had been pried open with something like a flat-headed screwdriver. The nick was still bright."

"Forensics caught that too, Jaymie. Give them a little credit, will you?"

I had to admit, I was kind of surprised. "OK. So what do they think?"

"They think it's not that important." He shrugged. "They claim the nick on the frame and the wipe marks on the sill could have been made any time over the past week or two."

"Bullshit, and they know it. No more than twenty-four hours. There was virtually no dust on the inside or the outside ledge. And there was a big june bug . . ." I made a face. "Never mind. It's pretty clear there's an agenda in play."

"Hold on. Yeah, something's going on at the top. But the guys on the ground are just doing their jobs. You have to see it from their point of view, Jaymie. A young woman is brutally murdered. A crazy guy is found sitting beside her body, mumbling and staring at a bloody knife on the floor. That's a lot more compelling than a missing splinter in a window frame."

"I'd have thought that's part of a detective's job. You know, to not be compelled."

"Sometimes common sense has to be listened to, doesn't it?"

I shrugged. "All I know is, those carvings performed on the body after death, the hair stuffed in the mouth . . . to me it looks like the killer wanted to appear to be crazy. It wouldn't be the first time somebody tried that trick. And now you're telling me there were no prints on the knife. So either the killer wiped it, or he was wearing gloves. We know Danny wasn't wearing gloves. Are you telling me he had the presence of mind to wipe it clean?"

"I'm not telling you anything. It's not my case."

I followed him out through the gate. "Mike? I appreciate what you've given me," I began.

"Uh-oh. She's buttering me up. Here it comes." He stopped and turned to me. "What else do you want?"

"I was just wondering—any chance of me seeing the interview transcripts? That's what I really need."

"Nope." He unhooked his sunglasses from the neck of his shirt and slipped them on. "Sorry, Jaymie. No chance in hell."

I thought of a quick retort, but swallowed it. No need to alienate the guy, after all. "One more question then, OK? The Apollo Guild—what's your take on it?"

"Hard to say." Mike shrugged. "Like I told you, supposedly it's a charity, a way for the wealthy to help disadvantaged local kids. But the way I see it, it's also an excuse to party, prestige for the wives, et cetera. The usual society crapola." He put out a hand. "Here, let me look at that list for a second."

I was happy to comply.

"OK, see here?" He tapped the yellow paper with an index finger. "If you want to start somewhere, I'd start with this little prick. He caught my attention for sure."

"*Jared Crowley,*" I read. "No alibi?"

"Oh yeah, clever Jared was up at the park too. I just *wish* he was guilty."

"Tell me about him."

"Crowley's not a high-schooler like the others. He's older, what they call the 'Guild Super.' Basically, he organizes the kids. He's twenty going on forty, if you know what I mean. A real wise guy."

"OK, I'll give him a look. Thanks, Mike. I want to move fast, before the public has Danny Armenta tried and convicted."

"Too late for that. You should go online to the *Independent* and see what people are saying about the case."

"Think I'll pass."

We walked out through the gate and into the warm sunshine, heading for the parking lot. "So, you've got four wheels today? Taking the El Camino out for a spin?"

"Not exactly. . . . Here, this is my ride."

Mike bent down and peered into the station wagon. "What the hell, Jaymie. Have you taken up housecleaning?"

"No, what I've taken on is a personal assistant, thanks to you. Gabi Gutierrez, the woman you sent to me? This is her car. She wanted to hire me, but she's got no money. So guess what? Now she's working for me, whether I want her to or not."

Mike threw back his head and laughed. "I figured that was her plan. You know, I like her."

"Well, she certainly likes you. 'The big hot cop.'"

"Hey, that's me. Now, if only you could see me that way."

I pretended to look out over the city as I slipped on my own sunglasses. See him that way? If only I couldn't.

I thought about Mike as I drove away in the cleaning mobile. He'd given me a list of names, and revealed forensic evidence. It wasn't like him to break rules, unless they needed breaking. Mike had smelled something he didn't like, I was sure of it. Something that stank.

Chapter Six

"Our lovely little city is so dangerous these days." Darlene Richter glared at her Italian limestone floor and rubbed at a miniscule blemish with the toe of her black suede pump. "First Minuet is kidnapped, and then that poor girl is murdered."

"Ah, yes. . . ." The two crimes were definitely in the same category. I sternly reminded myself to think about the fat retainer check, still uncashed, languishing in the desk back at the office.

"Your personal assistant praised you highly, Ms. Zarlin. Ten thousand dollars seemed a bit steep, but if you are all she claimed, the amount is well worth it." Mrs. Richter lifted her coiffured head. "Minuet is precious to me. I hope you understand how strongly I mean that."

Darlene Richter, I guessed, was somewhere in her early sixties. As a young woman she must have been a knockout. Even now, in spite of a certain sharpness bequeathed by the surgical knife, she was a head-turner. Her platinum-weave hair was cut to look as if it had been slightly tousled in a breeze at the beach. And her outfit, a beige linen suit and turquoise silk blouse, made a clear statement: I am relaxed and in perfect control.

"I understand. I'm fond of dogs too, Mrs. Richter." Dogs. An image of the toothy Dexter came to mind. Two days ago, the mutt had greeted me with a proud tail and roadkill dangling from his salivating muzzle.

"The phrase 'fond of' hardly does justice to my feelings for Minuet, Ms. Zarlin. But I suppose it will do."

Ten thousand dollars or no ten thousand dollars, it was time for the conversation to get real. "How did you happen to hire me, Mrs. Richter? Dognappings aren't my usual line."

She folded her arms beneath her artfully supported bosom. "I thought I'd explained to your assistant. I visited someone in your building—Saffron Sayers, the woman who reads pet auras. She'd done Minuet's chakras, and I thought she might have some insight as to where my little girl might be. Frankly, Saffron wasn't at all helpful. But as I was leaving, I noticed your sign."

"OK, I see." So I had a mutt's chakras to thank for my new affluence. Well, what could I say?

"But we're wasting precious time, Ms. Zarlin. Come with me. I've something to show you."

Darlene Richter led me from the foyer into a formal living room. Three sets of tall French doors looked out over a European-style garden. Twin rows of towering Italian cypresses flanked a stone staircase descending to a lower level, a lawn of wispy long grass. "That is the last place I saw Minuet," she pointed. "Out there, in the meadow."

"Excuse me, Mrs. Richter?" A middle-aged Mexican woman with patrician features stood in the doorway. "It is two thirty. I have finished."

"All right, Marisol. But did you remember to clean the screens over the stove top? The cook fried with olive oil twice this week. The greasy odor can be offensive, especially in the morning."

"Yes, ma'am." Marisol's gaze met mine, then skipped away.

"Yes ma'am you agree, or yes ma'am you cleaned them?"

"I cleaned them."

I studiously examined the view out the window.

"Very well then. I'll see you tomorrow at nine."

I saw an opportunity. "Mrs. Richter, I'd like a word with Marisol before she goes."

"I don't see—" But then she nodded. "Of course, if you think it might help. Marisol? This is Ms. Zarlin. She's going to help me find Minuet. I'll wait out on the patio while the two of you talk."

"She must pay you well," I said when Mrs. Richter had stepped outside.

Marisol smiled slightly. "Not too bad."

"What's it like, working for her?"

"Mrs. Richter? OK, but sometimes she's—" She grimaced, and stopped talking.

"Sometimes she's mean?"

"Yes, sometimes." But then Marisol shook her head. "Underneath, you know? Underneath Mrs. Richter is lonely."

"Because she misses her husband? I understand he died two years ago."

"Misses him? No, the opposite maybe." Her mouth twisted down. "The señor, he used to shout at her. He had girlfriends, sometimes he even brought them here to the house. A bad man. I think maybe she's been lonely for a long, long time."

"And the dog, Minuet—what happened to her, do you think?"

"What, the dog? I don't know, maybe it ran away." Marisol gave an exaggerated shrug. "Listen, that little dog. It's just a perro, you know? It only wants to be outside, play with kids. . . ."

"So you're saying Minuet wasn't all that happy being a pampered princess."

"Princess? Believe me, that dog is a dog. It goes pee-pee in her bedroom, sometimes even on the bed." She wrinkled her nose.

I noticed Mrs. Richter had turned and was watching us

now through the French doors. "Marisol, one more question. Do you think one of the gardeners—?"

Marisol's cell rang in her apron pocket. She pulled it out and peered at the screen. "My sister is here to pick me up. Sorry, I got to go."

"OK. But about my last question. King Charles spaniels are worth a lot of money, and landscapers have been known to kidnap valuable dogs before this."

"No. Not Mrs. Richter's gardeners. They been with her a real long time." She waved vaguely. "Maybe some other gardeners, up the road."

Minuet's playground was royal: an acre of manicured beauty. I accompanied Darlene Richter on a tour of the boundaries.

"You see, Ms. Zarlin? All solidly fenced. And beneath the redwood fencing, chicken wire sunk into the ground to keep out the rodents and rabbits."

"When are your gardeners here?"

"Mondays and Fridays. You're more than welcome to come by on Friday and speak with Jorge and his people. But I have to tell you, I trust them implicitly. Jorge is Marisol's brother, you know."

"Marisol didn't tell me that." A tiger swallowtail floated by on the breeze. "Mrs. Richter, I have to wonder. Could she be hiding something?"

Darlene Richter frowned. "It would be out of character, I'd think. I've employed Marisol for seventeen years now, Jorge for nearly that long. They certainly aren't perfect, but I've never had that sort of problem with either of them. They are both honest people."

We continued our walk inside the perimeter fence. The flower beds were meticulously maintained. Rake marks were everywhere, like wave lines in a Japanese garden.

Which meant I noticed immediately when we came on an area where the lines were smudged.

Following the smudge marks, I pushed my way through a stand of twelve-foot-high camellia bushes and knelt in the dirt. Sure enough, someone had sawn a neat little hole at the base of the redwood fence. Several long hairs, some white and some brown, were snagged on the splintered edge.

"Mrs. Richter? There's something here you'll want to see."

"Gabi! Get over here fast," her sister Vicky begged over the line.

"I'm at work. And anyway, this morning mi jefa borrowed my car. Is it something to do with that toilet that floods?"

"What are you talking about, toilet? He's here, Gabi, here at my place. And if Danny isn't gone in one hour, the manager's gonna evict us. Take a taxi, I'll pay."

"Vicky, they can't evict you so fast."

"What are you saying? The manager knows we got no papers. He can call INS if he wants!"

"OK, OK. But Danny's out of jail? How can he be out?"

"How do I know? The bail bond guy dropped him off. This was Danny's last address—the guy gave me some kind of rubbish like that."

"Vicky, listen to me. Is he . . . is he crazy?"

"Of course he is. What do you think, he got all better in jail?" Gabi heard her sister take a quick breath. "But he's not crazy-crazy, if that's what you mean. Danny's real quiet. But he's talking to himself like he does, you know?"

"Well maybe if you just—"

"Gabi, listen to me! He can't stay here no more. And Alma, she won't do nothing, she just sits and stares at the floor. You gotta come and get him. Alma and the kids too, or Danny will just follow them back again. And I'm telling you, you better get over here before Arturo shows up."

"Arturo, Arturo," Gabi grumbled. "What did you marry that guy for, anyway?"

"Never mind about that. I'm telling you Gabi, you better come fast."

The moment Gabi slammed the taxi door, she heard trouble. Shouting and clanging. She hurried into the center of the complex, then halted in her tracks. Eight or ten of her sister's neighbors—some of them supposedly friends—were shouting outside Vicky's door and banging on pots and pans.

"*Out! Out! Out! Out!*"

"Stop it! Stop it right now!" Her heart tightened with fear as she ran forward. "Leave my family alone!"

"Family. Some family you got!" one woman shrieked. "We have kids here. Daughters! We want him out!"

The door to Vicky's apartment had opened a crack. Gabi saw an eye—Vicky's eye—peeping through.

Gabi was the big sister, she had a role to fill. She turned back to the wild-eyed women. "OK. I'll take Danny out. If you back off, hear me? Go back to your telenovelas!"

"You've got thirty minutes," somebody yelled. "The manager's already gone to call the evicters."

She felt like a holy woman, leading her little band through a terrible wilderness. Gabi could see the blinds twitching as she took Aricela and Chuy by their hands and walked through the apartment complex courtyard. Behind her, Alma crept along with Danny. Alma seemed almost in shock, and Gabi had been afraid her sister would not be able to put one foot in front of the other. But somehow, probably for Danny's sake, Alma was inching forward.

They were nearly to the corner when the *hissing* began. A door flew open, then nine or ten more. No words were spoken, there was just the terrible hissing sound, like snakes or poisonous gas.

Gabi had called a different taxi, the white guys' taxi company, less likely to know who Danny was. "Get in, fast now," she urged the children.

The driver turned to look at Gabi, who'd taken the seat beside him. "Where to?" He was suspicious, she could see it in his squinty eyes.

"Can—can we go to your place, Tía?" Chuy sounded really scared.

Now Gabi began to panic for real. She turned to look at her family in the backseat. Alma and Danny both looked like zombies. No, not her place! *No.* Because Danny would never get better. He'd be a poor sad scary guy for the rest of his life. If she let them into her home, her private sanctum, they might never leave.

"My office," she pronounced. "101 Mission."

As they pulled away from the curb, *splat!* An egg hit the windshield.

The driver halted and stared at the yellow smear. "What the fuck?"

Next a tomato hit the hood, and then something ugly and brown. Now the driver stepped on the gas.

"You'll have to pay to get my car cleaned!"

But Gabi shook her head. "Nothing to do with us. They don't like you, maybe you overcharged somebody in the neighborhood?"

I was thinking about the hole in the fence as I drove out of Montecito and back into town. When I got to Mission Street, my musings came to an end. I had to circle the block three times before a park opened up. By the time I'd wedged Gabi's barge into a space more suited to a golf cart, I was sweating under my arms.

A devilish little tyke of six or seven was attempting to balance on the handrail alongside my office steps. The shrub below the rail was flat as a doormat.

"Hi!" the boy said.

"Hi yourself! Are you—"

"My nephew Chuy," Gabi answered from the doorway. "Chuy, get off there right now. Go inside. And say you're sorry about the bush."

"Sorry." The boy grinned.

"Bushes grow back." I peered past my assistant: there seemed to be more people inside.

"Miss Jaymie?" Gabi stepped down and grabbed my arm. "I gotta talk to you before you go in."

"Ah. What's going on?"

"Come on, let's walk over there. Chuy, get lost."

"Listen," Gabi said urgently once she'd steered me into a far corner of the courtyard. "Something's happened, I'm really in trouble."

"Let me guess. You have to babysit every day from now on. You're going to bring your niece and nephew with you to the office. Look, I love kids, but—"

She shut her eyes. "No. . . . Something way worse."

"Gabi? Open your eyes and just say it."

"OK. It's—it's Danny. They let him out of the jail! You won't believe it: some rich lady put up his bail. Some rich lady as crazy as he is."

"Celeste Delaney. I went to see her, Gabi. I asked her to do it."

"What?" Gabi stepped back. Her dark eyes flashed. "Why didn't you ask me first? Tell me, at least? Now I'm the one who's gotta figure out what to do!"

I realized I'd made a mistake, a serious one. "I should have told you. You're right about that and I'm sorry. But Danny was going to be hurt in there, Gabi, maybe even killed. The cops weren't going to protect him."

Waves of warring emotion battled in her eyes. "I don't—I don't want Danny to die, but I can't—I just can't—"

"Hey. It's OK." I put an arm around her shoulders and gave her a squeeze. "Let's go inside and talk."

But Gabi shook her head. "We gotta talk here first. Danny's in there. And my sister Alma, and Aricela too. That's what I'm trying to tell you: when Danny showed up this morning at our sister Vicky's apartment, the manager said if he didn't get out right away, she was calling the evicters on the whole family. Now Vicky's husband Arturo, he's OK but he's kind of a tough guy. He—"

"I get it, Gabi." I caught sight of a face materializing in a nearby window. The dog-aura lady was listening in. "Let's go inside anyway."

"OK, but one more thing first. I'm ashamed to tell you. But Danny can't—please, he just can't—"

"Come to live with you," I finished for her.

"How did you know?" Her voice fell to a whisper. "He scares me. My own nephew, he makes me afraid. Don't ever tell Alma, I'm so ashamed."

Now I understood why Gabi was so willing to work for me for free. She longed to help her family, but she couldn't offer what they needed most: a place to live.

"Gabi? Don't worry. We'll make it work out."

Chuy was back at the steps again, staying off the railing but now jumping from the top step to the ground. He made re-sounding grunts each time he landed. "You'll break your legs," Gabi warned weakly as we entered the office.

Inside, a woman who looked like a smaller and quieter version of Gabi sat hunched in the visitor's chair. A girl of about twelve stood beside her, stroking the woman's long dark hair. And a young man lay curled on the couch, his back to the room.

"Hey, Danny," I said softly. There was no response.

Gabi's sister didn't raise her head, but the girl met my gaze. "Hi. I'm Aricela. This is my mom."

My heart went out to the kid. She was trying to be an adult, trying to take charge. "Hi, Aricela. I'm Jaymie."

"Alma? Miss Jaymie is here!" Gabi spoke brightly and loudly, as if she were announcing the arrival of the Archangel Gabriel.

Alma Armenta raised her head and looked at me. Her eyes were utterly blank. "Hello," she said in a dry husk of a voice.

"Hi, Alma." I extended my hand, and after a long moment, Alma held up hers in response. It felt lifeless in mine, deathly cold on this warm summer day.

"My son . . . my boy, he . . ."

"Yes, I know. I'm just glad Danny's out of jail." I looked at the little circle of anxious faces. "Kids, why don't you run over to the bakery with your tía? Grab yourself sodas and pick up some pastries for all of us."

Once Gabi and the kids were gone, I pulled Gabi's chair out from behind the desk and sat down. "Alma, can you tell me what happened today?"

Danny stared hard at the upholstery. Tiny lines, gray and black, cut into the bluish fabric. Then the same series of lines crossed the first set, at an angle. The pattern repeated over and over and over. He stared harder, and the lines got squiggly. They danced and rearranged themselves every time he blinked.

The voices in the room droned on, like bees. No, flies. More like flies. Those voices were outside his head. The Voices that were inside were quiet now. Gone away or maybe sleeping . . . or maybe pissed off with him. Maybe really, really angry. He listened to the outside voices drowsily:

"He doesn't remember. . . ." That was his mom. ". . . back on his meds. In the jail they took them away. . . ."

"Do you think . . ." That voice he didn't know. But the lady was . . . nice. She visited him in . . . the scary place. Jail.

A gray fog descended.

It's foggy today, Danny thought, and he strained to hear the foghorn just outside the harbor. The foghorn he could hear at night in his bed, his own safe place.

"We can't go back," he heard his mom say. "Because they . . ." The fog thickened, muffling all the words.

What was out there, in the fog? Something bad—something so terrible—Danny lurched upright. He stared at the two weird faces now looking over at him. The eyes and noses shifted and slid to the wrong places. The way they looked at him, they made him horribly afraid. Were they devils hiding inside good people? Moving inside the people he knew, messing with their faces, taking them over?

"Lili Molina," one of the devils said.

"LILI!" Danny screamed in terror. "ARE YOU OUT IN THE FOG? LILI, LILI, WHAT HAPPENED TO YOU!"

"But Jaymie, where will you sleep?" Alma looked limp with exhaustion. "You're giving up your bed."

"Don't worry about me. I'll be in the studio, right next door." I smiled reassuringly. "I'll just get a few things out of the bedroom, then leave you to relax."

Alma slumped. I could see her giving way, inch by inch. "God bless you," she mumbled.

"Yes, thank you," Aricela piped up in her high clear voice. She and Chuy were already settled in front of the TV. Dexter, never one to miss an opportunity, was curled up between the kids on the couch.

Scooby-Doo seemed a little young for Aricela, but no doubt the show was helping her escape from the day's ugly events. Being drummed out of your home by an angry mob of neighbors was not something any kid should have to experience. I wasn't sure Chuy grasped what had happened, but Aricela understood all too well. I knew she would never forget.

I stuffed PJs and a fresh change of clothes into a duffel bag, then glanced into the smaller guest room on my way out. Danny lay curled into a fetal position on the single bed. He'd drawn the hood of his gray sweatshirt tight around his face.

Chuy looked up from the TV when I walked back through the living room. "Can Dexter stay with me?"

"I'd better take him to the studio for the night, Chuy. He wants to be let out early—five thirty in the morning. You'll still be sound asleep."

"No-oh," he mock-wailed, his voice rising and falling on the single syllable. "He likes me. He wants to stay!"

"Mijo," Alma admonished wearily.

"Dexter will be waiting at your door when you get up in the morning, Chuy," I said. "You can count on that."

I had to call several times before the mutt grudgingly slipped off the couch and followed me out. When I closed the door on the little household, he remained on the step with his nose pressed to the crack. "Tomorrow, Dex. They need you, God knows they do."

Inside the studio, I tossed my things on the table and drew the papasan chair up to the window. The mutt dropped down on the rug with an ill-tempered grunt.

Dusk was gathering in the Channel, and a few faint lights twinkled out on the rigs. I leaned forward and turned the old aluminum crank. Salty sea air, tinged with the odor of the oil that welled up naturally out in the Channel, flowed into the studio.

As it always did in this room, my brother's memory rose to greet me. "Brodie—" My voice caught in my throat.

I could barely make out Santa Cruz Island now, drifting off into the purple night. Loneliness, cold as the channel waters, seeped into my thoughts. To break the mood, I stepped outside and filled my lungs with the sweet prom-night perfume of the Victorian box tree spreading over the garage.

I would give up the studio tomorrow, I decided. Danny needed a separate and quiet space.

I looked over at the house. A light glowed in one of the windows. Tonight, at least, the Armentas were safe.

After five or ten minutes I returned to the studio, switched off the light, and stretched out on the futon. I told myself to relax, but my mind raced like a squirrel trapped in a cage.

Daphne. Daphne and Apollo. . . . How exactly had the story gone? Abruptly, I was wide awake.

I flipped the light back on, fired up my laptop, and searched. Just a press or two of a key, and I came upon a retelling in Edith Hamilton's *Mythology: Timeless Tales of Gods and Heroes*. The ancient myth blazed to life on the modern device:

> Daphne flew on, even more frightened than before. If Apollo was indeed following her, the case was hopeless, but she was determined to struggle to the very end. It had all but come; she felt his breath upon her neck, but there in front of her the trees opened and she saw her father's river. She screamed to him, "Help me! Father, help me!" At the words a dragging numbness came upon her, her feet seemed rooted in the earth she had been so swiftly speeding over. Bark was enclosing her; leaves were sprouting forth.

Rape. Once more I switched off the light and lay down in the dark. It wasn't so difficult, I discovered, to put myself in Daphne's place, to feel her panic and dread. But to think like the one who believed he possessed the right to rape . . . that was a challenge.

Rejection would be intolerable to such a being, and a rebuff would only add fuel to a smoldering fire. God or man, the rapist nursed a seething fury—and a lethal drive toward revenge.

I would pay another visit to the murder scene in the morning. Yes, the killer had taken great care to hide his identity. And yet—enthralled and distracted by his own ferocity—he could not have failed to leave a clue.

Chapter Seven

At eight the next morning, the mist was so heavy it pin-pricked my cheeks. I stopped in the yard and listened to the foghorn groaning out in the harbor.

Dexter stretched, extending one hind leg gracefully, then the other. The cow dog looked over at me and whined.

"You'll have to talk to your new family about breakfast, Dex. I've got business to attend to."

The unpainted garage at the back leaned sideways, and as always, the warped doors stood ajar. It took some elbow grease to lift and move them all the way open. I cursed under my breath as a redwood splinter stabbed into my palm.

I hadn't driven the blue and white El Camino in months, but I knew it would start with no problem. Brodie had always taken much better care of his vehicles than himself, and Blue Boy—Brod's name for it, not mine—was in great shape considering its age.

I slipped sideways into the garage, praying that none of the resident black widows would decide to hitch a ride in my hair. I squeezed into the cab and managed to shut the door. For a moment I just sat there in the gloom, allowing memories of my brother to wash over me.

"Hi!" The passenger door edged open, and Chuy slipped sideways into the front seat. He tipped his penny-bright face up to me. "Can I go with you? *Pleeze?*"

I returned his grin. "You don't even know where I'm going."

"Don't care! I'm going too." He wriggled down in the seat and snapped on the belt. "Come on, boy, hop in."

I had to laugh as Dexter skinnied in and somehow squeezed himself into the shoe-box-sized space at the kid's feet. Chuy closed his door and turned back to me. "OK, we're ready—let's go!"

"You two are my sidekicks, for sure. But this morning I'm afraid I've got work to do." I backed out of the garage and angled around, pointing the El Camino down the hill. "Tell you what. Take Dex back in the house and give him breakfast. I promise, this afternoon I'll take you both to the beach."

I'd expected to use my lock-picking skills at the warehouse, and had pocketed several tools for the job. But I was surprised to find the side door unlocked. The moment I stepped in, I heard two people, male and female, talking. Their voices were strained and intense.

I eased the door shut and walked softly down the concrete hallway, past the door to the dressing room. I paused at the entrance to the shadowy main work space. The hulking float, now partially dismantled, leaned against the far wall.

The voices were coming from a far wing of the warehouse. I crossed the cavernous room and entered a rabbit warren of narrow hallways. Following the voices, I halted just before a half-open door.

"Come on, baby. You know it's just you and me. Fuck all of them, right?"

"That's what I thought!" The female voice was peevish, high-pitched. "But I saw you, Jared! I saw you leave with her."

"OK, but it wasn't my idea. Lili asked me to drive her. I just dropped her off so she could change. Damn! I came back right away, I didn't even wait for her. Fuck, Shawna, you saw me—"

"Hey—I don't think you like, *did* anything," she said quickly. "I'm not saying that. Yeah, I saw you come back. But they're going to find out you gave her a ride."

"No they aren't, Shawnie." His voice was syrupy now. "Nobody's going to find *anything* out unless you open your mouth."

"Lili didn't ask you to drive her back here just so she could change. That's stupid, why would she do that while the party was still on? She probably wanted you to get into her pants! And you didn't say no, not you."

"OK, you need to shut up. You've got it wrong. Like I said, Lili just wanted a ride. They told her to come back and change out of her costume. It's worth a lot of money, they didn't want her running around in it."

"Who's *they*? You're the Guild manager."

"Who? Damn, I don't know." Jared's voice faltered a little. "The Triune, maybe."

"Oh, the *big* dicks." Now Shawna's voice was a tease.

"Never mind about the big dicks. Listen, I want you to keep your mouth shut about all this, and if you don't, you won't be getting any from me for a while."

"And what if I do what you want?"

"If you do what I want, we can still play."

"Play—like now?"

"Hell yeah, we could now."

"I've got to get to work, you know."

"Forget about the French Press. You and me are gonna do some pressing right here."

"You're funny. This early in the morning?"

"What do you think, baby?"

"I think if you say Lili Molina was an ugly little Mexican whore, you'll get whatever you want."

Shit. Did I have to listen to this?

I slipped back down the hall and out of the warehouse. On my way in I'd noticed an old tan BMW parked across the street, and now I wanted a closer look.

The car was clean inside and out. Anonymous, really. The only visible object was a black leather jacket, carefully draped along the backseat. I tried a door handle, but it was locked. I thought about breaking in but doubted it would be worth the trouble.

Instead, I drove up the street and parked a distance away, in view of the Beemer. I sat and thought about what I'd just learned. Jared Crowley had delivered Lili back here to change—and to die.

All hearsay, however, no proof. If challenged, Jared and Shawna would simply deny they'd ever had a conversation on the subject of Lili Molina.

Twenty minutes later, the lovebirds exited the warehouse and crossed the street to the Beemer. Shawna tossed her head, and her long black hair glistened in the sun. She looked like the most confident person in the world, but Shawna was one needy girl.

As soon as the vehicle was out of sight, I returned to the warehouse. The pair had locked up, and this time I needed to pick the lock. Once in, I passed through the warehouse to the room Jared and Shawna had just left. Several of Shawna's long black hairs lay on the grimy felted-down carpet.

I walked back to the murder room and found the door locked. I pulled on a pair of latex gloves and again used my tools to let myself in.

Except for the number thirteen and ladders blocking my

path, I'm not superstitious. But if ever a room contained a ghostly presence, this was it. The photos were gone, but the rusty blood outline remained. The air was hot and smelled of sweat and sick.

I crossed to the window. Mr. June Bug lay dead on the sill, gutted by ants. I scanned the room: what else had changed since my previous visit?

The screen, chair, and coat tree now stood upright. Lili's clothing was gone, no doubt to forensics. The scattered accessories and props were back where they belonged, in the storage bin, and the bin was shoved in a corner.

Once again I dipped under the costumes hanging in the alcove and straightened, my back to the wall. Here the air was thick with dust, mold, and that peculiar pong of cologne and old sweat. I switched on my pen light and located the spot where the dowel had been wiped clean.

No doubt about it. The costumes had been shoved aside, the dust rubbed from the dowel as the hangers parted. Forensics could have done it, I supposed.

I ducked back into the room. This was my chance, I reminded myself. I might not come here again. What had I missed?

I walked over to the prop bin and tipped it out onto the concrete. Then I dropped to my knees and spread out the heap of purses, hats, shoes—and belts, four of them.

I reexamined each belt, recalling the mark on Lili's neck. But none of these were a match—all four were too wide. Anyway, the forensics team would have gone through these items with a fine-toothed comb. I continued to rummage through the pile, not really expecting to find anything I hadn't noticed before.

But then my hand stilled. From the pile, I pulled out a thin leather cord, a heavy lace from a hiking or work boot. One end of the lace was stiff with dried blood.

This could be the ligature that the killer had used to stran-

gle Lili Molina. But where had it come from? The first time I'd
visited the dressing room, the contents of the prop bin were
spread over the floor. I'd sorted through the objects then, and
was pretty certain I'd have noticed a cord dipped in blood. There
was only one explanation: someone had visited the room and
planted the evidence.

In a rush of excitement, I nearly pocketed the thing. But I
stopped myself: that wouldn't do. After all, I couldn't turn in
the cord to the cops—how would I explain what I was doing at
the murder scene, how I'd gotten in? The best thing to do
would be to leave it in the bin.

I laid the bootlace on the floor and snapped a few pictures
with my cell. Then I reloaded the bin, tossing the objects in one
at a time, to make sure I hadn't missed anything. Handbags,
hats, a pair of old-fashioned pumps . . . and then, something
else. I sat back on my heels and stared at the object I held in
my hands.

It was a vintage megaphone, crafted of some sort of heavy
cardboard, the sort of thing a cheerleader might have used at
a sporting event many decades ago. No doubt a prop of some
kind, once part of a costume.

Why had the badly faded red and blue cone caught my attention? I had no idea. I snapped a picture of it too, before I
chucked it back in the bin.

I slid the El Camino keys into the ignition, then leaned back
in the old bench seat and stared at the stained cloth-covered
ceiling.

Tantalizing clues were surfacing. And maybe one or two of
these lures actually signified something. But I needed to slow
down: I knew I was getting ahead of myself. I turned the key in
the ignition, mainly just to listen to the engine's comforting
thrum.

The problem was, I wasn't beginning at the starting point.

How much did I actually know about Lili Molina? My next step—the one I maybe should have taken in the beginning—was suddenly clear.

I arched my back and tugged my phone from my jeans pocket. "Morning, Gabi. Just checking to see if you made it in on time this morning." I grinned and held the phone at arm's length as my PA gave me an earful.

"Seriously, I need Teresa Molina's phone number and address. Text them to me, will you? Please," I added. I'd rubbed the bobcat's fur in the wrong direction, and no doubt I'd be paying a price for the rest of the day.

I didn't much like the idea of showing up unannounced on Mrs. Molina's doorstep, especially as I was representing the boy accused of murdering her daughter. But when no one answered my call, I slipped the El Camino into gear and headed for downtown Santa Barbara.

I parked near the corner of State, got out and walked west on Ortega. The street was lined with big Victorians, some festooned with purple wisteria, all of them subdivided into apartments. A thumping boom box, perched on a windowsill, competed for air time with the sound of a crying baby. Battered old cars hugged the curbs, filled driveways and even front yards. Living was tight downtown, yet the rents were sky-high. No option for tenants except to pack in the roomies.

I halted and looked across the street at 536 Ortega, a once stately, now slumping Queen Anne with a dirty old rug hanging out of a second-story window. A huge Moreton Bay fig tree spread over the entire front yard.

Mike had said the Molinas rented a studio at the back of 536. I crossed the street and entered a narrow walkway running between the house and a wooden fence covered with peeling strips of yellowish paint. Another thirty yards along and I found myself in a garden filled with shrubs and flowers. In the farthest corner stood a converted Victorian summerhouse, no more than six or seven hundred square feet in size. Someone had trained a scarlet-flowered passion fruit over the door.

I slowed and drew in a breath to ground myself. I was about to enter a house of mourning, and my visit would bring fresh pain.

I pulled open the screen door and knocked gently, then allowed it to fall back into place. There was no sound of movement inside. Over in the main house, a man shouted in Spanish and a woman hollered back.

After a time, there was a scratching noise on the inside of the door. Then it creaked open and a once-pretty woman with a slack face and dull eyes peered through the screen. "Yes?" Her voice sounded lifeless, mechanical.

"Mrs. Molina?" I said gently. "I'm Jaymie Zarlin. Deputy Dawson suggested I talk with you. I am so very sorry for your loss." My words sounded formulaic, unfeeling. Suddenly I was ashamed to be standing on the doorstep, ashamed to be interrupting this woman's vigil.

"Talk with me?" Teresa Molina stood very still, as if she were made of lead.

"About your daughter, Mrs. Molina. If this isn't a good time . . ." Of course it wasn't a good time! What was I thinking? "I'll come back later. I'm so sorry to have—"

"No, please." She straightened and nudged the screen door. "No, I will talk. And there is something I need. Maybe—maybe you can help."

"I hope I can." I stepped in and gently closed the doors behind me. The cloying odor of church incense choked the air.

You could see where pictures had been taken down from the walls, leaving the nails. No rug covered the old vinyl floor. A single wooden chair with a rush-covered seat stood in the center of the room.

There was nothing to look at but the shrine. Two fold-up craft tables, covered with old crocheted cloths, were pushed against the walls to meet in a corner, forming a V. The possessions of Lili Molina were arranged on the tabletops.

"Please, go and look," Teresa urged. "That is all that remains of my beautiful daughter."

A single candle flickered in a jar painted with pictures of La Virgen de Guadalupe, and an incense burner wafted white strands of smoke. A collection of earrings, a pressed gardenia corsage, and a child's finger painting were among the objects artfully displayed. In the center of the shrine was a photo of Lili, not the self-conscious head shot you might have expected, but a picture of a giggling teenager with a green parakeet perched on top of her head.

"Your daughter was beautiful, Mrs. Molina. I can tell she had a good heart."

"Yes. Yes, she did." She motioned to me. "Come to the kitchen, please."

I sat down on a plastic-covered chair at the kitchen table, and Teresa sat facing me. It occurred to me that she was only a few years older than I. Already, her daughter had been murdered, and two years earlier, her husband had died in a gruesome accident. Life was giving this woman a very rough ride.

The small table held a laptop computer. "Claudia's," Teresa murmured. She lowered the lid and moved it aside.

I could see Teresa had something she wanted to say, but the words were not coming easily. She pushed a strand of hair off her forehead, and I noticed a diamond engagement ring on her left hand. The stones were not large, but the arrangement sparkled prettily in the dim light.

"The sheriff, Mr. Dawson?" she began. "He was good to us. He brought Lili's . . . things." Teresa uttered each phrase separately, as if she had to drag her thoughts to the surface, one at a time. "But something was missing. I wasn't thinking right, but Claudia saw."

I leaned forward to make sure I caught each of her words. "What was it, Mrs. Molina?"

"Always, Lili wore La Virgen de Guadalupe on a gold chain. Her father gave the medallion to her when she was little. She never took it off, not even when she had a shower."

"I promise you, I'll try my best to find it."

She let out a long breath, and her head tipped forward. "Thank you."

I looked at all the disarray: dishes piled high in the sink, an overflowing trash can. I didn't want to take advantage of this woman's despair. "Teresa? Before we talk further, I want to explain to you why I'm here. I'm a private—"

In rapid succession, the screen door and then the front door banged open. "Ma! Who's this?"

A petite girl of around fifteen stood in the kitchen doorway. She wore a man-sized white wifebeater draping a pair of baggy basketball shorts. The bottom half of her scalp was shaved, the long hair on the top half tied back in a severe ponytail. Her eyes blazed.

"Claudia, por favor . . ."

Claudia, who most likely weighed in at around ninety pounds, advanced on me. "Ma. Let me handle this."

"Mija—"

I rose to my feet, hoping to quiet the kid down. But Claudia wasn't fazed by the nine or ten inches I had on her. "Back off, bitch! What are you doing bothering my mom?"

"Miss Molina, calm down. My name is Jaymie Zarlin. I'm a private investigator representing the Armenta family."

"But—you never said that," Teresa objected.

"I was just about to tell you," I answered weakly.

"You're full of it." Claudia snarled. "Get the hell outta our house." Alas, the snarl was kind of cute, like that of a kitten.

I didn't want to embarrass the kid, but I had no intention of being bullied by a bantam chick. "There's something I need to say to you, Miss Molina. First, please take a step back."

"I ain't 'Miss Molina.' And I ain't taking no step back." Claudia balled her fists and raised them. "You got something to—"

"Claudia," her mother said wearily.

"Ma—"

"You're hurting me, Claudia." There was misery now in Teresa Molina's soft voice.

The girl jutted her delicate chin at me. "OK, what do you want? Say it and go."

"You loved your sister a lot. I can see that. Do you want the man who killed her to get away with it?"

Teresa moaned softly, then went quiet. Claudia's face froze in a mask, her mouth open in a silent O.

I was injuring them. I wanted to leave, but I couldn't. I couldn't for Lili's sake. "The truth is this: Danny Armenta was set up. If he's convicted, the killer will go free."

Teresa Molina broke into a sob.

I stepped forward and rested my hand on her shaking shoulder. "I promise I'll do my best to find Lili's medallion." I met Claudia's stare. "And I'll do everything I can to find out who did this."

As I crossed the small living room, I noticed that the candle at Lili's vigil had gone out, probably when Claudia slammed open the doors.

"Don't ever come around and bother my mom again, bitch!"

Claudia had caught up with me in the narrow walkway beside the big house. I turned in time to see her reach into her baggy shorts and pull out an old pearl-handled switchblade.

"You're taller than me, but that don't matter. White bitches like you are all *weak*." She raised her arm, released the blade, and jabbed the weapon at my face.

"Shit!" Claudia gasped. I'd grabbed her skinny elbow in midswing, wrapped it around her back, and tucked her hand up behind her ear. The knife clattered to the pavement.

"Sorry, I miscalculated a little." I dropped Claudia's hand down slightly to ease the pain in her shoulder.

"Fuck! I—*ouch!* OK! But don't think I'm gonna say sorry."

"Don't worry about it." I let the girl go. "My brother died a few years back. I lost it for a while."

Claudia lifted her shoulder and rotated it. "Damn," she muttered under her breath.

"That's a nice vintage knife you've got there. But you better put it back in your pocket."

She bent down to pick up the knife, closed the blade, and slipped it into her shorts. "It was my dad's. Smith and Wesson."

Above us, a window creaked. Claudia tipped back her head. "Hey bitch, mind yo own business!"

There was a hiss of disapproval, followed by the slam of the window sash.

I had to laugh. And to my surprise, I saw Claudia suppress the hint of a smile.

"OK. I need to tell you something, lady. Something my mom don't know nothin about. And don't you dare tell her, all right?"

"All right. Let's find a better place to talk, maybe out on the street."

"Yeah. Fuckin' goddamn chismosa!" Claudia yelled up at the window. "Nosy-ass bitch," she thoughtfully translated for me.

When we reached the sidewalk, I turned to her. "OK, I'm listening."

"The Stellatos. Know who they are? Rich-ass family my mom used to work for."

"I know them."

"OK. Well, I think maybe something bad happened to

Lili at their house. A couple months after my dad died." I saw her swallow hard. "You . . . heard about my dad?"

"Yes. I'm sorry, Claudia."

"Yeah." She glared at the pavement. "Well, anyway. One time the Stellatos, they had a big party. My sister went there to help my mom out. You know, dishwashing and stuff, like they were some kind of slaves."

"Uh-huh. So, what do you think happened?"

"I don't know. I thought maybe Mr. Stellato got mad at her. My mom always said he had a bad temper. Or maybe the rich kids at the party said some mean stuff. Once Lili started to tell me, but then she stopped. She never told Mom, I know that for sure. Anyways, a week after the party, they fired my mom. She wasn't too mad about it cause she got another job right away, and besides, the Stellatos gave her all kinds of money when she left—what do they call it?"

"Severance pay."

"Yeah, that's it. One time I asked Lili if Mom got fired cause of her. She got really mad and said to shut up. I don't know, it's weird. Maybe it doesn't mean anything, cause later Mr. Stellato got Lili into the Apollo Guild."

"How long ago did you say this was?"

"A long time ago. Maybe almost two years."

"Thanks for telling me, Claudia. It might help. Listen, I want to ask you a question. I noticed your mom wears an engagement ring. Is she getting married?"

"Yeah." The girl shrugged. "Margarito's OK, I guess. He gave Mom the ring a month ago. One good thing about him, he's got papers." She looked up quickly. "But my mom wouldn't—she'd never get married just because . . ." Her words faded.

"I understand. I'm glad for her." I took a business card from my wallet. "Here. If you want to, let's stay in touch. And please call me Jaymie, OK? I guess I'm old-fashioned, I like it better than bitch."

"OK." She accepted the card. "Do you really think that kid didn't—?" Her voice broke.

"I'm certain Danny didn't harm your sister."

"Armenta is weird. . . . No, it had to be hi-him!" There was an odd little hiccup in Claudia's voice. Suddenly she bent double, as if she'd been punched in the gut. "Lili," she moaned.

For a moment, uncertain, I hovered over the girl. Then I knelt down beside her and rested my hand on her shoulder.

"Get your hands off me!" She jumped up, eyes blazing. "And get the hell offa my street!"

Chapter Eight

Something bad had happened to Lili at the Stellatos'. I needed to know what.

The next morning found me tooling alongside the bridle paths in Hope Ranch, where H. R. Haldeman had lived before his death, where Snoop Dogg chose to kennel up now. Considering what I'd learned about Vincent Stellato, I'd decided not to call ahead. I was willing to take my chances: it was midmorning, midweek, and hopefully the man of the house was either at the office, running his statewide highway paving business, or busy negotiating a ninth hole.

The Stellato estate was located on Marina Drive, the street running along the cliff overlooking the Pacific Ocean. The mansions were invisible, hidden behind tasteful and pricey teak fences, ancient live oaks, and dapple-barked California sycamores. It occurred to me that the El Cam was maybe not the best calling card in this neighborhood. To gain entrance, I'd need to employ either subterfuge or my dubious charm.

As it happened, it would be subterfuge. A plumber's van had pulled up at the Stellatos' scrolly gate, and the driver was speaking into an intercom. When the gate swung open in a big arc, I drove in on the tradesman's heels.

The mansion was hidden, but close to the road. The first

thing I noticed about the structure was that everything seemed out of scale. Arches, windows, and chimneys were all somehow half a size too large. The architect had managed to turn a traditionally welcoming Mediterranean design into something arrogant and ugly. Even the paint color, a stippled yellow, set my teeth on edge.

The plumber's van continued on around to the back, but I pulled the El Camino right up under the giant portico, between a bed of waxy white gardenias and a dark red Mercedes, brand-spanking-new. I switched off the engine and stepped out: paradise greeted me. The house might have been hideous, but the grounds were lush and blooming, the warm air drenched with subtle fragrances and birdsong.

I shut the car door, turned—and sucked in my breath.

The biggest German shepherd on earth had appeared out of nowhere. Silent except for a low menacing growl, it took a step forward and bared its fangs.

Quietly, without looking the animal in the eye, I spoke to it. "Hey boy, good boy. Good dog, sit."

The thing did not sit, but leaped. As it dove past I felt a sharp nip on my leg, just hard enough to let me know who was in charge. The beast circled and prepared to make another pass.

"Freddy!" a woman's voice called out. "Freddy, please stop!" Freddy again showed his teeth and regarded me eagerly, as if I were a rabbit about to run.

"I'm so sorry! Did Freddy bite you?" A woman in her late forties, wearing pale-pink garden gloves and matching clogs, hurried up. "Lance, come out here! Lance, you have to call Freddy before he—"

"Before he kills again?" A handsome kid in his late teens leaned out of an upstairs window and laughed. In his right hand he dangled what looked like a joint. "Freddy, go back. Go on, git."

The dog slowly turned and moved off a few yards, then

dropped down on the grass, with what looked like ill-tempered regret. "Sorry lady," Lance drawled from above. He took a drag and puffed out a cloud.

"Lance, honey, how many times have I asked you to please, please not smoke those nasty cigarettes in the house." The woman smiled at me. She was pretty, in a faded sort of way. Even though her eyes and hair were dark brown, she reminded me of Doris Day. "He likes to roll his own nasty cigarettes for some reason or other. Kids. What do you do?"

"It's the economy, Mom." Lance grinned above us like a Cheshire cat. "Saves money to roll your own." He winked broadly at me.

"My husband wants Freddy to run loose, for security. But I just don't like it. I'm sorry if he frightened you." She cocked her head like a robin. "I'm Maryjune Stellato. Are you with the Master Gardener program? I called about my Quercus agrifo-lias. I must be overwatering. They just don't look—"

"No, Mrs. Stellato. I've been mistaken for many things, but never a master gardener. Actually, I'm here on a serious matter. Concerning the death of—"

"Oh. Oh my, I know exactly what you're going to say." Maryjune clapped her gloved hands to her cheeks. "Teresa's daughter, that poor girl." Her eyes brimmed with tears. "How is Teresa taking it?"

"Not so well, I'm afraid."

"No, no of course not. I sent flowers and fruit, and I wanted to go visit her, but Vince said—"

"Hey, Mom? Who's that you're talking to?"

Maryjune shaded her eyes and looked up. "This lady is here about Teresa's daughter." She turned back to me. "What did you say your name was?"

"Jaymie Zarlin. I'm a private investigator, and I've been hired to look into Lili Molina's murder." There was a sharp noise at the window, but when I looked up, Lance had gone. "I understand Mrs. Molina used to work for you."

"Yes, she did. But—but forgive me, I thought they arrested the boy—"

"A mistake. He didn't do it."

"Oh my. Tell me, how can I help?"

In this pretentious pile of stucco and concrete, I'd apparently found a genuine person. "I'd like to ask you a few questions, if you don't mind." I lowered my voice. Though I couldn't see Lance, I had a feeling he was still listening in.

"Absolutely. Absolutely anything I can do to help Teresa." She tilted her head to the open window. "Lance, honey? Ms. Zarlin and I are going into the garden to talk. Lance, are you still up there? Better put your car in the garage before Dad gets home."

So the Mercedes was Lance's, and Daddy was on his way home. I figured it might be a good idea to get my questions asked before Vincent showed up.

Maryjune removed her gloves and tucked them into the pocket of her gardener's apron. "Let's go sit in the Seaside Garden. It's the most soothing."

I followed the lady of the manor past beautifully tended flower beds, across verdant grass. We came on a gardener kneeling before a rosebush blanketed in red blooms so dark they were nearly black.

"Good job, Enrique. I know it's a fiddly business." Maryjune looked at me and giggled. "Don't imagine we dethorn all the rosebushes, Ms. Zarlin. Only the ones near the paths."

Imagine that, a life without thorns. "Um, please call me Jaymie." For the life of me, I couldn't think what else to say.

"I will, if you'll call me Maryjune." We sashayed around a few more corners on our plush emerald path.

"Let's sit here, Jaymie. This garden is completed—if ever a

garden is—and I won't be distracted with looking around and noticing what needs doing next. I'm kind of obsessed that way, you know." And she giggled again.

I just couldn't help myself: I found it impossible not to like the woman. We sat side by side on a weathered teak bench.

"I'd like to ask you about Teresa, Maryjune. I understand she worked for you up until about a year ago. Was she a good employee?"

"Oh my, yes. The best, you know? I trusted Teresa completely. She worked hard—too hard, I sometimes thought. At times she looked like a mother bird with a nest full of chicks, just worn to the bone. She worked here three full days a week, Vincent likes a clean house. And she had five or six other houses as well, can you believe that? She did it for her girls, of course. You know, Teresa is so competent, I always felt she could do more than clean houses. But—I hope this is OK to tell you— Teresa is *undocumented*."

"It limits her options, that's for sure. But tell me, why did Teresa leave? I understand you let her go."

"Oh . . . that was Vince." Maryjune reached out and twisted a dead leaf off a shrub. "He insisted. We argued about it, actually." She looked over at me. "We don't argue often. I don't see much point to it, you know? But that one time . . ."

"That time you did," I prompted.

"Yes, that time I stood my ground. Vince claimed it was too risky for his business, employing an illegal. But I thought that was nonsense. Nearly every house in Santa Barbara has a cleaning woman who is illegal, for goodness sake!" She shrugged. "So, now I have a cleaning *service*. It's very impersonal, and not nearly as good as Teresa was."

"How did Teresa take it—being fired, I mean?"

"Oh, she was upset. But then Vince talked to her and made it right." Maryjune glanced at me. "My husband has a bad temper, and some people think he's mean. But Vince can be generous. He gave Teresa a large check—six thousand dollars, I believe."

"That *is* a large check."

"Yes. I was glad he did it, and Teresa told me she was satisfied. So we parted friends, I'd like to think." Maryjune looked over the garden, and fluttered a hand. "This little nook is my favorite spot."

"It's lovely, Maryjune. You have an artist's eye."

"Well, it's all in grays and silvers, with shades of lilac. So many of my friends paint, you know. But I always like to say I—"

"Paint with plants." Lance Stellato ambled up to the bench and stood before us, blocking the sun. His face was in shadow, but I could confirm what I'd observed earlier: the kid was singularly handsome, with classic dark movie-star looks.

"Lance? Did you want something, honey?"

"Nope. Just keeping an eye on you, Mom." He laughed. "When Dad's not here, I'm the man of the house."

"Honestly, Lance," Maryjune said with a small frown. "Jaymie and I are just fine."

"I'm sure you are, Mom. You're fine with everybody, that's the problem." He shifted a little, and the sun shone in his face. He blinked, and I noticed his eyes were puffy and red. I glanced at the yellowish-brown stains on his fingertips.

"So, lady—you're a detective?"

"An investigator. I'm looking into the murder of Lili Molina."

"I heard. How come you're talking to my mom?"

The question sounded casual. But I could hear anxiety in his voice, in spite of the load of cannabis he had on board. "Because your family employed Mrs. Molina. I'm just trying to get a picture of what the Molinas were like."

"Kinda like in a detective show, huh?"

"Mm-hm." I turned to Maryjune. "Tell me," I said in an innocent tone, "did Teresa ever bring her daughters to the house?"

"Yes, when we had parties, you know? Just the older one, Lili—the girl who died. Teresa would never ask her daughter to serve or anything like that, but she did have Lili help out in the kitchen. I don't remember the younger girl at all, but Lili, yes. Such a sweetheart . . . In fact, not long before Vince let Teresa go, Lili was here." Maryjune shielded her eyes and looked up at her son.

"You remember her, don't you, Lance? The sweet Hispanic girl. It was your birthday party. I think the two of you got on quite well, if I remember. You and some of the others included her, didn't you? That was nice of you, dear. And Lili, she—"

"Mom." Lance scowled. "Dad wouldn't want you talking like this."

"Honey, if it will help, I don't see the harm—"

Lance turned on me. "So who hired you, lady? I thought they already caught the greaser who did it. Armenta, wasn't that it?"

"You're misinformed—Danny Armenta didn't do it. And to answer your question, I've been hired by his family."

A surprised "Oh!" escaped from Maryjune. "Goodness, I didn't—I wouldn't want to—"

"Danny Armenta didn't commit the murder," I repeated.

"Then who do you think—"

"Mom. *Shut up.*" Lance turned on me. "You need to go, lady. Hear me? Scat."

"Lance, honey, please. There's no need to talk like that!"

I'd have loved to settle pretty boy's hash, but this wasn't the time to indulge. I rose to my feet. "Thanks for talking to me, Maryjune. Just one more question. Your gardener, Enrique—does he have papers?"

"Enrique? No. No, I don't think he . . ." I watched as an uncomfortable understanding dawned on Doris Day's face.

Lance took a step forward. "Lady, I said *fuck off.*"

◆   ◆   ◆

On my way back to the office, sweet serendipity blew me a kiss.

My mind was still on the Stellatos when I turned a block too soon and found myself on a quiet Westside street off San Andres.

I coaxed the balky El Camino into a U-turn. That was when it happened: out of the corner of my eye, I caught a glimpse of two desperadoes. One was a small boy wearing flannel pajamas and purplish face paint, and the other was a tiny brown and white dog with floppy ears.

I knew a King Charles spaniel when I saw one. I pulled up at the curb, but before I could get out of the car, the pair had scampered off around the corner of an old wooden house.

I jotted down the faded house number stenciled on the mailbox, then sat for a moment and observed the property. It looked like no one was home: blinds were drawn over what was most likely a living room window, and a second window was draped with a sheet. The front yard was covered in sparse grass, neatly trimmed. A row of long-spined cacti, the edible type, bloomed in dainty apricot flowers all along an old wire fence.

I shifted the El Camino into gear and gave the house one last look—just as the blinds were parted by a small brown hand.

The next morning, two loud male voices filled the courtyard at 101 Mission. One, in mellifluous Spanish, promised *hi-gantic* savings. The other trumpeted like an infuriated football coach reaming the troops.

My office door was wide open, and both voices boomed from my private sanctum. I drew a deep breath and climbed the steps.

"Miss Jaymie, it's you!" Gabi cried out. She stood ramrod straight behind the desk, her arms wrapped tightly across her chest.

A short, rather heavyset man wearing a lime-green golf shirt turned and glared. "Hey. You're the one," he bellowed.

"Don't shout at me." But I couldn't even hear my own words, due to the other bombastic voice filling the background.

"Gabi," I mouthed, "turn off the radio."

Gabi edged from behind the desk, stiff-legged as a terrier ready to fight. She circled the angry man, her back to the wall, reached out to the radio, and switched it off. For a moment, the room was dead still.

"Sweet peace." I sighed. "Mr. Stellato?"

The guy seemed surprised I recognized him. It took the wind out of his sails, but not for long. He puffed himself up again and blared. "Yeah. And you're the girl detective, am I right?"

"Jaymie Zarlin." I smiled nicely. "Your son Lance takes after you, Mr. Stellato. What can I do for you?"

Vince Stellato took two steps toward me, which put us pretty much forehead-to-nose. My nose to his forehead, that is. "You can start by staying off my property, understand? Off my property and the hell away from my family."

Vince's orange golf cap, which read *Bandon Dunes*, was soaked in sweat. Large half-moons showed under his armpits. The guy was stressed. Who was he protecting—his wife, his son, or maybe himself?

"You have the right to ask me not to return to your house, Mr. Stellato. As to my speaking with your family members, that would be up to them."

"They don't wanna talk to you, get it?"

"Maryjune seemed happy to talk. And I never asked to speak to your son. Lance approached me himself."

"Cut the crap. You get the message." He took a step toward the door. Then for some reason he turned back, stuffed a hand in his trouser pocket, and jiggled change. "I just don't get it," he barked.

"Get what?" I kept my voice neutral. I wasn't sure what it

would take to get Vince Stellato to open up, but being combative definitely wasn't the answer.

"Why d'you want to help Armenta? The little prick did it. He's a nutcase. Even if you're some kind of bleeding heart, do you want to put a killer back on the street?" He glowered at me. "Lili Molina was a sweetheart of a kid. Maybe you oughta think about her, huh?"

"I've thought quite a bit about Lili, Mr. Stellato. But the fact is, Danny Armenta didn't kill her, or do anything else to her. He's innocent."

"How the hell do you figure . . ." Vince Stellato's mouth shut tight. In the interval of silence that followed, the parrot screamed.

"I don't believe you," he blurted at last. "You're meddling, trying to drum up business or something. Yeah, that's it. You're doing it for the money." He sneered into my face. "Whore."

"That's enough!" Gabi yelped. "My boss is not even getting paid."

"Oh yeah? Well, something's in it for her. Look, I don't give a damn." He shoved past me and stepped through the open doorway. "Just stay away from my wife and kid. I'm warning you."

"Warning me?" I said quietly. "Is that some kind of a threat?"

"You bet your sweet bootie it is." A breeze freshened and lifted the bill of Stellato's cap, flicking it off his head. I stifled a smile: except for a narrow rim of dark hair, the guy was totally bald.

"To hell with you, Zarlin!" Vince Stellato hopped down the steps and raced after his cartwheeling hat.

Gabi held two cups of fresh coffee, one in each hand. "I was so, so happy to see you walk in that door. You're pretty tough, I'm impressed!"

"Oh, there's plenty of bluff in that bully." I glanced over at the old secondhand printer as I accepted the coffee. It was spewing out color printouts, groaning under the effort. A page wafted to the floor.

"What's this?" I set the mug on the desk and bent down to pick up the flyer. A soulful spaniel gazed up at me. *Missing from Montecito!!! King Charles Spaniel called Minuet. Will pay reward for info leading to recovery. Guaranteed 100% confidential. Phone 987-6643, ask for Gabriela.* The message was repeated in Spanish.

"Actually, Gabi, I don't think—"

"Hang on, before we talk. You deserve a treat for what you just did. And guess what? Today I got your favorite, the chocolate-filled concha. Be right back."

While Gabi was in the kitchen, I pulled the stack of fresh paper from the printer, stopping the feed. Then I drew the client's chair up to the desk and took a slow sip of the richly aromatic brew.

"Here you go." Gabi set the pastry, nestled in a pink saucer, before me. Then she glanced over at the silent printer. It flashed a yellow malevolent eye. "Huh? Something is wrong?"

"No, I just took out the paper. The flyers look good, Gabi, but we need to hold off."

"What do you mean?" Gabi set down her coffee and fixed me with a keen look. "I was thinking sooner is better."

"There've been several new developments in the case. We need to reconsider our approach."

"Developments—you mean, like clues?" She settled herself in the desk chair. "OK, tell me."

"Well, here's one. When I visited Darlene Richter, I discovered a hole sawn out at the base of her redwood fence. A few brown and white dog hairs were caught on the wood. The dognapper could have called Minuet over to the hole, then dragged or lured her through."

"Good work, boss. I guess it was hard to find, that hole?"

"Sort of. It was hidden behind . . . hm . . ."

"Behind what?"

"Well, the hole was hidden behind some bushes. But in fact, you could see it if you just looked."

Silence filled the little room. Then the parrot struck up its favorite mantra: "Trust me, deadbeat. Trust me, deadbeat!"

"Miss Jaymie, what are you thinking?"

"I'm thinking someone was *meant* to spot that hole. Maybe it was made to just look like an outside job."

"So it was really a inside job? The gardeners, you think?"

"Could be." But now it wasn't a dognapping I was thinking of.

I was recalling a window with chicken wire sandwiched in the glass, a window that had been pried open from the outside alley. I'd thought I was clever, discovering that. But maybe I wasn't clever enough.

"You said several developments," Gabi probed. "What else?"

"Hm? Oh. Nothing I'm sure of yet." I'd decided not to tell her about the little boy and his pup until I knew more. Minuet wasn't the only King Charlie in town, and I could be miles off base.

"Even if you're not sure, you can tell me, OK? I never—" Just then her cell erupted in a salsa. "Alma? Que? OK, OK!" Gabi leaped up from the chair.

"Miss Jaymie, we gotta go right away! The cops are trying to get in your house! Come on, we'll take my car."

"Alma's been trying to call you," Gabi scolded as we pulled away from the curb. "But your phone is off, just like always."

"I need peace and quiet to think," I defended myself. "I do check it."

"When? At night after everybody who called is asleep, so you got a excuse not to call them back?"

I ignored this. "I live on El Balcón. Do you know which way to go?"

"El Balcón? I lived in Santa Barbara for twenty years, and I never heard of that street."

"Nobody has. It's more of a goat track. Get to Cliff, Gabi, and I'll direct you from there. Can't you go a little faster?"

"Yeah I can. Hold on to your horses, you'll see."

Deirdre Krause possessed a cherubic face and carried a layer of cute chubby-baby fat. One might even say she looked like a Renaissance angel. My, how looks could deceive.

The oversized tot had planted herself on my front step. A very large cop stood a few yards away, chewing his cud.

Aricela and Chuy peered around the partly open front door, eyes wide. I slammed the car door shut and crossed the yard in three bounds.

"Get off my property, Krause, and take your Rottweiler with you. You have no right to be here, harassing my houseguests."

"Hey, you just call me a dog?" Krause's slave boy looked at his senior partner for support.

"Houseguests, Neil, get that," she trilled. "Our guests say a lot about us, don't they?" Krause took a moment to pet her wavy blond hair. "I have to hand it to you, Zarlin, you're gutsy. Personally, I don't think I'd invite a psycho to move in."

I forced myself to draw in a deep, very long breath. Breathe it in, let it out. Deirdre was trying hard to provoke me, but I was determined not to let her succeed.

"Officer Krause, I repeat: you have no right to be here. I'm politely asking you to leave."

"Well, now, I'd love to." Deirdre's plump face fell into a pout. "But I have a responsibility to the citizens of our fair city. A responsibility to check up on the whereabouts of a certain suspect named Daniel Armenta who is out on bail—for a *very brief* time. I can and will obtain a search warrant if I have reason to think—"

"Fine, I get it. Gabi, can you help me out?"

"Anything," she stiffly replied.

"Who's this?" Deirdre bleated. "Another houseguest, I suppose? Got a police record, sweetheart?"

Gabi, with dignity, stepped forward. "I am Gabriela Rufina Martinez Gutierrez, Miss Jaymie's PA."

"PA? That's a hoot." Deirdre giggled. "And on second thought, maybe you don't have a record. In fact, maybe you have no records at all. Got papers?"

"That's harassment," I snapped. I'd never asked Gabi if she had papers. Obviously she didn't, because otherwise she'd be running some corporate office downtown. "Tell me something, Krause. Do you make it a habit to ask everyone who looks Hispanic if they have papers?"

"Believe me, if I had the time, I'd do just that."

How I wished Mike could see his admirer now. Deirdre's face was so pinched it looked shrink-wrapped.

"Gabi, go talk to Danny. Ask him to come to the window. He doesn't have to step outside, just show his face so the *peace officer* can see he's here."

"Will do." Gabi edged around the fuming Deirdre and shooed Chuy and Aricela in before her.

"Speaking of Rottweilers, Zarlin," Deirdre piped up. "I called the pound on that snappy little mutt you keep around here. They came right away."

In all the fuss, I hadn't noticed Dexter's absence. I had to fight to keep my voice steady as my blood pressure jackhammered. "That dog had better be all right."

"The safety of police officers, not to mention the public, comes before the welfare of canines. If I were you, I'd—"

An apparition appeared in the window. A pale face with large dark eyes stared out from the cowl of a hoodie. Then Chuy popped up beside his brother, chin on the sill.

"There's Danny Armenta. You have your proof. Now go."

"How do I know it's him?" Deirdre whined. "He's got that hood over his face. He could be any gangbanger in town."

"What, because he's Mexican? Danny was never a gang member, not even close." I stepped up to the window. "Danny, please take off your hood for a minute," I called through the glass. But he only looked at me blankly. "Chuy, pull down Danny's hood, OK?"

Chuy nodded vigorously, and disappeared. It took him a minute to drag a kitchen chair up to the window.

"There's your proof, Krause: Danny's red hair."

"I'll just document this," Deirdre sniffed. She snapped a photo of Danny—and of a grinning Chuy, making rabbit's ears over his brother's head.

Chapter Nine

"June gloom," Mike observed as we slogged through the sand at Ledbetter Beach. "I like walking in the fog."

"The foghorn sounds like a sick sea lion," I grumped. Pretended to grump, of course. Because actually I was in a good mood, happy to be with him.

"A sick sea lion? I was going to say it's romantic."

"Romantic," I snorted. "Might be, if I hadn't butted heads with Deirdre Krause this morning. Locking up my dog like that: I could cheerfully hog-tie the woman with baling wire."

"Jesus, Jaymie. Do we have to talk about Deirdre?"

"Why not? I need someone to gnaw on."

"Look. I'm not defending her. But did you know she grew up poor in East LA, with a crackhead for a mom and an abuser for a stepfather? Her childhood was a living hell."

"Hey, don't tell me that. How can I hate her?"

"Sorry." Mike grinned and tugged my ponytail. "Anyway, Dex probably appreciates you more after a few hours in the clink."

"He's no worse for wear, I have to admit."

"Let's go talk in one of the caves under Shoreline."

"OK. But you might have to dislodge an entrepreneur."

"We'll just shoo him away. I'm off-duty, and besides, that's a job for Harbor Patrol."

We reached the water's edge, then turned and walked westward up the south-facing beach. "The fog's so wet it's dripping off the end of my nose," I groused.

"Hey, come on now. Don't spoil the mood."

Spoil the mood? I was struggling to not get swept away. Mike and I were playing pretend: the pretense for this meeting was to exchange info about the murder investigation. Who were we fooling? Our minds weren't on work.

Within two or three minutes, we stood below the crumbling sandstone cliffs. The tide was pulling out, leaving behind a string of caves with wet, hard-packed sand floors.

"Jaymie, how about this one? If we climb, there's a dry place to sit."

"Why not," I heard myself say. I knew I had reasons not to get too close to the guy. Reasons I couldn't seem to recall.

The tide had swept the cave clean, but even so, you could smell urine under the sharp odor of brine. A century and a half ago, the caves were used by smugglers. Now dealers hung out here. Recently I'd heard Harbor Patrol had arrested a kid from LA in one of these caves. Fourteen years old, heroin-addicted, the boy was prostituting himself.

Avoiding the sea anemones clustered at the base, I scampered up a sandstone boulder. "Hey, try and climb up. But I warn you, I'm queen of the hill."

"No, you're a princess. Rapunzel, Rapunzel, let down your hair."

I laughed. "You're spreading it on pretty thick."

"All right, that's it. Out of my way, I'm storming the ramparts."

"Mike, I've got something to tell you," I said when he'd squeezed in beside me. "Something about the murder case."

"OK. Just be sure you tell me everything—don't edit like you usually do."

"Sure." I gave him a sly grin. "I'll tell you everything you need to know."

"What's new," Mike laughed.

"Seriously, listen. Did you learn that old song in kindergarten: *Go in and out the window, in and out the window . . .*"

"My mom used to sing that to me. She had a nice voice . . . kind of like yours."

I didn't know how to answer. Awkwardly, I skipped over it. "Uh . . . well. I thought about that song yesterday, it just popped into my head. See, I've got this dognapping case I'm working on—"

"You what?"

I ignored the question. "The dog—owned by a very wealthy client, I might add—was apparently pulled or lured out of her yard through a hole in the fence. But actually, I'm thinking it was just meant to *look* that way."

"You mean the dog was taken by someone inside?"

"You're quick," I teased.

"Smarty. But how's this connected to Lili Molina's murder?"

"It isn't. But it made me realize something." I picked up a broken shell and carved at the damp sandstone boulder. "The window was shut when the girls found Danny. Shut and latched, right? But like I told you, if you looked you could see where someone had pried it open from the outside. And the sill was wiped clean, as if an intruder had climbed through."

"Right. And that would mean the killer came in from outside and left through a door. We've been over this before, Jaymie. It sounds like someone who didn't have access, a stranger. A stranger who latched the window afterward, to make it look like an inside job. That's gotta be good for Danny Armenta, right?"

"That's what I thought, at first. But then the song started singing in my head: 'Go in and out the window.' . . . Don't you see?"

He shook his head. "All I see is you contradicting yourself."

"The window frame, Mike. It was just too obvious."

Mike groaned. "Jaymie—"

"No, listen. Here's what I think happened. At first, the killer wanted us to believe he'd climbed in through the window. He wanted us to think he was a stranger. But I'll bet you anything he entered the warehouse through a door."

"OK. . . ."

"Now, when the girls found Lili's body, the window was shut and latched, correct?"

"Yeah, yeah."

"Mike, don't get cranky. See, there was no good reason for the killer to *close* the window if he wanted to make it look like an outsider committed the murder—which he initially did want to do. But what if the guy changed his plan in the heat of battle? At some point, I think he realized Danny Armenta was in the building. That's when he saw an opportunity that was too good to pass up. After all, what better person to frame?"

"Hm. I see what you're getting at. And that would mean the killer knew who Danny was, knew he was mentally ill. An insider for sure. An insider like Jared Crowley, maybe?"

"Maybe." I brushed off my hands on my jeans.

"Jaymie? You know something else you're not telling me. Something about Crowley?"

"I'm not sure about anything just yet. When I am, you'll be the first to know."

"Sure I will." Mike sighed. "Listen. You be careful out there in crime land. It's no place to fly solo. And don't count on your good looks to get you out of trouble."

"Flatter me, I love it."

Mike dropped off the boulder to the firm sand. I began to

climb down, clinging to the wet rock until he plucked me off
the sandstone and into his arms. Before I knew what I was doing, I'd turned and melted into his body.

"I'm hot. Jaymie . . . don't tell me you aren't too."

"Very . . . very . . . warm," I admitted. Our mouths met.

We moved together against the damp wall of the cave. Just
then two middle-aged women walked past the entrance. They
looked at us, then glanced away. But their retriever dashed in,
squatted down, and pissed near Mike's boot.

We both started to laugh and couldn't quit. Then, just as we
got going again, a family with kids in tow walked past. "We'd
better quit or we'll get arrested," I said. "Lewd and lascivious."

"That pretty well describes me right now," he agreed.

"There's something I want you to do for me," Mike said as we
trudged back through the dry sand to the parking lot.

"What's that?" I asked carefully. I was cooling down, wondering what the hell I'd been playing at.

"I want you to come up to the ranch with me this weekend.
Dad always asks about you, you know."

I almost groaned aloud. I could feel him reeling me in like a
rainbow trout. How could I get my message across without
hurting him again? "Mike, listen. Your dad's a great guy. But I'm
not sure I should—"

"Before you answer, let me explain."

I heard an odd note in his voice and had the sense to back
off. "Something serious?"

"Yeah. Dad's got cancer, Jaymie. He won't be able to stay out
at the ranch much longer."

"Oh God. I'm so sorry." And I was. I'd met Bill Dawson
back when Mike and I were together. Old-time rancher and all-
around good man. We'd hit it off immediately, and over fish 'n'
chips out on the wharf, he'd let me know just how delighted
he'd be to welcome me into the Dawson clan.

"I'd really like to visit your dad. But—"

"But what?" He halted, set his hands on my shoulders, and turned me to face him. "It's lung cancer, Jaymie. Dad's not going to beat it."

I looked away, to where a homeless woman was curled up on the sand, a threadbare beach towel wrapped tightly around her and covering her face like a mummy.

"Mike, look. What are we together, you and I? Because your dad will ask me, you can count on it. And I wouldn't want to lie to him."

"We're not friends, Jaymie. I can tell you that."

"No. I guess not." My voice sounded small.

"Hey, come on. You know what we are." He stroked my hair, lifting it back from eyes. "Just step aside, damn it, and let it happen."

Vince Stellato had taught me one lesson: with this crowd, it was better to call ahead. I'd phoned Sutton Frayne for an appointment, and the move seemed to pay off: I was offered a welcoming smile.

"Miss Zarlin. You're more attractive than I expected," Frayne said gallantly. "Please, come aboard."

I hopped the gap between the dock and the *Icarus*. "My reputation precedes me, does it, Mr. Frayne?"

He tipped back his handsome head and laughed. "I've had an earful from Stellato, if that's what you mean. Somehow Vince missed your obvious charms."

"And I missed his." I knew I was being flattered by a grand master, but it was hard not to respond to the boyish grin.

"Well. Let's just say his was the greater oversight, and leave it at that." Frayne ran a hand through his hair, which naturally drew my attention to it. Strawberry blond, of all things, on a man of fifty or so. The guy was charming, but vain as a thirteen-year-old girl.

"I hope you don't mind meeting me here on the boat, Ms. Zarlin. This is where I prefer to hold all my meetings."

"Not at all." I looked over the deck, reminding myself to not be impressed. The *Icarus* was sleek and beautiful, and the yacht's owner, while not exactly beautiful, was very good-looking in an upper-crusted, blue-eyed sort of way. Sutton Frayne III wore khaki slacks and an open-neck navy silk shirt. His sleeves were rolled back to reveal forearms tanned to a perfect warm-toast shade. And Frayne was slim and obviously fit: the advantage of a personal trainer, no doubt, if not a personal gym.

"Let's talk in the cabin, shall we? We'll enjoy a glass of iced tea, and I'll tell you a thing or two about my friend Vince." He gave me a knowing half-smile. "You said on the phone you're interviewing people who had contact with the dead girl. But my guess is, you'd like to know more about Stellato."

"I'd appreciate hearing your opinion of him," I said politely.

"And for a pretty young woman like yourself, I'd be willing to oblige."

I followed Sutton Frayne down several steps, to a shipshape lounge gleaming with brass fittings and polished mahogany paneling and built-ins. He waved me to a chrome and black chair, something by a midcentury designer—original, no doubt. "Please, take a seat."

"Sure," I murmured. I couldn't take my eyes off an oil painting hanging on the opposite wall, over a narrow table. A impressionist still life, the painting depicted a footed green-glass bowl brimming with oranges, apples, and a banana. Cleverly, an identical antique bowl holding a similar collection of fruit sat on the table.

"That picture—it's wonderful." Wonderful but mildly pornographic, was what I was actually thinking. Plainly, the painting was not only a still life, but also a voluptuous depiction of female breasts. The banana spoke for itself.

"You have excellent taste, my dear. That painting is rather

valuable." Frayne glanced into the mirror over the bar and smoothed back a stray strand of hair. "Now, instead of iced tea, may I offer you something with a bit of a kick? A mimosa, perhaps?"

The mimosa was tempting. And the realization that I was tempted reminded me to stick to business. "Tea would be fine, thanks. I'm working today."

Frayne chuckled. "Unlike we idle rich, I suppose you mean." He bent down behind the bar and emerged with two crystal glasses and a carafe filled with a shimmery leaf-green liquid. "I have this tea sent from an exclusive Chinese import shop in San Francisco. Sparrow's Tongue makes the best iced tea in the world."

Frayne dropped several ice cubes into each glass with a pair of silver tongs, then poured the tea over the rocks. "Sugar, Jaymie?"

"Half a teaspoon," I answered cooperatively. I wasn't sure when I'd morphed from Ms. Zarlin to Jaymie, but I let it go. After all, I wanted to get the guy to talk. "Sparrow's Tongue? Sounds very exotic."

"Very exotic, and very expensive." He handed me my tea, and somehow our fingertips touched.

"Anyway. You asked about Vince." Frayne dropped into a leather butterfly chair and draped one long leg over the other. "You've opened a can of worms with my friend, that's for sure. Vince was on the phone with me for thirty minutes last night. The man can rave, that I'll admit."

"I didn't mean to step on his toes, Mr. Frayne. Frankly, his reaction to me seems kind of excessive."

"I wouldn't read anything into it. I've known Vince Stellato for years. Both his parents were Sicilian, and everything about the man is excessive and *passio-na-te*. And after all, I believe you did invade his home, his castle, without his prior knowledge."

His eyes met mine and he smiled warmly. "May I call you Jaymie?"

"You already have, Mr. Frayne."

He laughed, revealing beautifully capped teeth. "Call me Sutz. Everyone does."

Dear old Sutz was trying his best to seduce me. And the more he did it, the more it annoyed me. "Did Vince tell you I'm representing Danny Armenta's family?"

"Yes. Yes, he did." Frayne frowned slightly. "And especially now that I've met you, I have to admit I'm flummoxed. I'm not at all sure why you've taken this on. A dollar's a dollar, is that it?"

"No. That's not it." I allowed a bubble of silence to expand between us.

Frayne opened his hands, palms up. "Well, then . . . what?"

"My reasons have to do with justice. Danny Armenta is innocent."

He frowned again and shook his head. "Is that what the police think? Or just you?"

"I couldn't say what the police think, Mr. Frayne. Do you mind if I ask you one or two questions?"

He leaned back in the chair, spreading his arms. "I'm all yours. I've got an appointment, though, at two."

For his hair, his nails, or his tan? I resisted the urge to ask. "Oh, this will only take a few minutes." I creased my brow like a bimbo, hoping this would encourage Sutz to open up. "Where were you on June twenty-first, between the hours of one and four P.M.?"

"Ah, the detective's shopworn question." He smiled ruefully, as if I'd disappointed him. "I was at the Wiederkehrs', of course. The Guild Triune hosts an annual get-together after the Solstice parade. Tradition, you know." He knitted his fingers together and hooked his hands over his knee. "The Stellatos were there, plus dozens of Guild members-at-large and their families. Actually, I took along Caroline, to give her an outing."

"Caroline?"

"My mother, Caroline Frayne. She seldom leaves Stonecroft, her home." Frayne's foot, shod in gleaming Italian leather, twitched rhythmically. "There's not much more I can tell you."

"But maybe there is." I took a minute to rearrange the cushions behind my back. "For example, I'd like to ask if you saw anyone leave during the course of the party."

"Leave? No. No, I can't say I did. And to answer the question I think you're really asking, as far as I could tell, Vince Stellato was there the whole time."

"How about Lance?"

"Lance? What, Vince's son? I don't remember—yes, I think he was there." Frayne abruptly waved a hand and rose to his feet.

"Look, I'm sorry, but you need to go. You're making me rather cross: I'm not the sort of fellow who's comfortable gossiping about his friends and their families."

"To the gangplank with me, huh?"

But Frayne didn't smile.

A few minutes later, he led me off the boat and back along the dock to the electrified gate. He punched in a code and stepped aside. "Hopefully we'll meet again, Jaymie. I'm sure you're a great gal and I'd like to get to know you better. Under more social conditions, perhaps?"

"I'm not much of a socializer, Mr. Frayne."

"I'm sorry to hear that." He closed his hand around mine, exerting a slight but somehow intimate pressure. Ol' Sutz was now back in his groove: his palm felt cool and dry.

Heavy wine-colored drapes swathed the windows, shutting out the light. Mesmerized, I stared at the silent silvery women, long dead, smiling to reveal their square little teeth as they danced hootchie-cootchies across the two-story-high walls.

"Get down on your knees, Ken, and this time do it right," Celeste Delaney snapped.

Much as I disliked the arrogant Ken doll, I felt a twinge of compassion. I looked away from the walls and observed the tableau: Ken kneeling on the oak parquet floor to sweep up the crumbs with a clothes brush, catching them in his meaty hand.

"There, that's the way, head down and bum up," Celeste Delaney crooned. "Whatever were you thinking, Ken, bringing a long-handled broom?" She looked over at me and smiled.

"I demand perfection, my dear, and I get it. My staff care for me very well indeed, for they understand their generous remunerations will cease upon my death. I have left them absolutely nothing in my will. That would be unwise of me, don't you think?"

"You could be right."

"Ken, you missed something. Even my old eyes can see it. Over there," she pointed.

"That's just dust," Ken muttered.

"*Just* dust? Well don't *just* leave it there, man!"

Ken looked up and met my eyes. Judging by his expression, the guy was furious. But he resumed his downward-dog position.

"Will that be all, Miss Delaney?" His voice was rigid.

"For now. Off you go."

Ken walked stiff-necked toward the door, until he was behind the old woman's back. He turned and glared at me, then opened his hand and tossed the gleanings back into the room.

"So, my dear Jaymie. How do you like this private theater of mine? I spend much of my time here, reliving the past."

"It's very impressive. Like being in the movie yourself."

"Yes, it does draw one in. Here I can manage to forget what

year it is—bah, what century it is—for hours on end." She pointed a shaky finger at a nearby chair. "Sit down, won't you? I'm pleased you came straightaway. I think you will find our little visit worthwhile."

"I'm sure I will, Miss Delaney." I walked over and perched on the edge of an uncomfortable wingback chair facing the throne. "Thank you for posting Danny Armenta's bail. He and his family are staying with me, and I can tell you he's beginning to do better."

"Better? What, do you mean he's communicating?" The old woman seemed more alert today. Or maybe the little drama with Ken had brought her to life.

"Danny's talking to me, yes. Until now I haven't asked him what he saw on the afternoon of the murder. But I'll be broaching the subject with him in a day or so." I thought this would please Celeste, but she frowned.

"I understand the police remain convinced he is the guilty one. I do read the papers, you know, and I have my connections. I am not unfamiliar with what is going on"—she waved vaguely at the draped windows—"out in the world. And I must admit I have asked myself: should I have assisted a possible killer to obtain bail?"

"You don't need to worry about that, Miss Delaney. Your decision to help was the right one." I leaned forward in the backbreaking chair. "I'm certain now that Danny was set up. My job is to discover who did it, then obtain evidence of the killer's guilt."

"If the killer was not the mad boy, then no doubt it was a drifter, someone passing through."

"I considered that, Miss Delaney. But I don't think it was the work of a stranger."

Celeste turned her attention to the flickering wall. "Have you ever watched *Chinatown*, Jaymie?"

I followed her gaze. Now the ghost women were waving

long scarves, wrapping them around their long, snake-like necks.

"The movie with Jack Nicholson? Yes, I saw it a few years back."

"Noah Cross in real life was Mulholland, you know. My father, Jackson Delaney, knew him well. Daddy also did business with the Chandlers of the *Los Angeles Times*." She swiveled her raptor's head and peered at me. "May I give you a piece of advice, my dear? The members of our Apollo Guild are powerful men. Hardly the sort to appreciate a little detective poking about in their affairs."

I caught my breath in surprise. *Little detective*: Celeste had delivered a sharp, stinging slap. Like Ken, I thought wryly, I'd just been shown my place. "Yes," I said carefully, "I suppose I see what you mean."

"You *suppose*? Hmph." She waved her stick dismissively. "Tell me this, then. Have you made any progress at all, with the case?"

Was this why Celeste had summoned me here today, to receive a progress report? Well, half a mil in bail money entitled her to it, I supposed. "I think so, Miss Delaney. But these things take time. Right now I'm focusing on the Apollo Guild, trying to gain an overall picture of how it operates."

"I see. So is that why you went to see my nephew, Sutton—to gain an overall picture?"

So that was what all this was about. I should have realized Sutz would tell his aunt about my visit to the *Icarus*.

"Yes. Mr. Frayne was very helpful. I also spoke with the Stellato family."

"So I understand. You are curious about the Triune members in particular, it seems to me. Have you contacted the Wiederkehrs?"

"I did, but Mrs. Wiederkehr turned me down. Too busy, she said."

"I'm hardly surprised she turned you away. I knew Brucie Wiederkehr's father. The man was soft. But Cynthia Wiederkehr, she is in fact a Caughey from Montecito. My, my, her father was a tough old sot!" Celeste Delaney picked up a silver bell resting on the arm of her chair and rang it vigorously. "Did you know my father was once a member of the Triune? A founder of the Apollo Guild, as a matter of fact."

"Actually, I didn't know that."

"No? You must do your homework, Jaymie. I'll give you an introduction to the Wiederkehrs, but I will not do your work for you. What sort of detective are you?"

I couldn't help myself: I burst out laughing. "Sorry, Miss Delaney. The help just isn't what it used to be, is it?"

Celeste Delaney looked as if she was about to strike me with her silver-tipped cane. But then she laughed too. "You have spunk, I must give you that."

The door eased open, and a servant, the woman who'd helped Ken deliver the coffee to the garden, stepped into the room. Her face was acne-scarred, her figure voluptuously heavy. "You rang, Miss Delaney?"

"Of course I rang, Nancy. What have I told you? Never state the obvious."

"I apologize, Miss Delaney."

"Yes, well. I'm not sure you can help it, but do try to remember. Now, there is an envelope for Miss Zarlin sitting on the demilune table in the east hall. Bring it here."

"Yes, Miss Delaney." As Nancy backed out of the room, I half expected her to genuflect.

"Now, I apologize, my dear, for revealing the less cuddly side of my nature today. I fear I am quite irascible. Arthritis of the neck—painful, you know."

Again the door crept open. "Ah. Here she is. No, not to me, silly woman. Give it to Miss Zarlin."

Nancy's eyes met mine in the few seconds it took her to hand me the manila envelope. They were filled with hate. Was it hatred of Celeste Delaney, or of me?

"A gift for you," Celeste explained when the door had closed on her servant. "What they call a computer disc, I believe. I contains valuable information, information that my connections assure me will aid you in *focusing your inquiries*, as they say."

She struggled to her feet, leaning heavily upon her cane. "I find I rather like you. You've quite the dogged nature, haven't you?" A corner of her mouth twisted up.

"You know, little detective, I rather think I shall keep you on."

The garden outside my open office window was dusted in gold. Deadbeat was either murdered at last, or stowed away undercover. In the peaceful quiet, I could hear a drowsy medley of birdsong.

My old routine was to pack up and bike on home around five. If I had more work to do, I'd do it at El Balcón, looking out over the Pacific with a glass of wine close at hand. But now that I had guests, things had changed. Chuy and Aricela liked to spend the evenings tearing in and out of the house with Dex and generally fooling around. More often than not, they drew me into their shenanigans. I was learning to finish my work at the office.

I removed the disc Celeste Delaney had given me from my messenger bag and inserted it into the computer. I whistled under my breath as I peered at the downloads: the files held nearly five hundred photos, all taken either during the Solstice parade or immediately afterward, in Alameda Park. I could hardly believe my luck.

And how the hell had Celeste Delaney come by this treasure

trove? The kids in the Guild had been asked to turn their cell phones in to the police. I stopped smiling as I realized Celeste's tentacles had reached into the hallways of the SBPD.

Sobered, I sacrificed a few dozen trees to the cause and printed all the photos snapped in the park. Then I knelt down and spread the nearly three hundred pages over the office floor in a wide arc. One by one, I studied them.

Each photo had the name of the photographer printed at the bottom, together with the time the picture was snapped. I scanned through, smiling to myself. Five or six photos showed kids displaying their tongues at the camera, and several featured smart-alecky young women baring their breasts.

Quite a few were of Lili Molina, and it wasn't hard to see why: she'd looked stunning in her costume. But I thought I could see a troubled look in her sequined eyes.

I pulled out all those of Lili and arranged them by time. The last photo of her was taken at 3:02 in the afternoon.

Once more, I scanned all the other snaps to double-check: none showed any of the Guild Triune members or their relatives. What the rich guys were claiming was probably true: they'd all been engaged in their upstairs celebration of Solstice at the Wiederkehrs' estate. As for Jared and Shawna . . . I pulled out twenty-three photos of the great god Apollo, yet only one of sour, unpopular Shawna. The snap of Shawna was taken at 2:33, the last shot of Jared at 2:43. So both were taken well before Lili disappeared from the park.

I riffled back through the photos to see if I'd missed anything. Abruptly, my heart sped up as a squirt of adrenaline kicked in.

My eye had fallen on a photo of three costumed guys hamming it up for the camera. On the far edge of the photo was Shawna Sprague, facing right. She was taking a picture with her own cell. Caught in the act.

I went back to make certain: Shawna hadn't submitted anything at all to the cops. So she'd been clicking away, all right, but hadn't complied with the request to turn in cells. *Why not?*

Maybe Shawna had something in her phone that implicated Jared. Photos of Jared—with Lili, perhaps?

I returned to the twenty-three snapshots various kids had taken of Jared Crowley. In six of them he was talking into his cell. But there was no evidence he'd actually taken any photos— and why would he? Jared wasn't interested in anyone but himself. Even so, all the Guild members had been asked to turn in their phones, and Jared, like Shawna, hadn't complied.

Jared had mentioned the French Press coffee shop the other day in the warehouse. I looked up the number in the phone book and punched it in. A dude-type voice answered. "Hey. French Pah-ress."

I raised my voice an octave, hoping I'd sound seventeen. "Yeah, can I like talk to Shawna?"

"Shawna? Uh, she like works mornings. I think nine to noon."

"OK, thanks." I hung up. In the morning I would treat myself to a fancy coffee drink. Now it was time to go home.

I found myself wondering what was in the oven at El Balcón. In spite of her depression, Alma managed to cook like an angel. And after dinner, I'd let myself be talked into playing Wiffle ball in the dusk: kids-plus-dog against me.

Maybe tonight we'd have a new participant. Last night, for the first time, Danny had stepped outside the studio to watch us play.

The next morning, the order line at the French Press extended out the door. This was the place to be: a pair of high-heeled, sharp-tongued business girls stood shoulder to shoulder with a dreadlocked homeless guy and some other fellow who looked screen-familiar. True to Santa Barbara tradition, the actor was studiously ignored.

I observed a scowling Shawna while I waited in line. She wasn't taking the orders, which, with her people skills, was no surprise. Shawna was good at working the espresso machine, though. She operated with precision and speed. A hapless co-worker bumped her, and she snarled at the fresh-faced boy to give her space.

Shawna was strong, and I noticed her hands were not small. I'd assumed a female couldn't have inflicted the damage Lili Molina's body had received. Now I found myself second-guessing my assumption.

I ordered a dry cap, then walked around the corner of the bar to the espresso machine. Shawna glanced up at me, and her scowl deepened. She would have frown furrows by the time she was forty.

"Did you want something?" she asked icily.

"I'm not after an extra squirt of whipped cream, if that's what you mean. I want to talk to you, Shawna." I watched as she faltered. Shawna was, after all, still a kid.

"Who are you? How do you know my name?"

"I'm Jaymie Zarlin, and I'm investigating the murder of Lili Molina."

"Damn!" Shawna jumped back as a cloud of steam hissed from the machine. "Look what you made me do!"

"Shawna?" An older woman with a bleached-blond pony-tail, apparently the manager, appeared out of the back.

"It's under control." Shawna glared.

The woman turned away, then glanced back over her shoulder. I had a feeling Shawna would not last out the summer at the French Press.

"Why should I talk to you," she muttered. Her face was dark red.

"Try this: because it would be better to talk to me than to the police. They might not understand why you didn't turn in your cell like they asked."

"I have no idea what you're talking about."

"Sure you do. Look, I understand you want to help your boyfriend, OK? All I want is to ask you a few questions." Jared wasn't her boyfriend, any idiot could see that. But this was what Shawna wanted to hear, and if it helped loosen her tongue, I was happy to dish up the fantasy.

Shawna glared at me a moment longer. Then she called over to the manager, who was rinsing a large carafe at the sink. "I'm taking a break."

The woman frowned. "OK, Shawna. But next time *ask* me, don't *tell* me, OK?"

I followed Shawna out through the back entrance to a partly enclosed alley. The space reeked of fermented wine, or maybe the contents of a wino's stomach.

"It stinks out here. Let's make it quick." Shawna reached into her pocket and withdrew a packet of cigarettes. She didn't look at me, just lit up and took a deep drag.

"Well?" she said shortly. She still hadn't met my eyes. "My cell is my own private property. If I don't want to turn it in, I don't have to."

"Sure. It's just that everyone else turned theirs in right away. I mean, why not, if it might help find Lili's killer? That's how the other kids saw it."

Shawna rubbed at the asphalt with her foot. "I don't have anything to hide. I didn't take any pictures, OK?"

"I know that's not true. Listen, the police have a photo of you taking a picture of Jared. I've seen a copy." In fact, the photo of Shawna taking a picture didn't show Jared. But who else would she have taken a picture of?

Shawna dropped her cigarette to the asphalt and watched it burn down. A curl of smoke rose up near her toe. "OK, so I have pictures of him. So what."

I pricked up my ears. She'd said "pictures," plural. "Maybe you have pictures of Jared and Lili leaving the park together," I said quietly.

Shawna wrapped her arms across her chest and bent forward. Her shoulders shuddered. I placed a gentle hand on her arm, but she wrenched away.

"Believe me, Shawna, you don't want to shield Jared. If he was involved in Lili's murder, you could go to prison too."

"What do you think it's like?" she blurted. "To be adopted and Asian, except you're not skinny and cute, and not very popular—" Her eyes brimmed, but then she stopped. She shut it off like a faucet, just like that. "Jared loves me! And I love him. Is that OK with you?"

"You think he did it, don't you, Shawna?" I was sorry to do it, but I had to keep tightening the screws. "You think he killed Lili, but you really don't care."

"That's not true."

"I'm going to tell you something, Shawna. Unlike you, I'm pretty sure Jared's not guilty."

She looked at me in surprise.

"I don't think he's guilty, but I know at least one cop who does. Show me what you've got and maybe I can help." I was bending the truth a little. I was fairly sure Jared Crowley was innocent, but it was possible I was wrong.

Shawna stared at me for a long moment. Then she reached into the pocket of her skin-tight jeans and tugged out her cell. "I'll show you. But you have to promise me you won't tell the cops. And I don't want Jared to ever know I showed you this."

Did the cops include Mike? Surely not. This wasn't his case, and he was a friend. "I promise."

Shawna punched a few buttons, then held the phone out

for me to look. "No, you can't hold it. I'll scroll through. I'm not giving my phone up to you or anybody."

I stepped close, shielding the screen from the glare of the sun. "Angle your hand so I can see better." And then, I did see.

First in the sequence was a photo of Jared, the bleached Apollo, intently studying his cell in the park. Next, a picture of Jared talking urgently with Lili: Apollo imploring the goddess Daphne. Then the god and the goddess, walking away together.

And a fourth photo, from a distance: Jared and Lili, getting into the old tan BMW. So there it was: evidence that Jared Crowley had most likely delivered Lili to her death.

"Shawna, tell me something. Why did you take all these photos of Jared?"

She shrugged. "At first I just wanted some pictures of him, you know? But then, when he started talking to Lili . . . I guess I got kind of jealous." She looked up and glowered at me. "Anyway, it isn't a crime."

"No, of course it isn't." My fingers were itching to grab the camera and sprint off with it. Instead I pulled out my notebook. "Shawna, read me the times of those four photos at the end."

"This is the last thing I'm telling you." Shawna bent her head, worked her cell, and intoned: "3:12 . . . 3:14 . . . 3:15 . . . 3:19."

She glared as she shoved the phone back in her pocket. "Now leave me alone! And if you tell the cops, I'll wipe it all in a second, I swear to God."

I needed to talk with Jared, fast. Shawna had no good reason to reveal our conversation to him, but I figured that wouldn't necessarily stop her.

I switched on my cell, ignored six messages, and punched in my office number.

"Santa Barbara Investigations. Gabriela Gutierrez, PA to Jaymie Zarlin—speaking!"

"By the time you spit all that out, the person on the other end of the line will be long gone."

"Miss Jaymie! Haven't seen you today. What's up?"

"Right now I'm tracking Jared Crowley to his lair."

"Jared Crowley? Hold on." I heard her shove her chair over the oak floorboards. "OK, I'm standing in the kitchen now, looking at the wall. Jared . . . Huh. Looks innocent. Nice and clean-cut."

"Those are the types you need to take an extra-hard look at, Gabi. I've got a few questions for Mr. Clean-cut. Grab the interview file there on the table, would you? I need his address—somewhere on Cota, I think."

"Cota, are you sure? He'd stick out like a sore thumb in that neighborhood. A white sore thumb. Hold on. It's not on the table 'cause I filed it away like it should be." I heard the squeal of the old filing cabinet drawer. "OK, here it is. You're right: Jared Crowley, 441 West Cota."

"Got it. Thanks."

"Wait, I got something to tell you. Mrs. Richter called. She wants to know if you found out anything yet, about Minuet. She sounds very worried."

"Next time she calls, you can tell her I've picked up the scent and I'm hot on the trail."

Chapter Ten

Maybe I had a few questions for Jared Crowley, maybe I didn't. What I actually wanted was to chat with him, to get a sense of the real person hiding behind the fresh face and curly Apollonian mop.

I entered the four-hundred block of Cota and slowed the El Cam to a cruise. This was a century-old residential neighborhood, filled with small working-class houses set tight to the street. Maybe the address was bogus: a business of some sort occupied 441. I parked at the end of the block and walked back, disguised, I hoped, behind my sunglasses and nonchalant air.

An older woman sat hunched over a commercial-sized sewing machine set up in the front window of 441, a small, dilapidated Victorian. The seamstress didn't look up as I sauntered past. What could she possibly have to do with Crowley?

A cracked asphalt drive ran alongside the house. I continued on to the corner, then turned back, retracing my steps. This time I slipped down the drive and walked to the back.

Over 17 percent of Santa Barbara residents are illegally housed, and I'd seen hundreds of converted garages, sheds, and gazebos. But I'd never come on anything like this. Five plywood cubicles, not much bigger than coffins, sat behind the house. Each cubicle had a single door secured with a padlock on a hasp. There were no windows, no vents in the roofs.

The tan BMW was parked in the asphalted space. Sitting in the Beemer and talking on his cell was Jared Crowley.

He caught sight of me immediately. So much for subterfuge.

As I approached, Jared said something hurriedly into the phone, then tossed it onto the passenger seat and switched on the engine.

I leaned down to the open window. "Hi, Jared. I'm Jaymie Zarlin." I spoke in a friendly, offhand tone.

"That's nobody as far as I'm concerned. What're you doing here?"

"You gave this address to the police. Supposedly it's your residence." I assumed an innocent expression. "But you don't really live here, do you? These look more like storage sheds."

"Like it's any of your business. What the fuck do you want?"

Oh my, this one was sure of himself. "Just to talk. Got a second?"

"Not for you I don't."

"Maybe you should rethink that. My visit concerns the murder of Lili Molina."

He must have suspected as much, because his face betrayed no surprise. Jared Crowley was one cool customer. The only weakness about him was his chin: delicate and pointed, like a young girl's.

"What's it to you?" Then he softened his tone. "You a cop?"

"No. I'm working with the police, though." Alas, an out-and-out lie.

Jared hung his arm out the window and tapped impatiently on the metal chassis. "Lady, I'll give you one minute."

I couldn't help it. I laughed at his chutzpah.

He swiveled his head and glared at me. Our boy was fuming.

"Look. I'm sure you're very busy, Jared, so I'll be brief. We now have evidence that Danny Armenta didn't kill Lili. That's why we need to re-interview people, dig up more info." I hoped I sounded official. I also hoped Jared would betray himself in some way. I didn't think he was guilty, at least not of the murder. But *something* was there.

"If Armenta didn't do it, then . . ." Jared dropped his guard and met my gaze. I found myself looking through two blue windows into what should have been a soul. Instead, I saw an empty room.

Rapidly, he shifted his eyes. "Well, I sure as hell didn't kill her. Lili and me were friends." He set a hand on the key in the ignition. "OK, lady, you've had your time. Now step back. I wouldn't want to run over your toes."

I tailed the BMW eastward along Cabrillo Boulevard, past the bevy of volleyballers, onto the 101 exit heading south. Brod's El Camino stuck out like a sore thumb, but fortunately Jared had no idea what I was driving.

He cruised along in the middle lane, seemingly in no hurry to get wherever he was going. I hoped he was heading for Carpinteria, not LA. Still, I had to admit it was a gorgeous day to tool down PCH, the ocean breezes teasing my hair, the solstice sun warm on my cheek. Imagine, I called this work.

I couldn't exactly say why I was following the great god Apollo, what I hoped to learn. But he was hiding something, and I wanted to find out what it was.

To my disappointment, Jared didn't turn in at Carp. Ventura was the next stop. Enjoy the ride, I reminded myself.

Then, a few miles south of Carp, Jared pulled abruptly into the center divider and made a dangerous crossing across the northbound lanes of traffic into the tiny community of La Conchita. The hamlet was so small I'd forgotten it even existed.

I had no chance to follow the Beemer. I continued south

another two or three miles before I was able to make a relatively safe U-turn and head north. Then I right-turned into the collection of salt-faded little houses, and pulled up at a mom-and-pop store.

If ever a community could be said to be tragic, La Conchita was it. In 2005 the cliff above the houses had sheared off, burying houses and taking nine human lives. All you had to do was look at a satellite image to understand that the landslide would continue, as layer after layer of sandstone sloughed off and rumbled down onto the narrow marine terrace below. La Conchita was a microcosm of coastal California, just compacted in space, concentrated in time.

I opened the squealing aluminum screen door to the shop. An enormous man wearing a Hawaiian muumuu sat behind the counter on a sort of hand-fashioned double chair. "Help ya?" His tone was friendly, but his eyes, nearly buried in flesh, were sharp.

"Just a soda," I smiled. Best to buy something, I figured, in exchange for the information I hoped to receive.

"Back there against the cool box, under the bologna sandwiches. We keep the sandwiches cold or they go off real quick. No preservatives, ya know. Sure you don't want one to go with the sodie pop?"

No way was I going to eat a nasty bologna sandwich. But maybe I'd buy one all the same. I pulled open the heavy old glass door and grabbed a can of soda and one of the cellophane-wrapped sandwiches.

"So what's a little lady like you doing here?" The man punched the register and rang up the tab. "We don't get a whole lotta visitors. Right across from the beach, but the wrong side of the freeway, see?"

"Yes, I see what you mean." I extracted a bill from my wallet, then dropped the change he gave me into a jar. The jar bore a faded inscription on a strip of paper taped to it: *For the families of the victims of the La Conchita Disaster.*

"Thanks. Every little bit helps," he recited in a drone.

Probably his beer fund, I figured. "Can I ask you a question?"

"Shoot," the man said. As he smiled, his eyes narrowed and then disappeared.

"I'm supposed to meet somebody here, but I've forgotten the address. My friend drives a tan BMW. You don't happen to know what house that would be?"

"Know the name of this fellow you're supposed to meet?"

A fair enough question. "Sure. Jared Crowley."

"Just checking. We get all sorts." He reached across the counter and patted my hand. I resisted the urge to pull back.

"Jared and Summer live over on Las Olas. One block up, turn right, four blocks along. I forget the number, but that don't matter. It's the little house with a whole bunch of plants out in front. Summer is sure into plants. Bag?"

Summer. Bad news for Shawna: Jared had a girlfriend stashed away. "No need." I picked up my soda and sandwich and turned for the door. "Thanks for the info."

"No problemo, little lady. Don't think anybody's ever asked me about that boy Jared before. But Summer, now, people come in here asking about her all the time. Especially the males of the species, know what I'm sayin'?"

"Maybe." I halted and turned back to the shopkeeper. Might as well get to the point. "Are you saying she's a prostitute?"

"Hell no. Summer's a masseuse, a real one." He let one heavy eyelid droop in a wink. "For all I know, little lady, you could be some kinda cop."

As soon as I turned into Las Olas, I spotted the Beemer. I pulled over when I was a block away, and lifted my binocs from the glove box. Jared sat in the driver's seat, staring blankly ahead.

Just as I was beginning to wonder how long I should wait, a shiny silver SUV backed out of a driveway farther along. It passed Jared, heading in my direction.

The SUV was a Lexus, brand-spanking-new. The driver, a guy in his forties, was puffing away on a cigarillo, a smirk on his face. A satisfied customer if ever I'd seen one. So Jared Crowley's girlfriend was a working girl? That I wouldn't have guessed.

I returned my attention to Jared. His car was moving forward now, turning into the drive the Lexus had just exited. I waited several minutes, then cruised slowly up the road.

The Beemer was parked at the top end of the rutted dirt drive, and Jared was nowhere to be seen. This was the place, all right: the tiny front yard was choked with row upon row of struggling potted plants.

I drove past the small stucco house and circled several blocks. Then I made another approach. Jared's car hadn't moved. But now, a thin woman wrapped in an old pink bathrobe drifted about in the tiny front yard. A cigarette dangled from the corner of her mouth. She was watering the pots, dragging a hose.

The woman looked up and met my eye as I passed. She was probably not much older than me, but Summer was fading fast into autumn. Her fair skin was blotched, and her curly hair was more white than blond.

Blond curly hair. Eyes a washed-out blue. And that telltale delicate chin. Jared Crowley looked a hell of a lot like his mom.

The next day was Friday. Siding with my heart instead of my head, I'd agreed to spend the weekend with Mike and his dad at the Dawsons' ranch. But there was something I needed to look into before I left town, something I'd been putting off.

I hadn't driven the El Camino down Micheltorena Street since I'd scared away the little boy and his pup. Instead, I'd contented myself with pedaling by on my bike, on my way to and from the office. The boy and his spaniel were nearly always outside, but you had to look hard to spot them. Mostly they played behind a dense clump of Carolina cherry, remnants of an ancient hedge. But I was pretty sure I knew what would lure both dog and boy into the open.

"You're good for something, Dex," I said as I slipped a collar around the ornery heeler.

"Can I come?" This was what Chuy always asked now, every time I got ready to go out. When I could, I said yes. Today I was about to say no when I stopped myself. Dear Lord, forgive me: I looked at the cute little guy and saw lure number two.

"OK, Chuy. Go ask your mom."

The three of us drove down to San Andres and parked outside a shop selling ice cream. "We'll get ice cream after we go for a walk, Chuy. Dex needs practice on a leash."

OK, it was low, fibbing to a kid. Especially since I wasn't at all sure it was for a good cause.

"What's your favorite kind of ice cream?" Chuy pranced beside me, taking two or three steps to my one.

"Coffee, maybe. Or chocolate."

"Yeah, I like chocolate. But my favorite is . . . bubble gum!" He looked up at me. "Did you ever have bubble gum ice cream? I did."

We were approaching the house. Dexter, who was supposed to be a heeler, was on point, straining at the leash.

"Bubble gum? Maybe. What color is it?"

"Blue! OK, did you ever have—"

We'd reached the corner of the picket fence. Suddenly a flurry of brown and white fur hurled at Dexter, yapping wildly. Dexter's hair rose up on end and he pretended to be a big dog, growling deep in his chest.

"Dexter, stop!"

The heeler was just pretending. He quit and wagged his tale at Minuet.

"Hey, that dog's really cute—" Chuy began. Then he fell silent. The little boy had stepped out in the open.

For a moment, I stopped breathing. The first time I saw the child, the only time I'd had a good look at him, I assumed he'd been playing with face paint. But now I saw it clearly: a huge disfiguring birthmark covered more than half of his face. The little boy's right eye was surrounded by the discoloration, and he appeared to be peeping out through a hole in a purplish scarf.

"That boy, he—he—" Chuy began.

I gave Chuy's shoulder a quick squeeze. "Just say hi, OK?"

"Hi," Chuy called out in a tiny voice.

Even Dexter seemed to understand. He sat down and was quiet.

"Hello," I said softly. "What a nice little dog you have. What's her name?"

The boy took several more steps in our direction. He wasn't much older than Chuy, I saw. Maybe a year.

"Chica." His expression revealed both friendliness and fear. "I'm not s'posed to talk to people."

"We won't stay very long. Where did you get Chica?"

"My tía got her for me."

Chuy stepped up to the picket fence. "Do you—do you— want us to bring you some bubble-gum ice cream?"

My heart expanded with pride.

"So you're going to tell Minuet's owner where to find her pooch." Mike stretched his arm across the back of the bench seat.

"I should. It's her dog, after all, and she loves it. And there's the matter of the ten-thousand-dollar retainer. But you know what? That little guy needs the mutt a lot more than Mrs. Got Rocks does."

We were beginning the abrupt ascent up Cuesta Grade, and Mike set both hands on the wheel. "Want my two cents' worth?"

"You know I do, deputy."

"Have a little trust in human nature. Tell your client everything, and let her decide what to do."

"Darlene Richter's self-centered and spoiled. But I guess you're right."

The grade steepened and the pickup slowed. Mike stepped down on the gas. "You don't trust other people much, do you."

"Not a lot." I folded my arms across my chest. "Not after what happened to Brodie."

"Can't say I blame you." He reached over and squeezed my hand. "You know, I still remember the first time I met your brother—if you could call it a meeting. Brodie was way off meds and squirrelly as hell. Did I ever tell you the story?"

"I don't think so."

"Well, I responded to a call out in Noleta: a crazy guy had stolen a dog. Turned out it was Brodie. He'd felt sorry for a mutt tied up in the rain. Trouble was, the owner'd left the dog outside while she'd gone into the grocery store, and she freaked when she spotted a homeless dude strolling off with her pet." Mike smiled. "I liked your brother straightaway, you know? Bought him a hamburger and drove him back into town."

"Brodie was hard not to like." I fell silent and gazed out the truck window at the golden-furred hills. It was June, and the spring grasses had burned to the color of toast. Gradually, my mind relaxed and let go.

"Still thinking about Brodie?" Mike asked after a time.

"Not really. Just Zening, I guess."

"As long as you're not thinking about that shyster lawyer."

"Zave Carbonel?" I laughed uncomfortably. "What made you think of him? I told you, he's just a friend. I don't spend time angsting about him."

"You better not spend time angsting *with* him, either." Mike had tried to make a joke but his voice was gruff.

"Zave doesn't angst."

"You know what I mean." An uncomfortable silence filled the cab.

Yep, my conscience was pricking me, and it looked like I'd

have to give up certain aspects of my relationship with Zave. I felt a tinge of carnal regret.

"Listen, Mike." I squeezed his strong-muscled arm through his blue denim work shirt. "Henceforth, Zave Carbonel is not a person you need to worry about."

"Henceforth." He stared straight ahead. "So you *were* involved with the guy."

"Not exactly involved . . . Do you really want to know?"

"Maybe . . . not." Mike cleared his throat. "Not if you say it's over."

I thought of teasing him, making light of it all. But I realized I didn't want to do that. "You have my word."

After a few prickly minutes had passed, Mike spoke. "While we're talking about heavy stuff, there's something I need to say to you."

I mock groaned. "OK, what now."

"This murder investigation." He tapped the steering wheel. "You need to be more careful, Jaymie. If the killer thinks you're getting wise, he may try to force you to back off."

"Just let him."

"No, you don't get it. We're not talking about some dognapper here. The man who raped and killed Lili Molina is an extremely dangerous animal. And with all of law enforcement believing it's Danny Armenta, you and your contrary suspicions will shine like a lighthouse. The killer's going to take notice."

"Know what?" I shimmied my butt closer and pecked him on the cheek. "I always wanted a big brother to protect me."

"I'm telling you, don't make light of it. I know what I'm talking about."

"Welcome to Little Panoche Ranch, sweetheart. You're prettier 'n I remembered." Bill Dawson's right hand was gnarled as an old juniper root, and just as hard and dry.

I grinned up at him. Bill was bent over, but still topped

out at around six foot four. I had to tip back my head to meet his Nordic-blue eyes. "Ah, so flattery runs in the family, Mr. Dawson."

"Bill, for Chrissake." He laughed. "Come on in the house, Jaymie. It's hotter 'n a pistol out here today."

"Am I included?" Mike asked as his father took me by the arm.

"Sure, we'll put up with you, son."

Mike and I walked slowly, matching Bill's pace. We crossed the neat gravel drive and climbed the steps to the wide porch encircling the redwood ranch house. A deep overhang provided immediate relief from the sun.

"Damn radiation. If the cancer don't kill ya, they make sure the treatment does." Bill stopped for a moment to regain his breath, then motioned for Mike to open the heavy hand-carved front door.

"Make yourselves at home, kids." He waved his hand vaguely. "I'm not much of a hostess. That was Peggy's department. With me, it's mi casa es su casa. After that you're pretty much on your own."

I looked around the large open living and dining room. The space was expansive, floored in rich dark oak, and lined floor to ceiling in what I guessed was western red cedar. "What a beautiful house."

"I'm glad you like it." He glanced at me sideways. "Seeing as it might be yours one day."

Mike crossed the room carrying our duffel bags. "Stand up to Dad, Jaymie, or he'll use his tactics on you all weekend."

"Hey now." Bill Dawson grinned like a kid caught with his hand in the cookie jar. "All for a good cause."

"See what I mean?" Mike laughed. "Can't help himself. I'll just take these bags upstairs."

I noticed a family portrait displayed on an old walnut buffet, and bent to study it. The four Dawsons were on horseback.

There was a young Bill, his back ramrod straight. Beside him was Peggy Dawson, a petite and pretty woman. Her Native American heritage showed in her eyelids, straight nose, and warm olive complexion. Mike and Trudy, aged around eleven and nine, looked like a mix of both parents. Both kids had inherited Bill Dawson's height and Peggy's looks and complexion.

"Peggy was a beauty," Bill said quietly. "She's on Sugarfoot there, her favorite mare. Damned if that nag didn't love her."

"I wish I'd met her." I smiled up at him. "I mean Peggy, not the horse."

"Oh, you woulda liked Sugarfoot just fine. But you and Peggy—the two of you would have been thick as thieves. Peggy, she . . ." He shook his head roughly, as if to clear it. "'Nough of that. Let's go rustle up some cold drinks."

In the kitchen, Bill opened the refrigerator door and studied its contents. "I shoulda told Mike to stop off at the market on the way up. Haven't got much."

"We did stop, Bill. The food's in the truck. Nobody's going to go hungry."

"Good. So it's soda or a beer, what's your fancy?"

"Soda for now. Once the sun goes down, my answer will be different." I noticed a sign hanging over the kitchen sink: *My house was just cleaned—I'm sorry you missed it.* "Peggy had a sense of humor, didn't she?"

"You bet. She needed it, married to me all those years." Bill set two Cokes down on the table, then rummaged in two different cupboards. "I don't normally use a glass, but Peggy woulda offered you one. She had a place for everything. I try to keep it the way she had it, but . . . I don't know. . . ." A silence gathered.

"Don't worry about a glass, Bill. The can's fine." I noticed a collection of yellowed and curling photos of grandbabies, Trudy's kids, stuck to the fridge. One showed Grandma Peggy cradling a newborn in her arms. A lump formed in my throat. "You must miss her a lot."

"Hell yes. Peggy's been gone six years this fall, but I still catch myself listening for her to pull in through the gate. Guess I'm nothing but a lonely old man." He looked out the kitchen window. "Mike told you all about the cancer, Jaymie? Stage four."

"Yes." I rested my hand on his arm. "I'm so sorry you're having to deal with this, Bill."

"I'll be joining her pretty quick now," he said quietly. Bill covered my hand with his own. "Then I won't be lonely no more. It'll be about time."

Rough and ready though it was, the big cattle ranch cast a kind of spell. That evening, under a nearly full moon and a sky bristling with stars, I followed Mike along a beaten foot trail. Shep, Bill's old border collie, was on point. We'd only been walking for a few minutes when, without warning, a great horned owl screamed and lifted up out of the tall dry grass, clutching a limp dark creature in its claws.

"We disturbed her," I said when my heart rate dropped back into normal.

"It's her world at night," Mike said softly. "We're the intruders."

We walked on for another five minutes, our flashlight beams flitting through the coyote brush. When Mike finally halted, I nearly bumped into him.

"This is it, Perlina Point. There's quite a view in the daytime— you can see all the way over to the San Joaquin Valley."

We stood on flat rocky ground, near the edge of a cliff. Beyond gaped a great yaw of blackness. "If you and Shep weren't here, Mike, I might have gone right on over the edge."

"I know. That's why it was named after my grandmother, Perlina Sepulveda." We switched off our flashlights, and Mike shook open the bedspread and let it float down. Straightaway, Shep flopped in the center.

"One time when Grandma was little, she was playing hide-and-seek with her brother and sister when she ran up here. This ridge used to be covered in even denser scrub, and she never saw the edge. But a fawn was curled up right here in the bushes, where the doe must have hidden it. Grandma stopped running to look at it."

"So the fawn saved her life." I sat down next to Shep. The stubbly grass and sharp gravel jabbed through the blanket and my jeans.

"Sure did. And made mine possible, I guess you could say." Mike dropped to his knees. "Shove over, Shep."

I laughed when the collie, refusing to move, snuggled up tight to my hip.

Mike stretched out on his back. "That dog always did have to be in the center of things."

"Look at those stars," I admired. "Hey, did you see—are those—"

"Bats. We're serving them dinner, attracting the bugs."

"You, not me."

"If you say so. But mosquitoes prefer clean people, didn't you know?"

Mike rolled to his side and reached over the dog to grab my arm. As he pulled me down, Shep finally got the message and moved to a corner of the bedspread.

"Mm. Jaymie, your smell's driving me crazy."

"You and Bill. Full of sweet talk."

"Enough about my dad. You'll make me jealous." Mike propped himself up on an elbow and began to unbutton my shirt. "It's been a long time, Jaymie. And I don't really know why."

I laced my fingers behind his neck and pulled him close. "Because it's so good it hurts."

We stood under the stars and undressed one another. Mike drew me to him, and my breathing grew deep and fast.

"Shep, get the hell outta here," Mike growled.

✦   ✦   ✦

Afterward, we lay close beside each other, gazing up at the stars. Mike cradled my head in the crook of his arm. "I want to tell you a family secret. But you have to promise not to turn it into a joke."

"I wouldn't do that."

He kissed my cheek. "Hey, there's the Big Dipper."

"Yeah," I said in a drowsy voice. "What's the secret?"

"It has to do with this ridge. Something my mom told me, a week before she died." He sounded hesitant.

"Mike? You can trust me."

"OK, here it is. She told me this is where I was conceived."

A cold breeze rose up from below, bearing the sharp scent of the chaparral. In the silence, a coyote called from the next ridge.

Can't you see what he wants? a voice reasoned in my ear. *You don't belong with this man and you know it.* I rolled out of Mike's embrace and drew my knees up to my chin.

"Hey. Is something wrong?"

"Mike . . . that's a wonderful story. But maybe there are some things I'm just not . . . ready to know about." Coming here, making love on this spot—he'd planned it, whether he was conscious of it or not. All part of the Dawson family saga, of which I was apparently going to be the next chapter.

"Jaymie, don't pull away like that." He turned me back to him, and I didn't resist.

"I'm sorry, Mike." My voice caught in my throat. "Honestly, it's my problem. It's not about you."

"Shh. Let it go."

I wrapped my arms around his neck and pulled him close. We began all over again.

The truth was, I was fighting not to fall in love with everything and everyone connected with Little Panoche: Mike, Bill, Peggy's memory, even Shep and every square inch of the rolling land-scape. In spite of my misgivings, every hour I spent on the ranch brought me closer to Mike.

Sunday morning, the two of us packed a lunch and climbed on fat-tired motor trikes. We planned to spend the day explor-ing the far reaches of the old rancho.

Early on we surprised a small herd of deer, all standing statue-still and staring at us with dark liquid eyes. Then, through Mike's binocs, we watched a pair of coyote pups playing rough-and-tumble on a rocky hillside. But later, as the scorching sun seared a trail up the sky, only hawks and slow-moving cattle were evident. The red-tails glided lazily on drafts of hot air ris-ing above the chaparral-blanketed ridges.

In the middle of the afternoon we bounced up a grass-slick hill. Mike signaled to stop. Below, curling through a small val-ley, was a ribbon of vivid yellow-green.

"There's the creek, Little Panoche. In the winter that drib-ble of algae can widen to fifty feet." He dismounted and pointed. "Can you see over there, partway up the far side of that hill?"

I raised the binoculars to my eyes. "It's a little shack, isn't it? No . . . looks like an adobe."

"The Sepulveda Adobe. My great-great-grandfather built it in 1863. Dad built an iron roof over it a couple years back, to keep it from melting away. I'd take you over there, but it's get-ting late—it's further than it looks."

"Has it ever been restored?"

"Back in the 1950s my grandma had some things done to it. She had the good sense not to change much." Mike shrugged. "Dad's not all that interested. He makes sure it doesn't deterio-rate, but that's about it. Course, it was Mom's family that built it, not his."

He kicked at a dry mound of clump grass. "That was Mom's goal, before she got sick. She wanted to restore the adobe to the way it originally was."

"That's something you want to do for her, don't you?"

"Sure. And I will." A gentleness filled his eyes and he looked away. The sweet smoky odor of sage, crushed by our tires, welled up around us.

"To hell with the time," Mike said abruptly. "What does it matter if we get back late? Let's go take a look."

Twenty minutes later, when I pressed my hand to the old mud and straw wall, the spell of Little Panoche was complete. Unbidden words popped out of my mouth. "Someday I'd like to help you restore this. If you want me to, that is."

Mike leveled his dark brown eyes on me. "Kinda contradicting yourself, wouldn't you say?"

Chapter Eleven

On our way home, we stopped in Pismo for a fish dinner and snagged a table looking out over the harbor. Mike's good mood had returned, and we lingered over a relaxed meal. It was nearly eleven by the time he dropped me off at the bottom of El Balcón.

"I wish you'd let me drive you up to the house."

I pecked him on the cheek. "It's late. I don't want the truck to wake up the Armentas."

"OK. Now, remember what I told you: keep your eyes open. And don't go poking your nose where it doesn't belong."

"Don't worry, I can take care of myself," I answered drowsily.

Half-asleep, I wandered up the steep road, breathing in the cool, skunk-perfumed air. The big lopsided moon reflected a wavering path on the water.

Dexter was probably inside, curled up on Chuy's bed. I was used to the mutt charging down El Balcón at full tilt to challenge and greet me. But ever since Deirdre's unannounced visit, Chuy had wanted Dexter close, especially at night. The dog loved the attention and was more than willing to oblige.

It was good the moon was near full, because the light at

the top of the drive was off. Either Alma had forgotten to switch it on when she went to bed, or the bulb had burned out.

But as I passed under the light standard, my shoes crunched on glass. I bent down to look: the bulb had shattered. Something was wrong.

I looked over at the house, and was reassured to see that the front hall light was on. The window set in the top of the door glowed welcomingly, a warm yellow hemisphere in the dark.

I stepped onto the path of crushed shells that lead around to the kitchen steps at the back. When I rounded the corner of the house, I halted.

Something dark had been flung down on the steps. Perhaps it was a shrugged-off jacket—or a pelt. A *pelt?* Now my heart stopped cold. I took three more steps. The object moved slightly, and whimpered.

Dexter, Dex! I couldn't cry out—the children mustn't see or hear any of this.

I whispered, "Easy, boy. Easy, Dex."

The dog's muzzle was bound in plastic packing tape. His black nose poked out, sucking hard for air. I lifted him up, and the pathetic whimper slid up the scale to a thin high scream. I felt something wet and sticky on his back and side—then I saw his leg, dangling at a crazy angle—there was blood, lots of it.

I ran to the garage with Dex in my arms, stumbling twice in the dark. Thank God the sagging doors never quite closed. I edged in sideways and, gently as I was able, laid the little fellow on the floor of the passenger seat. The sounds he made nearly broke me.

I lifted and dragged the double doors all the way open, fumbled for the key on my ring, jumped in, and backed out.

I didn't look down until I reached the street lights on Cliff Drive. Then in a glance I saw it all: the dog's leg was snapped, the white bone sticking up at a sharp angle. He'd been butchered.

Dexter lay still. I jerked to a stop, leaned down, and held my fingertips close to his muzzle. Thank God, I felt the faint breeze of his breath. I tried to unwrap the tape, but my fingers were numb, useless sticks of dough.

I stepped on the gas. Ignoring stop signs and lights, I raced through the empty streets of the town.

The emergency vet was young, just out of vet school. "Dogs are tough. That's why medical researchers use them for experimentation." She looked upset.

"So he's going to make it." I spoke firmly, as if my voice would make it so.

"Dogs are tough," she repeated. "He's stabilized, and unless he develops a raging infection, he's got a fighting chance. Call the office in the morning."

"You put him on antibiotics, right?"

"Of course I did." She frowned.

"Sorry," I mumbled. "Didn't mean to tell you how to do your job."

"Speaking of jobs, aren't you a detective? I think I read your name in the paper."

"Investigator."

"Then investigate and find out who did this." She dragged off her bloodstained gloves. "Somebody wanted your dog to die a slow and tortured death."

I drove home and let myself in through the front door. I listened carefully: all I could hear was Chuy, snoring softly. I headed to the kitchen for a scrub brush.

"Jaymie?" It was Aricela, blinking her eyes and tugging her old T-shirt down over her shorts.

"Sorry, Aricela. I didn't mean to wake you."

"It's OK. But Jaymie, we couldn't find Dexter when we went to bed. We think maybe he ran away."

I'm no actress. But for her sake and mine, I needed to pull

off an Oscar-winning performance. "Don't worry about it, sweetie. Sometimes Dexter just wanders off. Go back to bed, OK? He'll turn up in the morning."

"OK." The girl smiled shyly. "Jaymie? I really like staying with you."

"I really like having you here too, Aricela." I turned away so she wouldn't see the tears in my eyes. "Now you better get some sleep, OK?"

I waited until Aricela had returned to bed. Then I took the brush from under the kitchen sink, switched on my flashlight, and went out to find a hose nozzle in the garage. The last thing I wanted was for the kids to discover the blood in the morning.

I washed off the steps and the path, diluting the blood and flushing it into the dirt. Then I bent down and scrubbed, the brush in one hand and the flashlight in the other. I scrubbed until my arm ached, then rinsed and scrubbed some more.

It was after one in the morning by the time I finished, but I noticed the lights were on in Danny's studio. Before I went to bed, I needed to make sure he was OK.

I walked over and tapped on the door. "Danny, it's me, Jaymie. Can I talk to you for a minute?" I'd made it a point to say a few words to him every day. Little by little, he was starting to trust me.

I'd installed a dead bolt for him, so he'd feel safe. I heard it slide back, and the door opened a foot. "Hi, Danny."

"Hi." He opened it further. His dark red hair hadn't been combed in days.

My heart went out to him. Danny had been taking meds for nearly two weeks now, and he was no longer psychotic. But I could see in his eyes that he was frightened and confused.

"I got home late and thought I'd check in with you. Did your weekend go OK?" I could see, over his shoulder, that the TV was tuned to a nature show.

Danny nodded, once. "Yeah. . . . I guess so."

Back on meds, he was remembering. No doubt he was beginning to recall Lili now, and the terror he'd witnessed. I knew this was a dangerous time, the point where mentally ill people can be vulnerable to suicide.

"Where's Dexter?" He looked past me into the night. "My sister said she—she couldn't find him."

"Probably out hunting for gophers and rats. He'll come home soon."

"When—when—Dexter comes back, he can stay with me if he wants." A faint flicker of pleasure lighted his face. "He likes it in my room."

"That's a good idea, Danny." A lump formed in my throat. "I'm sure Dexter would love to stay with you."

"It was meant as a message to me. What happened to Dex was my fault."

"Your fault?" Gabi, who had a job to go to later in the day, tugged her French-maid outfit over her hips. "No, Miss Jaymie. That's bad negative self-talk."

"Huh?" I almost managed a smile. "What are you reading these days?"

"*Positively Positive: Self-Talk-n-Walk Your Way to Fulfillment.*" She poured a cup of steaming black coffee and set it on the kitchen table, then went to the ancient fridge and took out a container of half-and-half. "You need coffee, extra strong. And a big chocolate croissant."

"Yeah. That should fix everything."

"Pastries, coffee, and positive self-talk. You can't lose on that combo." The seams of her uniform strained dangerously as Gabi sat down in the chair opposite me. "Miss Jaymie? You're real mad, I can tell."

"Mad? I'm fucking furious."

"I never heard you use the *f*-word before."

"If I had a stronger word, I'd use it." I drowned the stern coffee in the half-and-half.

"Did you tell the kids what happened?"

"No way. As far as they're concerned, Dexter wandered off. Tonight I'll tell them I checked the pound and found him there, injured. I'll say I took Dex straight to the vet's, and they're taking good care of him now."

"What about Alma?"

"I didn't tell Alma either. I told her about the smashed light, though. She needs to know someone was around, so she can watch out."

"I gotta be honest, I don't like dogs that much. They make my houses all dirty with their hair and their feet, they lick themselves down there and then they try to lick you in the face. *Pft!* But still, to make God's creature suffer like that . . ." Gabi frowned and ran her fingernail along a crack in the tabletop to dig out the dirt. "Anybody who would do that to a perro could do it to a person, I think."

"You've got that right."

"So. It's not your fault, but what do you mean, it was a message?"

"What happened to Dex was a warning to me to back off. I've been talking to people, Gabi, asking awkward questions. It's no surprise the killer heard I was poking around." I shoved my chair back from the table and stood. "Or maybe I've got it wrong. Maybe I've made an enemy just because I'm protecting Danny, letting him stay at my place."

Gabi got to her feet and gave her uniform another tug. "What are you going to do now?"

"Continue. Push on."

"That's positively positive for sure. But I am the one who hired you, Miss Jaymie. And I say you should be very careful."

"I hear you."

"Sure you do." Gabi raised an eyebrow. She carried the cups

to the chipped sink and turned on the tap. "Did you tell Mr.
Mike what happened to your dog?"

"Not yet. He might . . . interfere."

"Hm. Alma told me you went to visit his father this weekend. If you were Mexican, that would mean—"

"It means never-you-mind. Now, I gotta move on. I'm going
to see Celeste Delaney, and I don't dare be late."

"Just tell your boyfriend what happened to your dog, right
away. I'm begging you, Miss Jaymie. He'll be real mad if you
don't."

Gabi was right about that: Mike would be furious. Besides,
he had a right to know.

I dialed his number as I shut the office door behind me and
descended the steps. "Mike? It's me, Jaymie. I've got some very
bad news."

More often than not now, my bike was left languishing in the
breezeway at El Balcón. Maybe I was just getting lazy. But driving a car had its advantages, such as transporting me to Sheffield Drive, Montecito, in ten minutes or less, minus the sweat
bath. I needed to be there by 2:30, Marisol's quitting time.

A battered old Datsun was parked under the shade of a
towering eucalyptus, across the road from Darlene Richter's
home. The woman in the driver's seat was younger than Marisol, her features softer, but clearly kin.

I continued up Sheffield and made a U-turn, then pulled up
to one side of Mrs. Richter's gates and switched off the engine. I
leaned back in the seat and stared at the torn fabric under the El
Camino's roof.

I didn't much like what I was about to do. But I'd avoided it
long enough.

Marisol, outfitted in her severe black uniform and carrying
a black handbag, appeared at the smaller pedestrian gate. She
stepped through, then firmly pulled the gate shut after her. As

she began to walk in the direction of the Datsun, she glanced over and caught sight of me.

I hopped out. "Marisol, can I speak with you, please?"

"No—no." She took a step away. "I'm sorry, I'm in a hurry. My sister . . ." She waved vaguely.

By this time I was standing beside her. I touched her arm lightly. "Please," I said more firmly. "It's important for us to talk."

"But I—I'm in a hurry." Then she grew still. Her hands fell to her sides in defeat.

"Marisol, I'd like you to look at this photo. I printed it off my phone."

As Marisol studied the picture of two little boys eating cones filled with blue ice cream, and two very hopeful pooches sitting alertly at their feet, her face collapsed.

"Oh no. Are you—are you going to—"

"Let's talk, just for a few minutes. In my car, OK?" Oh, I felt like a criminal, all right. The poor woman had folded like a puppet with slashed strings.

"Please, don't—"

"Tell your sister she can go, Marisol. I'll drive you home."

"Not home. To my next job, on Hot Springs." Instead of crossing the road, she dialed her phone and spoke rapidly in Spanish. Her sister stuck an arm out the window and waved, then drove off.

Marisol raised an eyebrow at the El Camino, then climbed in and placed her bag in her lap. "That picture." Marisol turned to me. "Who is the other little boy?"

"His name is Chuy. His family lives with me. It was his idea, actually, to give your nephew an ice cream cone."

"So you know Beto's my nephew." She shook her head. "That little devil. He's supposed to stay in the backyard or inside the house. I love Beto, but he never does what you say, and he talks too much. He told you everything?"

"Pretty much. The ice cream made us friends for life." I pulled into the road.

"That's because he doesn't have any friends," she said sharply. "At school, what the kids did to him, you don't know! At first they spit on him. Then one day a bunch of them pushed him down on the ground and rubbed gravel and dirt in his face. Where were the teachers, that's what I want to know! The kids kept rubbing and rubbing till Beto was bleeding and screaming. So my sister decided, no more school. She told the principal Beto went to live with his father in Mexico."

"So that's when you and your brother decided to give him a dog—a friend."

"It's a nice little dog, and we knew Beto would love it. It really doesn't like living with Mrs. Richter, that is the truth." Marisol shrugged. "I don't know who's more happy now, Beto or the dog."

"It's going to be hard for him to let Minuet go." I tried to disguise the regret in my voice. "Couldn't you get him another dog, maybe from the pound?"

"That's what we should have done in the first place, I know. But we didn't think, 'cause that little dog was just perfect for him. And now it's too late. He loves Chica, he says she's the best dog in the world." Marisol stared at the purse in her lap. "I know you have to take the dog back. Go ahead. But even if you report me to Mrs. Richter, please, I'm asking you, don't tell her about Beto. If the school hears, they'll send CPS. My sister will lose her son."

"Look, I'm not going to report Beto or you either, OK?" I turned into Hot Springs Road. "But there has to be something better for Beto than staying at home. He's a kid, he needs friends—human friends, his own age."

"Yes, he needs friends. Not bullies." She scowled. "What, you think my sister has money for a private school or something?"

"Private school kids wouldn't behave any better." I glanced over at Marisol. Tears had sprung to her eyes. "Listen, I have a plan. A plan that trusts in the goodness of human nature."

"Human nature is not good. You learn that when you're on the bottom of the pile."

I slowed down the car. "What number am I looking for?"

"304. Down more." Marisol placed the photo on the dash. "So what happens now?" she asked in a resigned tone.

"Tomorrow I'll give Mrs. Richter your sister's address. I won't mention you or your brother, and I'll fib—I'll tell her Beto's family found the dog wandering in the street." I pulled up at the house.

Marisol put a hand on the latch, but she didn't move. "It will be so hard for my nephew. Outside of our family, the only thing that loves him is that silly dog."

"That's where the goodness of human nature comes in. I'm going to show that picture to Mrs. Richter. When she sees Beto's birthmark, she might realize he needs the dog more than she does. She doesn't seem like a bad person."

"Huh. I know my boss better than you do," Marisol snapped. "The señora has no children, no family. She will grab that stupid little dog in a second. It's her baby, that's what she always says."

"Maybe you're right. But maybe not," I said lamely.

Marisol shoved open the door and got out of the car. Then she bent down and glared through the open window. "What do you know about human nature, anyway? Do you clean people's toilets every day of your life? Do you have to—to—let the señor have sex with you or else lose your job? Humans," she hissed, "are ugly and cruel!"

I sat there, stunned, as Marisol strode away to the house, queenly in her righteous anger.

Let the señor have sex with you or else lose your job. My, yes. Yes indeed.

+   +   +

Bright and early the next morning, Mike filled the office doorway. He was in uniform, achingly commanding. "Jaymie? Let's
talk."

"Good morning to you too," I winced. The night before, I'd
only half slept while my brain churned over the case.

Ignoring my sarcasm, Mike stepped into the room and took
charge of the space. "Hey, Gabi. How's it going?"

"It's going good. But I just remembered I gotta go to the
store." She started tossing things into her big beach bag.

"Gabi, don't let him push you around. Just because Mike's
here, it doesn't mean you have to—"

"We're outta napkins, Miss Jaymie, OK?"

Mike dropped into the puffy recliner Gabi had recently acquired, over my objections, via Craigslist. "Let Gabi go, Jaymie.
She doesn't want to listen while I chew on her boss's ear."

"Miss Jaymie? I'll be back in one hour. Anything you want
from Smart and Final?"

"Nope." I perched on the edge of the desk and waited until
the screen door had banged shut behind my PA. "What's up at
work?" I asked nonchalantly.

"We're cleaning up a big meth operation, over at Seis Pinos
Ranch." He brushed the topic away with a sweep of his hand.
"How's Dex this morning, still getting better? I called the vet
yesterday and they said he's out of the woods."

"Yes. The operation went pretty well, thank God." A shud-
der went through me just thinking about it. "They had to take
his leg, Mike."

"I heard, sweetheart." His tone softened. "He'll be fine.
You'll see."

"I know. And I'll be fine too, after I find out who mutilated
him."

"That's what I'm here to talk to you about."

"What—do you know who it was?" My heart began to pump faster at the thought of revenge.

"No, and this is where you listen to *me* for a change." He picked up the chunk of sandstone on the desktop and smoothed it like a baseball. "Jaymie, this time I mean it: you need to back off. The game's way too dangerous now."

"No. No way am I backing off!"

"I'm saying you will. Leave the revenge to me." Mike morphed into a cop. He straightened to his full height and leaned forward slightly, towering over me. His voice turned quiet and hard. "I'm responsible, because I got you into this business in the first place. And I'm not letting what happened to Dex happen to you. Got it?"

I'd seen Mike like this once or twice before, and I knew I'd come up against a wall I couldn't go through. I would need to find a way around the obstruction. "I'm willing to compromise," I said carefully.

"Compromise? What do you mean?"

"I'll forget about revenge—*if*. If you'll help me poke around behind the scenes."

"What do you mean, 'poke around'? Didn't you hear me?"

"Just a little evidence-gathering, Mike."

"Well—maybe. Depends on what kind of evidence you're talking about."

"Nothing risky." I swear, I batted my eyelids. Then I worried: was I being too obvious? But no, apparently that was impossible: Mike was smiling sweetly now. Thank God for male gullibility.

"Hey, hold on. Why do I feel like a steer with a ring in its nose?"

"Oh, come on. That's just your paranoia talking. Listen, as a sign of my sincerity, let's gather some evidence together."

He raised a skeptical eyebrow. "What have you got in mind?"

"How about a trip to the morgue?" I said brightly.

"Uh-huh. Because you know you can't get in there without me." Mike folded his arms over his chest and shook his head. "Yeah, I'm a steer, all right. Neutered and fattened for slaughter."

"You're no steer. Only men with cojones can allow a woman to take the lead."

He tipped back his head and guffawed. "Know what? Deirdre Krause has nothing on you."

Chapter Twelve

"I'm taking you to the morgue like I said I would, right?" Mike raised his hands from the wheel in protest. "All I'm asking in return is for you to let me give you shooting lessons. And when you've had them, I'm buying you a gun."

"I always thought I was safer without a gun."

"And maybe that was true in the past. Not now. Lili Molina's killer is hard-core."

"Please don't say he's a crazy lunatic, Mike. Just do not say that."

"I don't think he is." Mike frowned. "This one's a cold-blooded executioner who plans ahead."

"You believe me now, don't you? You agree it's not Danny."

"Yeah, I've seen the light. OK, here we are." Mike pulled into the morgue lot, parked, and turned to face me. "Look. Are you sure you're cool with this, Jaymie? I know you're no shrinking violet. But still, you saw the pictures from the murder scene—"

"I'm fine with dead bodies, Mike. I've been to the morgue a few times before this."

"OK, then. Let's go."

The morgue was like every other county building, run-down after years of tight funds. There was a whiff of an odor just inside the door, though, that announced this wasn't city hall. I'd noticed it on my other visits: a smell that was both acrid and cloying at the same time. Formaldehyde, maybe? It reminded me of tenth-grade biology lab.

Mike showed his badge to the teenager behind the desk. She paused her texting but kept one eye on her cell. "Help you?"

"Dr. Jorgensen's expecting us."

"I'll buzz you in. You know where to go?"

"Straight down to hell." Mike looked over at me and smiled apologetically. "Gallows humor. Joking's good in a place like this."

"A laugh never hurts," I agreed.

He held open the heavy door. "You look almost eager, Jaymie."

"I've got one or two theories in mind. I want to see if I'm on the right track."

"Funny place to bring a date, Mike." The guy who met us at the end of the hall was blond and good-looking, except that his mouth was soft and sulky.

"Vaughn. This is Ms. Zarlin," Mike said sternly. "She's helping with inquiries into the Molina case."

"Vaughn Jorgensen at your service." The guy actually winked.

"Glad to meet you, Vaughn."

"I need her to take a look at the vic," Mike interjected.

"Is this on the record?"

"Come on, Jorgensen. Remember that little slipup of yours a while back?"

Jorgensen shrugged and turned back to me. "The pleasure's all mine, Ms. Zarlin. Are you the sensitive sort?"

"Only around the living." I smiled. "And please call me Jaymie."

Mike gave a grunt of disapproval.

"Well, Jaymie, your timing's good. I just completed the

final autopsy on Molina. Unfortunately for me, I'll have to send in Samuels. I've got to go to some joke of a meeting down at county."

Jorgensen unlocked the steel door, passed through, and held it open. "But please call me *Dr.* Jorgensen. Most women are hot for doctors. How about you?" The guy was just kidding around, but this time Mike actually growled.

"I hadn't really thought about it," I said, mainly to annoy Mike. "I suppose I could be."

"Excellent." He gave me a wink. "Hope to see you again soon, Jaymie. Anytime, anywhere."

"Anywhere but here," I corrected, waving at the long white room. The two of us laughed.

"He's a jerk," Mike groused as the door swung shut. "Jorgensen was flirting with you."

"But you said joking's good in a place like this."

"To you it's a joke, but to Jorgensen it's foreplay."

"Look who's the sensitive one."

The door opened again and a motherly round-faced woman in her forties stepped into the lab room. "Hey, Mike. How's it going? Haven't seen you here in the crypt for months."

"Nina, how are you? This is Jaymie Zarlin. Jaymie, Nina Samuels."

"Hi Jaymie. No wonder Vaughn had that big stupid grin on his face just now. Stupider than usual, that is." She set a file down on the shiny stainless countertop, then selected a key from the ring attached to her belt. "Are you ready, folks?" She waited for each of us to nod.

"Not that anybody could be ready for this one." She handed us gloves from a dispenser on the wall, then unlocked a cabinet and drew out a long steel tray on rollers.

Almost tenderly, Nina folded back the heavy white sheet. There lay the small and delicate body of Lili Molina.

"If you aren't used to this, Jaymie, the trick is to not dwell on the victim's face. Work to keep it impersonal." She studied me for a moment, then turned to go. "You'll be OK."

Mike watched me as I pulled on the gloves and approached the corpse. Against Nina's suggestion, I examined the badly bruised face first. Next the neck, down to the slashed torso. I was determined to be methodical, unemotional. Several times I had to remind myself that the body was an object now, no longer a girl.

When I'd looked at the hands and feet, I took a step back.

"Finished?" Mike asked quietly.

"Not quite." I moved around to the other side of the tray. "I need to lift and turn the upper part of the body. I want to see the back of the neck."

"Here, I'll help. Damn, these gloves are kid-size." It took Mike a minute to wrangle them onto his hands. "What are you looking for?"

"I want to confirm that the ligature marks match the bootlace."

"Hold on. Bootlace? I haven't heard anything about that."

"Oh . . . I guess I forgot to tell you. I went back to the dressing room, Mike. I found a bloody bootlace buried in the prop bin."

"The hell you did! How could the police miss something like that?"

"They didn't. The killer returned it later on, after the police had searched the room. He needed for us to find it, don't you see? Danny never left the dressing room, after all. If he's going to be convicted as the killer, then the ligature has to be in the room."

"OK. But if the killer knew he was going to frame Danny, why did he take it away with him in the first place?"

"He's not perfect." I shrugged. "In the heat of the moment he probably stuffed the thing in his pocket." I bent over the body.

"OK, Mike. You can see the marks . . . can you hold Lili right like that for a moment?"

"You said her name," Mike said uncomfortably.

"Sorry. But look, there they are at the nape of the neck. And something else. Very faint, but you can see it in two places. There, and there."

Mike bent closer as I held Lili's long dark hair out of the way.

"That looks like a different kind of abrasion," he said. "Something very thin."

"Right. Those are the marks of a necklace. The killer yanked it off, breaking it." Together we eased the body back down.

"Jaymie? I'll tell you what I bet it was. A chain holding a medal of the Virgin Mary. When I spoke with Mrs. Molina, she told me Lili always had it on, and it was missing." He met my eyes. "But you already knew that."

"Teresa told me too. La Virgen de Guadalupe. Know what I think? When we find that medallion, we'll find Lili's killer."

"Let's see what Jorgensen says about it." Mike grabbed the folder off the counter and flipped through the pages. "Yeah, here it is . . . but he doesn't say much. *Evidence of the links of a fine chain.*"

I held out a hand for the report. "Can I take a look at that?"

After two or three minutes I closed the folder and laid it on the counter. "Well, I'll tell you what *is* news: Lili wasn't a virgin before the rape."

"That's news? Come on, Jaymie. She was seventeen, and this is the twenty-first century."

"I'm getting to know this girl." I shook my head. "She wore the medallion in honor of her father. And Lili was modest, not into boys. A serious kid."

"So you think the fact that she wasn't a virgin means something?"

"Yes, I do."

"You've got an idea, don't you." Mike struggled to pull off the skintight gloves. "You going to share? Or is it going to be like the bootlace?"

"When I've confirmed it, you'll be the first to know."

"No. Let the PD do the confirming." He frowned. "Jaymie, are you listening to me?"

I took pity on him. "I will be careful, I promise you. And if I'm in danger, I'll let you know."

There was one line of inquiry I was determined to run to ground. And I knew where to go for the answers: Dos Pueblos High.

School had just let out, and doors were slamming on Porsches, Mercedes, and Lexus SUVs. Hormones and powerful motors revved. The contents of the DP parking lot spoke volumes: these days it was the teachers, not the students, who arranged to have someone drop them off down the street so nobody would see their cheap broken-down cars. Or maybe the teachers did what I was doing now: elected to ride a bike. They could call it green.

I cruised up and down the aisles, scanning for a dark-red Mercedes. But I spotted Lance Stellato before I located his car. He was ambling along with three other kids, laughing at something. None of the group carried backpacks or books.

I followed behind, pedaling slowly. When they reached the Mercedes, parked to one side of the lot under the spotty shade of a jacaranda, I sped up.

"Hi, Lance," I said rather loudly. All four teenagers turned and stared at me. The lone girl in the group found her tongue first.

"Look at that bike—retro, how cool!" Her tone suggested my bike was anything but.

The other two kids guffawed, and Lance sneered like James Dean. "You. What do you want?"

"You know her?" the girl asked. "Wow, Lance, she's almost as old as your mom!"

I kept a calm face. "I need to talk to you, Lance."

"Maybe she deals," one of the boys said. For a moment I thought he was kidding. But he gawked at me, looking especially thick-witted and hopeful.

"Hey guys," Lance said quickly. "Sorry, no ride today."

The kids grumbled but moved off. Then the girl caught sight of somebody else and shrieked. "Jazz! Jazzie!"

"OK, lady." Lance lounged casually against his car. "What the fuck are you doing here?"

"Know what, Lance? You do sound like your dad. Except with him the attitude's real, and with you it's an act."

"I should slap you upside the head."

The kid was a punk. I knew he'd back down. "Go ahead, try."

He hocked up some phlegm and spat near my shoe. Near it, but not on it. "Speak up fast, or I'm gone." Unbeknownst to Lance, a purple jacaranda blossom chose that moment to float down and rest gently in his dark wavy hair.

"I'm not the one who's going to talk. Tell me, where were you on the afternoon of June twenty-first, between the hours of three and four?"

"That's easy. I was at that dumb-ass party we go to every year. The one Sarah Wiederkehr's parents put on."

"Uh-huh. But I'll bet you didn't stay the whole time. You had better things to do, right?"

"Nope. Sarah scored some weed. She took a few of us to that tank house they have in the back. We got stoned." Lance was bragging, convinced he was cool.

"You're a very bad boy, Lancie. Now I want to hear what you have to say about what happened a year and a half ago, between you and Lili Molina."

"How did you—" Shock registered on his face. "Nothing," he sputtered. "Nothing happened."

"You sure? Because maybe I do have something to say to you, Lance. Maybe I need to explain that Danny Armenta didn't kill Lili. He was framed. My job is to find her killer, OK? And right now, you're one of my favorite suspects."

An Austin Mini tooted as it raced down the aisle. "Hey Stellato, your mom's hot!" someone called. A wolf whistle followed.

"But I wouldn't *kill* anybody." Lance had turned white. White with shock, or was it with fear?

"Well, you don't seem like a killer. But I know you hurt Lili a while back, so until I understand what that was about, I can't rule you out."

The parking lot had emptied. I noticed a female security guard watching us from the school steps. My time with pretty boy was growing short. "Speak up. Otherwise I'll take my suspicions straight to the cops."

"We had sex!" he blurted. "Sex, OK? Big fucking deal! Why would I kill her for that?"

Let the señor have sex with you or else lose your job. Except it wasn't the señor, after all: it was the señor's son. And Teresa Molina had almost certainly lost her job over it, even though her daughter had given in.

I studied the young man's face. It was all written there now: anger, fear, shame. "Lance? So far you're telling me half the truth. Let's call it a start."

In the silence, a woodpecker thumped on the trunk of a frowzy palm. *Thunk, thunk, thunk . . .* The rotund guard pushed off and began to advance. I'd have to press.

"You forced Lili, didn't you? You got her alone, then you forced her. Lili Molina wasn't a girl who'd give it up just because you asked—*rich boy*." I carefully held back from one word: *rape*. I needed Lance to talk more.

"No! You're wrong, OK? I didn't force her. Lili wanted it, for sure. She just—she—"

"Needed a little push? Like you saying you'd get her mom fired if she didn't cooperate?"

"No. I don't know! Maybe . . . something like that." He yanked open his car door. "I don't need this shit. I'm outta here."

"One more question, Lance. The truth, that's all I'm after here. Who else knows about this?"

"Nobody. Nobody except my dad." He looked desperate. "I *liked* Lili, OK? She was nice. I *liked* her. My dad decided to fire her mom. That wasn't me."

"Sure it was, Lance. Your dad found out what you did. He got rid of Teresa to protect his little boy."

"I don't have to listen to any of this!" He threw himself into the driver's seat and slammed the door shut.

"Excuse me?" The security guard wore a polite but suspicious smile. "I know Mr. Lance here. But you look a little old to be a student."

Lance took advantage and peeled away.

I'd made a promise to Mike. But visiting Casa Arabe, yet another huge and beautiful Santa Barbara estate, hardly constituted danger. The morning after my consult with Lance, I paid the Wiederkehr family a call.

Casa Arabe was a grande dame reposing in acres of lavish gardens. Moorish fountains and walkways, torrents of purple and white wisteria, and twelve-foot-high copper-clad gates all murmured of money, taste, and more money.

To my surprise, Cynthia Wiederkehr had phoned me. She'd apologized for refusing to see me earlier, and suggested a time to come by. Well, maybe *suggested* was the wrong word, I thought as I waited beside a courtyard pond crammed with aggressive turtles. I'd been told precisely when to show up.

"Ms. Zarlin?" A tall willowy woman opened the door,

closed it behind her and extended a hand. "I'm Cynthia Wie-derkehr. Sorry you had to wait out here. Lalo should have asked you to step into the foyer."

I was fairly sure Lalo had done exactly as he was told. "Thanks for agreeing to speak with me, Mrs. Wiederkehr." I took her cool dry hand and felt it immediately slide from my own.

"Bruce and I want to help all we can in this terrible business. Besides, when the most powerful woman in the city makes a call, it's unwise to say no."

Surprise number two: Celeste Delaney had intervened.

Cynthia Wiederkehr then smiled graciously, but like her handshake, the smile slipped away quickly. "I'm expecting guests for a luncheon at noon," she briskly continued. "I want to answer all your questions, but I'll need to do it in an efficient manner." She nodded toward the path. "Let's walk around to the kitchen. If you don't mind, I'll continue with the prep while we talk."

I followed Cynthia along a tiled path, in through French doors to a kitchen larger than my house and studio combined. The stainless-steel appliances were massive, restaurant-sized. Twin double sinks were filled with water and stuffed with bunches of roses and ferns. Clippers in varying sizes were arranged on the granite countertop.

The lone sign of disorder made me smile: a big green inch-worm looped along the bull-nose edge of the counter. Cynthia noticed it, pinched it between thumb and forefinger, and dropped it in the trash.

"Ms. Zarlin, may I get you something to drink?" she asked as she rinsed her fingers and dried them.

"A glass of water would be fine."

She tucked a strand of her artfully cut blond bob behind an ear and tied on a barman's apron. "Please, fire away," she said as she took a pair of clippers into her hand.

Apparently the glass of water was not going to materialize.

"I'm not sure what Celeste Delaney told you, Mrs. Wiederkehr. But I've been hired by the family of Danny Armenta to find Lili Molina's killer." I watched carefully, but the expression on Cynthia's expertly made-up face did not seem to change.

"Yes, Celeste said something like that." Cynthia held a rose stem under the running tap and clipped it, then plunged it into a vase. "Does that imply you don't think the Hispanic boy did it?"

"The fact is, Danny Armenta is innocent."

"That's what you're being paid to think."

"Nobody pays to influence my thoughts, Mrs. Wiederkehr." I held my voice steady.

"But aren't you the only one who believes in his innocence?" She continued to attack the roses, but color had flooded her cheeks. Blushing was the one thing Cynthia apparently couldn't control.

"Not at all." I maintained my casual tone. "There's the killer himself, to state the obvious. And there are others who suspect or know the truth."

Cynthia Wiederkehr's forehead creased. I noticed permanent frown lines arcing down from the corners of her mouth.

"What does the boy have to say for himself?"

"Danny's still traumatized. He discovered his friend's mutilated body, after all. But he's beginning to open up. Any day now, he'll talk about that afternoon."

"Mom? Where are you?" A strident female voice sounded from another part of the house.

"In the kitchen, dear," Cynthia called. She seemed eager to break off our conversation.

"Mom!" A cross-faced girl of around seventeen appeared in the kitchen doorway. This would be Sarah Wiederkehr, only child of the doctor and missus.

Sarah was attractive enough, but she had a receding chin and wasn't as good-looking as her mother. Her long blond hair was marshalled into a French braid and she was dressed in what must be golf attire, though both the top and shorts were spandex-tight. She stared hard at me, ignoring my polite smile.

"Sarah, this is Ms.—I'm sorry, what was your name?"

I knew damn well Cynthia hadn't forgotten. "Jaymie Zarlin. You must be Sarah?"

"Hi." The girl had learned how to be dismissive from her mother. She'd no doubt learned a lot from Cynthia.

"Ms. Zarlin is a detective, dear. She's looking into the death of that Hispanic girl, the one who was killed at Solstice, you know?"

"Oh . . . yeah. Mom, I'm going to be late. I tee off at one and we're supposed to be there an hour and a half early, remember? My Lexie's still at the garage, so you need to drop me off." She shrugged. "Unless you want me to take yours?"

"Why don't you do that, dear. I've got my luncheon at noon, so I need to stay here." Both women seemed to be working hard at ignoring my presence. Quite the mother-daughter act.

"And why don't I ask my questions right now?" I made my voice sugar-sweet. "Then I can let you ladies get on with your busy day."

"Oh." Cynthia looked at me as if she were surprised I was still there. "Yes, all right then. Sarah, my keys are on the hall table."

"Actually," I said quickly, "I'd like to address my questions to Sarah, too."

At last, the real Cynthia Wiederkehr began to show. "No, absolutely not. My daughter will not be—"

"Mom, it's *fine*." Suddenly Sarah's voice was every bit as determined as her mother's. "Don't treat me like a little kid."

"Oh, honestly. If it weren't for Celeste—" Cynthia waved her hand dismissively.

I decided to take this for an OK. "I want to ask both of you what you observed at the solstice party you hosted."

"Can you narrow your question?" Cynthia snapped. "We'll be here all day." Sarah said nothing—but to my interest, her face registered discomfort. She was a tough kid, but at seventeen, most people don't know how to hide their feelings. It was an art Sarah Wiederkehr had yet to learn.

"Sure. To begin with, I'd like to know if either of you saw anyone leave during the course of the party, and then return."

"How could I notice something like that? Ms. Zarlin, one hundred and twenty-three people attended. I was far too busy coordinating the event to—to monitor my guests."

"Let me be more specific, then. I'm asking about the Guild Triune members and their families."

"Unh." Sarah had folded her arms over her middle, as if her stomach hurt. Cynthia glanced over at her daughter and froze. Then, like a dog on attack, she turned.

"*That is enough.* I am not prepared to have a total stranger come into my home and grill me concerning my friends. Really, I shall have to speak to Celeste Delaney. I think you must have pulled the wool over that old woman's eyes."

She was truly angry, and it was obvious why: Cynthia had sensed Sarah's anxiety, and was now protecting her young.

"Come on, Mrs. Wiederkehr. No one pulls the wool over Miss Delaney's eyes, do they?" I shrugged. "I didn't mean to upset you. My question was pretty straightforward."

"I just don't appreciate invasions into my family's privacy." Cynthia's glance flitted back to her daughter. "Though we've certainly nothing to hide."

"What's all this about, dear?" A tall thin man in baggy shorts and T-shirt stepped into the kitchen. He was sweating a little and appeared to have been working out. "I could hear you from downstairs in the gym."

"I'm Jaymie Zarlin, Dr. Wiederkehr. I apologize if I've upset anyone."

"I'm not upset," Cynthia interrupted. "I'm just in a hurry,

that's all, and Sarah has somewhere to be. Bruce, you could walk Ms. Zarlin to the gate."

He gave me a conspiratorial wink. "Better off out of it when the girls are in a rush." He crossed the room and held open the door to the outside. "Shall we?"

I could see why his patients doted on the guy. Dr. Bruce made you feel he truly wanted to help, wanted you to be every bit as happy as he knew you could be.

"I'm sorry," he said pleasantly as we passed back through the garden. "My wife is terribly particular in what she serves to her guests. Didn't your menu follow her instructions, my dear?"

"I'm not the caterer, Dr. Wiederkehr." I halted and turned to the gangly man. I noticed Sarah had inherited her unfortunate chin from her dad. "I'm a private investigator."

"You're—what?" He withdrew his warm hand from my shoulder. "But how did you—"

"Get inside your house?" I smiled engagingly. "Actually, Celeste Delaney called your wife for me. Don't worry, I'm not here to investigate your family, Doctor. It's just the solstice party I need to know more about."

"Celeste—that old crow." Dr. Bruce laughed, and his Adam's apple, which was large and pointed, bobbed nervously. "Well, you've explained it. Nobody dares turn down her requests, not even Cynthia." He beamed. "But please, don't tell Celeste I called her an old crow. I'd be socially dead in this town if she heard."

I smiled and played along. "She is kind of scary. And she's going to be very annoyed with me if I don't ask my questions."

"Go right ahead then, ask away," Dr. Bruce said in his best bedside manner. "But first tell me, why is Celeste even interested in that sad business? Just between you and me, she isn't what you'd call the caring sort."

I turned what I hoped were guileless eyes upon Dr. Bruce.

Two could play at his game, after all. "I wish I could tell you. But she's kind of secretive. Personal reasons, I guess."

"Celeste Delaney does play her cards close to her chest. Just when you haven't heard from her for ages and—sorry to say it— you think she might be dead, well, that's when she pops up." He smiled, rested his hand again on my shoulder, and squeezed. "Why don't we walk on toward the gate, Jaymie? I'm in no hurry, I just think it might be best if Cynthia sees you're gone. At times she can be a little . . ."

"Jealous?" I asked innocently.

"Jealous?" The affable mask slipped just a little. "No, edgy was what I was about to say." His hand slipped to my shoulder blade and applied forward pressure.

The good doctor had only one goal, and that was to send me packing. It was now or never. "About your party, Doctor. You host it every year?"

"Oh yes." He actually chortled. "In the old days, the party was hosted by both active and retired members of the Triune. Why, even Cynthia's father once held Solstice Rising. The name is rather pretentious, but that's what we've always called our private shindig, you know. My own father held the record for the most number of hostings, and by now I'm a close second. This property, which I inherited from him, is what you might call the perfect party pad."

"It's no small pad, Dr. Wiederkehr. So your wife's father was a member of the Triune?"

"Yes. Caughey, the good old stick, they used to call him. Because he was such a—good sport." Even Dr. Bruce heard the weakness of this comment, apparently. An awkward silence ensued.

"Well. Here we are, then." He punched a code into a panel mounted on a stone pillar, and the copper gates swung soundlessly open.

I made a step forward, then stopped and turned back. "Oh! It's been so nice talking with you that I forgot to ask my main question."

The smile had already slid from Dr. Bruce's face. I had to hand it to him: the guy tried his best to pin it back on.

"Well, go ahead then, Jaymie. But briefly, if you don't mind."

Time to stop being nice. And since he'd called me Jaymie, I'd follow suit. "I want to know about individual comings and goings at your party, Bruce. Particularly between two P.M. and four P.M."

"Well, you have to understand, I was quite busy. I—"

"Vincent Stellato, for example."

"Vince? Oh, that's easy. Vince never left. He was here with Maryjune, of course, and his son, Lance."

"You seem very sure."

Dr. Bruce forced a laugh. "You know when Vince is around. Let's just say he's the life of the party."

"I can imagine. How about Sutton Frayne? The Third," I added, allowing myself a smidgeon of sarcasm.

Bruce decided to try on a glower. "You know, it sounds as if you're checking my friends' alibis. That's ridiculous. Besides, we all accounted for our movements with the police."

"You don't have to answer," I said quietly. "It's entirely up to you."

"Oh, I don't mind—anything for Celeste." He shrugged his bony shoulders in an obvious attempt to seem nonchalant. "It's just that it's a waste of time. But for the record, let me be clear. Neither Vince nor Sutz left the party, as far as I'm aware."

"And their family members?"

His voice remained calm. "Now you really are crossing a boundary, don't you think?"

I had to hand it to the guy. He was playing the part of the uninvolved bystander to the hilt. Mr. Nothing to Hide.

Just then a car engine started up around the side of the mansion. Come on, Brucie, I thought. Answer the question, that's all I ask.

"All right. Let me get this over with, once and for all. Frayne has no family of his own, except for his mother, Caroline, and Celeste, who I'm sure you know is his aunt. He brought Caroline along that day, though I don't know why he bothered—the woman is practically gaga. To give her an outing, I suppose. I doubt Caroline moved out of her armchair the entire time she was here, and Sutz had to attend to her, off and on."

"And the Stellatos?"

"Vince, Maryjune, and their son were here the entire time. As was I, by the way. And if you are silly enough to wonder about Cynthia or Sarah: they did not leave at any point. I recall Sarah playing tennis out in the back with Frayne. That went on for over an hour." He smiled slightly. "I believe she thumped the old boy quite soundly."

"Youth often wins out in the end, doesn't it, Bruce?" A big gleaming white Lexus SUV curled around the drive and approached us. Princess Sarah on her way to golf.

It was pure instinct that prompted my next—and what I knew would be my last—question. "Speaking of the younger generation, how about Jared Crowley?"

The blood drained from the doctor's face, and he put out a hand to the pillar to steady himself. "What does he . . . I don't see what . . ."

I knew, of course, that Jared hadn't attended the party. It was Bruce's reaction I was after, and damn, had I scored.

"Dad, would you get out of the way? I'm in a hurry," Sarah shouted out the car window. The Lexus blasted on through, riling up a snake cloud of dust.

Chapter Thirteen

"Can't a man get a cuppa joe around here?" Mike grabbed the folding chair off the side of the ancient Vee-Dub and snapped it open.

A battered old drive-in restaurant tray emerged through the open window. "Fit this on here, will ya, Cowboy? Neuralgia's acting up."

Mike took the tray from the scar-gloved hand and wedged it into the door frame. "Sugar, Charlie, no cream."

"My brains ain't gone soft. I remember."

Mike turned his chair to face the beach and flopped down in it. "What's going on down here, Captain?"

"Can't fool me, Mike. You're a cop when you're not being yourself. Nothin's goin on here a-tall, and if it was, I wouldn't tell ya."

"Fair enough." A chipped mug steaming with thick brew appeared on the tray, followed by a silver sugar bowl and spoon. "That bowl must've been Annie's. Too fancy for an old coot like you."

"That sugar bowl *is* Annie's. Came from the Longstreet family, those sons-a-bitches."

"*Is*. I stand corrected." Mike swirled a spoonful of sugar into the mug.

"Say, saw your girlfriend not so long ago. She brought me horehounds, by the way."

"Sorry I'm empty-handed. I'm not as nice as Jaymie. Guess you know that by now."

"You and Jaymie are the yin and the yang. Annie thinks the same as me about you two."

Mike settled back in the chair and sipped at the sludge. It was Tuesday, and there were no tourists in sight. A few locals ambled along the hard sand just above the waterline, their mutts rummaging through the seaweed wrack. Maybe a dealer was plying his trade in the caves under the bluff, but Mike couldn't see it from where he sat.

"Actually, Charlie, it's Jaymie I came to talk to you about."

"Figured as much. Fine young filly. You won't do better."

"I know that. I'm stuck on her, I guess you could say. Just wish she was stuck on me."

"Give it time, Cowboy. You're the only one for her. She don't completely know it yet, is all." Charlie coughed harshly. "But you got somethin' else to say, don't you?"

"Yeah. Yeah, I do. Did you hear what happened to Jaymie's dog?"

"I heard. Some people are worse than animals. No animal woulda done that. Dexter gonna pull through?"

"The little guy's tougher'n shit," Mike said. "The vet had to amputate his hind leg, but he'll survive just fine."

"Dex was Brodie's bud. For Jaymie's sake, I'm glad he's gonna make it." Charlie coughed again. It sounded painful this time, like the ripping of strong Velcro.

"Charlie? Here's the thing. What happened to Dex was a warning. Jaymie's too involved in the Molina case. She said she'd back off, but I know she won't. I'm worried she's going to get hurt."

"Oh boy. You think the girl's killer hurt Dex?"

"Most likely." Mike got to his feet and thumped the empty

mug down on the tray. "But Jaymie won't listen to me. The more I say on the subject, the more she ignores me."

"You know why."

"Sure, I know. What happened to Brodie, she still blames herself."

"Nothin' to do with her. She did her best like always. It was a crime. A goddamn crime."

"You said it." Mike jammed his hands in his pockets. "She's trying to make up for it by helping the Armenta kid—and by the way, I encouraged her in the beginning. Why won't she get smart, though? This is evil she's brushing up against now, pure evil."

"Jaymie *is* smart, Mike. Smarter than the two of us put together. And she's brave." The scarred hand slipped through the curtain and closed, stiffly, around the empty cup. "Correct me if I'm wrong, but that's gotta be a couple of the things you love about her."

"No comment, Chief. That's kinda personal."

"No comment necessary, Mike. No comment at all."

Mike watched an angry gull chase a crow off the beach. The crow cruised off with the spoils, what looked to be a dead crab. "She dumped me, you know."

"What's that you say?"

"A couple of years back. Jaymie dumped me."

"Didn't know that, Cowboy. Thought the two of you were just takin' a breather."

Mike snorted. "Damn long breather, I'd say. It's taken me all this time to stop being pissed."

"Looks like the two of you decided to try it again."

"Mainly me. I thought, well, Brodie's been gone for a while now, you know? Maybe Brodie's death was what was bothering her the first time around. I decided to give it another shot."

"Yep," Charlie rasped. "'Cause she's worth it."

"Yeah, that and the fact that no other woman seems to

measure up. But I don't know, Charlie . . . something's still holding her back." Mike got to his feet. "Like I said, though, it's personal. I shouldn't be talking about it, not even to you."

"Don't worry about me. I don't go around flapping my lips in the breeze."

"I know that. Thing is, I can't wait forever. Life goes on, you know?"

"Life goes on," Charlie rumbled, "like it or not."

"Danny? It's me, Jaymie."

"And me!" Chuy pounded on the door with both hands.

"Not so loud, Chuy." Danny was continuing to improve, to come back to himself. Even so, his vulnerability was still raw.

But when the door opened, Danny was actually smiling a little. "Hey, Chuy. I can hear you."

Chuy pushed past his big brother and raced into the studio. "You got your own TV—*lucky*."

The studio had acquired a lived-in look. Apparently Danny didn't like to throw things away. His trash was stacked neatly on the small table—disposable plates and cups, even a small mound of chicken bones. And the pile of clothes in the corner was tidy enough, too. But it wouldn't take many more days before the small space would be overwhelmed by Danny's collections.

"Do you get *Curious George* on this TV?" Chuy asked.

"Probably," Danny said. "What channel?"

"I think twelve. Or maybe ten."

Danny picked up the remote from the bookshelf and handed it to his brother. "You try." He glanced at me. "Dexter . . . is he back yet?"

"Not yet. Soon, though. The vet wants to keep him two or three more days. Maybe they'll send him home on Saturday."

"What . . . happened to him?" Danny looked confused. He'd asked the question before, and I carefully repeated my answer.

"Well, when Dexter wandered off, he got hit by a car. It's sad, because I'm afraid he lost his back leg. But the vet says he'll be OK. I went to visit him today, and he's standing up. He'll be running around on three legs in no time."

Chuy had seated himself on the floor and was engrossed in a cartoon show. "Maybe a bad guy kidnapped Dexter, and took him up in a spaceship, and then Dexter pushed open the door with his paws and jumped out."

"That's a good story, Chuy, but it's not what happened."

"*Maybe,*" he replied.

"Danny, can we go outside for a minute? I want to ask you something." It was time for me to speak seriously with him, and I didn't want little Mr. Big Ears listening in.

It was evening, and just as we stepped out through the doorway, a large white shape lifted from a nearby cypress and drifted away like a slice of the moon.

"What—what was that?"

"A barn owl. So beautiful, and they're good to have around—they keep down the rats."

"Rats . . . we had rats at our other house."

I nodded in the semi-dark. "Santa Barbara is full of rats." I clasped my hands behind my back. "Danny, I want to ask you a question. I won't talk very long, because it's hard to think about. But there's something I need to know."

"O-OK."

"It's about the day Lili died. I know you didn't do it, Danny. I'm trying to figure out who did." I looked away, out over the darkening channel. The lights on the oil rigs twinkled like stars afloat on the water. "You said Lili came and said hi to you while you were drawing, and then she went off to the dressing room, right?"

"Uh-huh . . ." His voice was low and hesitant now, as if it required effort for him just to speak.

"OK. So tell me, why did you go down to the dressing room later on?"

"Somebody—somebody called me."

I bent my head to hear him better. I didn't want to step any closer, in case he felt threatened.

"Somebody called you? Did the person call out your name?"

"Yeah . . . he said my name."

"Was it Lili? Did Lili call you?"

"Lili?" He shook his head stiffly. "No. It was a man."

"OK, a man called your name. Did you recognize his voice? Was it somebody you already knew?"

"I don't . . . think so."

"Are you sure? Could it have been Jared—Jared Crowley?"

"Jared?" Confusion crept into his expression once more. "It wasn't a kid, it was a man. He had a real weird voice. He said it like this: *Danny, come here. Lili needs you to help her.*" Danny cupped his hands around his mouth and deepened his voice as he spoke the words.

"OK. Thanks, Danny. You're doing good. I'm sorry for this last question, but I have to ask. Are you sure the voice was real? Not a voice in your head?"

"It was a real person, really loud. And . . ."

"Yes?"

"The voices I hear in my head? They're real too."

I tossed and turned through the night, grappling with the details surrounding Lili's murder and the brutal attack on Dex. Finally, around 5:00 A.M., I tumbled into a deep sleep. At six thirty my alarm squawked in my ear. By the time I got to the office, my mood was what you'd call edgy.

"Good morning, Miss Jaymie," my PA called out cheerily. "That was Señorita Darlene on the phone just now."

"Morning," I grunted. I walked through to the kitchen, opened my bag, and pulled out a dozen or so crime-scene photos I'd printed from the disc Celeste Delaney had given me. "Oh yeah? And what did the rich bitch want?"

"She said she's coming around. Miss Jaymie? I don't think I ever heard you use the *b*-word before, either."

I taped the first photo to the wall. "Guess I've got a bigger vocabulary than you thought." I stepped into the doorway and set my hands on my hips. "I've got a task for you, Gabi. Add up our expenses on the dognapping. Subtract them from ten thousand dollars and draw up a check, made out to Mommy Warbucks, for the difference."

"Mommy who?"

"I'm talking about Darlene Richter."

"Wh-what! Miss Jaymie, excuse me, but this is a business, remember. Since Mrs. Richter, only two new cases came in: the Kimuras, their son's been missing for eight years and you're not gonna find him tomorrow, and another missing dog."

I grimaced. "You didn't tell me about the dog."

"I was gonna break it to you when the time was right. Word gets around, people hear how you found Minuet. You got opportunity knocking."

"*Please*. No more cases involving four-legged creatures. My life's absurd enough as it is."

"I don't know about no absurd. But Mrs. Richter, she's gonna drop by this morning to thank you, she said. She's so, so happy she got her dog back."

"Then you better get that tally sheet ready." I retreated to the kitchen and picked up the next photo in the stack.

"OK, you're the boss," Gabi called loudly. I heard something thump down hard on the desk.

Five minutes later she entered the kitchen. "OK, here's—*Dios mío!*" Her hand fell open and a sheet of paper, forgotten, fluttered to the floor. "No. Oh no."

"Gabi, I'm so sorry. I should have warned you."

"I didn't—didn't—those pictures are so horrible."

I slipped a hand under her elbow. "Take it easy. Let's go outside."

"No. I *won't* be a baby." She drew a shaky breath, then tugged a tissue from her pocket and blew. "I—I thought this investigating business might be kinda fun, but it's not, it's just . . . just . . ."

"Sometimes it's fun. Sometimes it's terribly sad."

"Oh my, that poor girl!" Standing in the kitchenette doorway was Darlene Richter, holding a large gourmet gift basket in her arms. Sitting prettily at her feet and wearing a turquoise-blue rhinestone-studded collar was none other than Minuet.

I found my voice after a lengthy moment. "Hello, Mrs. Richter. It wasn't necessary for you to come by."

"I realize that." She held forth the grand basket. "Minnie and I just wanted to let you know how much we appreciated your help."

"Thanks." Gabi jumped to her feet. "Here, I'll just set it on the table."

"What a terrible shame." Darlene Richter was staring again at the photos of Lili, and hardly seemed to notice as Gabi took the basket from her hands.

"Mrs. Richter, let's go into the other room, shall we?" I bent down and picked up the tally sheet from the floor. "I have a refund for you."

"A refund?" The woman still seemed unable to tear her eyes from the photos.

"If you please," I said firmly, "the other room."

I didn't invite Darlene Richter to sit in the client's chair. Shamelessly, I sat there myself, effectively leaving her no option but to stand. "I asked my assistant to total up our expenses on your account." I glanced at the page. "Your refund totals eight thousand and twenty-one dollars."

"No, Ms. Zarlin." Darlene smoothed her blond weave off her cheek. "As far as I'm concerned, we're even."

"Maybe *you* think so. The thing is, Mrs. Richter, there's a little boy who doesn't see it that way." I tried the filing cabinet and found it locked. "Gabi, would you please open this damn thing and get me the checkbook?"

"What my boss really means," Gabi said, stepping forward, "is that—"

"I know perfectly well what your boss means." Darlene Richter's green eyes snapped. "Don't bother, I don't want your check. The two of you can use the money to go out and buy yourselves some new clothes."

Gabi gasped. "My boss Mrs. Victoria Terbell gave me this outfit. She bought it at Saks and only wore it two times, one time to—"

But Darlene Richter had turned away. "You know, I had something to tell you just now, Ms. Zarlin," she said as she opened the screen door. "But on second thought—"

The door banged shut after the woman and her dog. She turned and scowled through the screen. "On second thought, you can just go to hell." She ran a fingertip along the edge of the frame.

"This door is filthy. What's your name—Gabi? If I were your boss, I'd have you sacked."

"I'm not a cleaner when I'm here," Gabi yelped. "I'm a PA!"

"Oh, and by the way. Victoria Terbell? She's well known for her taste—the absolute worst in town."

So Darlene Richter had something to tell me. What, something about Lili's murder? It wasn't likely that it amounted to much. On the other hand, to be honest, I needed all the help I could get.

But by the time I'd squelched my pride and made it out to the street, Minuet and her mistress were gone.

By the end of the day, I needed to unwind. My two confidants were happy to assist.

"Sangria. Best damn thing to come outta the sixties," Mike mused.

I sat down in the chair I'd carried in from the kitchen, and twirled the stem of my wineglass between my finger and thumb. "You know, I was thinking about what you said the other day, Mike. You were right: I need to share more. If something happens to me, no one will know what I've figured out so far."

"Knock on wood!" Gabi scolded as she tapped on the desk. "Nothing will happen to you, don't say stuff like that."

"Nothing's going to happen if you're careful," Mike added. "But I want to hear it, so share."

"Where should I start?"

"Let's start with Dex." Mike leaned back in the Craigslist recliner. "The attack on your dog was a warning, Jaymie. That's one thing we can be sure of: Lili's killer attacked him."

"It was a warning," I agreed. "And the person who butchered Dexter *could* be the killer. Or . . ." I took a deep breath. The sweet creamy scent of a nearby tobira bush was wafting in through the open window.

"Or?" Gabi prompted.

"Or, the killer could have manipulated somebody else into doing his dirty work."

"I guess that's possible." Mike leaned forward, balanced a smoked oyster on a cracker, and topped it with a chunk of cheddar. "But why look for a complicated answer when we've got a simple one that works?"

"I gotta agree with Mike." Gabi sipped her glass of the bloodred sangria. "Why wouldn't the murderer just do it all by himself? Safer for him that way."

"Because everything's layered with this guy. Don't you see? Nothing's straightforward, and that's how he wants it. Complications make him feel safe." I got to my feet and paced to the door and back.

"Look, here's the bottom line. I'm pretty sure the killer was an insider who planned to make it look like a passing stranger raped and killed Lili. When he realized Danny was in the building, he changed his strategy on the spur of the moment. He saw a better option, the opportunity to make the crime look like a psychotic act."

"He did a damn good job of it. The cops aren't looking past Danny Armenta. I hear the trial date's going to be set by the end of the week."

"Why can't they just admit the obvious? Lili's murder was fueled by cold and calculated fury." I dropped down in the chair again, tipped back my head, and stared at the cracks in the plaster ceiling.

"But you know what?" Gabi said quietly. "I don't see how Lili could've made anybody that mad."

"I've asked myself that too," I admitted. "Maybe she stood up for herself, you know? Maybe she resisted, and her resistance brought on the killer's rage."

"Well, I'm still stuck on the question of how Lili got to the Guild warehouse in the first place." Mike shrugged. "Until we—"

"Oh. That's one of the things I wanted to tell you," I interrupted. "I found out how Lili got there: Jared Crowley gave her a lift."

"What! How the hell did you figure that out?"

"Through Shawna Sprague, Jared's girlfriend. Look, I realize this seems to put Jared in the center of the picture, Mike. But I still have my doubts. For one thing, I know for a fact he dropped Lili off and went straight back to the park. There just wasn't time for him to have done all the things the killer did."

"What the hell, I'll play along for a minute. Who looks better for it than Crowley?"

"Wish I could tell you. Everybody has an alibi."

"Let's take a look at your suspects." Mike got up and went to the kitchenette doorway. "I see Stellato, Frayne, Wiederkehr—powerful men in this town. You know what they say: power corrupts. Then there's the one my money's on, that squirmy little asshole Crowley." Mike paused. "Now, that last one—Stellato's son, right? What's he doing up there?"

"Lance Stellato coerced Lili Molina into having sex about a year and a half ago."

"Oh no," Gabi gasped.

"The hell he did! I'll see he's arrested for that if nothing else. He—"

"Mike, no. He'd just claim it was consensual, and you'd never get a conviction. We have to stay focused on finding Lili's killer."

"Yeah, well, that kid's got a motive if ever I've seen one." Mike folded his arms and leaned against the door frame. "What else've you been keeping quiet about?"

"There might be something, as a matter of fact. Those interviews the cops conducted, Mike? I need to listen to the actual audio recordings."

"We've been over this before. Come on, Jaymie. You know I can't do that."

"Just listen and I'll explain," I pleaded. "Danny's improving, right? He's stayed on his meds, thank God, and he's beginning to move past the trauma. Last night he talked to me, just a little, about what happened that afternoon."

Gabi set down her glass and leaned forward. "Did my nephew hear something?"

"Yes. Danny heard the killer's voice. He went down to the dressing room because a man called out his name." I reached for my pack and took out my spiral notebook, then thumbed through the pages.

Somebody called me . . . a man. It wasn't a kid, it was a man. He had a real weird voice. He said, "Danny, come here. Lili needs you to help her."

I held up a hand. "Now let me read it again, in the voice Danny used." I dropped my own voice a couple of octaves: "*Danny, come here. Lili needs you to help her.*"

Gabi half rose in her chair. "Mike, you gotta get those recordings for her. It's crucial evidence!"

"No, it's not evidence. But yeah, it could be important." Mike walked over and set his empty glass on the desk. "Jaymie, like I said, I'm not handing anything over to you. I'll look into it myself. Now, you need to keep this latest development under your hat."

"But I *want* people to know about this, Mike. I want you and Gabi to tell people Danny's coming around, remembering things. That's what I'm going to do." I gave him a wicked little smile. "Tell Officer Krause. She'll spread the word, and I guarantee she'll love you for the tip."

Mike didn't bite. "You've got some theory about flushing out the killer, huh? Like he's a coyote or something."

"Yep, something like that. If the killer thinks Danny might ID him, he could make a move and show his hand. Otherwise, he'll just hole up till the trail's cold. See what I mean?"

"What I see is you waving a big red flag. Why do you think your dog's at the vet, for Chrissake?" He stabbed a finger in my direction. "The coyote knows you're the chicken that's scratching up a cloud of dust."

"Tell you what. No coyote should underestimate this chicken."

"There you go. Just what a coyote loves: an overconfident chick."

I biked home, then helped myself to a serving of melt-in-your-mouth chili rellenos. At dusk, Chuy and Aricela and I moseyed down to the beach, where the kids filled my pockets with damp sandy treasures. Later I chatted with Alma and then went to bed, just as a nearly full summer moon nudged over the lip of the Pacific.

I didn't see Danny that evening. I could have knocked on his door, but I didn't. It crossed my mind, and I decided not to bother him. I reasoned he'd come out if he wanted company. But maybe, because I was tired, I just couldn't be bothered.

If I'd knocked on his door, it might have changed things. We'd have talked for a bit, or Danny might have stepped out, played a little with his brother and sister. Later, he might not have felt the urge to go out. He might have stayed home that night . . . stayed safe.

If only. If only I had.

Chapter Fourteen

It's better to walk in the dark, Danny thinks. It's quiet at night, most of the people are inside their houses. In the daytime he doesn't go out, it's too crazy out there. Santa Barbara is dangerous, man.

He used to go out with Joey and Eric, sometimes Victor too. They were safe together, they weren't afraid of nothing. They used to go to the 7-Eleven. That's where all the homeless guys and the winos hang out, but it was cool. He doesn't know why, but his friends don't wanna go out no more—they don't wanna do nothing. Joey and Victor have jobs, maybe that's why. Eric, he says . . . he says he doesn't wanna hang no more, he doesn't want—

Whoa—that guy over there, he's following. What does he want? Maybe the guy's after him. But maybe it's what they told him about, that paranoid thing. Just keep walking, move on. . . . OK, the guy went the other way. He's not following now.

Yeah. It's better at night. If you walk fast and don't stop, nobody bothers you. But you have to keep moving, that's for sure.

Last night or maybe another night he walked out on the wharf, out to the end. The moon was almost full. He's gonna go to the wharf again, walk out to the end like he did before, then turn around and head back.

One good thing: he likes his new place. He never had a room all by himself before. He can sleep whenever he wants and nobody bothers him. Jaymie's nice. He hopes they get to stay with her for a really long time.

OK, stepping onto the wharf. The big rough boards under his feet. Not boards, more like square telephone poles. You have to wear shoes. He remembers one time when he was little—hey, it's that same guy. Is he following? He remembers one time—it's OK, the guy's gone, he just went to piss over the side.

He remembers one time when him and his primo, when they were little they ran out on the wharf in their bare feet. They both got bad splinters, Eddie got his pulled out at Emergency. Danny's mom pulled his out, and it really hurt. . . .

Past the ice cream store. They used to hang out there, it was fun. When there weren't any tourists around, Brittany Lopez used to give him free ice cream in a cup. She really liked him. Maybe if he went in there now, maybe she'd . . . Last time he went in, that was after, after he dropped out of school, she wouldn't really look at him. Then Brittany whispered to the other girl and the girl said he had to leave right away.

Look at the moon, how big it is. One corner's missing, so yeah, it's still not full. Look how there's a path on the water, not silver but gold, it looks like you could walk on it. Now the wind's ruffling up the waves, so it looks like a gold chain. He could paint that. . . . Hey, did he hear something?

The Voices, they went away when he started the meds. But they could come back anytime. They never really went away, if you listened really hard, you could hear—

"Danny."

Jesus. Jesus!

"Over here, Danny."

That voice, he remembers!

"Danny."

He spins around fast, tries to—tries to run, but the man's

faster. He pushes Danny hard with both hands on his chest and he's
falling. His back crunches on the edge of the dock, he twists and
grabs the planks but the man stomps on his hand, so hard he

SCREAMS

FALLS

COLD

PLEASE HELP ME PLEASE

CLAWS to the . . . CLAWS to the . . .

Fights to get up to the—get up to the—

so cold down here . . .

Can't . . . can't . . . can't . . .

can't

"So sorry to wake you," Deirdre's voice purred in Mike's ear.

He moved his cell a few inches away. For a moment there, he'd thought the woman was in bed with him.

"Deirdre? What the hell time is it?"

"Five forty A.M. Something's happened, Michael. Something I know you'll want to hear about right away."

She sounded almost eager. And that meant something was wrong.

"Hold on a minute." He returned his cell to the nightstand, sat up on the edge of the bed, and rubbed his face hard.

"OK," he said after a minute. "Shoot."

"Danny Armenta. You know, the Mexican guy who murdered the girl?"

Mike tensed. "I know who you're talking about."

"Well, he's dead. He drowned himself. A jogger found the body on the beach, maybe twenty minutes ago."

Now Mike was wide awake, so awake he nearly bolted for the door. "Where, Deirdre? *Where.*"

"Hey, take it easy. East Beach, near the volleyball courts. Looks like he jumped off the wharf in the night."

"Christ. Is the body still there?"

"Yeah. Forensics just arrived. And we need to get it off the beach before some family on vacation decides to take an early-morning stroll. I'm getting dressed and heading on over." She made her last statement in a low confiding tone, as if she were suggesting he might want to come over and dress her himself.

"Deirdre, hold on. Have you informed the next of kin?"

"Not yet. I'll go around myself, after I've looked at the body. I—"

"No!" Mike reminded himself to calm down, and took a slow breath. You couldn't move Deirdre Krause by pushing her, he knew that. Only sugar would work.

"I'll take care of that, Deirdre. You need to be there at the scene. Armenta was a prime suspect in a murder investigation. This has to be done by the book, no loose ends."

"I suppose you're right." She sounded flattered. "Michael, I've got to run. Will I see you down at the beach?"

"Count on it."

"Good. And again, sorry I had to wake you up. I can just imagine how cozy you were."

Fifteen minutes later, Mike parked his truck on Cliff and trudged up El Balcón. The day promised to be warm: already the sun blazed, and the blue waves flashed like mirror shards.

When he got up to the top of the hill, he turned and looked back across the harbor. He could see a tiny patch of green at the far end of East Beach. That would be the canvas awning forensics had placed over the body.

His cell rang and he jumped. Mike glanced at it: Deirdre again. He switched it off and slipped it back in his pocket. He had to take care of this now, or the bad news would be delivered by Krause. He headed for the house.

Jaymie needed to hear it first, he decided. She'd know what to say to the family. But Mike wasn't sure which bedroom Jaymie was using, now that she had a houseful of guests.

He didn't want to risk knocking on a window and having it be the wrong one.

Debating his next move, Mike stepped onto the small concrete porch. He paused, listening. He thought he could hear the TV. The kids must be up already, watching cartoons with the sound turned low. He hesitated, then tapped softly on the door. What else could he do?

Oh, man. It was the little guy who opened it.

"Hi! I thought—I thought maybe you were my brother."

"Hey, buddy. No . . . no, it's just me."

"Jaymie, wake up!"

I found myself looking into a pair of big round eyes, an inch or two from my own. "What is it, Chuy? Is something wrong?"

"That man is here. He wants to talk to you."

Suddenly I was wide awake. "Man? What man?" I sat up in bed.

"The really big one. You know, your boyfriend."

"Do you mean Mike?"

"Yeah. Mike." He nodded vigorously, then turned and high-tailed it out the bedroom door.

I grabbed my jeans off the chair and pulled them on over my underpants. Decided the T-shirt I'd slept in was OK, and didn't bother to search for my bra. Damn, it was early. Why was Mike—but then I stopped still. Dread seeped into my body. He would have news, and it wouldn't be good.

The front door was open. I looked out and saw Mike standing beside the garage. He was examining the hinges, testing them. He turned and looked toward the house. When our eyes met, his hands fell to his sides.

I walked quickly toward him, but I felt as if I was moving in slow motion. "What is it?"

"It's Danny, Jaymie. I got a call."

It made no sense. I looked over at the studio. "What about Danny? He's probably sound asleep."

"He's . . . not in the studio, Jaymie. He went out last night. And he didn't come home."

How would Mike know? But then I saw. I saw how Mike was easing me into it, easing me into a bad world I'd visited before, a hurtful place I didn't want to be. "Say it, Mike. Just say it."

"Danny's dead, Jaymie. They found him down on East Beach at dawn. He drowned."

Why was Mike holding me? I could stand up on my own. But then the wave toppled over me, the tsunami, for the second time.

"I can open the door for myself," I said when we got to the truck.

"Jaymie, listen to me. What's happened isn't your fault."

I glared at him till he looked away.

"After we view the body, we'll go by and get Gabi. We need to be quick about it," I said after we'd driven for a few minutes. "I don't want the police informing Alma and the kids. I have to come back and tell them myself."

"Take it easy. You did everything—"

"Why does this happen!" I exploded.

Mike pulled into the beachside parking lot and reached for me. "Jaymie, *listen*—"

"Don't," I hissed. "Don't try to pretend."

"Pretend what?"

"Pretend I'm not responsible for Danny's death."

"Responsible? You're the one who was trying to help."

"Trying. Yeah, trying, I'm always fucking trying." Tears stung my eyes like sharp little needles. "If I hadn't tried so hard, he'd still be alive."

I wiped my eyes on my sleeve, opened the truck door and stepped down to the loose dry sand. Mike was beside me, matching my stride as I plodded across the beach toward the green canopy.

Half a dozen cops and techs were clustered together. One caught sight of us and said something. All the heads turned in our direction.

"There's Deirdre," I muttered.

"I'll deal with Deirdre. You won't be doing anybody but her a favor if you jump on her."

The gaggle was still staring at us by the time we were within speaking distance. "Mike? I expected you to come on your own," Deirdre began. "Because actually, Ms. Zarlin here—"

"Officer Krause? I'd like to speak with you in private," Mike said evenly.

Yesterday, I'd have bridled at the way Deirdre now cooed and melted toward him as he walked her away. Yesterday that would have mattered. Not today.

I turned my attention to the body sprawled on the hard damp sand.

That's what I wanted it to be: just a body. An object, a thing.

But no, it was *Danny*. My hand flew to my mouth, too late to hold in a moan.

Danny lay entangled in his sweatshirt. A bit of tar-encrusted seaweed was stuck to his bluish cheek, a longer piece wrapped twice around his neck. And dear God, Danny's expression: his eyes were open wide, staring up at the sky, and his face was frozen in a grimace of horror and shock.

I promised myself, right then and there, I'd make certain Alma didn't see her son before the undertaker had done his job.

I knelt down beside him and reached for his free left hand.

"Don't touch," one of Deirdre's henchmen barked.

I ignored him. I had to make contact, to warm Danny with

my own flesh and blood. To pull him back to me, to his family, to the world of the living.

"Hey, didn't you hear what I said?" A rough hand grabbed my shoulder.

Do your job, I ordered myself. *You have only a few minutes here. Before Deirdre returns, observe everything you can.*

"OK, OK." I released Danny's hand.

It was clear he'd struggled mightily against death. The zippered sweatshirt bound his arms and torso like a straitjacket. There were no visible marks on his neck, though the seaweed could be obscuring something. And . . . my attention returned to his hand.

I bent close to examine Danny's fingernails.

"All right, lady, that's it."

Another swift look, and I got to my feet. I'd seen all I needed to see.

"This is the body of Daniel Armenta," I stated. "He lived with me, and I'm making the official identification. For your information, he didn't commit suicide. Danny was murdered."

I looked out over the channel, where the water glimmered like crushed foil under a mother-of-pearl sky.

The ocean had flung Danny's body up on the beach at high tide, then retreated. As if Mother Nature wanted we humans to witness just what we could do, to one of our own.

Mike switched on the big throaty engine. "We're headed over to the Westside. I phoned Gabi, and she's waiting for us." He turned to study me, one hand on the wheel. "They're saying it was suicide, Jaymie. But I just heard you call it murder."

"Right." I stared out the window. A group of kids were seated at a picnic table on the edge of the beach parking lot, sharing a before-school joint. "Danny didn't jump off the wharf, Mike. He was shoved."

"How do you know?"

"He fought like hell against death. There are splinters under his fingernails, and a bruise on the back of his hand. Forensics will be able to compare the wood splinters with the timbers on the pier. Danny must have grabbed the edge as he went over and held on for dear life. But the crush of a boot or a shoe forced him to let go."

"Christ. What else did you see?"

"The jacket, Mike. Danny struggled. He fought so hard in the water he literally tied himself up in knots." My own voice sounded hollow, robot-like.

"OK. But something doesn't add up." Mike backed the truck out of the lot. "If it wasn't suicide and he was pushed, why didn't he swim to shore? It seems like he could have made it, from the end of the wharf to the beach. Most kids in Santa Barbara know how to swim."

Abruptly I was sick of it all, sick to death. Danny, his blank glazed-over eyes staring skyward . . . "Mike, pull over."

I opened the truck door and leaned out, retching into the street. I'd had no breakfast, and nothing but a strand of sour spit dribbled from my mouth.

Mike offered me a bandana. "Here. It's clean." I shut the door and took it, wiping my mouth and chin.

"Well, not anymore," he tried to joke.

"I'll answer your question. Then I don't want to talk about it. I'm done."

"Sure." Mike lifted my hair off my sweaty forehead, as if I were a little kid.

"I'm pretty sure the coroner will find that Danny struggled and then drowned, with hypothermia being a contributing factor."

"This isn't San Francisco Bay, Jaymie, and Danny was young. It's cold, but people swim that distance all the time without wet suits."

"Yes, and how many of them are on an antipsychotic medication? Danny's meds could have lowered his core body temperature. What do you want to bet Danny's killer counted on that?"

The three of us sat packed together in the pickup. Nobody said much. Gabi, on my right, seemed shocked into silence.

Mike slowed the truck to a crawl as we turned up my drive. How I dreaded what was to come: we were bearing the worst sort of news.

Chuy's pert face appeared in the window, then disappeared. A moment later, he banged open the door and hurtled down the steps in his red and blue superhero pajamas. "Hi!" he yelled. "Mom's making pancakes!"

"How do I tell them?" Gabi's voice cracked. "What do I say?"

"We'll do it together," I replied.

The three of us climbed out. Mike picked up Chuy and gripped him in a bear hug, put him down gently, and turned away. "Damn . . ." He seemed about to break into tears.

"Mike, can you stay out here with Chuy for a little while? Gabi and I will go in."

"Yeah. Yeah, we'll pretend-drive the truck." Mike gripped my shoulder. "Good luck."

Inside, Aricela sat at the small kitchen table. Her spelling homework was spread out on the yellow Formica top. It struck me I'd never seen such a sunny, unclouded smile as hers at that moment.

Alma turned from the stove. "You're both just in time for—" She stopped and searched our faces. "What—what—is it *Danny?*"

When I nodded, her face crumpled, and the spatula clattered to the floor.

One week later, Alma, Aricela, and Chuy departed for Mexico.

"I must take my children home. Santa Barbara has some

very bad people, evil ones," Alma muttered to me at the bus station.

"I know we've talked about this," I pleaded. "But I have to ask you again. Don't you think you'd be better off staying here?"

"What, for money, do you mean? Better clothes for the kids?" Alma shrugged heavily. "That doesn't matter to me anymore. I have to go home, take my children back to where I was born."

The coroner had refused to release Danny's body. I'd promised Alma I'd take possession of the remains when the time came, and ship them on to Michoacán for burial. Thank God, Alma didn't seem to blame me for Danny's death. But it didn't matter: I knew.

I knelt down to talk to Chuy and Aricela. "I loved having you live with me. When you come back, please stay with me again, OK?" I stroked Aricela's satin-smooth cheek and gave Chuy a high five. I wanted to say something about Danny, but my throat swelled.

It was quiet Aricela who found words. "Jaymie? Danny told Mom he wanted to stay at your place forever. He really liked you, I know that for sure."

But Alma had the last word as she boarded the bus. "You know what the gangs have always called it? *Santa Bruta*. I think that is this city's true name."

The house was an empty shell now, still as a grave. My work was little more than a cruel charade, of no use or good to anyone. It was time to move on.

"Jaymie Zarlin! How are you, sweetie? Honestly, it's been what—nearly three years since I sold you that cute little bungalow?" Tiffany Tang's voice hadn't changed a dot, and neither had she. "I was so surprised to get your message. Ready for an upgrade, are we?"

"Not exactly, Tiff. Actually, I'm leaving town."

"You *are*? But where *to*, sweetie? Where could you possibly want to go after living here?"

"I haven't thought much about it. New Mexico, maybe."

"*New Mexico*? Isn't that a little far *inland*? You shock me, sweetie. I always say we cling to our cliffs like barnacles here, they have to pry us off with crowbars." Tiff was quiet for an unusually long moment. "Oh, I get it," she said at last. "You've met a man. Congratulations!"

"No." I stared out the window at Santa Cruz Island, wrapped in its misty white scarf. "It's not because of a guy."

"Are you sure? Because nobody leaves town unless it's for love. Or because they're broke, of course. But if you're broke, just do what most people do. Take in lodgers. You could move into the studio, couldn't you? Why, with that view, a two-bedroom on the Mesa? You could get at least thirty-five hundred a month."

"Tiff? I just want to leave town."

"Can't say I've heard that before." Her voice soured. "This is *paradise*, sweetie."

"Guess I'm sick and tired of paradise."

"Hm. I read something in the paper. It's this Solstice murder business, am I right? Rough patch for you, sweetie. Tell you what. We'll sell that bungalow of yours and you'll be so impressed with the money, you'll decide to turn around and buy— let's see—how about a cute little condo? No upkeep, Jaymie. I've got a great one over on—"

"Tiff? No thanks."

"OK, sweetie. OK. I'll do some comps, we'll talk. When do you want the sign to go up?"

"Yesterday," I replied.

Mike saw the sign at the base of the hill and slammed on the brakes. 12 EL BALCÓN, FOR SALE. An über-confident Tiffany Tang, purveyor of fine properties on the American Riviera, beamed forth in vibrant color. Through some trick of printing, she tracked Mike with her gaze as he committed a U-turn and barreled up the steep drive.

The sagging garage door was open all the way, revealing an empty space. No El Camino, so Jaymie was out. Still, he drove on and parked in front of the house.

Mike lowered his window and switched off the engine. He could hear the bark of a sea lion, probably coming from some unattended boat anchored in the marina.

An uneasy feeling crept over him as he studied the house. The curtains were pulled across the windows, although it wasn't yet dark. Had Jaymie jumped ship?

He pulled out his phone and punched in her number. No reply. A mechanical voice said, *The mailbox is full.*

"Fuck!" Abruptly, Mike felt punched in the gut. He shoved open the door and got out.

He stood still for a moment and listened to the wind whistling through the big flat-topped Torrey pine behind the garage. "Girl, don't you even think about running out on me," he muttered as he crossed the gravel drive.

When he pounded on the door, the grasshoppers fell still. He stalked around the corner of the house, ignoring the 270-degree view. The window off the kitchen was uncovered.

He put his nose near the glass and peered in. To his relief, the yellow Formica table still stood under the window. And if Jaymie had left town, she hadn't bothered to clean up first: the counter was stacked with dirty dishes.

Mike felt relief for about one minute. Then a fresh wave of worry washed over him. Had something happened, something bad? He rapped hard on the kitchen window and shouted her name. "Jaymie! Jaymie, are you in there?" The silence scared him.

In three strides, he was at the kitchen door. It was locked, but the old sun-and-salt-beaten wood was weak. He put his shoulder into it, and the door burst into pick-up sticks.

Mike half fell to the floor, regained his feet, and slammed through the rooms. The house was dead empty.

He returned to Jaymie's bedroom and stood beside her unmade bed. Blankets were thrown back, and clothes were scattered around on the floor.

Mike bent down and picked up a T-shirt he recognized. He pressed the dark blue fabric to his nose and mouth and breathed in. The fragrance of her, faint but unmistakable, only heightened his dread. *Please, let her be OK.*

"What in heaven's name are you doing?"

He spun around. Jaymie stood in the doorway with her hands on her hips. Her hair looked as if it hadn't been combed in days, but a very self-possessed expression filled her eyes.

"I thought you were—I—" He dropped the incriminating garment to the floor.

"Let me guess. You thought I was missing, so you decided to sniff my shirt. What, you planned to track my scent?"

"Uh—I—" He couldn't think of one reasonable thing to say.

"Yes?"

"I was praying, I guess." His throat choked. "Praying you were OK."

"Everything I touch turns to shit." I tipped back the amber bottle and let the last drip of beer trickle down my throat. "Can you take Dexter for a while, Mike? He'll be ready to leave the vet's in a day or so. I'm just not up to taking care of him."

"You're giving away your dog? Jesus, Jaymie. That's what suicidal people do."

"I'm not suicidal, and I'm not giving Dex away. I just—I think he might be safer with you for now."

"As far as that goes, I think you're right." The old aluminum lawn chair squeaked as Mike shifted his weight.

"Anyway, it's time for me to move on. Paradise just isn't for me." I cradled the empty in my hands.

"Paradise—the American Riviera—that's chamber of commerce crap, and you know it. The whole world is limbo, and this town's no different. Stuck somewhere between heaven and hell."

"Tiffany Tang wouldn't agree. You should read her copy: *a little chunk of paradise fell to earth at 12 El Balcón.*"

"It's what we make of it, I suppose." Mike leaned forward. "Jaymie? What can I do to help? Besides cinching up your bootstraps for you, that is."

I ignored his jibe. "Do? Nothing. No, wait a minute...." I worked at peeling the label off the empty. "There is something. It's not for me, it's for the case."

"What is it?"

"Remember I told you Danny said he went back to the dressing room because a man's voice called him? I told you he made it sound hollow and deep when he mimicked it, kind of like an announcer's voice."

"I remember."

"Later on, I thought of something I'd noticed in the dressing room."

Mike fixed me with his sheriff's stare. "What was that?"

"An old-fashioned megaphone. It had been tipped out of the prop bin."

"You're thinking somebody should check the mouthpiece for DNA."

"It's worth a shot. The killer could have grabbed the megaphone on the spur of the moment, and not thought about wiping it off later."

"I'll call forensics first thing in the morning," Mike replied. "They already picked up the bootlace and confirmed it was dipped in Lili's blood, by the way. They're going to wonder why I'm taking such an interest."

"You'll think of something to tell them, Mike." I shoved back my chair and stood. "Anyway. It's not my concern, not anymore."

"I can't believe you're talking like that." Mike drained his own bottle. "Say, where's the El Camino?"

"Gone to a new owner."

"What? You sold Brodie's car?"

"No, I'd never do that. I donated it to the homeless shelter," I said in a small voice. "They'll sell it and use the cash. That way Brodie's car will do someone some good."

"So, what, you're leaving town on foot?"

"I'm leasing a car, starting tomorrow."

"I don't know what to say. Brodie loved that car."

I leaned over the stone wall, into the night. I could smell the ocean, the peculiar and pleasant blend of brine and tar characteristic of the Santa Barbara Channel. "I might as well tell you, Mike. I'm not waiting for the house to sell. I'm moving out next week, putting my stuff in storage, and closing down the agency." Far below, a car alarm began to sound.

"Jaymie. Don't do it." Mike's voice had turned flat and hard.

"I have to get away from all this. I'm sorry."

"Are you?" He stood and kicked the chair away with his foot. "You know I love you. I've told you every damn way I can think of! Why do I stick around? Because I'm pretty damn sure you love me too. I don't see it all the time—you make sure of that. But you slip up now and then."

My eyes stung with tears I refused to release. "Mike, you and I—it's not possible."

"I just don't get it! What is the problem?"

I left the patio and headed back to the studio, where I'd spent the afternoon curled up on Danny's bed. I tried to close the door after me, but Mike pushed his way in. "Jaymie, for fuck's sake, tell me! I've got a right to know."

"OK, fine! Remember that night at the ranch?" I heard myself snarling like a cornered cat. "Up on the ridge?"

"I remember."

"You were thinking about us having a kid—I know you were."

"I thought about it, that's all. One day in the future, you know?"

"That's what I'm trying to tell you. . . ." But then, I shut my mouth. In spite of my decision to leave town, I didn't think I could bear to never see Mike again. That wasn't part of my plan.

"Say it, Jaymie. I'm fed up with guessing."

I felt myself cave in. "I don't want to have children. Not with you or anyone. I'm just no good at caring for others."

"If you loved me, you wouldn't say that. Wouldn't think that!" The color drained from Mike's face. "Do you love me? Answer me, damn it to hell!"

"I—" Suddenly, I was mute. My mouth gaped open like the mouth of a beached fish.

After a moment, he turned his back on me and walked out the door.

Loneliness slipped into the studio. Loneliness—and a kind of relief. What I'd said to Mike was true, but there was more, further back, deeper inside me. Thank God I didn't have to go there now.

An hour later Mike sent me a text: *I'll pick up the dog from the vet's when he's ready. You're right about one thing—he's safer with me.*

Chapter Fifteen

The next morning, I stumbled up the office steps carrying an armload of knocked-down boxes.

"Miss Jaymie! At last you're here. You—"

"Gabi, can't you see my arms are full?" I peered at her through the screen door.

"Sorry!" Gabi squeezed past me to hold the door open. "What's all this?"

I sidled in and leaned the boxes against the wall. "I've got more out in the car. Be right back."

"Wait, this looks like—like moving day."

"Be right back," I repeated.

By the time I'd retrieved the rest of the boxes from the rented Honda and returned, Gabi had the coffeepot on. Two plump pastries, oozing with chocolate, rested on two pink Fiesta ware plates.

"Miss Jaymie, let's please sit down *right now*, OK?"

We faced each other across the big desk, Gabi in the command position (she had a new favorite book, *Feng Shui for Sure*) and me in the hot seat, as Gabi had taken to calling the visitor's chair.

"You haven't been in for five days. I'm so glad you're here, 'cause two new people already called. One was—"

"Gabi." I set my pink cup in its pink saucer.

"Miss Jaymie, before you say anything—"

"Gabi? Me first."

She dropped her head in defeat. "You're the boss."

"If you say so." I smiled a little. "You're a great PA. It's what you were born to be, and I'm going to help you find another position. Because—"

"Now I'm going to interrupt you for sure!" Gabi jumped to her feet, nearly upsetting her coffee. "I got no papers, you know that. Cleaner, dishwasher, campesina. *That's* what I was born to be!"

Now it was my turn to study the floor.

"I never thought you were a quitter, Miss Jaymie. Other people, never you." The silence swelled.

"People are dying," I finally said. "They're dying because of me. First my brother. Now Danny. Even my dog nearly died. I need to back off and mind my own business."

"Miss Jaymie, I got something to say. First, a dog is a dog. And anyway, it survived. And then . . ." Gabi obviously didn't know what else to say after that.

"Yeah, the dog survived. Minus a leg." I shook my head. "Let's face it, I'm not much of an investigator. I get too involved."

"You get involved, all right." Gabi pushed her cup away. "'Cause you're human, you know? And worse, you're a woman."

A lump formed in my throat. But the last thing I wanted to do was to feel sorry for myself.

"Please, I'm begging you," Gabi persisted. "Wait a little while, OK? You got new customers, more business coming in—"

"I've already given written notice to the rental agency. I'm sorry, Gabi, but we're out in less than three weeks. I plan on leaving sooner than that, but you can suit yourself. Would you hand me the checkbook, please, and a pen?"

Moving in slow motion, Gabi unlocked the top desk drawer with a key on her ring and removed a smaller key. She used that key to open the filing cabinet, then removed a locked security box. "This is a really good system I invented. But what does it matter now?" She unlocked the security box with a key she removed from a magnetic key-keeper stuck under the cabinet drawer, and opened it. Finally, she slid the checkbook across the desk.

I wrote out a check in silence, ripped it from the book, and handed it to her.

"Five thousand dollars," Gabi squeaked. "Made out to me?"

"Your half of the retainer from Mrs. Richter. Another case I botched, by the way. The rich bitch got her dog back and the little boy is lonely again."

"No. You can't give me this."

"Why not? I wouldn't have gotten it in the first place if it wasn't for you."

Gabi bit her lip and stared at me. I could see she was thinking.

"OK, I accept. Thank you." She started to say something more, then abruptly closed her mouth and dropped the check in her bag.

Already, the little house on El Balcón didn't seem like mine anymore. The same mellow evening sun glazed the kitchen window in smoked gold, the same vinegar tang from the ocean drifted in through the open back door. But except for a few sticks of furniture, the small rooms were stripped bare of all that belonged to me.

I dropped down onto a kitchen chair, folded my arms on the table, and rested my head. I'd worked hard all day packing my life away—and Brodie's life, too.

The van was coming in the morning at 7:00 A.M. sharp, to transport the stacked boxes to a storage facility. I was shedding my identity, the way a snake wriggles out of its tattered old skin. The new rattler would turn in the Honda for an RV and hit the road, heading who knew where.

I pushed away worries about gainful employment. I could always get a job writing meaningless newsletters or sending out urgent bulletins about tiny bugs, as I'd done for the grape growers. I'd been pretty good at that.

My eyelids felt heavy. A fly buzzed at the glass, seeking a way out into the declining day.

I must have fallen asleep. When I jerked awake, it was twilight. I raised my head and listened: I could hear a clanking of gears. Something—too big for a car, too small for a truck—was laboring up the drive.

I went to the front door and opened it. An ancient Vee-Dub van, painted white and glowing like the moon in the semi-dark, nosed over the rise.

In the driver's seat was a disturbing apparition. The body was draped in a sack-like garment, and a dark hood covered its head. Two eye holes were cut in the shroud, and the holes turned to meet my gaze.

Charlie and Annie.

The van pulled up, and clunked and sighed to a stop. I descended the steps and walked up to the open window. "Charlie?"

"Come for my horehounds," the voice rasped. "Last chance, I hear."

My eyes filled with tears. "I'm sorry."

"Sorry? Only be sorry if you planned on runnin' off without saying good-bye."

"Sorry, no horehounds." Now I was crying for real.

He extended his scarred hand through the window. "Take it easy, Jaymie. Take it slow."

I took his hand in my own. It felt like a leather garden glove, all rough ridges and bands. "Charlie, do you want to come in?"

"No thank you, Jaymie girl." He chuckled. "As they say, I don't get out much."

I smiled back at the hood, then looked away.

"So what's this I hear about you ditchin' town?"

I couldn't ever lie to Charlie. It would be like lying at the pearly gates. "I'm slinking away," I admitted. "Leaving the scene of the crime, in more ways than one."

"Hmm." In Charlie's scarred throat, this syllable sounded like the rumble of distant thunder. "Like I always say, Jaymie, deep down you know what's best."

In the silence, the foghorn sounded: a heavy fog bank advanced on the coast.

"Just stopped by to say we'll miss you, Annie and me. Been an honor."

"No, Charlie. The honor was all mine."

He waved my words away. "Now, you're sure about this? Sure you're doing what you know's best? Annie wants me to ask you straight out, just to be double sure."

"It's best all the way around."

"Right then, Jaymie. You know your own self." The twin black pools glittered. "Until our paths cross again, may your way be smooth."

"Charlie, wait. I need you to understand." I reached in and grasped his shoulder, so bony and thin beneath the sacking. "What good am I to anyone? I have to let go, leave it behind."

"Not possible, Jaymie. The past is part of you, all the good and the bad mixed in. You'll never leave it behind, not none of it." Gently, he removed my hand from his shoulder and held it. "We gotta be brave. We gotta keep plugging away, face our mistakes. That's all there is to it."

When the Great American Novel had dipped down the drive and disappeared from sight, I went inside and shut the door.

I poured myself a glass of velvet-red wine and wandered back outside to stand in the flower-and-ocean-perfumed night. As I sipped the elixir, a cricket sang its heart out and rats skittered in the brush covering the bank.

Without warning, the big white owl swooped out of the blackness and landed at the very top of the cypress. I held still as the rodents fell silent and the tree branch bowed a little under the exquisite weight of the bird.

Then I drank all the wine so it wouldn't be wasted, pouring the sacred sweetness down my throat and pressing my mouth to my sleeve. When I looked up, I saw the heart-shaped face looking down on me.

"*Forgive me*," I whispered. "*I gave up, but it won't happen again.*"

I went inside and started unpacking.

Humpty Dumpty was going back together, but he wouldn't look quite the way he had before the great fall.

I tried not to fret about Mike. He'd sent me another text stating he'd collected Dexter and paid half the hefty vet bill, and that was the last I'd heard from him. I knew he was furious with me. But I'd been honest with the guy, hadn't I? What he did now was his call.

Tiff Tang was philosophical about the loss of a potential commission, and ripped up the contract. But the El Camino was another story. I contacted the homeless shelter and offered to buy Brodie's car back, but they'd already sold it. The new owner, a sixties guy with a booming voice, remained firm on the phone. "She's a great little ride, and now the deal's done, I don't mind telling you Dudette was a steal. These babies are hot down here in Laguna Beach." His laugh was a snortle. "Guess the sellers weren't so up on what's cool."

"No, I guess not." I sighed. "So there's no way I could persuade you to sell—*Dudette*—back to me?"

"Try me in a year or two, sweetheart." He snortled again. "That's about how long it takes me to wear out my girlfriends, know what I mean?"

The rental agency witch sneered a similar song. "I'm sorry, Ms. Zarlin, but your office suite has already been leased. We do have a refund check waiting for you, your deposit money—

minus the cleaning fee, of course. Plus we had to do some re-
pairs on the unit, so I'm afraid . . ." I held the phone out from
my ear: the woman's staccato sounded like bubble wrap popping.

I thought longingly of my office kitchen, swirling with the
perfumes of strong coffee and Mexican pastry. "I'd like to talk
to the new tenants. Who are they?" Meaning, maybe I'd con-
vince them to change their minds. I could describe the termite
clouds, the general air of decay, and the angry women and men
who stormed in and out of the repo business next door.

"It would be unethical of me to reveal that information,"
Ms. Kraft said starchily.

"I get it. You raised the rent."

"In fact, no. The market would not sustain that at present.
But the new tenant did pay six months in advance."

"Whatever," I huffed. "But don't allow him to move in even
five minutes before the end of the month, or I'll toss him out on
his ear."

But changes had already begun in my absence, I realized as I
wheeled my bike into the bungalow court.

My screen door was spray-painted pink. The solid door,
now a purplish-blue, was open halfway. Indignant, I prepared
myself to do battle. The new tenant had moved in early, just as
I'd suspected he might.

I propped up the bike on its kickstand, yanked back the
squealing screen door, and took a bellicose step inside.

What—was I dreaming? Within, all seemed business as
usual: a delicious aroma welcomed me, and Gabi appeared in
the kitchen doorway with a laden tray in her hands.

"Miss Jaymie! I was so happy to hear your message, that you
would come in today. I got your favorite pastries to celebrate.
How do you like the doors?"

"Very nice," I said faintly. Looking past Gabi, I could see the
kitchen was also transformed.

"Popsicle Pink and Plum Purple. Let's sit down at your table! I haven't painted the front room yet, next weekend maybe. I got lotsa paint. My prima's brother-in-law is a painter, he had some left over and gave me a good deal."

"Let's . . . sit out here in the office, shall we?"

"Uh-oh, a little too bright? Mexicans like bright colors. Pink and purple are my personal favorites," Gabi added unnecessarily. She stepped forward and set the tray on the desk.

"You know, it's very exciting for me." She smoothed her paint-speckled hands down her thighs. "I always wanted my own office. My very own!"

My mouth fell open. "Are you—you're not—"

"Yes! I'm the new tenant. I used the check you gave me, the money from Mrs. Richter, you know?" She sat down in the command chair behind the desk. I observed that a newfound dignity had entered her bearing.

"I thought maybe I'd run my cleaning business out of here. Hire one or two people. And I got a new name: Sparkleberry Cleaning Service."

"That's very—nice." I dropped into the hot seat, so appropriately named.

"It is, isn't it? Sparkle, you know, cause everything's so clean? And berry, 'cause of my favorite colors." Bright-eyed, she studied me over the rim of her cup. "Miss Jaymie, listen. I got this idea. It's against the contract, but who cares. Do you want to sublet from me? Cause something is telling me you're gonna stay."

I sputtered the coffee. "You mean share an office with—*Sparkleberry?*"

"Sure. Look at it this way." Gabi beamed. "Your rent will be half what it used to be. I'll still be your PA for free. And your office will always sparkle! That's what they call a win-win."

"I'm just not sure the two businesses are—uh—compatible."

"Oh they are, believe me. I clean people's houses, and you clean up people's problems."

"Well, that's a thought." I cleared my throat. "One thing's for sure: next time I'll think twice about quitting."

"I would if I was you," Gabi smiled sweetly. "Because your sublease will be for one full year."

I had to laugh. "OK, I hear you. But I have a request of my own. As subleaser, I've got a few rights. The painting's done, OK? Enough with the purple and pink."

"No problem! I hold the lease, Miss Jaymie, but you're still the boss."

Had I detected a sly little smile?

It was just after one in the afternoon, and the Molinas' cottage garden was quiet, drowsing in sunshine. Bees droned in the citrus trees. A blue jay scolded me raucously, protesting my presence.

I'd decided to visit Teresa when Claudia was at school. The last thing I wanted at this point was a confrontation with the Tasmanian devil. It was time for me to pick up the strands of the investigation, and this was the place to begin.

The door was cracked open. I knocked and it fell away. "Teresa? Hello, are you there?" I called into the drape-shrouded room.

I'd hardly expected to find a fully recovered Teresa already moving on from her daughter's death. Still, I was taken aback: the woman who shuffled to the doorway didn't look like the same person I'd met before. She was gripped in a deep depression.

Teresa wore a man's worn flannel robe, which bagged open to reveal a food-stained nightgown. Her skin was puffy, discolored under the eyes, and her mouth was slack. She looked as if she hadn't slept for weeks. Her eyes were sharp, though, burning.

"Teresa," I said gently. "May I come in?"

"I . . . forget who you—" Her voice was a croak.

"I'm Jaymie Zarlin. If you don't mind, I'd like to talk with you for a bit."

She nodded slightly and stepped aside.

Misery had settled into the room, staining the atmosphere like smoke. Every curtain was drawn, and the only light came from the single candle flickering on the altar. An unpleasant smell lingered. My gaze fell on the birdcage covered with an old tablecloth.

Teresa gestured with a limp hand. "Lili's bird—it's dead in there. It couldn't go on living . . . it had to be with her."

Her words chilled me. "Teresa can we talk in the kitchen?"

Without answering, she shuffled ahead of me.

The square kitchen table was littered with food-encrusted dishes and a dirty cat's bowl. Teresa eased herself onto one of the chairs and I sat in the other, facing her.

It was all I could do to stay put and not hop up and clear the table. I felt an urge to scour: the kitchen, the house, and even Teresa, who needed a shower and a shampoo.

"I'm sorry, Teresa. I can see how terribly hard this is for you."

Her head slumped.

"I won't stay for long, not unless you want me to. But I have something to tell you." I wanted to hold her hand while I talked, but the table was so covered with crap I couldn't reach her.

I got up and moved my chair around to the end of the table. When I took Teresa's hand in my own, I nearly dropped it in surprise: it felt tissue-light, freeze-dried.

"Teresa, do you know about Danny Armenta?"

She nodded once, without raising her head. "Dead."

"Yes, I'm afraid so." I pressed the fragile hand. "I want you to know he didn't harm Lili, not in any way." No need, I decided, to tell her Danny had been murdered too.

"Then tell me who . . . who . . ." Her voice trailed off as she raised her head and met my eyes.

"I don't know yet. That's why I need to ask you more questions, Teresa. Because I promise you, I *will* find out who did it."

"It won't bring my baby girl back."

"No, it won't. But they're going to close the case, Teresa. The killer will go free. That matters, doesn't it?"

"Yes." Her voice grew stronger, harsh. "Yes, it matters. Ask me anything."

"Thank you. First, about Lili's costume. It was made down at the Guild, right?"

"Yes, the girls made it down there. But Lili brought it home the night before the parade, and I worked on it too."

"Why did she bring it home?"

"The seams were scratching her, driving her crazy. They used the wrong kind of thread. I opened it all up and sewed it with nice cotton thread, soft."

"And in the morning? Did she try it on here at the house?"

"Yes, she said she tried it on and it was good. I was already at work, but she called me and told me." Teresa dropped her eyes again to the floor. "Lili loved her costume."

"I'm sure she did," I said quietly. "So, what I'm getting to is this. Was there any reason she might have wanted to change out of it in a hurry—after the parade?"

"No, I don't think so." A shadow of a smile flitted across her face like a moth. "She loved how she looked in it."

"That's what I thought. Now, there's something else I need to ask you about, Teresa. The Stellatos. I know you worked for them for quite a while."

"Twelve years. But not for over a year now."

"Twelve years? You must know quite a bit about them."

"I guess."

"Would you mind telling me a little?"

"Well . . . Maryjune, she's a nice lady. Her husband—" Teresa shrugged. "Mr. Stellato gave me a lot of money when he fired me. But he's mean. He yells a lot at his wife."

"What about Lance?"

"Lance? Lazy. Always a messy room."

Clearly, Teresa had no idea Lance had manipulated Lili into having sex. I decided there was no need to tell her now.

"About Vince Stellato. Does he have any girlfriends?"

She slowly withdrew her hand from mine. "I don't know if I should . . ."

"Teresa, listen to me. Personally, I couldn't care less about Stellato. But you have to understand: this is how I fit the pieces of the puzzle together."

"OK, I'll tell you. Mr. Stellato, he has a girlfriend—just one. All the time I was there, the same one. Sometimes she even called the house."

"Do you know the woman's name?"

"No. None of my business."

"Does Lance know about her, do you think?"

"He knows." Teresa nodded. "One time he even mentioned it to me. He said it was like his dad had two wives."

"You've been very helpful, Teresa. What can I do for you?"

"There's nothing. Nothing anybody can do."

"How about Claudia? How is she?"

"Claudia?" Teresa shrugged. Leaning heavily on the table, she raised herself to her feet. "OK, I suppose."

I followed Teresa back into the living room, where she halted. I understood she wanted me to join her at Lili's altar.

Several new items had been added since my earlier visit: concert tickets, a small makeup bag, and a blue pottery bowl holding three mottled oranges glowing in the candlelight.

"You haven't found La Virgen de Guadalupe," Teresa murmured. It was a statement of fact, not a question. "The medallion belongs here."

"I haven't forgotten, Teresa. I will find it, as I promised."

"When you find the killer, you will find the medallion." Teresa's voice was growing more anguished.

"Yes. Yes, I think you're right."

Teresa plucked one of the oranges from the bowl, and I

smelled the sharp scent of citrus as her fingers dug into the rind. Her face contorted with pain. Then, with both hands, she ripped open the orange.

I gasped: was it some trick of the candlelight? The interior of the fruit was dark, the purplish color of clotted blood. As Teresa dug her fingers further into the flesh, the bloody juice trickled over her hands to her wrists.

"Teresa, that orange—what's—wrong with it?"

"It's a blood orange. They grow in my garden. It looks so pretty on the outside, doesn't it?" She was panting hard, as if she'd run a long race. "Like life, that's what I think. Pretty on the outside, but inside, so ugly and cruel!"

Her hands fell open, and the mangled fruit dropped to the floor.

I climbed into the Honda, pulled the door shut, and closed my eyes. Life was brutal, all right. I couldn't argue with Teresa on that. The innocent ones were ground down, buried. Then the corrupt waltzed over their graves.

As Charlie said, you just had to keep plugging away.

I snapped the elastic band off my notebook. Next on my list was Jared Crowley. He was no innocent, I was certain of that. But was he corrupt? Time to find out.

I reviewed what I'd jotted down. Working backward: at 3:19 P.M. on the day of the murder, Shawna had taken a photo of Jared and Lili getting into the BMW at the park . . . 3:15, a photo of Jared and Lili walking to the BMW . . . 3:14, Jared talking to Lili, probably telling her she had to go to the Guild warehouse to change out of her costume . . . 3:12, Jared studying his phone. Abruptly, I choked.

Jared studying his phone. Damn! I thumped a fist on the dash, frustrated at my own slow-wittedness.

Fixated on Shawna's snaps, I'd forgotten all about the primary function of a phone, which was not to take photos but to communicate. Jared studying his phone? Sure. The guy was most likely reading a text message.

And if that message ordered Jared to drive Lili down to the warehouse, the sender could be Lili's killer.

I grabbed my own phone as I switched on the ignition. "Gabi, I need you to check something. If I remember right, Jared Crowley works at Olio e Vino. Would you get me their number?"

"Miss Jaymie? First I think you better come back to the office." Gabi's voice was tight as a rubber band. "We got a little problem here."

"I know you speak Spanish and I know you aren't deaf. Now sit up and get your feet off that chair!" It was Gabi's voice, all right, but I'd never heard her so mad. I paused on the office steps, just outside the screen door.

Then, an insolent girl's voice sounded: "Say the magic word and maybe I will."

"The magic word is *now*! I'm telling you"—I drew open the door just as Gabi jumped up behind her desk. She saw me and her face flooded with relief. "Miss Jaymie, thank goodness you're here!"

"To the rescue," I sighed. "Hey, Claudia. What's up?"

"Nothin'." The kid nonchalantly pulled a pair of earbuds from her pocket and stuck them in her ears. Her feet remained where they were: pressed firmly against the chair arm.

"Miss Jaymie," Gabi said airily. "You know what this girl reminds me of?"

"Now, Gabi—"

"Tinker Bell. So dainty and small, you know? Tinker Bell the fairy, that's who."

Apparently Claudia had no problem hearing through the earbuds. She leaped to her feet, her face scrunched and red. "I'll make you sorry you said that."

"No you won't," Gabi snapped back. "Now sit down the

right way with your feet on the floor, and shut up if you want to stay. Otherwise I'm calling a cop I happen to know."

I listened, fascinated, reluctant to intervene. Two worthy opponents, head-butters, one with youth and energy on her side, the other with age and all the cunning the years can bring.

"Call all the cops you want," Claudia said archly. "They don't scare me."

"Oh they don't? What do you weigh, maybe ninety pounds after Thanksgiving dinner?"

"Ninety-four," the girl shot back.

"Ninety-four, my, my. Well, this cop I know—he's Miss Jaymie's boyfriend, by the way—he weighs maybe two and a half times what you do." Gabi settled back into her desk chair and raised an eyebrow at me. "Oh yes, I'm really sure she could handle him."

Claudia curled one corner of her lip in a snarl. "Jaymie, I came here to talk to you. Do I hafta put up with this shit?"

I parked my messenger bag on the corner of the desk. "I need to go over something with Gabi first. Then you and I will talk."

"What*evah*." She hopped up and walked over to the open window. Deadbeat started to shriek, and Claudia shrieked right back.

"Gabi," I shouted over the din. "I need you to call a restaurant, Olio e Vino, and ask—" But Gabi wasn't listening. She was staring at Claudia's back. I followed her gaze: a tattoo of a snake crawled up Claudia's neck from under her white T-shirt.

Gabi shook her head sadly at me. "That one's not like a girl. She wants to make herself *ugly*."

Claudia spun around. "I heard that. You got a problem with the way I look?"

Gabi ignored the question and asked one of her own instead. "You're never gonna get a boyfriend, looking and acting like that. Don't you like boys?"

"Sure, they're OK. I just don't wanna fuck them."

Gabi sucked in her breath. "This is a place of business! In here you don't talk like that!"

"Claudia," I said firmly.

"OK, OK. Hey. I wanna glass of water."

"In the kitchen. Glasses are in the cupboard over the sink." Fortunately, a week before I'd taken down the disturbing photos of Lili's mutilated body and tucked them away out of sight.

The kid disappeared. The cupboard banged shut—of course—and the tap ran, for way longer than was necessary. "Jesus, please help me," Gabi muttered.

"OK, Gabi, let's get down to business." I sat in the hot seat.

"No, *listen*," Gabi insisted.

All I could hear was the sound of cellophane rattling. "She's stealing my chocolates," Gabi hissed. "The little *rata!*"

But then, just as I groaned in frustration, there came from the kitchen a sharp cry of pain.

I shoved back the chair and ran to the doorway.

Claudia stood before the wall, her skinny arms wrapped tightly around her thin chest. She was staring at a captioned photo of Lance Stellato. "It says—it says he—forced my sister to have sex. *Forced*—"

"Claudia, listen to me."

With a high-pitched scream, Claudia ripped the photo from the wall and turned on me. Fury rampaged in her eyes. "He raped her!"

"That was almost two years ago. Listen to me—" I stepped forward and grasped the wildcat by her shoulders.

But she twisted out of my grip and bolted for the door. Before I could react, she was gone.

Chapter Sixteen

It was an evening in midweek, and the national economy was struggling. Even so, the upscale Olio e Vino was packed to the gills with the dinner crowd.

I stood in a doorway across the street, observing the scene in the restaurant. The view in through the huge plate-glass window was excellent: apparently those who could afford to pay through the nose for a few tattered scraps of radicchio were happy to be observed by the peons in the street.

Everyone inside Olio was putting on a show, but no one more than the waiters, and no waiter more than Jared Crowley. Dressed in a freshly ironed white shirt and black slacks, his crisp blond hair gleamed platinum under the halogen lights. Even from this distance I could see how he affected an indifferent attitude toward the more submissive diners, and employed an obsequious touch when dealing with the dominant types.

Twenty minutes into the show, Jared disappeared. Another waiter responded to a crooked finger from one of Jared's tables. I figured my prey must be on a break.

I crossed the street and entered the rarified atmosphere. Chatter and laughter, lights and delectable odors assailed me. I'd missed dinner, and my stomach sat up and begged. I tried not to think about food, glorious food. Because what did I have at home waiting for me, a frozen Salisbury steak?

"May I help you?" The hostess, who was probably also the manager, wasn't sure if I'd come to eat or to present a problem. A hard edge ran just under her polite words. My jeans and T-shirt were not standard attire at Olio, but Santa Barbarans tend to be scruffy, and no doubt it could be tricky to distinguish the casual rich from the truly impoverished like myself.

"I'd like to speak with one of your employees. Jared Crowley."

The hostess was in her fifties and rather handsome, in a plastic-surgery sort of way. Time for more work, though: the scoop neck of her sleeveless silk top revealed a good five inches of sagging cleavage. "I'm sorry. We ask our employees to conduct personal business outside work hours." Her eyes had narrowed.

"I understand, but this is urgent. It shouldn't take long."

"Well, if it's urgent . . . what did you say it's about?"

"I didn't, actually. It wouldn't be appropriate for me to say."

She shrugged. "Oh, all right. Jared's out in the back, taking a break. Make it quick, though. He needs to be on the floor in five." She nodded at a swing door, then turned away.

I pushed through the door and found myself in the kitchen. A cook, one of four, was furious about something. He slammed a raw chicken breast down on the floor, then glared at me, challenging me to object.

"Where can I find Jared Crowley?"

"What?" he yelled. But then he pointed toward a heavy door set in the back wall.

I went through and found myself in a small, poorly lit yard paved in concrete. The space contained a metal table and chairs and an urn for cigarette butts, nothing more. A cyclone fence separated the space from an alley.

Jared sat at the table. The tip of his cigarette glowed orange-red.

"Chasing me down to my place of employment," he said smoothly. "I don't think I like it."

"Sorry about that, Jared." I made my voice as slippery-smooth as his. "Actually, that's not true: I don't much care if you like it or not."

He pulled the cigarette from his mouth and stubbed it out on the tabletop. "What the fuck do you want."

"You know what I want. Information. And just so we understand each other, with what I already know about you, I could go straight to the police."

His face became a smooth unreadable mask. "Who says you haven't?"

"I do." I dropped into the opposite chair. "Know why?"

Jared curled a corner of his upper lip, but kept silent.

"I know you're involved, but I doubt you killed Lili Molina. I think you know who did, though."

"I'm not involved in anything. And how the fuck should I know?"

"You lied to me, Jared."

A group of drunken young people wove by the fence. "Make nice now," one of them taunted. I let the silence return.

"I lied?" he sputtered at last. "That's bullshit, lady."

"Is it? You said Lili asked you to drive her back to the warehouse the afternoon she was murdered. That's just not true, is it. You drove her, all right, but it wasn't her idea to go."

"Go fuck yourself." Even in the half-light, I could see the look of a hunted animal creep into Jared's eyes. "I—did—not—kill—Lili. Get it?"

"Maybe not. But the person who texted you probably did." The only sounds now were the rasp of a cricket under the table and the muffled traffic noise out on the street.

"Look, Jared. Let me be plain. I know somebody texted you and told you to drive Lili down to the warehouse. Either you followed her inside and raped and killed her, or the person who texted you was already inside, waiting."

In fact I'd no idea what the text message had said, and I couldn't even be a hundred percent certain he'd received a text. But I needed to make Jared Crowley shake in his pointy-toed boots, to shake so hard that something fell out. "Who contacted you, Jared? Tell me, and you'll do yourself a big favor."

Jared jumped up and shoved back his chair. It crashed to the concrete pad. "It's bullshit, total bullshit. Leave me alone, will you?"

"A name, Jared, that's all I want. One little name." I stood too, and stepped sideways to block his exit. Then the light dawned. "Hey. Somebody has something on you, don't they."

In a flash, he pulled his arm back to punch me in the face. I caught his wrist and twisted his arm hard. Jared Crowley let out a small and pleasing scream.

I put my mouth to his ear. "Give me a name or I snap it."

"Go to hell!"

I was on the verge of reacting badly to the god Apollo. Quickly, before I could fall to temptation and damage more than his fragile ego, I let him go. He and I had traveled as far as we could.

I reentered the kitchen and passed through to the bustling restaurant without looking back. Then I kept on going until I'd melted into the shadows on the far side of the street.

Three minutes later, when Jared Crowley scampered out the front door and down Anapamu, I followed.

He didn't catch sight of me as I trailed him to the city lot. I climbed in the Honda as he hurried over to his Beemer. I'd parked close by, and when he exited the lot, I was right on his tail.

"Who the hell is she, Wied? She talks like an undercover cop or something."

"Jari, she's nobody, absolutely nobody. Believe me, I had Zarlin checked out."

I pressed my ear tight to a sliver of a gap in the wall of the plywood box. It sounded like Bruce Wiederkehr, of all people. He stood mere inches away.

"No, she's connected to the cops. Gotta be. She knows stuff—"

"Her boyfriend's a detective in the county sheriff's department. That's as close as she gets."

I planted one hand on the wall to keep my balance. So Dr. Bruce had been sticking his long skinny beak into my business. I'd been sticking my nose into his, but that was different.

"Zarlin knows nothing," Wiederkehr continued. "She's got one connection that matters, just one. Zave Carbonel."

"Never heard of the dude."

"No, Carbonel doesn't operate on your level, Jared. But believe me, there's nothing for you to worry about. The lady detective is clueless." He chuckled a little. "Get it? The detective is clueless."

"The fuck she is!" Jared's shrill squeal drilled my ear like a dentist's tool. "She knows you texted me, Wied, OK?"

"I did what?"

There was a pause in their conversation. I tried to shift in my uncomfortable position, and somehow knocked my knee against the wall.

"What was that?" Jared snapped.

"Nothing, Jari. Nothing at all." Dr. Bruce sounded as if he was soothing a frightened toddler. "Things go bump in the night."

"Shut up. And don't act like you don't know what I'm talking about. You texted me and told me to drive Lili down to the warehouse."

"I *what*? What the heck are you talking about? First, I don't 'text.' And second, what did that girl have to do with me?"

"Don't ask me, prick. But you did it, OK?"

"Jared, what are you playing at?" Dr. Bruce's voice grew stern. "Is this one of your little games? Because if it is, it's not funny."

"Oh right. Yeah, man, I'm playing a game." There was another long pause. "Here. Take a look at this, Wieder."

"OK, but what's it got to do—"

"Need your specs, old man? Sent from your fucking phone. See the date? See the time? Let me read it to you: *Sweetie, find Lili Molina right now and drive her down to the warehouse. Tell her to change out of the costume, it's valuable and we don't want her screwing around in it. Be sure to wait for her and then drive her back to the park. Love you, Wied.*"

"But that—that was sent during the party. Have I ever called you 'sweetie'? Somebody must have—" The doctor dropped his voice, and I strained to hear.

"—tell me you didn't—you didn't drive Lili down to the Guild."

"Yes I did! You told me to drive her down. I did what you said. I didn't wait for her, though—why the fuck should I? But you were there, all right. You raped and killed her." Jared laughed harshly. "I have to admit, I didn't know you had it in you."

"I *don't* have it in me. And you damn well know I don't. In fact—"

Again, there was a lengthy silence. I held my breath so I wouldn't miss a word.

"In fact what?"

"I don't have it in me, but I'm not at all sure you don't have it in you."

"What the—you're setting me up! You killed her and now—"

"Shut up, will you? I think I heard something."

"Things go bump in the night," Jared sneered.

The door at the front of the container abruptly slammed open. Thankfully, I was standing at the back in pitch dark. I faded into the shrubbery lining the broken-down fence.

"There's nobody out here," Jared said to the night. The ply-

wood door closed with a hollow thump. I waited a moment before I returned to my post.

"OK," Jared was saying. "If it wasn't me—and let's say for a
second it wasn't you either—then who the hell sent the message? Somebody at the party, somebody who got hold of your
phone. One of your so-called friends, that's who."

"I sincerely doubt that." Bruce Wiederkehr's voice was careful now. "But someone at the house on that day . . . it's possible,
I suppose. A cleaner, a caterer, a gardener—"

"Yeah, right. Or it could have been one of your rich dick
buds, or one of their kids, or—or your own kid. How about that,
Wieder? It could have been your darling Sarah." He said the
name Sarah in a snide, sexy tone.

"Stop. Stop right there. I've told you before, Jared, my family's off-limits. I put up with your smart-aleck remarks, I pay
your ridiculous blackmail demands. But there's one thing I—"

"Yeah, yeah. *One thing I will not tolerate.* I've heard it all before. And another thing you can stuff is the blackmail shit. You
think it's ridiculous? If one of your buds or relatives or whoever
it is wasn't blackmailing *me,* I wouldn't have to ask *you*—"

"Oh, come *on,* Jared. Somebody keeps threatening to out us
if you don't pay up? I'm not sure I believe a word of it. If you—"

"I've showed you the notes, haven't I?"

"Faked. I'm pretty sure of it, Jari."

"Screw off. Find somebody else to play your sick little games,
old man!"

This time the plywood door crashed open. I heard Jared,
muttering, hurry over to his car. He roared out of the small
space and screeched down the drive.

Blackmail. So somebody knew all about Jared and Bruce,
and was making a little money off their secret. Making a little
money—and maybe having fun tightening the screws.

After a moment, I again pressed my ear to the crack and

heard a strange noise. It took me a moment to understand: inside the plywood box, Bruce Wiederkehr was weeping.

"Jaymie Zarlin." Zave smiled across his football-field-sized mahogany desk. "Enter the lair."

"Hi, Zave." I made a mock bow. "Good of you to grant me an audience." The undraped walls were glass, edge to edge and floor to ceiling. I spun slowly in a circle, drinking in the three-sixty panorama of the clay-tile-roofed city, terra-cotta mountains, and dark blue channel waters.

"This has to be the best view in town."

"I thought you didn't like coming to my office. Too public, wasn't that the complaint?" Zave walked an end run around his desk and reached for me.

"I had to see you in a hurry." I ducked out of his embrace. "No foreplay, OK? I'm here about a serious matter."

"Whatever you say." Zave halted his pursuit and held up both hands, palms outward. "Sorry about Armenta, by the way. Was it suicide? I hear maybe not."

"Definitely not."

"Hm. The police got a cover-up going? Surprise me and say no."

"Maybe. Or maybe they just don't want to admit they made a mistake." I shrugged. "You're the one who knows how the cops operate."

"What I hear is they're in one hell of an unholy hurry to shut the case down. The DA is mighty unpopular, and she doesn't need another black eye." He tapped his desktop. "Come close and I'll spell it all out."

"Zave . . ." I felt myself flush.

"What, strictly business? Ain't no such thing between you and me. We changed all that a couple years back, remember?"

I met his gaze full on. "How about this, then: I'm very fond of you and I always will be. Also, it's true I want something from you: information. But the thing is, Zave, I will not pay you with sex."

He tipped back his sleek head and laughed, then sat on the edge of the desk and leaned forward. Our eyes were now level. "Prostitution is a time-honored profession, Jaymie."

"You're not going to take this standing up, are you, Zave?"

"Very funny, sweetheart." He nodded appreciatively. "But let's cut the crap. You've finally admitted it to yourself, haven't you? Once again, you've fallen for the dep-u-ty."

"Rest assured, he's out of the picture," I stiffly replied.

"Oh. Like that, is it? OK, so what other explanation is there—it just doesn't 'feel right' anymore between you and me?"

"Something like that."

"Tell you what. I'll believe it if you'll let me put it to the test."

"What test?"

"You heard of the carbon test. Well, this is the *Carbonel* test." He rose to his feet and drew me to him, pressing his body tight to mine and kissing me long and slow. Actually, it was humanly impossible not to respond.

"Zave," I squeaked when we at last came up for air. "Please, I'm asking you as a friend!"

"Aw shit." He stepped back and grinned. "I'm warning you, girl, *you'll come a runnin' back. . . .*"

I laughed breathlessly.

"OK, Jaymie, have it your way. So now I'm going to walk around and sit behind the barricade. I'm putting on a different hat. Comprende?"

"Yeah, comprende." I did understand, and it made me wistful. Playtime with Zave had always been fun.

"So, Ms. Zarlin." Zave rapped on his desk with a pen. "What can I do for you? I'll give you five minutes."

"Damn it, Zave!"

"Sorry, Jaymie. Just teasing. I'm a little hurt, that's all."

"Don't be. Friends forever, as far as I'm concerned."

"I'll buy that for now. So what's up?"

"I need more information about certain members of our local uppity crust. Specifically, Vincent Stellato and Sutton Frayne the Third."

Zave thrummed the fingers of his right hand on the desk. "Members of the Triune. What do you want to know?"

"I want to know if they have girlfriends. Current or recent past. I'd like the women's names and addresses."

"Girlfriends. So that's why you're not asking about Wiederkehr too."

I raised my hands in admiration. "Is there anything you don't already know?"

Zave shrugged and leaned back in his chair. "How soon do you need it?"

I couldn't resist teasing him. "Fast as it takes us to you-know-what. And that's pretty damn fast."

His eyes narrowed dangerously. "Oh, my. Now you just ain't playin' fair."

"I don't wanna be rude, but I never heard of you." Crystal Makler held onto the door frame and swayed a little. "What did you say your name was?"

"Jaymie Zarlin. There's no reason you would have heard of me, Miss Makler."

"That's *Missus* Makler, honey. I was married. Not for long, but long enough, I can tell you." She nodded four times, slow. "Who gave you my name, anyways?"

"A friend."

"Oh yeah?" Crystal attempted to repin her updo with one hand, but a few more bleached strands tumbled to her shoulders. "OK, what do you want? The sun's hurting my eyes."

"I'd like to talk with you about Vincent Stellato."

"That *wop* son of a bitch! What, did something happen to

Vince?" She scowled. "I hope something bad happened to him. . . . I guess."

"Last time I saw Mr. Stellato, he was just fine." I handed Crystal my card, and she squinted at it.

"You're what—a PI? Great, just great. See, this is not something I need, not at the moment. Nothing personal, but bye." She wiggled her fingers at me, then closed the door in my face.

"Uh, Mrs. Makler?"

"Who hired you—Maryjune?" Crystal shouted through the door. "Why should she give a rat's ass after thirteen years? Was it Vince? Does Vince think I'm gonna sue or something? Actually, maybe I will sue the bastard. He gave me this place, but I should probably get more, putting up with that jerk for so many—"

"Mrs. Makler," I shouted back. "It's not about you, not at all. Please let me explain, and then you can decide if you want to talk or not."

After a minute, the door opened again. "Guess it's your lucky day. I'm kinda sick of hiding in the house and dumping Bacardi in my Cokes. A little company would be nice. So Vince didn't send you?"

"No."

"How about mealymouthed Maryjune?"

"Nope." I suppressed a smile.

"Well, it's gotta be about money somehow. I've lived on this earth for forty-eight years." She paused. "Forty-eight years, but listen, honey. As far as Vince is concerned, it's forty-three."

"OK."

"So, who's paying you to be here?"

"Fair question. I was hired by the family of a person named Danny Armenta. But I'm also doing this now off my own bat."

"Don't know Danny. Look, I'm starting to feel kinda woozy. I need to put some food in my stomach. It's the damnedest thing. I'm hardly eating at all, but I'm still putting on weight. It's

my slow metabo-bolism. Come on in. It's dumb to let someone you don't know into your house, but God help me, you've
got an honest face. Pretty one, too."

"Thanks." I stepped inside and followed Crystal down a
short hall to the kitchen. She pointed at a maple chair.

"Sit down, why don't you. What's your name again?"

"Jaymie."

"OK. Cuppa coffee, Jaymie?"

"That'd be great."

A minute later, she caught me observing the room. "Checking it all out, huh?"

"Sorry. Force of habit."

"Look, I'll save you the trouble of working things out. Here's
the nitty-gritty." Crystal plugged a coffeemaker into the wall.
"I'm a waitress at Nonni's. That's where me and Vince met. We
were together nearly thirteen years, off and on, as of June twenty-
fifth. *Were*, not *are*. He broke up with me on June twenty-sixth,
the son of a bitch. And this time it's for real. Know how I
know?" She opened the cupboard and reached for the filters.
The stack toppled down to the counter. "Shit!"

"This time it's for real?" I prompted.

"Yeah. Because *this time* he gave me the house. Had the pa-
perwork all ready, the prick. Quitclaimed this place to me, free
and clear. And that is not Vince, let me tell you. Vince isn't
cheap, but he likes to keep his hand in, know what I mean? He
likes to be in control."

Crystal plonked down opposite me. "This time, we're toast."

"I'm sorry, Mrs. Makler."

"Oh, call me Crystal, for Chrissake." She rubbed at her eyes.
"Know what? I think I'm depressed. We were good as married
for thirteen years, except for the times we split up."

I decided to give her a push. "Well, that would make Vincent a bigamist. One wife set up large in a mansion in Hope

Ranch, the other stashed away in a worn-out sixties tract house in Ventura."

"Do you want my cooperation or not? Because talking like that is sure as hell no way to get it." Crystal glared at me, then burst out laughing. "But it's true enough. Know what? I like a straight talker."

With a practiced hand, she poured the coffee into a pair of turquoise-blue cups. "So. What's this all about? Maybe I'll answer your questions, maybe not. First off, who's this Danny guy?"

"Did you hear about the rape and murder of Lili Molina, up in Santa Barbara? 'The Solstice Murder,' they're calling it now."

"Sure. It was all over the news. And Vince told me about it, right before we—" Crystal halted midsentence. "So that's why you want to know about Vince. It's that board thing he's on, isn't it."

"Yes, the Apollo Guild Triune." I tasted the coffee: it wasn't half-bad. "Danny Armenta was the boy they arrested for the murder."

Crystal dumped four heaping teaspoonfuls of sugar into her cup and stirred. "He killed himself, didn't he? Suicide?"

"No, that's not true." I set the cup down in the saucer. "Danny was murdered too. And my job is to figure out who killed them both."

"OK. Hold your horses right there." She waggled the spoon at me. "Look, I hate Vince with a passion, OK? But I gotta tell you, it wasn't him, if that's what you're thinking. No way José."

"Why not?"

"Oh, he's nasty when it suits him." She shrugged. "He's mean to his poor little wifey and mean to me too, if I let him. It's always Vinnie's way or the highway. *But.*"

"But?"

"See, Vince would never *kill* anything. Too sentimental. I

had this old cat that got hit by a car. I was ready to put Ziggy down, but not Vince. Oh no, he paid I don't know how much to get that cat's leg set and his shoulder stitched up. Course, Ziggy was so damn mad he pissed on everything from then on out, the couch, the bed, you name it. But Vince didn't care." She shook her head. "The man couldn't kill a gopher, I swear to God."

"OK, I hear you. But sometimes men kill after they rape, because they don't want the woman to identify—"

"Stop right there. Rape? Not Vincent Stellato, not ever."

"Crystal, I know Vince is a bully. How can you be so sure he'd never rape anyone?"

"Look. I hate it that I'm defending the bastard. But it's just the plain truth. Vince wouldn't rape cause he wouldn't see any reason to do it. If some woman refused to have sex with him, he'd just figure she had some kinda problem."

"Not short on self-confidence, huh?"

"Honey, Vince thinks he's irresistible. His mom was a lot like Maryjune, from what I've heard. And Vinnie was her little darling. . . . He believes women love him to bits. Actually, what they love is his money." She thought of something and laughed out loud.

"What is it?"

"See, Vince doesn't understand what part of his pants women want to get into. It's not his fly, like he thinks. It's his back pocket, where he keeps his wallet."

"He wouldn't be the first old guy to make that mistake."

"Oh, believe me, honey. When you're a waitress, you learn a helluva lot about men." Crystal sipped her heavily fortified coffee. "Anything else you want to know?"

"Did you ever meet his son, Lance?"

"Uh-huh. Vince brought Lance into Nonni's every once in a while. The kid never guessed who I was, least I don't think he did. See, Vince liked to talk about the kid, and he wanted me to see him so I'd, you know, have a picture in my mind."

"What about Maryjune? Did you meet her?"

"Sister Maryjune? Yeah, I made sure I bumped into the nun once or twice. And I gotta admit, a couple times I called the house just to stir up trouble. Once I even phoned and told her straight out that I was Vince's girlfriend." Crystal grimaced. "I'm not proud of it, you know? But that was years back, when I was young and stupid. In love with the jerk."

"It's funny, though," I said. "Maryjune doesn't seem to think her husband has a mistress."

"Yeah, well. About three years ago, Vince told her he gave me up. That's when he made me promise to quit calling. I guess she believed him, the ninny." Crystal tried to run her hand through her tangled coiffure, then gave up. "I used to hate that woman. I thought that softness of hers was just a big act. But you know what? I think she's probably a pretty nice person." Crystal winked at me. "Unfortunately, if you know what I mean."

I laughed. "Yeah. It's hard to dislike the Maryjunes of this world. Look, Crystal, do you think Lance could have killed Lili Molina?"

"What?" Crystal leaned back in her chair. "Lance is just a kid. He's real spoiled, but . . . hey, don't ask me. I don't know him at all." She frowned and set her cup on the table.

"Look. I don't want to make things up and get people in trouble. Just because I know Vince inside and out doesn't mean I know the rest of them, capish?"

"Capish." I shut my notebook and snapped the elastic band. "You've been helpful. Thanks for your time."

"Know what? I'm feeling better now. You kinda took me outta myself."

"Sorry for the crack I made about your house. Actually, it's a palace compared to mine. I like it, especially the sandstone fireplace."

"No offense taken. Now that Vince is out of the picture, I can decorate it any way I want, can't I?" She walked with me to the door. "I could do it that new midcentury style. He'd hate that for sure."

"Crystal, before I go. Can I run three more names past you?"

"Shoot."

"Jared Crowley, Bruce Wiederkehr, Sutton Frayne. Did Vince ever talk about any of them?"

"Crowley I never heard of. Wiederkehr, yeah. Vince called him a pansy. But Frayne—what a turd!" Crystal flushed and put out a hand to the wall, to steady herself.

"Hey, take it easy." I took her by the arm and led her back into the living room, easing her down to the couch.

"Jesus, my blood pressure. I've managed not to think about that asshole Frayne in months!"

"Breathe evenly. Don't talk till you feel OK."

After a minute or two, she looked up and met my eyes. "I'd love to tell you Frayne's the guy you're looking for, Jaymie. 'Fraid not."

"Just tell me what you know about him, then."

"Not much, actually, not so fucking much considering how he messed with me. See, about a year ago Vince and I were on the outs, OK? And somehow Frayne hears about it. So he comes into the restaurant where I work, makes a big play. The guy's handsome, kinda like Robert Redford used to be. I'm an idiot, being on the rebound, and before I can think straight he takes me down to the Coronado Hotel, wining and dining. Next he charters a plane, I kid you not, and flies us up to the wine country . . . that man is loaded. Loaded, I'm telling you." She picked up a glass figurine, a poodle, off the coffee table and cradled it in her hands.

"This is kinda embarrassing. But actually it's funny too, now that I think about it. See, outta the blue, the guy dumps me. One night he comes by the house and calls me a broken-down slut, yadda, yadda. And get this: he claims that's why he

couldn't get it off with me anymore, because I was so—so—
'dirty and used up.'" Crystal shook her head and laughed.

"Nice guy," I observed.

"I've known my share, honey. I have known my share."

I was getting into the Honda when Crystal opened the front
door again and hurried down the walk. "Hey, Jaymie. I got a
hunch Robert Redford maybe did the same thing to that Wiederkehr guy's wife. Just something he said once, something like
'that woman's so damn hungry it's disgusting.'" Crystal made a
face. "That bunch. It's like incest, know what I mean?"

Chapter Seventeen

I'd just left Ventura and pulled onto the PCH when Mike called. I was so deeply immersed in my thoughts that I didn't respond to the ringing at first. When I finally picked up, the phone had gone to voice mail.

Mike's words didn't exactly radiate friendship. He wanted to meet me in an hour at the Mission, but he wouldn't say why. I texted him back with a yes.

I arrived early, so I parked and wandered into the Mission rose garden. The beds had just been watered, and delicate French perfumes wafted up on the warm moist air.

I drew in a slow deep breath to calm myself. Nature took its sweet time, and I needed to do the same. A few feet away, the rich earth bubbled as a mole inched forward in his safe dark world.

Mike's truck approached up Los Olivos. When I waved, he lifted his hand an inch above the wheel.

I watched as the truck pulled into the parking lot. Mike got out, then walked around to the passenger side. When he reappeared, he was cradling something in his arms. He set the something down on the asphalt. It began to move forward, like a broken rocking horse.

Dex! With every step, the little mutt halted. Patiently, Mike stayed at the dog's side.

I began to walk toward them. But Mike called out, "Wait there on the grass."

Fortunately Dexter was on the lawn before he realized it was me. He gave a sharp bark and broke into a gallop, forgetting he had only one hind leg. The cow dog pitched forward and landed on his muzzle. I put a hand over my mouth: it hurt just to see.

"Whoa, boy. Take it easy." Mike lifted Dex to his feet.

I didn't know if it was the dog's stumble or the man's gentle response that caused my eyes to prickle with tears.

"Dex." I knelt down and pulled the mutt close. He slobbered on my cheek. I looked up at Mike. "I want my dog back."

"He likes riding shotgun. You're not getting him, not for a while."

"Come on, Mike. You just like having a regular bed partner," I teased. But my words were met with a flat-out glare.

"Listen," he said curtly. "Did you hear what happened an hour ago? Claudia Molina."

"What! Please don't tell me she—"

"No, the girl's fine. Except for a black eye and bloody knuckles." Mike gouged out an errant weed with the toe of his boot. "It's Lance Stellato who got the worst of it."

"What? They fought?"

"Yeah. They're both cooling their heels in juvie as we speak. They got into it in the high school parking lot. She had an old knife on her, and I guess she scratched him up a little."

"Her father's switchblade. You know why Claudia went after Lance, don't you? She found out what he did to Lili a year and a half ago. My fault. Claudia was in the office—she read it on the board."

Mike shrugged. Subject closed, apparently.

I gave Dex one last ear rub and got to my feet. "He's better off with you for now, I admit. I'm not sure I could protect him."

"The question is, can you protect yourself?" He scowled and looked away. "Not that it's any of my concern."

"Mike? Can we talk? Because if—" I saw his expression, and my voice withered midsentence.

"I've got something to say to you, Jaymie. For once, it's not the other way around."

"OK," I said in a small voice. I knew this wouldn't be good.

"You and I are done." His eyes were gleaming and hard as two slivers of obsidian. "You don't need to worry, I won't be chasing you anymore."

I'd expected a tongue-lashing, but not this. "Mike, I don't really see—"

"You didn't think about me, not for a minute, when you decided to run off." With each word, his voice grew louder. "I got a real good look at how much I mean to you."

"Mike, I—"

"I risked my job for you, do you know that? It was stupid, handing that info over to you. Damn stupid. But I trusted you, Jaymie. Trusted you, damn it!"

"And did I betray your trust? How? I haven't told a soul!"

"How? I'll tell you how. Something goes wrong, and all of a sudden you're hightailing it out of town. No discussion with me, not even a heads-up." All traces of Mike's impassive stoniness were gone: his furious voice boomed out over the rose garden. "Like I'm nothing to you, nothing but a way to get what you want!"

"Don't blame me. I didn't chase after you!" I was getting a little warm myself. "Why did you give Gabi my card in the first place? Admit it, all that talk about seeing justice done was bullshit. Just a ruse to start up with me again!"

"A little of both." Suddenly deflated, Mike shrugged heavily. "What does it matter now? It's finished, that's all. Not that it ever was on."

I looked over to where Dexter was lying on his belly, digging furiously in the soft dirt of the rose bed. "At least he's having fun."

Mike shrugged in dismissal. "Dex, time to go."

The dog shoved his muzzle into the ground, then pulled back and looked at us: tiny pink mole hands waved on either side of his jaws.

"Mike, please. Can't we be—"

"What, friends?" His voice was flinty, his mouth drawn in a tight line. "No, we damn well can't. And you know it."

Dexter stood there with his prize. He looked at me, then looked at Mike striding off, his head bent, hands stuffed in his Windbreaker pockets.

"Go, boy," I said softly. "He needs you even more than I do right now."

A tense-looking Cynthia Wiederkehr hovered just inside the old teak gate. She wore beige linen slacks and a taupe silk top, accented by a black pearl necklace and matching earrings. I caught a whiff of her understated, elegant perfume.

"Did you park behind the hedges, as I asked?" The woman clasped her hands together, as if to keep them from flying off. "I don't particularly want my family to know we're meeting."

"My car's hidden, Mrs. Wiederkehr. There was a gardener back there, though."

"Armando, no doubt, having a smoke." Cynthia wrinkled her aquiline nose. "Smoking isn't tolerated on the grounds, and I believe he has quite the nicotine addiction." She pressed the gate latch and waved me through. "We'll go to the tank house. I want our talk to be uninterrupted—and preferably brief."

I followed Cynthia through a natural section of the property, along a narrow gravel path. Insects hummed and butterflies lazed through the air. Though the area seemed overgrown and wild, each shrub and tree was perfectly placed.

"Wonderful garden," I said to Cynthia's back. Sure, the woman had an army of worker bees. But still, she deserved some of the credit.

"Two acres of California natives, nothing else." Cynthia

strode forward, educating the air. "Montecito Elementary School uses this area for their nature study. The native plants attract native insects and birds, of course."

We circled an ancient live oak and entered a clearing. An old two-story-high redwood water tower, weathered to a soft silvery brown, stood at the center. Cynthia stopped and turned to me. "Are you interested in native species, Ms. Zarlin?"

"Sure. I wish I knew more." Surprisingly, I was beginning to like this woman, silk, pearls, scent, and all.

"I know what you mean. Our California flora and fauna are so diverse." Her voice softened. "Just recently we discovered a population of southwest blind snakes living right here, under the tower foundation." She took out a key ring and stepped onto the sandstone threshold. "They're beautiful, silvery. And so small— they fit in the palm of your hand." She opened the door and stepped through, motioning me to follow.

The single airy room was filled with lab tables and chairs. A large whiteboard was mounted to one wall. "So this is a classroom?" I asked.

"Yes. The base of the tower, this space, was originally a storage room. I had it converted for the school. The water was drained out of the tank upstairs nearly a hundred years ago—in 1923, I believe."

I followed Cynthia across the orange and blue vinyl floor to a rough-hewn door, which opened into an enclosed redwood staircase. We climbed to the second level and stepped out onto the original open catwalk, which circled the tank. A few steps along we came to a door set in the tank wall. A new padlock secured an old iron latch.

Cynthia fiddled with the padlock. "That's odd. It's turned back to front, and no one comes here but me. In fact, I have the only key." Then the door fell open, and we entered a circular high-ceilinged room.

The floor was made of thick redwood planks, blackened

with time, and the walls and ceiling were lined in cedar. The heavy exposed beams in the ceiling were also of redwood. A series of tall, narrow fixed windows looked out to a wavering blue and green world.

"A magical space," I murmured. Then I told myself to cut it out. It wasn't my job to praise the possessions of this wealthy woman.

"I suppose it is, yes. Anyway, the tank house is private, and that's why I've brought you here." Cynthia walked to one of the windows and stood looking out, her back to me. "You know, when you asked about Sutton on the phone yesterday, I wasn't really surprised. Somehow I knew my indiscretion would surface." She turned toward me. Her figure was dark now, illumined from behind.

"I decided to speak with you because there's something I want you to know about him. Something you might find useful."

I heard a bitterness under her words, and knew exactly why she'd agreed to talk to me. Cynthia couldn't care less about being helpful. No, what she wanted was revenge.

"Sutton Frayne isn't what he seems, is he, Mrs. Wiederkehr."

"No. No, he's not. Dear old Sutz is something of a manipulator. It's—somewhat embarrassing, actually."

"I'll be discreet."

"I certainly hope so." She let out a puff of air. "It was like this: Sutton pursued me for five or six months. He wined and dined me, he took me to cozy little hideaways."

"And then?"

"And then?" She lifted one shoulder in a shrug. "Once he got me on the hook, he dropped me. He had the nerve to drop me flat."

"Did he say why?"

"Not really. He had the gall to blame me, though—I didn't measure up in some way or other."

"Do you mind if I ask you a personal question?"

"You can try. I may choose not to answer."

"With Frayne . . . how was the sex?"

Cynthia barked out a short laugh. The bark was high-pitched, like a shih tzu's. "Sex? In Sutton's case, we'd have to define the term, and I'm not going to—"

"Tell her, Mom!" a high girlish voice rang out from the open door.

"Sarah! I thought you were going out!"

Sarah Wiederkehr wore black calf-length tights and a pleated skirt that barely covered her ass. "Armando. He told me this—this *person* came in through the back gate. I'm kind of surprised you'd bring her *here*. Isn't this where you used to meet Sutz?"

"But—how did you know?"

The young woman strode across the room and flipped a switch. Harsh light flooded the room. "He told me all about it, Mom. He told me how you came on to him, how he didn't want to say no. How pathetic!"

"Sarah, for God's sake, what do you know about these things? You haven't even—even—"

"What, you think I'm still a virgin? You know nothing about me, nothing! I have a *lover*, OK?"

"Sarah! Who is he? Tell me the boy's name this instant!"

"He's not a boy. He's a man, an older man, and it's none of your business! You're so out of it, Mom, and your head's stuck in the sand. You don't even know about Dad!"

"What do you mean? There's nothing to know about Bruce. He—"

"Dad's *gay*," Sarah spat.

I could hear their rough breathing, as if mother and daughter had just taken time out from a bout in the ring. Their eyes were locked, and both seemed to have forgotten I was there.

"Don't you dare say that," Cynthia rasped. "I'm married to him. I think I'd know."

A charged silence swirled in the circular room.

When Sarah finally spoke, her voice had changed: she sounded like a little girl. "You didn't want to know, Mommy. I always knew, but you never wanted to know."

"That's not true," Cynthia said dully.

"Yes, you know it is. These days Daddy likes that horrid bleached-blond boy. . . ."

Cynthia suddenly sprang to life. She spun around and focused on me like a rattler about to strike. "You. What do you want from us? Why in God's name are you here?"

"You know why, Mrs. Wiederkehr. I'm investigating the murder of Lili Molina. I came to ask you questions pertaining to her death."

"But why us?" Cynthia snarled. She needed a sponge to absorb her rage, and apparently that sponge would be me. "Answer me! What could my family possibly have to do with the murder of a little Mexican whore?"

"Mrs. Wiederkehr." Now I struggled to rein in my own anger. "You're talking about an innocent young—"

"Get out! And get off my property, you little nobody!"

"I screwed up, Gabi. I got tag-teamed by a mother-daughter duo."

"Screwed up? Sounds to me like you learned really a lot."

"Oh, I did. Information buzzed around me like a swarm of Africanized bees. But I never got the answer to my main question."

"What was that?"

"'How was the sex?'"

"Hm. So you think Sutton Frayne's got some kinda problem?"

"Could be. He seems to make it a habit to turn against his sexual partners. I suspect it works in the beginning for him, as long as he's in control."

"Well, I can see why you never found the right moment to ask about that." Gabi filled the office sink with hot soapy water and pulled up her sleeves. "So you burned your bridges, huh?"

"Yeah. I won't get much more out of Cynthia."

"Rich stuck-up bitch."

I grinned. "The worst kind of bitches are the rich ones, aren't they." Then I rested my head in my hands and groaned. "I've got to start eliminating suspects, Gabi. The more I look into this business, the guiltier everyone seems."

Gabi swabbed the cups and saucers energetically. "So maybe they *are* all guilty. All in it together."

"They can't all be killers." I picked up a dish towel and a dripping cup.

"Rich people got stuff to hide. Cause they got the power to do bad things."

"No doubt about that." I raised a hand and popped up one finger at a time. "Lance Stellato has something to hide: he manipulated Lili into having sex with him. Vince has two things to hide: his girlfriend, Crystal, and the fact that his son abused Lili. Married gent Bruce Wiederkehr—well, he's having sex with Jared. Jared, he's having sex with Bruce, and they're being blackmailed. Sutton Frayne the bloody Third: he plays nasty games with the wives and girlfriends of his friends."

"If you ask me, the women are worse." Gabi yanked the plug, and the water gurgled down the partly clogged drain. "They act like nothing's wrong. Otherwise, the men would have to behave better."

"Hm. What you just said about the women . . ."

"Miss Jaymie? You're gonna wear a hole in that cup."

"What? Oh, here." I thrust the cup and towel into her hands, and reached into my pocket for my phone. "You talking about women made me think. There's one I've got to make contact with."

◆   ◆   ◆

"These are hardly the sort of matters I discuss on the phone, Jaymie. Surely you, as an investigator, can understand."

"I'll come visit you if you like, Miss Delaney."

"That is inconvenient, I'm afraid. In fact, I am planning to go out myself this afternoon, to visit an acquaintance around four. I suppose I could stop at your office or home on my way there. We could go for a little drive and talk in my car."

"Yes, of course. I'll be at my office. Can I give you directions?"

"No, I know where it is. Well then, half past three."

"Get out of the vehicle and walk on the beach, Ken. Exercise is important for the aging body. Make certain you cleanse your clothing and breath of cigarette smoke before you return."

The back of Ken's neck purpled. "Yes, Miss Delaney," he said tonelessly.

"He hates me, of course," Celeste Delaney observed once Ken had closed the driver's door. "It's best that way—no misunderstandings." She turned to me. "Don't you agree?"

"If you hold absolute power, Miss Delaney, I can see how that would work."

Celeste Delaney laughed thinly. "Observant of you. If the balance of power slips, well then. All hell breaks loose."

"After me, the deluge?"

"Indeed, and already the waters are rising. But the rich will continue to get richer for a time longer. Certainly there will be time enough for me." She plucked at the afghan covering her lap. "Do you see what is happening, as I do? Society has begun its decline. Our institutions are crumbling, both those that do good and those that are evil. For better or worse, chaos awaits at the door."

"There are times when I see it that way," I admitted.

"Times when you are honest with yourself, you mean." The old woman gave a short laugh. "Now, you said you wanted to ask about Sutton. My curiosity is piqued. Whatever for?"

"I do understand he's your relative, Miss Delaney. But I have to go where my inquiries lead me." I watched Ken advance along East Beach, a wisp of cigarette smoke trailing after him. "Apparently your nephew is not the easygoing fellow he seems."

"No? Well, I don't suppose any of us are what we *seem*, my dear. So, you want to ask me about him. But to what purpose? Sutton is not a suspect, surely."

"I can't rule anyone out. Not yet," I said carefully.

"You disappoint me, Jaymie. Why are you overlooking that vulgar boy Jared?"

Celeste Delaney had an ear to the ground, that was for certain. "Crowley's still in the picture."

She inclined her head in my direction. "And the Stellatos, father and son? My sources tell me they may have had what is called *motive*."

How the hell did she know all this? The sun was beating down on the shut windows, heating the limo like an oven. I'd broken out in a sweat.

"Vince Stellato was at the Wiederkehrs' party—he has an alibi. He was front and center most of the time. Lance's alibi is wobbly. He was at the party too, but a lot of the time he was out of sight. I get the sense he liked Lili, though. For what it's worth," I added lamely.

"Oh, intuition can be useful, as far as it goes. Though it does not trump facts, as I'm sure you'd agree. But if all these people are innocent, as you seem to believe, might that not lead us back to Danny Armenta? Alas, now we cannot speak with the poor demented boy. . . ."

"It wasn't Danny, Miss Delaney. That I can promise you. And the money you put up for bail will be returned later this week. Again, thank you."

"You know, I was thinking about that, Jaymie. You should have a portion of the money."

"Me? What for?"

"You've worked so very hard, my dear, and asked for nothing for yourself. I have my connections, naturally, and they tell me the case is soon to be closed. It is only right you should receive some compensation."

"Miss Delaney, would you mind if we opened a window?" I needed to slow things down, to *think*. What game was Celeste playing at—and why?

"Oh, are you too warm? I'm sorry, but I am elderly, you know, and must avoid drafts." She rearranged the afghan in her bony lap. "So what do you say, Jaymie? I was thinking in terms of fifty thousand dollars."

Fifty thousand dollars? To me, a king's ransom! And certainly too much to have no strings attached. "Miss Delaney? Exactly what are you asking me to do?"

"To do? Simply to move on, my dear. To close your little investigation. Come now, you and I know that no one associated with the Guild killed that girl. A preposterous thought! Yet by investigating, you are troubling people, creating suspicion. And my dear, I simply can't have you troubling *my crowd*."

I admit I was tempted. The investigation was going nowhere, and fifty thousand dollars would pay for so much. I could keep Gabi on, invest a portion for the Molinas and the Armentas. It would change their lives. College fees for the kids, for example. I dreamed for a moment. . . . And then I woke up.

"I can't do it, Miss Delaney." I shrugged. "It's a matter of uncovering the truth."

"The truth? The truth is this: once upon a time, Jaymie, your self-centered actions and inactions contributed to the death of your own brother. What drives you now is not a thirst for justice, my dear. It is guilt."

"What? How do you know about that?" Abruptly I was squishy with sweat, struggling to think straight.

"Stupid girl." She swiveled her head to face me. "I am growing impatient with you. Do you not see by now that I can

discover anything, should I choose?" Her face grew dark, suf-
fused with blood.

"Get out! Walk back to town. Lesson one: the powerful
ride, the powerless walk."

The black limo, silent and smooth as a hearse, whisked by
me a few minutes later. It came so close, I felt the wind of its
passing on my bare ankles.

"I'm coming over." Mike sounded tense. "There's something I
need to show you."

Shamelessly, my spirits lifted just at the sound of his
voice. "Will you bring Dexter?"

"Dex goes everywhere with me now. I registered him as a
service dog."

"Dexter, a service dog? Are we talking about the same mutt?"

"Dogs get trained to do all sorts of things nowadays, Jaymie.
Like sleep with a diabetic kid. If the kid's blood sugar drops too
low, the dog trots down the hall and wakes up the parents."

"That's wonderful. But I can't see Dex working out. He
thinks a little too much, know what I mean?"

"Yeah, Dex would be calibrating the kid's sugar intake and
the time of his last shot. He'd figure the kid had another hour,
easy, and go back to sleep."

The joke wasn't very funny. But I laughed, just happy Mike
was actually talking to me again.

"Jaymie, before I come over I just want to say . . . I've decided you're right, we can be friends. I mean, why the hell not?
We're grown-ups."

"Uh—OK." There was something else, I could hear it. His
words were peaceable, but his voice was strung tight as a banjo.

"So, I want you to hear this from me." Seconds passed. "I'm
thinking about—whatever they call it now. Dating."

I drew in a sharp breath, and my blood pressure zinged. He

hadn't wasted any fucking time! "So who's the lucky lady, or isn't it any of my business?"

"There's no lucky lady. I just think it would be a good idea. You know, to move on."

"Is that all you want to talk to me about?" I snarled. "Because if it is, you don't need to come over and bother me with it."

"No, it's not. Like I said, it has to do with the case. I just wanted to set matters straight. I don't want there to be any—you know—misunderstanding between us."

My, wasn't he on the high road. "Whatever. Suit yourself."

My heart began to thump out an angry rhythm when I heard Mike's truck powering up the drive. Maybe I was getting what I'd asked for, but that didn't make it any easier to accept.

I went to the front door and opened it. Mike got out, then lifted down the scrappy little cow dog. Dexter hop-skipped one way, then the other, nose to the ground. Then he looked up and saw me standing there. He raced forward and stumbled.

"Dex, how are you, boy." I knelt down and wrapped him in my arms. "He looks happy, I have to admit," I mumbled into the dog's fur.

"He's got scars, though. And not just the visible kind." Mike followed me inside, Dexter tight on his heels.

"Want a cup of coffee?" I tried to keep my voice flat.

"What the hell, Jaymie? It's seven P.M. No beer in the fridge?" His voice was so damn hearty. Trying out this new friendship thing, I supposed.

"I'll get you a Sierra Nevada." I disappeared into the kitchen, my face hot. I didn't know if I wanted to hug the guy or show him the door. It was confusing, and I damn well didn't like it.

When I returned to the living room with the beer and a rawhide chew, Mike was smoothing out a piece of paper on the coffee table. "So here's what I want to talk to you about. Recognize this guy?"

I tossed Dex the chew, and the pup scuttled out of the room. I sat at the far end of the couch and picked up the paper. The picture was blurred, but I knew instantly who it was.

"Ken. Don't know his last name, but he works for Celeste Delaney. Real sweetheart."

"Ken Utman. I knew Utman was here in town—I've seen him around a few times. But I didn't realize he works for Delaney now, not until this morning."

"How do you know him?"

"Utman's a dirty cop from LA Narcotics: he was on the take and in the trade, too. He was fired down there, hell, must be five years ago now. A buddy of mine from downtown phoned to tell me Utman came into the station today and met with Chief Wheeler."

I sat forward on the edge of the couch. "Celeste must have sent him. He's her errand boy."

"No doubt of it. Right after Utman left, Wheeler called in the detectives working the Molina case."

"And? Don't keep me guessing."

"Basically, the chief told everybody to wrap it up pronto. Far as he's concerned, Danny Armenta killed Lili Molina, then killed himself. End of story."

I frowned. "Why should Celeste Delaney's opinion matter to the chief of police?"

"Come on. Were you born yesterday?" Mike took a swig of beer. "Maybe because she's powerful enough to have his operating budget diced and chopped? Or because she has the clout to get the city to fire him?"

"OK, I get it." I stared at Utman's ugly mug. "One thing's for sure, Celeste has changed camps. She was all for helping Danny in the beginning. That was back when I was looking for an outsider. But now that she knows I've put the Guild Triune under the microscope—"

"What—you told Delaney that? No wonder she's calling a halt!" Mike banged down his bottle and got to his feet. "Jesus, you're taking a risk."

"I don't see why. I—Mike? Where's Dex?"

"I might have left the door open. Guess he's outside, just sniffing around. I'll get him." His words were casual, but he moved quickly. I followed him out the door.

We hadn't walked more than a few paces, calling for the cow dog, before Dexter scuttled out from under the truck. His tail was tucked between his legs.

"Something's spooked him," Mike said.

"Maybe he wandered around to the back—to where he was tied up. I've cleaned it twice, but he can probably still smell everything."

Mike opened the cab door and lifted the little dog up into the driver's seat. "Let's go take a look."

Usually I avoided the site of Dexter's torture. But I nodded and followed.

"Those dark stains on the steps. Is that Dexter's blood?"

"Yeah. He was spread-eagled, tied to the posts." My throat constricted. "The tendons in his hind leg were severed. In other words, he was butchered."

"And his muzzle—you said it was wrapped in tape."

"Yes. He could breathe just enough to die a slow death. I— damn!" I pressed a hand to my mouth. "I can't believe I was so dumb."

"What?"

"I was so freaking upset, I didn't think to ask the vet for the tape after she removed it. Plastic tape—stuff sticks to it. Who knows what evidence got tossed?"

"When things get personal, it's hard to think straight."

"Isn't that the truth." I knelt down and ran my fingers through the long grass sprouting at the edge of the steps. Suddenly my pulse took a hop.

"Look at this! The gods must be smiling." I extracted a crunched ball of clear tape from the grass. "This is it, the same tape the guy used on Dexter's muzzle."

"The asshole must have tangled that part, then rolled it into a ball and tossed it."

"Maybe," I replied. "Let's go inside and have a closer look at it."

In the kitchen, I placed the ball of clear tape on a clean paper towel. There was no point in trying to unravel it. The adhesion was too strong.

I found a magnifying glass in a drawer. "Dirt. Seeds, probably grass. And something else. Reddish-brown . . . fabric? Some sort of fuzz?"

"Dexter's fur?" Mike was so close I could feel his warm breath on my cheek.

"No. Too short, wrong color. OK, I think I know. Material off a glove, maybe a leather gardening glove. And—*shit!*" I jerked up and we bumped heads. Mike winced and I looked away.

"OK. Before you head-butted me, Jaymie, what did you see?"

"Look for yourself." I handed him the magnifying glass.

"Two curly blond hairs approximately one and a half inches long." He peered closer. "Dark roots, not quite black. More the color of a bay horse."

"Uh-huh. And notice: the roots aren't more than an eighth of an inch long."

He looked up at me. "Why is that important?"

"Because the god Apollo bleached his hair about one week before these fell out of his scalp." As I spoke my voice tightened with anger.

"Jared Crowley," Mike snarled. "I'll murder the little bastard. I'll kill him tonight!"

Oh, I wanted to share the sentiment. But right away, I knew it was all wrong. And I needed to get that message through to Mike, before he blew the case to bits.

Chapter Eighteen

We walked down to the south-facing beach and then headed west, into the setting sun. The burning orb lingered, bobbing on the horizon as if it were a balance beam. Just friends . . . It was strange, and it didn't feel so good to me.

I glanced over at Mike. "Calmed down yet?"

"My blood was up, I admit it." Mike picked up a stick, tossed it ahead for the dog. "Still is. Just seeing Dex hobble, I get pissed all over again."

"Remember what you said about things being too personal to think straight?"

"Sure. We need to keep quiet for now, run those hairs for DNA to be certain. Let Crowley be, for the moment. But this is evidence, Jaymie. Crowley tortured Dex and most likely killed Lili. Maybe even Danny, for Chrissake!"

"I'd love it if it was that simple." I hopped over a heap of drying seaweed, and a cloud of black gnats rose up and buzzed my ankles. "But something's not right. It's too obvious, just too damn obvious! I feel like I've been handed the killer on a plate."

"Don't do this, Jaymie. For once, just accept the fact: it *is* simple."

"No." I shook my head stubbornly. "Like I said, this killer needs things to be complicated. Complicated and misleading."

"Damn it, Jaymie. He's not some genius!"

"Not a genius, no. But he's smart, real smart. My guess is he somehow obtained Jared's hairs and stuck them on the tape. I'll bet he also planted hair on the tape that got tossed at the vet's."

Mike groaned. "Come on. Do you really think the killer's that clever?"

"Absolutely. He's a chameleon, deceptive. It's in his nature, his way of hiding: nothing can be what it seems."

"OK, OK. Going with that theory for a moment, how about this? Jared's the killer. He's so damn clever, he pretends to be someone else—implicating him."

"You're making my head hurt." I laughed a little. "But no, Jared wouldn't do that. He's sly, but he hasn't got the nerve. If he were guilty, he'd never do anything to turn the spotlight back on himself. By the way, there's something I haven't told you about Jared."

"Sure there is."

"Bruce Wiederkehr and Jared are lovers."

Mike stopped dead in his tracks. "How the *hell* do you know that?"

"It's kind of a long story. But the thing is, somebody out there knows all about their relationship. Jared's being black-mailed. Of course, Wiederkehr's the one paying up."

"Shit, Jaymie. You've been keeping all this to yourself?"

I ignored his question. "My point is, the blackmailer could very well be the killer—and the one who stuck Jared's hair on the tape."

Mike toed a broken sand dollar. "A blackmailer wants cash. That eliminates most of our suspects, doesn't it? Apparently they're swimming in it. Everyone except Crowley, that is. Maybe he's actually the one wringing the dough out of Wiederkehr."

"Possibly. But there are other fruits of blackmail, remember. Like causing the victim to squirm, and enjoying his pain." I looked out across the channel to the now-dying sun. "You know, I've always wanted to see a green flash at sunset. Most often it happens in the tropics, but they say every once in a while it happens right here."

"It's getting late," Mike observed. "I've got to go."

I wanted to ask him where he had to be, but I kept my mouth shut. A lover might have the right to ask such a question, but not a mere friend.

"No green flash," I said as the sun plunged away.

"I've been wanting to do this for ages." I carefully pried a loose chunk of sea glass from the Vee-Dub dash, dabbed on glue, and pressed the translucent blue piece back into place. "It isn't until you actually work on this that you realize how seamlessly it all fits together. Your van belongs in the Smithsonian."

"Annie has the artist's touch," Charlie rumbled from somewhere in the back. "You're the only one she trusts to work on it, Jaymie."

"Well, at least that's one person who trusts me. It's a short list these days." I paused and studied the next item: a seventies Matchbox car, its paint worn off by surf and sand. "Truth is, Charlie, I'm stuck."

"You're talkin' about the murders now?"

"Yeah. I'm stuck in other ways too, but that's the one I'm most worried about."

"Hm. Knowing you, I bet you already walked down every avenue."

"More than once. And I've learned plenty about certain people. Stuff they'd prefer to keep under wraps."

Charlie sucked noisily on a horehound. "So the investigation just goes round 'n' round, like one of these damn roundabouts they're building all over town."

"Round and round. A handful of suspects, and I can't seem to shorten the list."

"There's a way outta that stuck situation, you know. You're

doin' it all on your own. You gotta ask other people for help, let in some fresh air."

"Other people, they let you down." I ran my hand under the dash. "Wow. Annie even lined this part under here. Feels like shells."

I opened the van door and stretched out along the floor on my back, my legs sticking out into the parking lot.

"Yeah, we remember when she worked on that, don't we, Annie? Hard on the back, it was."

I ran my fingers over the rounded cowry shells. "It's all intact under here. Doesn't get the sun on it, I suppose."

I was about to leverage myself out when something pink caught my eye. Glued way in the back, all by itself, was a tiny plastic treasure chest. It was the sort of toy a kid might get from a gum-ball machine.

"Charlie? Do you know about this? There's a little pink treasure chest up in here."

"Might know something about it."

"Should I open it? Looks like the clasp really works."

"Well . . ." He was quiet for a long moment. "Why not."

I hesitated. Something was in there, all right. Something that mattered. Maybe something that was just plain none of my business.

"Jaymie, it's OK. Annie says take a look."

With thumb and forefinger, I popped it open. A small object dropped out and hit me on the nose, then rolled to the floor of the van.

"Hold on." I backed out like an upside-down crab, then knelt on the pavement to scan the van floor. "Can't really see—" I shifted, the sun angled in over my shoulder, and something winked back at me.

"Oh, how about that!" I picked up the tiny gold ring and held it up to the light, admiring the miniature diamond surrounded by what looked like ruby chips. "Charlie, what—" But then I stopped short.

It was a ring for a child. A little girl.

I turned and stared at the tattered gauze curtain. "Did Annie put this ring in the treasure chest?"

"Who else? It's all Annie's work."

"Tell me what it is, Charlie. Don't make me guess."

"Well. S'pose Annie would want you to know." He coughed heavily. "Long time ago now, Annie and me, we had a baby girl. Named her Bonny. We kept ahold of Bonny for nearly a month before they took her off us. Claimed we weren't fit parents. We was living pretty rough then, up in the hills. But I always reckoned somebody wanted Bonny, somebody with clout. She was a real beautiful baby."

"What a terrible sorrow to carry with you."

"It was worse on Annie. Hard."

"And this ring, was it Bonny's?"

"Yep. Annie came from money, you know that. The Longstreets. She had a little cash of her own stashed away. When Bonny was born, Annie designed that ring and sent the design to a jeweler's. But the ring didn't arrive till after our baby was gone."

"I'm so sorry. Did you try to find your daughter later on?"

"Dozens a times. Wrote letters to agencies, that kinda thing. Nothin' ever came of any of it."

"Must have been tough on both of you."

"Still is, Jaymie. Still is."

I sat in the seat, carefully cradling the ring in the palm of my hand.

After a time, Charlie cleared his throat roughly. "But Annie, she's got an idea. She thinks it's time for us to pass the ring on."

An uncomfortable feeling swelled up inside me. I looked out to the sea, rolling in, rolling out, over and over and over.

"Annie's handing the ring over to you, Jaymie. To keep for

your little girl. And she says if you have boys instead, keep it for your granddaughter."

"Charlie, I—" My throat was so tight it hurt. "I'm just not the right one."

"You're the one, all right. I don't care to argue with you, girl. But if Annie says you're the one, why, it's you."

"But what Annie doesn't know . . . is that I won't be having any kids."

Charlie was quiet for a time. The whole world was quiet, except for the surf pounding the shore.

"OK. But it don't make no sense to me, 'cause I was a foster kid. There's a million kids out there in the world nobody wants—why, you'd love one or three of those kids no problem, I know you would."

I didn't answer until I was sure my voice was steady. "I'll take the ring, Charlie. I'll keep it safe and hand it on to the right person. Tell Annie I promise to do that much."

I hopped out of the way as Gabi pivoted and nearly ran over my foot with the purple vacuum.

"Sorry," she shouted with what was obviously barely restrained patience. "My two jobs don't mix so good when I'm in a hurry!"

"Just for one minute," I shouted back, "would you mind switching it off?"

"One minute? Sure." Suddenly it was quiet in the big empty room. "Miss Jaymie? You never chased me down at one of my houses before. It must be important."

"You're never at the office, and I need your advice."

"I want to be there—it's where I belong." Gabi let out a long deep sigh and released her grip on the vac handle. "But Sparkleberry still only has one employee, me. I tried those three girls, they didn't work out. One showed up when she felt like it and the second one had a big mouth. And the third, Kathy, the one I really liked, stole my other vac, my favorite, right out of my car."

"You've had some back luck," I agreed.

Gabi hesitated. "But it's not just that, I gotta be honest with you. Nothing's happening, Miss Jaymie. New clients call, I tell you about them, you don't follow up." She shrugged. "What's there for me to do, except maybe keep a seat hot?"

"That's how it's going to be, until I find the killer. Patience is part of the job."

Again, Gabi sighed loud and long. "Let's go make some expresso, Jefa. I finally figured out the señor's machine."

After a hiccupping start, the shiny contraption, big as a car engine, cooperated. We carried our cappuccinos into the ultramodern living room and perched on the hard rectangular furniture.

"I've been selfish." I took several sips of my drink, and noticed Gabi was smiling at me.

"You got a mustache. But what did you say?"

I wiped my mouth on my sleeve. "I said I've been selfish."

"That's what I thought you said. But no, it's one thing you are not. Stubborn, yes. Selfish, no. So what are you talking about?"

"I can't expect you to live on nothing, Gabi. Me, I'll live on boxes of noodles until—until I look like a noodle. But it's not fair to ask you to do the same."

"I still have a little money left over from the five thousand you gave me. I'm OK for now. I just—I just don't like doing nothing, you know? I don't like to be useless."

"Believe me, neither do I." I set my cup on the big glass coffee table and rubbed my face hard. "I'm running around in circles, and I hate it."

Gabi had spotted a spiderweb, very small, on the rock fireplace. She jumped up, grabbed her long-handled duster, and swiped at the gray strand. "Keep talking, Miss Jaymie. I'm all ears."

"Well, a friend of mine said I should ask other people for . . . ideas." I leaned back in the stiff uncomfortable couch and gazed at the ceiling. "Oh, hell. He said I need to ask for help."

"Good advice! I thought you'd never say something like that." Gabi propped up the duster in a corner. "Listen, I been biting my tongue. It's about Mrs. Richter. That's the only thing I seen you do I don't agree with, sending her off like that. She had something to tell you—didn't you hear?"

"I heard, but she took off, and I didn't feel like chasing after her. . . . You know what? I didn't think any more about it." An uncomfortable feeling crept over me. "Damn, did I screw up?"

"I think maybe you did."

"See, I thought she deserved the cold shoulder. That little boy . . . life is so lonely and hard for him with that birthmark. What friend did he have but the dog?" I stood and walked to the huge plate-glass window that looked out over the city below. "I still get pissed when I think about it."

"Sometimes we gotta compromise, you know?"

"I'm not a great compromiser. But you're right, Richter had something to tell me—who knows, maybe it was something about the case. I'll have to eat crow, Gabi, that's all there is to it."

"Eat a crow?" Gabi stared me. "What, are you crazy now?"

"Just an expression. You know, like eating humble pie."

"*Humble* pie?"

"Yes, humble pie. Definitely not my favorite flavor."

"English!" Gabi scowled. "It's like a boxer. I never know when it's gonna give me a punch."

How did she do it? Already my spirits were lifting.

"Listen, I'm done here." Gabi untied her apron and lifted the strap over her head. "I know you turned in the Honda to save money, so use my car to go see Mrs. Richter. We'll put your bike in the back and you can drop me off at the office. You don't wanna show up on that bike, Miss Jaymie. Impressions are important, you know."

"Ms. Zarlin. I wondered when you'd turn up."

Something was different about Darlene Richter. And what

was she doing out in her front yard with a butterfly net in her hand?

"You mean, like a bad penny?"

"No, I wouldn't say that." She stepped closer and I saw what had changed: she wore no makeup, and gray roots showed at her temples.

"I've come to apologize." I'd expected those words to stick in my throat. But Darlene smiled up at me, her hand shading her bright-green eyes from the sun. I found it wasn't so hard to speak after all.

"I see, Jaymie. And what are you apologizing for?"

"I was wrong to be angry. You had every right to take back your dog."

"I had every legal right, but no moral right. Isn't that what you felt?"

"Something like that."

"And if you had been in my place, what would you have done?"

I thought of Dex, and flushed. "Taken my dog back," I admitted. "But I wouldn't have felt too good about it."

"Well, neither did I." She smiled. "Call me Darlene, will you? Because honestly, I'm just Darlene Owens from King City."

To my surprise, Darlene Owens took me by the arm.

"Let's go around to the back, shall we, Ms. Zarlin? I only came out front because I spotted your car."

"Call me Jaymie," I said meekly.

We were halfway around the house when Minuet appeared, scampering toward us. A blue rubber handball was clenched in her teeth.

"She looks happy," I admitted. This was an understatement: the froufrou little thing looked delirious with bliss.

"Yes . . . and far too excited. But there's not much I can do about that."

We turned the corner of the house. Two figures, one large and one small, knelt beside a flower bed a hundred yards away. The little one looked up, then jumped to his feet and shouted. "Chica! Chica!"

Minuet-Chica raced back to the boy like a windup toy. "I do worry that little dog will have a heart attack," Darlene murmured. "But I suppose she'd die happy." She led me over to the pair.

Beto wore a miniature beekeepers' white suit and hat. He grinned widely at me. "Hi! I'm helping my tío."

"Good for you, Beto. I can see you're working hard." I couldn't seem to wipe a silly smile off my face.

"Yeah! But Chica, she keeps digging holes." He giggled.

"Jorge? This is Jaymie Zarlin. She's the lady who found Minuet."

Beto's uncle, the dog thief, looked up and appraised me. "Hi."

"Hi." I wasn't sure what else to say. "Looks like you've got a couple of helpers."

"Yes, and no." Jorge broke into a slow grin.

"I'll take them inside in a few minutes, Jorge." Darlene turned to me and dropped her voice. "The doctor doesn't want Beto outside at all, actually. He's taking medication to prepare him for his procedure, and he can't be in the sun. But you try telling that to a seven-year-old. So I looked online, and sure enough, I discovered they make beekeepers' outfits in kids' sizes."

"His procedure?"

"Let's walk to the house, shall we?" Darlene waited until we were out of earshot. "Beto knows about it, but of course he's a little scared. I don't talk about it too much in front of him. The truth is it's surgery, not just a procedure."

"For his birthmark? I'm amazed it's even possible to remove it, Darlene."

"Oh, let me tell you." She pushed her hair out of her eyes. "The first two doctors said nothing could be done. But I took him—the whole family, actually—down to UCLA. And they told a different story. They won't be able to completely remove it, but it will be better, so much better that people will just ignore it."

My throat tightened. "This will change Beto's life. He'll be able to go to school and have friends. . . ."

"Yes. It's going to be entirely worth it. And it will be safe: he'll have one of the best cosmetic surgeons in the world."

"I told my assistant I was coming here to eat humble pie. I didn't know how true that was." I met her gaze. "Sorry for my rush to judgment."

"It's easy to accept your apology, Jaymie. Because if it hadn't been for you and your work . . ." Darlene laughed. "Let me put it this way: if it weren't for you, I'd still have perfect hair. I never seem to have time anymore for the stylist."

She patted my arm. "Let's go inside. I do have something to tell you, something connected to the murder case. It won't be easy to say, and I don't want one of these pint-sized tornadoes interrupting us."

"What a wonderful bedroom, Darlene. A separate apartment, really." I looked about me, admiring the peach walls and warm cherry cabinets. Lime-green and rose-colored protea flowers drank from a crystal vase, and beside the arrangement, a heap of glowing lemons filled a matching crystal bowl. In the far corner, a bevy of bright tropical fishes darted about in a large cylinder-shaped saltwater fish tank.

"I created this little world for myself when my husband was alive. Frederick was . . . intrusive, shall we say. I put a lock on the door, and at night I used it." She motioned for me to sit in a turquoise club chair and settled herself on a matching love seat draped with a bright paisley shawl.

"Well. I hope you understand what I'm going to tell you. You seem like such a strong person, Jaymie. I don't suppose you'd let anyone take advantage of you."

"Maybe it's that way now. But when I was a kid, it was different."

"I know what you mean. Somewhere along the line, I made myself tough too. I had to. But you pay a price for toughness." She laughed a little. "Do you remember the story of the children who brought springtime to the giant's garden? I believe it was written by Oscar Wilde."

"Sure." I smiled. "Kids will do that to you if you let them."

"Yes, they certainly will. Beto and his sister have changed me." Darlene folded her hands and studied them. "It's not easy for me to tell you this. I'll say it, and then if you don't mind I'll go outside and get Beto. Sylvia will be here soon, and I want to fix them their afternoon snacks."

"You're babysitting the kids?"

"While their mother's at work." She drew the bright shawl over her lap. "You know, for twenty-five years, I've carried this inside me. I haven't spoken of it ever, to anyone. I'm not even sure how to begin."

"You've already made a good start."

"Yes, maybe I have. Well, here it is: in 1983, I was chosen to be Daphne."

The room grew suddenly still. I could hear Beto through the open window, singing a song out in the garden. "I didn't know."

"Yes. And when I walked into your office that day and saw the photos on your wall. . . . It all flooded back to me, all the anger and shame." Darlene balled her hands into fists. "I won't stop now. I owe myself that!" She threw back the shawl and got to her feet.

"I grew up in a poor family. My father was an alcoholic. My mother barely existed, caught in a cycle of abuse. All I ever wanted was to leave King City and get away from my family. And I did make it down here to Santa Barbara. I got a job as a maid at the Biltmore, and started my first semester at City College. I planned to become a beautician." She walked to the window.

"Oh dear. I see Beto has pulled the beekeepers' hat off his head. Maybe I should go out and—*no*. What I should do is finish this, once and for all." She turned and faced me.

"Have you noticed that Daphne is often poor and alone, as I was, or from a single-parent family? So there are no repercussions if—" She let the half-uttered thought hang in the air.

Nearly a full minute passed before Darlene completed her sentence: "If she is raped."

"Christ!"

"Oh, I'm not saying there's a conspiracy or anything." She shrugged. "I'm sure most of the Daphnes go their merry ways. But the opportunity is there, isn't it? Opportunity, power and entitlement, and a sick sort of tradition. And every once in a while, some twisted bastard decides to act on it."

Oh, Lili, I thought. Lili . . . "Why don't the victims go to the police? Are they afraid?"

"Certainly. In my case, the threats were veiled, yet made clear enough. Besides, the girls would get nowhere with the police, believe me. But you know, there's something else." She made a face of disgust. "Something that still makes me ashamed."

"You've no reason to be ashamed, Darlene. None at all. And I think I know what you're about to say."

"I'm sure you do. After the crime is committed, the victim is somehow rewarded. With money, or a scholarship, or, in my case, with a wealthy suitor. So the girl finds herself trapped in a double bind: she'll receive a great deal if she keeps silent, and she'll be punished if she talks."

"Who committed the crime against you?"

"Samuel McDermott." She laughed harshly. "Good God, the man was a zombie. I thought he'd never pass on. I seemed to run into the old half-dead bastard everywhere I went. And he always enjoyed reminding me of 'our little secret.'"

She curled back into her love seat. In the softly filtered light, Darlene Richter looked like the vulnerable girl she'd once been.

"Thank you for talking to me about this. I'm so mad at myself for not listening to you."

She shook her head. "I'm sorry, Jaymie. I wish I could have been more help."

"Darlene, listen to me. You've given me a key to the lock." I got to my feet. It was time to go.

A no-papers Mexican girl with a dead father—Lili would have appeared to be the perfect rape victim, I thought as I piloted the barge through the downtown streets on the way to the office. But in fact, Lili wasn't as vulnerable as the rapist had thought. For one thing, the Molinas were on track to become citizens, thanks to Teresa's engagement. With Lili, a threat of deportation wouldn't have worked, and she wouldn't have wanted anything the killer could offer her. But more than that: Lili Molina was brave.

Maybe Lili had said something the rapist didn't like. Maybe she'd infuriated him by simply saying *no*.

The moment I stepped into the office, a tornado engulfed me.

"Miss Jaymie! She says you called her. She says you told her to come over and poke around in the computer. But I said"— and Gabi's eyes flashed me a warning—"I said, no boss would do that without telling her PA first."

"Hey!" Claudia popped up like a jack-in-the-box in the kitchenette doorway. "You're lucky I waited. I don't put up with this kinda shit. I—"

I raised my hands in the air. "Stop. For the love of God, both of you stop."

To my amazement, they fell silent. For the moment, I held back the twin walls of roiling water. "You two listen to me. We have to pull together. We're in the home stretch." I turned to Gabi. "This girl, pain in the ass though she is, has lost her only sister."

Gabi blanched. "Oh. Oh, I know that, and—I'm sorry, mija."

I looked over at Claudia and saw she was listening, at least. "Claudia, let me tell you something about Gabi. She's lost her nephew. And Danny is still accused of a murder he didn't commit. By the way, Gabi offered to work for me for no money if I'd help him. So see?" I looked from one to the other. "We're all on the same side."

"I'm so sorry!" Gabi rushed over to Claudia and wrapped her in a hug. For a moment Claudia was stiff as a board, but then she hugged Gabi back.

I sat down in the hot seat and waited for the hugs to subside.

"Thanks, Jefa. We both needed that." Gabi returned to her driver's seat, and Claudia perched on the corner of the desk.

"Claudia, before you get started, fill Gabi in. Do you understand your assignment?"

"Yeah, course I do. When do you need it by?"

"Yesterday. So if you have to bring a sleeping bag here, do it. This may take time."

"I'll keep her company," Gabi volunteered. "I got two fold-out pads I can bring over. What else can I do?"

"Keep Claudia fed. Pizza should do it. And keep your phone on, 24/7, in case I need help."

"If it's dangerous," Claudia piped up. "You need me along."

"Me too," Gabi added, though she sounded a little less sure.

"Thanks. But right now, I need both of you here."

Chapter Nineteen

"Charlie, you'll have to forgive me, no horehounds today. Too distracted, I guess."

"Course I forgive you. What's on your mind?"

"The murders. Let's face it, I'm a rank amateur. I've cracked open Pandora's box, and now I don't know what to do next."

"Slow down, Jaymie. Cuppa joe?"

"No thanks, Charlie. Not today. Here's how it is: I think I know who killed Lili and Danny."

"Good for you." The curtain swayed. "How'd you figure it out?"

"A dash of intuition, and help from my friends. But if I told the authorities I'd solved the case based on intuition and chats with my buds, I'd get laughed right out of town." I dropped my head into my hands. "What do I do now?"

"You already know the answer to that one."

I felt like I deserved a dunce hat. "I have to . . . find evidence?"

"Yep. You gotta go out and rustle it up. Got any good evidence in mind?"

"Uh, well—" At that moment, a spark leaped a gaping synapse in my brain, and—at long last—the lights flashed on. "As a matter of fact, it so happens I do."

Evidence. Lili's medallion. Hadn't I known it from the beginning? When I found the Virgen de Guadalupe, I'd find the killer, too. Thing was, I'd gotten it the wrong way around: I knew the murderer's identity but hadn't yet found the medallion. And I needed it. I needed that proof.

I hadn't discovered its hiding place yet . . . but I could make a damn good guess.

"You just don't go away, do you?" Cynthia Wiederkehr stood before one of the narrow tank room windows, smoking. Several squashed butts lay at her feet. She glanced sideways at me as I entered, then returned her gaze to the window.

"Hi, Cynthia." I pulled the door shut behind me. "I thought you hated cigarette smoke."

"Oh, I do. With all the hatred of a recovering addict." Cynthia was dressed as classically as always. But everything about her looked rumpled and out of focus, as if she'd been picked up and savagely shaken.

"Explain something to me, Ms. Zarlin. Why did I agree to meet you today?" She dropped the cigarette to the rough unfinished timbers, and ground it out with the toe of her polished pump. "Masochism, I suppose."

"I doubt that. You're a smart woman, and my guess is you're trying to piece the puzzle together. You want to know the whole truth."

"The truth?" Her laugh was a whinny. "What truth is that? The truth that my daughter's having an affair with an older man, and I knew nothing about it? The truth that my husband's a fag—smitten with some bleach-haired bimbo of a boy?" She half turned to glare at me. "Thanks to you, I already know about as much of the truth as I can stomach."

"I'm not interested in your husband's sex life." I softened my voice as best I could. "I'm interested in identifying a killer. And as it happens, all the suspects on my short list used you and your party as an alibi."

"You call yourself a detective?" She cast a look of scorn on me. "If you want to find the killer, look at Jared Crowley. Actually, I was wrong just now when I called him a bimbo. Crowley is sharp, a con artist. Hardly the choirboy he appears."

"I know plenty about Jared. He looks guilty, all right—because he was so expertly set up."

I watched Cynthia as she circled the room. She was hurt, but something more was going on. She seemed almost afraid.

She halted in front of me. "Look, I know you want something from me. Otherwise you wouldn't be here. Say it and go."

"I want you to show me Sarah's jewelry box."

Cynthia paled and her mouth fell open. "Sarah's—but why—" A dull dark tide of blood crept up her neck. "No. I will not let you get your dirty hands on my daughter. That's where I draw the line. You won't drag Sarah into this!"

If there's one emotion you need to treat with respect, it's the passion of a mother protecting her young. I'd have to find a way to turn Cynthia's fury to my advantage, or cease and desist.

"Cynthia, I'm not accusing Sarah of anything. The opposite, actually. I suspect your daughter was used to hide evidence without her knowledge. You'll be helping her if you let me look at her jewelry."

"But who—" Then she gasped. "How dare he! How dare Bruce use his own child—" She stuck a pointed finger in my face. "*You. Come with me.*"

Sarah's room was oddly juvenile. All yellow and pink, decorated with fanciful butterflies and birds. A big canopied bed, swathed in acres of blush-colored netting, stood at the center.

"We haven't got long." Cynthia closed the door behind us. "Sarah's taking a summer school class, and she gets out in ten minutes. She'll come straight home to change."

I watched as Cynthia went to the nightstand, opened the

middle drawer, and removed a miniature key. "She keeps her jewelry chest locked, of course. To avoid tempting the maids."

I gritted my teeth. Eyes on the prize, I reminded myself. Eyes on the prize.

The mint-green jewelry box sat on a long dresser. I stood beside Cynthia as she opened the leather box with the tiny key and lifted the lid. A melancholy ballerina twirled to a twangy waltz.

"I don't see anything unusual in here." Cynthia stirred the jumble with a finger. It was all fine jewelry: I saw three or four diamond tennis bracelets, an emerald set in a platinum ring, a sapphire and diamond pendant, and warm glowing pearls.

"Do you want to take a closer look, or are you satisfied now?" Cynthia was obviously relieved.

Satisfied? I was disappointed: so much for my vaunted intuition. "Sarah doesn't keep her valuables anywhere else, does she?" Actually, I doubted it. What I'd just seen was a king's ransom. Surely there wouldn't be more?

"The really valuable pieces are in a vault downtown. Her everyday earrings are on a stand in her bathroom, but other than that—oh. Sarah does have a miniature treasure chest. She used it when she was little—I doubt she's opened it in ages." Cynthia closed and locked the jewelry box, and carefully replaced the key in the nightstand drawer.

"Listen. After I show you the treasure chest, you'll have to go." She opened a door leading into a large walk-in closet and switched on a light.

"I'll have to speak with Lupe," Cynthia muttered. "It doesn't look as if she's cleaned in here for some time."

I followed her into the long narrow space. Clothes were wedged into tightly packed racks, and a jumble of shoes littered the floor. The closet was filled with the smell of Sarah: a brash perfume covering the fuggy odor of sweats.

"How funny. I thought I'd have to rummage for it, but here it is, right out on this shelf." Cynthia raised the lid of the carved wooden box, and paused.

"Where on earth did she get *this?*"

In a flash I stood beside Cynthia. And there it was, nestled in a child's collection of trinkets: a gold medallion on a gold chain. I leaned closer: the medallion was etched with the image of La Virgen de Guadalupe.

"This medallion belonged to Lili Molina. She wore it night and day." I took it into my hand. "Look: you can see where the chain has been repaired."

"Bruce—how could he. How *could* he!" Raw fury sprang up in Cynthia's eyes, and she let out a thin scream.

Quickly, before the situation could deteriorate further, I turned back to the box. I nudged aside sparkly rocks and old pennies, objects a young and innocent girl had collected. A moment later, a chill ran through me like a surgical knife.

There, at the bottom of the treasure box, lay three more pieces of jewelry. I picked up each item in turn. A gold engraved cross. A cheap expansion bracelet, chrome with rhinestones. And a tarnished silver necklace, finely wrought, of interlocking *x*'s and *o*'s. I cradled all four items in the palm of my hand and met Cynthia Wiederkehr's stricken gaze.

"I don't recognize any of those things," Cynthia moaned. "I'm done with that man, done!"

"Cynthia," I began. "There's something I should tell—"

"Those were gifts to *me,*" Sarah Wiederkehr said icily from the closet doorway. "To me from my boyfriend, do you hear? Put them back. And get out of my room this instant, both of you hags!"

"Sarah! I don't understand. What—"

"I'm so sick of you, Mom. You still pretend I'm a little girl, and you know perfectly well I'm not!"

I was trapped in a closet between a livid mother and her

enraged teenage daughter. Before the Molotov cocktail exploded, I needed to get the hell out. "Excuse me, Sarah. I need to go."

"Not with my stuff you don't." She moved to block me. The golfer needed a lesson, and I forced her aside with a sharp elbow in the ribs.

"Hey, that hurt! And you're stealing!"

I stared her down. "You aren't hurt and I'm not stealing. I have four objects here I'm turning in to the police as evidence in the murder of Lili Molina. If you cooperate, I'll say the killer asked you to keep these for him. If you don't cooperate, I'll tell the full truth."

"Killer? What do you mean, killer? I just—" Sarah's mouth gaped.

Behind me, still stuck in the closet, Cynthia let out a bleat. "Sarah! What is she talking about? Does this have something to do with your father? Sarah, I demand—"

"Dad? It doesn't have anything to do with Dad!" Sarah spun around and screamed at her mother. "*Shut up. For once why don't you just shut up!*"

"I'm your mother, I've every right—"

"It's Sutton. Is that all right with you, *Mommy Dearest?* He never even liked you. Didn't you know? All the time it was me he wanted, he just used you so he could be close to me!"

Cynthia sagged. Then she buckled at the knees and slumped to the floor.

I climbed into Gabi's station wagon and pulled the door shut. Then I removed the four sacred objects from my pocket and rested them side by side in the passenger seat. The medallion, the cross, the bracelet, the necklace. I knew exactly what they were: trophies taken by Sutton Frayne from his victims. One trophy per rape. Possibly, one trophy per kill.

And I knew something else: although Sarah probably had

no knowledge of the jewelry's original owners, she hadn't simply stored the pieces away. No, I'd bet my sweet life on it: she'd worn them when requested. The rhinestone bracelet, the cross, the necklace of *x*'s and *o*'s, and Lili's medallion: Sarah wore them when she and charming Sutz had sex.

I reached over into the back and grabbed one of Gabi's yellow rubber gloves, slipped the jewelry into the fingers, and tucked it into a bucket holding brushes and rags.

Then I switched on my cell and phoned the office. "Gabi, any results?"

"Not yet. Miss Jaymie, she won't stop to eat nothing, I'm trying to tell her—"

"Forget about food. Tell Claudia to keep digging into Frayne's past. She needs to comb through the newspapers, find every single rape and rape-murder committed wherever he's lived. Sutton Frayne, Gabi. He's the one."

I turned the key in the ignition and began to move forward down the Wiederkehrs' private lane. Out of nowhere, a gunmetal-gray limo pulled sideways across the exit into the road, blocking it. The vulture-like face of Celeste Delaney peered at me through a side window.

I braked and fumbled blindly for the power-lock button, just as Ken Utman wedged his shoulders out through the limo door. Then an even larger man, a thug I'd never seen before, rolled out from the front passenger side and walked around the limo to stand beside Ken.

Celeste rapped on the glass with her stick, then dropped the window an inch. Ken bent his neck and angled an ear to the opening. Then he straightened and said something to his companion, the mountain of flesh. They started toward me.

I was tempted to run the goons down, and maybe that's what I should have done. Instead, I stepped on the gas and surged past them.

The limo was stretched sideways across the lane. There was a gap between the rear bumper and a stone pillar supporting the wall—but I realized too late that the gap was a foot too narrow for Gabi's wagon. I jumped on the brake and stopped several feet short of Celeste Delaney's door. The woman had nerves of steel: all this time, she hadn't taken her black eyes from me.

I must have missed the power button, because Ken yanked my door open with ease. I swiveled around and managed to place a swift kick squarely in his gut. I'd aimed lower, but this did the job and sent him tottering. The other goon opened the passenger door, and when I turned to confront him, the butt of a gun whacked against my cheekbone. I yelped in pain.

"What's the matter, Utman? The little girl hurt ya?" Mountain Man laughed.

"Get out, Zarlin," Ken snarled behind me. He grabbed my shoulder and dragged me to the ground. I scrambled to my feet, but the other guy had already circled the station wagon and trained the gun on me.

Ken's face was red with rage. He frisked me roughly, removed my cell, and stuffed it into his pocket. Then he frog-marched me over to the limo.

"She wants you treated nice—for now," he spat in my ear. "I couldn't care less, so behave yourself or there'll be a little accident."

"Remember, Ken, she's the boss." I hoped my voice sounded cocky, but maybe it didn't. I was terrified.

The guy with the gun opened the limo door, and Ken shoved me into the seat facing Celeste. "You want Hurley to sit back here with you, Miss Delaney?"

"Absolutely not. I cannot bear the sight of the man. Did you recover the trinkets?"

"They're not on her. Too big to stuff up her—" Ken stopped himself. "We'll come back later and go through the car. Or she coulda stashed them in the yard on her way out."

"If you go onto the property, be discreet." She turned to me. "How are you, my dear?" Her smile was tender, for a flesh-tearing raptor.

"Just fine, considering I'm being kidnapped." I was determined to be plucky. Showing fear to Celeste Delaney was not a good idea. For one thing, this was the aunt of Sutton Frayne.

"You really are brave, aren't you? Most commendable, I would say."

The two front doors thumped shut, and the glass partition whirred into place. The limo glided into the road, so smoothly that we seemed to be rolling forward on a sheet of stainless steel.

"I have to admit I rather admire you, Jaymie. Tell me, this business about the jewelry. How did you know where to find it?"

I knew I should say nothing. But my anger was growing, and apparently I wasn't going to keep my mouth shut. "Sarah had revealed she had a lover—an older man. I'd guessed Frayne had snagged her. After all, what better way to raise merry hell than to screw your friend's wife and daughter? I knew Lili's murderer kept the medallion as a trophy, and once I figured out your nephew was the killer, I put two and two together. How jolly to have a teenager wear your victim's jewelry while you fuck her—wouldn't you agree?"

"Vulgarity does not become you, Jaymie. I think you are losing your cool, as they say. But it is understandable, I suppose, under the circumstances."

"Where are we going?" I demanded.

"You shall see soon enough." She tapped me lightly on the neck with her cane. "Soon all your questions will be answered, little detective. Then you will need to question no more."

Her head tipped to one side. It was odd: Celeste's face was beginning to look like a totem, the wooden mask of a vulture. Was fear causing my mind to play tricks on me?

We rose in elevation as the limo slipped up the winding

roads of Montecito, where large secluded estates backed into mountain ravines. Twenty-foot-high hedges of Victorian boxwood hid the properties from view.

We glided to a stop before a pair of tall iron gates topped with spikes. Ken stuck his arm out the window and punched in a code. The gates swung back. "Stonecroft," Celeste observed. "Barely tolerable in midsummer, and a miserably cold cave in the winter. A mausoleum for the living, in a way."

The crushed granite road snaked through redwoods and ferns, then ended in a circular drive. A gray stone mansion, three stories high, loomed in the crook of a steep hill. The shaded slate roof was thick with mold-blackened moss.

"Come closer, Jaymie. I have something to tell you, something for your ears alone."

I can't say why I obeyed my captor. Maybe it was my unquenchable curiosity, the kind that killed the cat. Whatever the reason, I did lean toward Celeste, and allowed her claw to grip the skin of my neck as she breathed an odor of carrion on my cheek.

"You have tried so very hard, my dear, with so little reward. Before you go, I should like to do something for you. I am going to introduce you to Daphne. The very *archetype* of Daphne."

The elderly housekeeper who opened the door was dressed in a gray skirt and black sweater. She glanced quickly at me, then stepped back and stared at the floor.

"Janet," Celeste snapped as she entered. "Is she in the sitting room?"

The lady visibly cringed. "Yes, Miss Delaney. Today, she—"

"That will do, Janet. I don't need to hear how her bowels are behaving, or some such thing. Take the boys to the study."

"Yes, Miss Delaney." The woman twisted her hands.

I had an urge to leave a trail of bread crumbs behind me. "Hello," I said firmly. "I'm Jaymie Zarlin."

"Hel-Hello," Janet faltered.

"Never mind about her," Celeste ordered. "You come with me."

Everything about the interior was massive and heavy. The floors were stone, the walls paneled in dark oak. This was not a California house, but a structure that belonged in the East. Perhaps it had been built by a wealthy industrialist, before the Great Depression.

Leaning on her stick, Celeste tapped her way over the stones like a blind person. But her path was unerring, across the hall and down a long corridor. We entered a great kitchen, large enough to serve an army. A teakettle, the only item that spoke of life, whistled away on the concrete counter. "Janet is thick as a plank. Look at that: the idiot's left the kettle boiling. Pull out the cord."

As I did so, it crossed my mind that the boiling water was a weapon I could use to free myself. But my curiosity was growing, conquering my fear.

Celeste hobbled toward a door at the far end of the kitchen. "Open it, will you."

The door opened into a simple room, no doubt originally planned as a breakfast room off the kitchen. It was furnished with a scattering of chairs and small tables, and a big old television set, which crackled and hissed in a corner.

Sunk into a motor-powered recliner facing the TV was a large pale-skinned woman with wispy white hair. "Why, Ce-Celeste—" Her flaccid cheeks quivered as she attempted to speak.

"Really, Caroline." Celeste hobbled up to the woman. "Your sweater is food-stained. Make yourself presentable, can't you?"

Caroline. So this was the mother of Sutton Frayne.

"But, Celeste . . . I didn't know you were . . . were . . ." Poor Caroline. She tried to smile at me, but her expression collapsed in defeat.

"Were what, coming to visit? What if I have? Now pay attention. This is Miss Zarlin. Miss Zarlin, my sister, Caroline Frayne."

"Hello, Caroline."

"Hello, I—I—"

"Honestly, Caroline, pull yourself together," Celeste scolded.

Caroline looked down at the knitting abandoned in her lap.

So, where was the fabled Daphne? I glanced around the room, almost expecting her to pop up from behind a chair.

"What are you looking for?" Celeste asked in a sly tone. She leaned heavily upon her cane, watching me now. "Or should I say, whom?"

"You said you'd introduce me to Daphne. I was just wondering . . . *Oh.*" I looked again into the sad lost eyes of Caroline Frayne.

"Yes, what year was it, Caroline?" Celeste leaned down and shouted into her sister's ear. "What year was it you were selected to be Daphne, and raped by Daddy's old friend?"

"But Celeste," Caroline said in a shivery voice, "you said— you said we must never—"

"For heaven's sake, close your mouth," Celeste snapped. "Every time you open it I must wonder what fresh inanity will issue forth."

The television crackled on and on.

"Well. As it happens, the half-wit is right—we tell no one. Except for Janet, even the staff do not know." Celeste hobbled to a chair and eased herself down. "She was impregnated, you see, and Daddy arranged for an idiot to marry her quickly. But even Reggie Frayne could not tolerate her in the end."

Celeste pointed her cane at me and cackled. "Oh my, if you could see your face!"

Apparently I'd been called upon to bear witness to the shame and suffering of nearly six decades. I turned to Caroline. "I'm sorry. Truly sorry for what happened to you."

"You are sorry for her? But why?" Celeste patted her hair with a shaky hand. "Father took care of my doltish sister from then on. Though I daresay that was only fair. You see, it was Daddy who had arranged the rape of our Daphne. He told her it was an ancient solstice tradition, the sacrifice of innocence, and she should be honored to play her part. But in fact, Caroline was sacrificed in exchange for a business favor—the oil rights to a large parcel of land in the Los Angeles basin. Oh my"—she laughed again at my expression—"you do find it shocking, don't you?"

"Caroline," I said gently. "You never told anyone?"

"I—I—"

"Certainly she did not," Celeste interrupted. "In our day, a girl kept quiet about such things. She remained silent out of shame, I suppose, but also out of respect for the family and the tribe." Celeste turned to her sister and again raised her voice. "Isn't that right, Caroline? You kept quiet about what Jack Caughey did to you."

Jack *Caughey?* "What, do you mean Cynthia Wiederkehr's father?"

"Certainly I do. Cynthia is Sutton's half sister, and that clever daughter of hers, Sarah, is Sutton's niece."

I was quiet for a moment as Celeste's words sank in. So Frayne had sex with his sister and then with his niece. I glanced over at Caroline. Her face had grown blank, and she seemed to have abandoned her body.

"Don't look to her for answers," Celeste said. "You'll come up empty-handed."

The stark cruelty of her remarks nearly took my breath away.

"I'd have drowned the infant at birth, had it happened to me," Celeste continued. "Still, it all worked out, in a way. I was able to take a strong hand in Sutton's upbringing, especially after my grandson's death."

"How did you know I was at the Wiederkehrs' today?" I asked quietly. "Did Cynthia phone you?"

"Cynthia? Hardly. Caroline, ring the bell. Caroline, I spoke to you!"

Caroline crept back into her skin and looked confusedly about.

"The bell, you fool!"

Sharp high rings stabbed at the air.

"No, it was Sutton who phoned me, of course. He was up in Carmel when Sarah called him, quite distraught. Apparently you upset the girl. He is on his way here now, as we speak."

"You never cared about Danny, did you? That was just a ruse."

"You *are* catching on!" Celeste clapped her hands together. "Great God in heaven, why would I, of all people, trouble myself over an impoverished Mexican boy? All that matters to me is my lineage, and Sutton is my only living heir. You know, my nephew thought you were an idiot, nothing to worry about. But I suspected otherwise. You were determined to get that boy out of jail, and one way or another, I knew you'd succeed. Paying the bail was merely a way for me to keep an eye on you, my dear, to keep 'in the loop.'"

"And supplying me with the photographs from the parade and the park? A diversion, I suppose."

"I rather prefer the term 'red herring,' don't you? It has a whiff of the literary about it."

"You knew Sutton was guilty. You knew from the start."

"No, that's not so. But I suspected as much. You see, I know what he is capable of."

"Celeste," Caroline said in a quavering voice, "what is she talking—"

"Shut up," Celeste barked. She turned back to me. "There's no harm in telling you now. Yes, I know my nephew rather well. Something happened while Sutton was in college, you see, involving a coed."

"He raped a girl, didn't he. Did he kill her?"

Caroline let out a cry. "Celeste, what is she—"

The door opened and Janet stepped into the room. "Did someone ring?"

"Tell Ken and his dog to come in, Janet. Tell them the package is ready." Celeste smiled. "'The package.' That's what they say in the movies, you know."

But I had no intention of becoming anybody's package.

I jumped up and ran for the door, pushing Janet aside as gently as I could. I jogged down the hall, turned right and then right again. I found myself in a utility room with no windows or exit.

At that moment I heard a commotion: Ken and his dog. The hunt was on, and I was the fox.

I hurried back into the hall and jogged around a corner. Here the hall ended in a series of steps. I peered down and saw another door, which looked as if it might lead to the basement. I took the chance and raced down. Miracle of miracles, the door swung open onto a small landing. I stepped through, pulled the door shut behind me, and turned the bolt.

The half-basement was gloomy and vast. A row of small windows set just above ground level allowed in a little light. No doubt there were electric lights too, but it wouldn't be smart to switch them on. A strip of light around the door could announce my presence.

I felt my way down the steps, sliding my hand along the rough wooden banister. I was so focused, I felt no pain when a splinter drove into my palm. By the time I reached the cellar floor, my eyes had adjusted to the low level of light.

The cellar was crammed with many decades' worth of discarded tools, boxes, and massive pieces of old furniture. Places to hide—but what I needed was a way *out*.

The windows were fixed in the wall and too small. Even if I

managed to break one without being heard, I wouldn't be able to squeeze through. Heavy footsteps above. Stuck! My heart hammered in my chest.

Now the feet pounded directly overhead. I wound my way through the debris to the back of the space. And there I saw it: a fine beading of light outlining a pair of angled double doors. It was an old wooden cellar hatch, built into the wall. But as I made my way toward it, the doorknob rattled at the top of the stair. Time was up.

I found an old Victorian sofa, tipped it over, and slipped my body into the inverted V between the seat and the back. Dust filled my nostrils, and I felt as if I might choke. I coughed several times, then covered my mouth with my hand as a heavy body slammed against the cellar door. I knew the old wood could not withstand the force.

With the third onslaught, the wood splintered and the door burst apart. Immediately, a strong beam of light passed over the room, shining for an instant into my narrow den. Then the room was flooded with harsh light. "Zarlin!" Ken bellowed. "You wanna make it easy for yourself, get your ass out here!"

A minute of silence crept past.

"Hurley. You start down that end," Ken ordered. "I'm telling you, the bitch is in here somewhere."

I listened to Mountain Man stumble through the furniture, grunting a little. "Fuck!" Then there was a crash.

"What the hell happened?" Ken snarled.

"Stepped on a fuckin' rake."

Ken laughed. "Maybe it'll knock some sense into ya."

My heart was beating so loudly I was afraid they'd hear it. But Ken and the dog were making too much noise of their own, shoving over boxes and equipment, upending small pieces of furniture. As they moved through the room like twin bulldozers, their frustration seemed to mount.

"Set off a smoke bomb," Hurley suggested. "Smoke 'er out."

"Frayne wants to talk to her, didn't you hear?" Ken snapped. "He doesn't want her half-dead."

Ken stood very close to me now. The beam of his flashlight crept over the sofa. Would he think to shine it into the crevice? I shut my eyes so they wouldn't reflect the light.

When the beam crossed my face, I saw the light through my eyelids. I was shivering with fear, like a small animal run to ground.

But somehow, he didn't see me. They searched on for another four or five minutes before Ken called a halt. "Fuck. She musta gone upstairs."

"Hell, that's what I said in the first place," Hurley groused. "But you said—"

"Shut the fuck up, will you?"

They crashed through the shattered door on their way out.

I remained hidden in my upholstered cave for five minutes or more. I thought about old houses I'd visited in my childhood—houses with cellars. Those cellars had all had a hatch opening onto a farmyard or garden bright with sunshine. I fervently prayed that this hatch would not let me down.

When I crawled out from the sofa, the house was quiet. Ken and Hurley must have been searching two floors above. I moved carefully through the jumble, now even more chaotic thanks to my pursuers' search, and made my way to the hatch.

The golden light edging the small double doors was soft and bright as a monk's illumination.

I picked up a crate and set it below the hatch. Then I stepped up and gave one of the flaps a two-handed push. It budged a little, but something outside held it firm.

Of course something held it shut—most likely a hasp. If I was lucky, the hasp wasn't padlocked. I hopped off the crate and began rummaging through the chaos: there had to be something, some tool I could use.

It took me another three or four minutes to locate just the thing: a heavy file, probably used to sharpen garden tools.

First I had to widen the gap with the file, and that made some noise. But it wasn't long before the file slipped all the way through. I worked it along the gap.

Sure enough, some sort of narrow bar crossed the gap at midpoint and held the doors firm. Another few minutes of poking and prodding, and sweet success was mine. Apparently there was no lock, because I heard the hasp fall away.

Carefully, I lifted one of the flaps and shoved. It banged as it fell back against the wall of the house, possibly loud enough for someone upstairs to hear. I had no time to waste.

I hoisted myself up and over the hatch sill, and tumbled no more than a foot down to the cushiony lawn. I was tempted to lie there for a minute, breathing in the sweet smell of fresh grass and crushed clover, the warm sun on my—

"Up, bitch!"

I raised my head and found myself looking into the snub nose of a gun.

Chapter Twenty

"Hurley, I've got her. Get over here," Ken grunted into the mic attached to his collar.

"I see you kept a few little toys when you got kicked out of the force," I said cheerfully. I didn't want Utman to know how frightened I was. "That was forward-thinking of you."

"Open your smart mouth again, Zarlin, and I'll hurt you and like it. Now turn around and start walking."

"It wouldn't be wise to mess with me, Ken. Frayne likes to do his own hurting, you know."

I crumpled to my knees and gasped for air. He'd whacked me hard between the shoulder blades with the gun.

"I said shut the fuck up!"

Hurley appeared around the corner of the house, moving at a slow trot. "Where was she?"

"Creeping outta the cellar like a mutt. Now tie her hands. Then gag that smart mouth of hers. I don't want to listen to the shit that comes outta it."

Hurley bent over and cuffed me with zip-ties. He yanked me up by my wrists, and in spite of myself, I cried out in pain as the plastic cut into my skin. A filthy cloth was wrapped around my mouth and knotted at the back of my head.

"Step aside. I'll take over now." Ken prodded me in the small of the back with the gun. "Move it."

I thought about running. But as if he'd read my thoughts, Ken's hand gripped the back of my neck like a vise. "Don't try anything, I'm warning you." My arms felt as if they were about to pop out of their sockets.

He goaded me forward with the gun, around the corner of the house to an old Suburban parked under a cypress. I looked over at the house and glimpsed Janet watching our little parade through an upstairs window. I tried to plead to her with my eyes. But she put one hand over her mouth and melted back into the room.

Ken picked me up like a log and tossed me into the backseat. My head hit the opposite door, and my vision dimmed.

"Hold the gun on her," I heard him order. "And pay attention for once. She's a helluva lot smarter than you."

The two thugs sat in the front. Hurley was wedged sideways in the passenger seat so he could train the gun on me. We screeched out of the drive and headed uphill.

"So what does Frayne want us to—"

"Shut up, stupido. Not in front of her," Utman barked.

The trip was short. For no more than three or four minutes, the Suburban ground up an unpaved road. Dust choked my nostrils. Then we were off road for another few minutes, bouncing wildly before the vehicle jolted to a halt.

The two men jumped out. Hurley opened the door and dragged me out feetfirst. My head hit the ground hard. He yanked me upright and gave me a shove. Again I fell, and again he yanked me to a vertical position. My cheek was gouged, and I tasted blood.

"Hurley, quit screwing around," Utman snarled. "Let's get the job done. He'll be here in thirty minutes, and he wants us long gone."

"Wonder what he's gonna do," Hurley snickered.

"Quit wondering, bright boy."

Each of the men grasped one of my arms, and between them they hauled me forward, into a clearing surrounded by a circular stone wall. I was fading in and out, struggling to take in my surroundings.

I could see that the wall was open at four equally spaced points. Each of the four curved sections bore a stone mask of a lion with a spigot protruding from its open mouth. If circumstances had been different, I might have thought how entrancing the space was, a kind of Greek ceremonial garden. But as the men dragged me toward a big four-by-four post set in the center, I began to fear I was part of the ceremony.

Hurley held me against the post while Ken produced a wheel of plastic clothesline. He proceeded to lash me to the stake, round and round. He severed the line twice, and continued to wrap me until I looked like a mummy. The lashings were so tight across my chest I had trouble expanding my lungs.

"He's gonna have fun with her," Hurley leered. "Think he'll let us watch?"

"I said shut up, didn't I?" Ken turned on him with a growl. "You forget all this, 'cause if you don't, you'll pay a big price."

"Hey, I was just saying." Hurley fell silent, but the lewd smile lingered.

"Keep your trap shut and get the gas can outta the back. He wants it left by the wall over there, in the shade."

Gas can. Dear God, I hadn't expected this. A wing of panic brushed me.

Utman waited for Hurley to do as he was told. Meanwhile he stared at me, a smirk playing on his thin lips. "Guess this is it, huh?"

I didn't want Utman to know how frightened I was. I focused on the large mole, ugly as a tick, growing on Utman's chin.

"Don't worry, Zarlin." Ken lifted a corner of his lip, exposing a yellow canine. "I'll tell the deputy you said good-bye."

I heard the doors slam. The engine revved, and the Suburban roared back down the hill.

Gradually, the delicate sounds of nature returned to the clearing: bird chatter, lizards scuttering in the dry grass. And another natural sound: the whoosh of a hot summer wind.

Tinder-dry grass. Gasoline. Hot wind, which would morph into a sundowner in an hour or so, roaring down the canyons, through the city to the sea.

Fire. I wasn't the only one in danger now.

But at the moment, it was my own personal danger I was worried about. Utman had said Frayne was thirty minutes away. That was ten minutes ago.

I struggled against the clothesline, but Utman had a talent for bondage. I fought down the panic crowding up in my throat. Panic wouldn't help, and precious minutes were ticking by.

I forced myself to breath slowly, even and deep. Breathe in, breathe out, breathe in. . . . A scrub jay, blue as a flake of sky, hopped down from an oak and proceeded to scratch at the duff near my feet.

There had to be a way out, had to be! Again, panic crept up on me. I made a sound in my throat, a garbled choking sound. The blue jay halted and looked at me, tipping his head. My eyes brimmed with tears.

Then I heard something. I held my breath and listened hard. There it was again, a murmur of voices. Not on the road, but below in the chaparral, to my left.

A minute later, two silver-haired, red-faced women entered the enclosure. They were linked arm in arm, breathing hard. I let out a muffled cry.

Caroline stopped and leaned against the stone wall. Janet

raised her hand in greeting, then bent forward. The two of them didn't move for a time.

When they finally approached me, I saw their expressions. Fear was written there, yes. But there was a kind of triumph too, and I knew I was witnessing a true rebellion. I just hoped their hearts and lungs allowed them to survive the revolt.

"Try—to—hold—very—still—my—dear," Janet said, still breathless. She lifted a pair of sewing scissors from her apron pocket, inserted the blade under my gag, and cut. Meanwhile, Caroline silently patted me on the shoulder. At last the filthy rag fell away.

"Thank God," I gasped. "How did you know where to find me?"

"We overheard those horrible men talking. But we haven't much time," Janet cautioned. "Sutton will be here soon." She fished about in her magic pocket and this time removed a Swiss army knife. "Now those plastic thingamabobs on your wrists."

"Janet will have you free in no time," Caroline encouraged me. "She has very strong hands because she's had to work so hard all her life."

I gave out a grunt from the pain as the blood rushed into my hands. "Give me the knife, Janet, and I'll cut the rest." Within seconds, the snaking clothesline lay in a heap at my feet.

"Now you must come with us," Caroline said urgently. "The path is actually quite short, compared to the road. And it's all downhill!"

"Jaymie must run on ahead, Caroline. She's much quicker than we are."

"I'm in your debt," I said to both women. Then I turned to Caroline. "This must be especially hard for you—Sutton's your son."

Her face collapsed. I'd said the wrong thing.

"Caroline has been hurt by Sutton, in ways we can't even talk about. It's why I've always stayed, you see. To protect her."

Janet patted my arm. "We couldn't bear seeing him hurt you as well."

Caroline took my hand in her own. "Run, Jaymie. Fast as you can."

"Do you have a car I could use?"

"We only have the Suburban," Janet replied. "Those men will probably leave it behind at the house when they take Celeste away in the limo. But I don't drive anymore, and Caroline never did—I'm afraid they have the only key."

"If I'm lucky, they'll leave it in the ignition. Will the two of you be OK?"

"Oh, yes. I told Celeste that Caroline felt unwell, and that I needed to take her upstairs for a lie-down. Celeste can't climb the stairs." She broke into a smile. "When Caroline and I get back, we'll have tea and cookies to celebrate. No one will ever suspect that we've—well, rescued you!"

A red-hot needle jabbed my knee as I set off down the path. Damn—I'd injured it, probably when Ken knocked me to the ground. But I blocked the pain from my mind and pushed on: there was no time to lose.

Within minutes, I'd arrived at Stonecroft. I halted on the edge of the vast lawn.

A spider-like Celeste Delaney inched from the house, leaning heavily on her cane. Utman waited beside the limo, holding open the door. Hurley stood apart, smoking.

"Come on, come on. Hurry up and get out of here," I muttered under my breath.

I circled the lawn, staying at the margins, inside the shrubbery. I was looking for the Suburban. Then I spotted it, pulled up near the garage.

Time was short: Frayne would arrive very soon. And once he continued on up the hill and discovered my escape, he had two options: he could try to find me and kill me, or he could run.

Neither of those options was acceptable, not to me.

Celeste took her sweet time getting to the limo. Once she was in, Utman shut the door and hurried around to the driver's side. I wasn't the only one who wanted to keep out of Frayne's sight.

Utman barked something at Hurley, who tossed his butt, then slouched over to the front passenger side. The limo was moving before Hurley's door closed.

The dust hadn't yet settled in the drive as I hobbled across the lawn. The Suburban was unlocked, but there was no sign of a key. I looked everywhere: in the glove box, under the seats and the floor mats. *Nothing.* Had Utman stuffed the damn thing in his pocket? I slammed the door in frustration.

Unable to accept defeat, I was down on all fours checking under the chassis when I heard a powerful engine roar up the drive. Thank God I was hidden by the Suburban. I backed out and slipped into the shrubbery.

Sutton Frayne opened the door of his sleek black Maserati, stepped out, and surveyed the grounds. The strong Santa Ana wind ruffled his strawberry blond hair. He wore beige slacks and a blue chambray shirt, and looked ready for a garden party. The only detail that didn't jibe with a summer fruit salad was the ugly gun in his hand.

He stood there for a moment, studying the big house. Then he turned and looked over at the Suburban. I froze: Frayne seemed to be staring straight through the vehicle and the bushes and meeting my gaze.

He placed the gun on the roof of the Maserati and pulled a cell phone from his pocket, then punched in a number. I could hear him talking, but I couldn't make out the words. He ended the call, returned the cell to his pocket, and locked his car. I heard two musical clicks.

Then Sutton Frayne picked up the gun and headed straight for me.

At least, it seemed like that for an instant. Thank God, he was actually heading for the Suburban, eight or ten feet from my hiding place. I willed myself not to cough or move. I barely breathed, and if I could have stopped the beating of my heart, I'd have done that too.

When he reached the vehicle, I caught a whiff of Frayne's cologne. That scent—I'd smelled it before ... *in the dressing room*. Where Lili was raped and murdered.

But Frayne wasn't thinking about Lili Molina now. I'd little doubt he was intent on his next project: me.

He opened the driver's door, reached down, and popped the hood. Then he walked to the front of the vehicle, lifted the hood, and leaned into the engine. A moment later, he stepped back with the prize: a key on a ring. Under the hood—I should have thought of that!

I got a good look at Frayne as he tooled off in the Suburban. Old Sutz was smiling. He was smiling at the prospect of burning me at the stake.

I jogged down the mountainside as fast as my injured knee would allow. I kept out of sight as best I could, hugging the bushes and staying off the road.

By now Frayne would have discovered my escape. Was he racing up and down the back roads of Montecito, hunting for me? Maybe, but I feared he'd first go back to Stonecroft, and that had me worried. Brave women though they were, Janet and Caroline would not withstand Frayne's interrogation. And once he'd forced the truth out of them, what would he then do to the two good souls?

I was certain of one thing: Frayne would go into hiding if he couldn't eliminate me. After all, I knew everything now. And an organized killer like Frayne would already have his exit plan firmly in place.

Above all, I couldn't allow the man to escape. Four pieces

of jewelry, signifying four brutally raped women: I was sure
of it now. Lili Molina was dead. Were the others alive?

And I was sure of something else: if Frayne was not caught,
there would be other victims to come.

After ten minutes, I came to a crossroad. I slipped back into
the bushes and sat down to massage my knee.

When I stood once more and stepped out on the road, I
glanced back up the hill. My overheated blood turned to ice.

Above Stonecroft, a plume of smoke unfurled on the mountainside. *Fire.*

Fire in the dry season. Fire and a powerful Santa Ana wind.
Sutton Frayne had literally set up a smoke screen to cover his
escape.

I studied the billowing smoke cloud. Soon the fire would
arrive at Stonecroft, where two elderly ladies were sharing a
celebratory cup of tea.

I looked frantically around me. Every goddamn house in
Montecito was surrounded by high gates topped with spikes. A
steel-gray Jag approached and I waved frantically. The woman
driving scowled at me with disapproval.

I jogged on, hardly caring now about the pain. A house without a gate, I prayed. One trusting household, just one.

And then, there it was: a pretty house with a crunchy gravel
drive, a hedge of purple bougainvillea—and no gate. I ran up to
the door and banged on it. Meanwhile a large brindle dog with
yellow eyes bounded silently around the corner. I had no time
for pleasantries, and ignored him. He touched my bare calf with
his cold wet nose and turned away.

"Yes?" The door opened halfway and a thin blond woman of
about my own age peered through. She was beautifully put together, as if she were modeling that afternoon for *American
Riviera* magazine.

"There's a fire up on the mountain!" I pointed. "Please, call
911."

She looked at me doubtfully, her glance shifting to my hair. I put a hand to my head and discovered a stick with leaves attached. "Look. It's a long story, and I don't have time. Please, just make the call. And this is really important: two older ladies are trapped in the Stonecroft mansion, just below the fire." Doubt lingered in her expression.

Impulsively, I reached out and grabbed the woman's arm. My hand left a dirty smudge on her pale blue linen blouse. She looked at the mark and cringed.

"If you'll just step out here, you'll see it! Promise me, will you phone?"

"Yes, all right. I'll phone."

"And after that, can I use your cell to call for a ride?"

Her face changed. "I really don't think so. I don't even know you. Maybe you should—"

"OK, OK." I backed away. "Never mind about that. Just call 911 and don't forget to tell them about the women at Stonecroft. *Please.*"

I'd only make matters worse by sticking around. I turned to go.

At that instant, through the bougainvillea, I saw the black Maserati rip past. It did not slow.

In less than ten minutes, the Montecito fire brigade roared past me, heading up the mountain. Before long, other fire engines followed: Santa Barbara, Goleta. As I neared the lower Riviera, a stream of cars joined me going down. Two women trotted past on horses. Nobody had forgotten the recent big fires: the Tea Garden, the Jesusita, the Gap. I was witnessing the beginning of a fresh exodus.

When I reached the city streets, I slowed to a hobble. The pain in my knee was persistent now, too strong to shove out of my mind. The traffic was slow, but I needed a lift. I stuck out my thumb several times, but no one gave me so much as a second glance.

I needed to call Mike, to warn him about Frayne. I stopped a kid skateboarding past and asked if I could use his cell. "Sure. But the networks are jammed." I tried Mike's number several times, then Gabi's, before I gave up. I limped on.

Dusk was creeping into the city, and the wind had reversed its direction and was accelerating. I allowed myself one long look up the hill. The smoke rose in towering pillars, and in the gathering dark you could see angry orange lines racing along the ridges. The devil's playtime had arrived once again.

Think, I ordered myself. Think like a cold and calculating killer. Where in hell would you go?

If I were Frayne, I'd want to get as far away, and as fast, as I could—but no. Maybe not so far after all. I'd only need to cross the border. Mexico would be my kind of country: a land where cash is king and no questions are asked. Just feed the mordida, señor, then do as you please.

Mexico, and perhaps later, points further south. Once Frayne got to Mexico, he'd be free—free of the law, free to rape and kill. And the fastest and surest way for him to get there was in his boat.

I took off at a gimpy trot through the city streets, heading down to the marina. Twilight was deepening, and small crowds were gathering at vantage points to watch and photograph the fire. People pointed their cell phones, not saying much. Quiet, waiting. Waiting to see how far down the mountain the fire would rage.

Frayne hadn't bothered to hide the Maserati: I found it parked near the marina at a crazy angle. He was in one hellish rush to get out of town.

I stepped off the parking lot to the sand and sank to a sitting position. I was exhausted, and by now my injured knee felt as if it were pierced with a red-hot skewer. But I knew I had very little time.

I tore off my shoes and then my socks. Bare feet would be

best: silence was everything. I filled one sock halfway with sand, and tied the top in a knot.

The wire gate at the head of the dock was locked as usual. Cleverly designed to foil intruders, the gate was edged with razor wire and extended out over the water on both sides. I was thinking about easing myself into the brine and swimming around it, when a thoroughly drunk couple tottered up.

"Hi!" I said merrily. "I left my keys at home. Can I come through with you?"

The guy looked me up and down. "Well, I don' know," he deadpanned. "No socks, no shoes, no serv-serv—"

The woman shrieked with laughter. "He's jus' kidding. Come on!"

I entered hard on their heels. The gate clanged shut. The couple engaged in a sloppy kiss and I moved around them, fading into the dark.

The *Icarus*'s berth was out near the end of the dock. I'd gone fifty yards before I got a good look at her. The lights were off, but the beam of a strong flashlight shifted about on the deck. I edged closer, hugging the shadows.

Now I could make out Frayne. I watched as he strapped a storage box to the rail, then untied the line to the dock and tossed it on board. A minute later he descended into the cabin, closing the door behind him. Even then he didn't switch on a light, but continued to work by flashlight. I could see him through the portholes, preparing for departure.

It was now or never. I whispered a prayer for assistance, figuring it couldn't hurt.

I crept forward and jumped the widening gap between the *Icarus* and the dock. I landed with a thud and froze, willing myself not to scream with the pain in my knee.

I held my breath as the agony subsided. Nothing had happened. So far, so good.

I slipped across the deck, pausing with each step until I

reached the gas tank at starboard. Thank God, the cap wasn't locked. It took some elbow grease, but I managed to unscrew it.

The daylight was nearly gone. Only a reddish light tinged the horizon, just enough to see by. I untied the knot in my sock, weighing the sand.

But then I heard a noise above me. Frayne was in the wheel-house. Fearing he might see me, I crouched down on the deck as the engine roared to life and the cabin lights flared.

The *Icarus* backed out of its berth, swerved right, and headed out of the marina. Within minutes we were in the harbor, heading for the open channel. I'd have to work fast.

I turned my attention back to the gas tank. The boat had slowed, but I couldn't waste time wondering why. As I reached for my sock, the sand spilled onto the deck. Damn! I worked frantically, pushing it into a little pile.

"Sand play, investigator? Freud would have approved."

Slowly, I turned. Pointing straight at my head was the barrel of a gun. "Mr. Frayne—"

"Shut up. Raise your hands over your head." Frayne bent down until his face was inches from my own. His heavy cologne made me gag.

"Seasick already?" He lifted my lip with the tip of the barrel. "No, it must be fear."

Fury boiled up in me. "It's the smell of you, Frayne."

Quick and smooth as the strike of a snake, the gun lashed the side of my head. I sagged to all fours.

"On your feet. Get down below."

My brain swirled as I descended the cabin steps. Frayne was right behind me, his gun prodding the small of my back. I clung to one thought: the *Icarus* must not leave the harbor.

"Ever tried bondage, sweetheart? I'd start right now, but we'd never get out of the channel." Frayne flashed his movie-star smile. "See that Saarinen chair? I'm going to tie you to it.

It's an original, so please don't puke or shit in it later, when we play our games. Actually, you might find you enjoy the experience. I know I will."

"What kind of monster are you?" Unfortunately my voice wasn't as confident as I wanted it to be.

"'Monster'? I expect a little respect from my girls, if that's what you mean. And if I don't get it, the sluts get what they deserve. That's reasonable, wouldn't you say?"

My brain had cleared well enough for me to grasp one vital fact: if I let Frayne tie me up, I was as good as dead. All I could think to do was to talk. "Just tell me something, will you? Why were you blackmailing Jared? Not for the money, obviously."

"Obviously. For the fun of it, I suppose. I knew the little freak would turn around and ask Wied for the cash. I enjoyed seeing them sweat."

"What do you have against Bruce? It wasn't enough to screw the man's wife and daughter? Your sister and niece, by the way."

Frayne tipped back his head and laughed. "Jaymie, you're showing off. And you are clever up to a point, I have to admit. But speaking of Crowley, you never noticed his hair stuck to the tape I used on that ugly little mutt of yours."

"Oh, I saw it, all right. I just didn't fall for it. You tend to overplay your hand."

Frayne's smile disappeared. "Oh, I wouldn't say that. After all, everyone cooperated so nicely. That idiot Crowley delivered the girl to the warehouse for me, just as I'd devised. And I'd planned to implicate a drifter—in fact, I had one likely fellow picked out—but the Armenta boy offered me an opportunity too good to pass up."

"So why did you kill him?" I fought to keep cool. I wanted to scream in his face, gouge out his eyes.

"Well, you know the answer to that, Jaymie. Armenta was going to talk."

I knew I had to keep Frayne engaged, until I could come up with a plan. "Yes, you were clever, I have to admit. Your alibi, for example."

He looked amused. "And you never figured that out."

"I did, actually. An old-fashioned shell game, right? You thought if you kept rotating between your mother, Sarah, and various party guests, everyone would assume you were with somebody else during the hour you were away."

"Jaymie, I'm touched. You understand me."

"I understand you're sick, if that's what you mean."

But I'd gone too far. The muscles in Frayne's jaw tightened as he trained the gun on my chest. "Shut up. Question-and-answer time's over. Now put your ass in that chair."

As I turned toward the chair, I took a step closer to Frayne, bent low, and drove my head up hard under his chin. He grunted, and the pistol went flying as his neck snapped back. I scrambled after it, but just as I reached out to pick it up, he kicked me in the back of my knee—my injured knee. I screamed and fell on top of the gun.

Then Frayne made the mistake of trying to kick me off the weapon. In spite of the pain I was ready for that, and grabbed his foot and twisted, sending him crashing. He cursed, spitting with rage.

But as I struggled to my feet, I rolled off the gun, and Frayne grabbed it. Before I could lunge for him, the gun was pointing straight at my head.

"Get—back—up—on—deck. *Now*."

Cold ferocity shone in the man's eyes. I knew I was walking to my execution.

"First it's downstairs, then it's up. Make up your mind, Frayne. Admit it, I've rattled you."

"You know, I like that about you, Jaymie. You just never give up, do you. Not even when it's hopeless."

I ascended the steps with the gun digging into my back. A horrifying phrase entered my mind: *dead woman walking.*

"I'm sorry we're skipping playtime, Jaymie. It would have been fun, hearing you beg. Now get over to the rail."

I stood facing the mountains. The sundowner wind was now in full force. A tracery of fire illuminated the hillside. "You set that, Frayne," I shouted into the wind. "How dumb can you get? You burned your own family home—with your mother in it!"

"I set the fire so I could escape, to keep the plods busy. Caroline? I did her a favor. The old cow's better off dead." The gun barrel dug into the small of my back. "Step closer to the edge. I don't want your blood messing up my—"

At that moment, the *Icarus* pitched. I saw my chance.

I grabbed Sutz by his chambray sleeve and launched us both over the side.

The cold sent a shock wave through my brain, and I sank. When I surfaced, I could hear Frayne sputtering nearby. I sucked in a big breath of air and dropped under again, trying to breaststroke away from the boat. When I came up I could still hear him, but we were farther apart.

"I'll kill you," I heard him scream. "I'll kill you just like the others!"

I closed my ears and began the long swim to shore.

The California Current, flowing down from the North, twines its icy fingers into the Santa Barbara Channel. The cold water, and all I had been through that evening, gradually took its toll. I thought about Danny, and wondered if I'd still be alive by the time I washed up on the beach.

Then a wave hit. I bobbed under, swallowing seawater. The second time it happened, I thought about staying down.

And at that moment—the moment when I began to give in—the magical dream began.

A boat lit with garlands of party lights waltzed out of nowhere on the choppy waves. It came so close I could hear Louis Armstrong crooning on board. I used what strength I had left to bleat for help.

Somebody called back. Louis fell silent, and a beam of light struck me full in the face.

The party boat maneuvered side on, and a chorus of voices urged me to catch hold of the rope ladder.

I managed to grab it and hang on as four or five people reached down and hauled me on board. I was immediately wrapped in a silvery cape. Then an elixir of steaming clam chowder was held to my lips.

"There's a killer out there," I croaked. "Call Harbor Patrol."

"Jaymie, you're a superhero." Mike leaned in through the squad car window and gave me a shoulder squeeze. "A wet one," he added with an odd little smile. He looked as if he couldn't decide whether to laugh or cry.

"What I feel like is a drowned rat. I just want to go home and curl up in my dry little bed."

"It won't be much longer now," Mike replied. "Listen, I just talked to Gabi. Wait till you hear what Claudia dug up about Frayne. Thank God the Coast Guard pulled that scumbag out of the drink—drowning would have been too easy on him."

"But will the charges stick? We're still short on physical evidence."

"The report came in yesterday: Frayne's saliva was on the megaphone, just like you said it would be. Matched his DNA. He slipped up—wonder why?"

"Arrogance, I'd say. Frayne probably thought we'd never connect the megaphone to the murder."

A pretty young woman wearing a summery cotton dress— and Mike's Windbreaker—stepped up to the squad car window. "Hi, Jaymie. I'm Mandy Blaine. I think we met once? I work in the sheriff's office."

Oh, how I wanted to say, *Fuck the hell off!* And if I hadn't been so exhausted, that's just what I might have done.

But I heard myself say, "Sure, Mandy. How are you?" Because of course I remembered her. I remembered her because she was the only nice person in that viper's nest, the one to go to if you needed some help. I glanced over at Mike. His hands were stuffed in his pockets and he was studiously looking out to sea.

Suddenly I was conscious of my hair hanging in wet clumps around my seawater-washed face. Hell, for all I knew, I had seaweed stuck in it.

"Mike's told me all about what happened, and I think it's awesome, what you did." A small frown crossed her face. "Oh, I didn't mean *all* about it—he would never talk about confidential stuff!" And I swear to God, she turned and squeezed Mike's arm.

"Does she have to be so damn nice?" I muttered. I pulled the silver cocoon up over my head, leaned back, and shut my eyes.

Postscript

"Jaymie, Jaymie. I arrange a surprise trip to our fiftieth state, with only a few strings attached. Last night you see your green flash. And back in SB, all turns out for the best: the case against Sutz is airtight. What more could you want, petulant one?"

I opened my eyes and looked deep into his. We were sharing a beach towel, lying on our sides face-to-face. I reached up and brushed a silvery glitter of Big Island sand from his cheek.

"Not everything turned out for the best, Zave."

"Hey. I thought we agreed not to talk about the deputy."

"I'm not talking about him. Or thinking about him, either." That was a flat-out lie, but it was best to pretend.

"So what's subpar? The pile of evidence surrounding Frayne is reaching to the sky. He's not buying his way out of this one, and there will be further charges on down the line." Zave propped himself up on an elbow. "Did I tell you? Janet and Caroline are happy campers over in Casa Serena. You know, they took your suggestion and left Celeste off their approved-visitors list. I think they're secretly glad Stonecroft burned."

"It's good they've settled in. And Casa Serena will benefit in a big way from Caroline's donation. Thanks for taking her on as a client."

"No, baby, thank *you* for the rec." Zave ran a finger under the edge of my bikini bottom. "So I repeat, what's not good?"

I sat up and looked out over the bright turquoise sea. Pert little waves flirted and danced. "Well, the Armentas. Gabi told me they aren't doing so well in Mexico. Chuy's OK, but Alma and Aricela can't seem to get past Danny's death."

"It's early days, Jaymie. Time will heal."

I shut my eyes against the relentless glare off the water. "Lili and Danny are dead. The truly innocent ones, you know? And Celeste Delaney—not a scratch on that she-monster."

"Time to let it go, sweetheart." Zave took me by the shoulders and gently pressed me down on the big beach towel. His hands drifted over my body. His caresses were so sweet they made me shiver, in spite of the scorching sun and the black sand steaming all around us.

Zave bent down and touched his lips to mine, then fell back on the towel and groaned. "Let's go take a nap in the condo."

"OK. In a few." I got to my feet, wobbled a little, then skittered across the scalding beach to the water. I let out a sigh as the cool wavelets lapped at my ankles.

The horizon, a smudged line of dark blue chalk, marked the mating of ocean and sky. I shaded my eyes with a hand and turned to look to the east.

Two thousand four hundred miles from here, as the seagull flies, a small city looking westward was ending its workday, the residents shoving their chairs under their desks and heading outdoors. I could almost see the red-tile roofs climbing the steep terra-cotta mountains, and the sparkling blue harbor guarded by a line of ancient islands, a barricade of mythic whales.

At 101 Mission, in a run-down bungalow court, a woman in a hot pink tracksuit at least one size too small was shutting down her computer, rinsing the coffeepot, and turning keys and spinning locks in a secret, intricate ceremony I would never fully comprehend.

"Zave," I called across the sand. "After that nap in the condo?

"Yeah, baby?"

"It's time to go home."

Acknowledgments

I want to thank my talented editor, Kat Brzozowski, for taking a risk and choosing to work with me, and for so generously giving me her discerning assistance.

My agent, Becca Stumpf, is the agent every writer dreams of. She's whip-smart, warm-hearted, and wise. Thanks for all your help, Becca.

Thanks to each and every member of the extended Reich family, for never once suggesting I get a real job. To yachtsman Tom Reich for telling me how to sabotage a boat, and to Kevin Reich for educating me on the subject of cool cars. To Corey Reich, for inspiring us all.

Muchas gracias to Monica Carrillo and Imelda Irabien, who helped correct my cultural shortsightedness.

To Shelly Lowenkopf, Story Magus, thank you for mentoring me and always prodding me toward the thornier path.

Loving thanks to Casey Dellabarca, who put up with a distracted writer of a parent for many years, yet thrived.

To all of you who have trusted me and shared the stories of your lives, I am grateful.

Most of all, thanks to my partner Salvatore Dellabarca, for

his support and love. Thank God Salvi's not a writer—what stories he could tell!

A portion of the author's proceeds from this book will be donated to The Rosalynn Carter Fellowships for Mental Health Journalism (www.cartercenter.org).